THE PHOENIX AWAKENING

THE PHOENIX AWAKENING

AMANDA MERCEDES SOTOMAYOR

PREFACE

Close your eyes and imagine a life like mine. You're taken away from everyone and everything you love. Your life is a written book, but you have no idea what it's about. You're young and scared with no one to turn to. You trust no one until they prove they can be trusted. Because of the dangers ahead, you have no choice but to remain distant, yearning, and desperate to live a normal life. Hunger, pain, and death surround you. You scream for help, but no one hears you. There's a hollow hole where your heart is supposed to be. You are forced to embrace a life you never wanted. They say you choose the life you live. But that's a lie. It was chosen for me.

Chapter 1

THE BEGINNING

When I was a baby, my father left my mother, leaving me with her and my older sister, Fawn. Fawn left six months ago with some guy she met at school. My mother was a junkie named Tracy Doyle, and so was my father, but he left before he could do any harm. My mother was beautiful, with long hair, caramel skin, and a great body, but she had low self-esteem. Drugs will do that to you She had boyfriend after boyfriend. Heck, she sometimes had more than one boyfriend at the same time. I honestly couldn't keep track of all the ones she had. She was also a prostitute and had her johns come to the house for her service. After they had their way with her, they left. One day, a guy named Earl decided he would do differently.

Earl was fat, nasty-looking, hairy everywhere, had a bald spot in the middle of his head, and smelled like cigarettes and alcohol. His teeth were stained yellow with brown guck between them, and he always wore stuff that was too small for him with his butt crack hanging out. Tracy fell asleep after she and Earl did their thing, and she was high off whatever she was on, like always. Nothing could wake her up.

I was watching TV alone when Earl came and sat next to me — too close for comfort. Uncomfortable with him taking up all my personal space, I got up and headed to the kitchen for a drink.

"Can you get me a beer?" he said.

"Sure," I say, and sit on the other side of the couch and hand him his beer, hoping he would be on his way to wherever he had to go. But he remained sitting there. He kept staring at me, smiling freakishly. "I think you should be going since you and Tracy are done," I tell him.

He laughs sarcastically, then gives me a sinister grin before speaking, "How old are you?"

"Not old enough for you! Please take your beer and leave!" I snap. Earl completely ignores me when I tell him to leave; he continues to talk to me. "You're way prettier than your mama, and you look a decent age to me." He moves closer to me and rubs the left cheek of my face. Instantly, I jerk my head back and jump up, but he grabs my hand and pulls me back to the couch.

"I'm not. I'm only ten and just turned it a week ago! Get off me and leave now, or I'm going to scream." I panic, becoming scared and careful not to look him in the eye.

"Like I said, girl, it's a decent age." He quickly releases me and hikes his falling pants up by the belt, his butt crack still hanging out. "So go ahead and scream. Your mama ain't waking up, and no one can hear you. The only thing it'll do is turn me on," he says, quickly grabbing my hands again. He rolls his tongue out of his mouth while pressing his body up against me, my hands still trapped in his. I try to fight him off me, but it's no use. I knew what would happen, and he knew what he would do to me. He was going to rape me!

I scream, and he forces a kiss, thrusting his tongue damn near down my throat. My tongue immediately tastes what his body always reeks of, cigarettes and alcohol. I bite his tongue as hard as I can. I gag as blood rushes into my mouth. I've upset him. He bitch-smacks me and tells me to sit fucking still. He wasn't going to be done for a while. I cry and beg him to stop, but he doesn't. Instead, he chuckles and sticks his dirty sock in my mouth, rips my pajama bottoms off, and forces his horrible-smelling penis inside me.

I was a virgin at the time and dry as hell. The pain I was experiencing was unimaginable. I feel blood gushing out of me. The feeling of shame shadows me; the fight-back spirit in me unearths.

Suddenly, I manage to kick him off me and try to run, but it was no use. He catches me, tackles me, and splits my legs wide open from behind. His hand slams my face to the floor. Ol' man Earl smothers me with a throw pillow to muffle my screaming. "You stupid bitch! Shut the fuck up!" he yells, penetrating me harder and harder with every strike.

I wiggle my head from under the pillow. I gasp for air and use my eyes to look around for anything or anyone for help, but no one is around. My mother is too high to hear me, passed out from snorting a line. It feels like Earl is raping me for hours, but it's only been ten minutes. He finishes, lets out a big exhale, and collapses on my back, breathing hard. I feel blood gushing out between my legs again as he pulls out. His breath hovers at the back of my neck. He kisses my left cheek and whispers, "Until next time." he smirks. "And if you tell your mother, I'll kill her in front of you," he threatens while pulling up his pants, his butt crack still hanging out. He leaves.

I was in so much pain, but I run to the door to lock it, scared that he would come back into the house to finish me off. I look around and see a trail of blood coming from me. I lie on the floor in a fetal position, collecting myself. Hours later, I crawl to the bathroom, get in the shower, and watch blood mixed with shower water go down the drain. I whisper a prayer because I feel he will be back soon. I don't want him to kill Tracy. I know she's not the best mother in the world, but sadly, she's all I got. She does her best to make ends meet; I know it's not easy.

She's a drug addict who needs help. I can't leave her. Even if I left, where would I go? I have no friends or family. I'm all on my own and alone. I can't tell anyone this happened to me. Tracy might be a bitch, but she's my mother. She would never tolerate Earl raping me, but he would kill her, and I can't have that either. There's a knock on the bathroom door; I freeze. "Unlock the fucking door, bitch!" Tracy yells.

"Just a minute," I say, then I unlock the door. Tracy falls into the bathroom, messed up from whatever she's on. She uses so many drugs it's hard to keep track of everything she's on. I'm so out of it myself from Earl assaulting me that I forget I'm still wearing my pajama shirt, now soaked and dripping all over the bathroom floor.

My mom is so doped up she doesn't notice. She probably didn't pay attention to the trail of blood in the front room either.

Months pass, and Earl comes by every day. He also rapes me every day. He makes me wear these god-awful, whorish-looking dresses. He gives Tracy drugs so she can be out of it. I lie there helplessly day in and day out, praying and begging God to make him stop, but Earl never stops. Things get worse, and finally, I become fed up. I start to plan my escape. I search the kitchen for the most giant knife I can find. I place the knife between the couch cushions, ensuring I can get to it quickly.

It's four o'clock, and Earl always comes around eight at night, so I have some time. I layer myself in clothing. It's not much since I don't have a lot. He'll tire if he has a few layers to tear through, giving me more time to escape from him. If he comes after me, I'll threaten to stab him and will do it if I have to.

I wait for him to arrive. I watch TV, become tired, and fall asleep. I never fall sound asleep though, because of the nightmares. Earl raping me hunts me in my sleep. No matter how hard I try not to think about him, it's impossible, and there he is, terrorizing me through the night, inciting my bedtime tremors and nighttime panics. My night terrors are so vivid that I can even smell his horrible scent and feel my skin crawl when he comes near me. This time, the odor is more intense. The stitch awakens me; Earl's breath is barreling in my face.

I spring up. I'm awake and slightly annoyed; he's caught me off guard. I can't believe I dozed off. I shift to the side of the couch where I hid the knife. "Nice to see — you happy to see me," he breathes in my face.

"Yeah, too bad I can't say the same," I say while trying to hold my breath. He goes to grab my hand to have his way with me, but I move it away and yell at him to get off me. Without him noticing, I take the knife from the couch. I stand up and face him.

"We're going to do it the hard way, I see," he says with a menacing stare.

"No! Not this time. I've had enough of you raping me. It ends tonight, you perv!" I shout.

He laughs sadistically, "It's not done until I say it's done, and believe me baby — I ain't near done."

I reveal the knife. "I said, it's done. Now leave and don't come back!"

"Careful, love, I don't want you cutting yourself. We both know you ain't got no guts to stab or kill me."

"Oh, I do now. Keep trying me," I tell Earl, maintaining my stance while stepping back a little. He moves in closer; I back up more until the heel of my foot runs into the wall. I must cut him because I'm not playing with him. He bucks at me; I swing the knife but miss. He laughs and bucks again. I swing the knife again; this time, I don't miss. The blade slices his forearm, drawing a nice line of blood.

"You bitch! Ahh, you fucking cut me, you little cunt!" he wails in agony, panting heavily.

"I told you to leave, and you didn't!"

"Didn't think you had it in you, you little shit… but it won't happen again," he mumbles while turning towards the door, looking like he's about to leave. He freezes mid-turn and, with all his might, swings his arm back and hits me up against the wall, knocking the knife out of my hand. We struggle for the knife, but he grabs my hair in his hand and yanks it with his wounded arm. Digging my fingers as deeply as possible in his cut was a waste of effort. He bellows loudly and throws me the opposite way of the knife. I become paralyzed, scared to move.

He has the knife now. I don't need to turn around to see that he does. Should I run? He hoots with laughter, the power now entirely in his hands. He tells me to strip, "You have a lot of making up to do…" I slowly turn halfway around, look at him, and beg him for mercy. "Shut up! Look at my arm! You ain't have none for me."

"You were going to rape me again!" I pause, hyperventilating. "I had no choice. Please don't, I beg you," I cry.

"Turn around." I shake my head from side to side, pleading with him not to hurt me.

"I said turn, bitch! And start stripping! Start with the shirt first!"

I slowly take off all four shirts. Earl unfastens my bra and tells me to lie on the floor. He whips out his thing, pisses on a spot on the floor where he wants me to put my face in. I cover my fully developed chest with my arms. I make a run for it, but he catches me by the arm and slams me face-first on the floor. Earl shoves my face in his piss and sits on my back. He runs the blade of the knife across me, ready to cut me at any moment.

"You thought you could kill me or make me run," he taunts.

"No, no, I swear, I…"

He cuts me off, "Shut up! I ain't tell you to speak! I got something for you now." He applies pressure to the blade on the upper part of my back. I scream as loud as I can and kick, but I'm trapped between the floor and him. He maneuvers himself, no longer sitting on my back, takes my arms, places them parallel in front of me, and sits on them with his knees. "I think it's time for you to get a tattoo. I think *'YOUR MINE'* is a perfect one to get." he snuffs cruelly.

I feel the blade pierce my back, my skin tearing. Earl digs more, carving me from the opposite end but making sure the words are right side up. I never felt anything so painful. I scream, and he punches me in my head every time, the pain insufferable. The blood gushes from my back and runs down to the floor. Earl carves *'YOUR MINE'* on my upper back from the left side of my spine to the right. He turns me around and rapes me; my back oozes blood When he finishes, he pisses on me and throws rubbing alcohol all over me. I screech loudly and curl into a ball.

"Next time, you know better and won't do that again, I hope," he says, slamming the door behind him. I lie there for hours before crawling to the bathroom and entering the shower. I never knew a shower could be so torturous until that day. I put on an oversized shirt and some sweatpants; a bra was too painful. I hurry to clean the piss and blood from the floor before Tracy wakes up. I didn't want to smell it anymore; the foul smell was nauseating. It was making me sick.

Scrubbing was killing me. Blood leaks out from my sliced back with every stroke of the sponge. I move my arms to scrub the piss and blood off the floor. I scrub harder and harder for the blood to come out to get it as clean as possible, but my body's soreness makes me stop. I literally feel like I'm about to die from the pain. The sharp, incessant pulses radiate from my upper back to my shoulders and through my neck. My head throbs from a series of headaches. To make matters worse, my lower back and upper arms start to ache and burn, all connected to the very spot Earl engraved.

Bedtime is difficult. I'm only able to lie on my stomach. Despite my best efforts to clean the blood and urine, the odor lingers, like Earl is still smashing me face-first into his bodily fluids. I lie there facing the wall, the wall staring back at me. I want someone to come and kill me; just take my life right now. I'm now his, and there is no way out. My back even says so.

I begin to hate my father and sister for leaving and not taking me with them. I'd never have gone through this if they hadn't left me. I have a drug addict for a mother and no one to turn to, no one to protect me or vent to. I need someone, but I have no one. Part of me hates Tracy. If she weren't a junkie or a prostitute, I would've never gone through this. I wish they were here to make him stop.

Why me? Why is it just me by myself? Why did God allow this to happen to me? I never did anything wrong. I've always tried to do the right thing. I even stuck up for Tracy when Fawn was calling her all kinds of names to her face before she left. Fawn was right about everything she said, but Tracy is our mother, and her oldest daughter's words hurt her. While these thoughts run through my mind, eventually, I fall asleep.

"Get the fuck up before you're late for school, you stupid bitch!" Tracy yells as she walks out. I open my eyes and cringe in pain. I can barely get up. My bed shirt is stuck to my back where Earl did his carvings. I don't go to school the entire week. I leave the house and wander around, walking to nowhere, but I can't stay home. Everything is a blur. I don't pay attention to anyone, and I don't hear anything when I go walking. I'm like *The Walking Dead*; my whole body in pain. I've heard people talk about how when they're in so much pain, it eventually becomes numb, but this pain doesn't numb out — not physically, anyway.

Mentally. I'm numb. I'm not here. I've checked out. Psychologically, I need help. In my absentmindedness, I find a box big enough to hide under in the back of an alley. I collapse under it. I don't know what it is about this box, but it makes me feel safe. Maybe it's because no one knows me here or where I am. I mean, Earl doesn't know where I am, and neither can he find me. I'm hiding. I'm in what I call a safe haven. I'm safer here than the place I call home.

In my makeshift shelter, anyone can snatch me up and have their way with me if they want to, but no one does. I'm safer here. My home is never safe if Earl is still alive. I drift off and sleep for hours. For once, I don't have any nightmares. It's the best sleep I've had since Earl. It's so peaceful. I don't worry about Earl coming to get me. This box is more secure than the front room I use for a bedroom at home.

Chapter 2

THE MOVE TO A NEW BEGINNING

One day, when Tracy came home, she told me to pack my bags. She said we're leaving this town and going far away. I was so happy. I didn't care where we were going as long as I was far away from nasty ol' Earl. Tracy also had a brand-new BMW that I knew we couldn't afford.

"How did you get this?" I ask her.

"My new lover got it for me; now let's go," she says with a dreamy-like smile.

"Let's go where? And when did you get this new lover?" I question her while getting into the car.

"Well, when I was away from home all that time, I was over at my boyfriend's house, and I swear this man is the one. We're going to be living with him now," she tells me, quickly trying to bypass the last part.

"What!" I yell angrily.

"We're…"

"I heard. I can't believe you!"

"We'll have a better life with this man. He's rich, kind, and cares about me, Dawn. We're old friends who've rekindled a flame. Wait until your sister meets him. She'll be so proud."

"Does he know about your drug addiction?"

"Yes, and he's going to help."

"Help like what?" I ask, hearing the irritation in my voice.

"Like… rehab."

I laugh at the thought. "Oh yeah? And what are you going to do with me? Throw me on the street?"

"No, but I got something better, you're going to be staying with—"

"Don't you dare say what I think you're about to say!" I yell from the top of my lungs.

"It's only until I get better. I swear, everything will be okay. I won't be on the streets anymore. He's going to take care of us, I swear."

"How could you without my permission?" I demand.

"Hey, I'm the mother and I—"

"Oh yeah? Since when? Because you've been a real shitty one lately."

"I'm going to ignore that rude remark. It's not easy being the only one raising two girls at the same time. Especially ungrateful ones at that," she says, starting to cry. She pulls over and puts the car in park.

"I know, Tracy. I'm sorry, I'll be more grateful. I promise."

"Well, good. You can start by driving. I need something to get my nerves out of whack," Tracy replies, not a tear in sight.

"Wait, what? Are you serious? I'm only ten!" I remind her.

"And you look like you're eighteen! So, quit yapping and get over here."

I hop into the driver's seat, unsure what the hell I'm doing. Tracy pulls a bag out from the back. I know it's her heroin kit. She sparks up right in front of me and passes out, never telling me where we're headed. I look for her cell phone to see if this lover boy of hers name is stored somewhere. Surprisingly, it starts ringing in my hand. Praying it's him, I answer it. "Hello?"

"Hey, sweetheart, did you tell her yet?"

"Umm, yeah, she did, and now she's high and passed out in the passenger seat, and I don't know where to go. So, can you be so nice and tell me where to go?"

"Yeah, I can tell you but aren't you ten years old?" he asks me, sounding confused.

"Yup, but I look older, according to Tracy, not to mention the drugs were calling her name."

"Where are you?"

Thankfully, we're pulled over next to a sign that said I-710. "On Interstate 710, Uhh… going North, I think, now can you please tell me where to go?" I beg.

"You're not driving anywhere. I'm coming to get the two of you now."

"Okay, thank you."

"No problem," he says.

I wait for two hours. Finally, a black Range Rover pulls up behind us. A muscular white man with nicely brushed short hair, dark shades, and all-white clothing hops out. He looks like a typical California guy with money. He approaches the driver's seat, where I'm sitting, and taps on the window.

"Dawn?"

"Yeah, and you are?"

"Your mother's boyfriend, Steve Sandino. Nice to finally meet you."

"Yeah, sure." I turn and look at Tracy in the passenger seat. "So, what are we going to do with her?"

"I'll carry her to the truck and put her in the back so she can lie down, and you can sit in the front with me if that's okay with you," he offers.

"Why don't you put her in the passenger seat and lay the seat back?"

"Because I'm putting the seats down in the rear so she can lie all the way down."

"I can lie back there with her."

"Yeah, but I've got stuff in the back of my car — only she can fit."

"Why would you keep stuff in the car knowing you were picking us up?" I question him.

"Because I didn't think it would be a big deal for you to sit in the front. It'll also give us some time to talk."

"I can talk to you from the back," I say, not knowing if he's another Earl.

"Yes, you can." Steve answers, calmly.

"What are you going to do with the car?" I blurt out.

"Send for it later. You ask a lot of questions."

"Because I don't trust you."

"You don't know me."

"Exactly. All I know is that you have a dick," I retort, looking him in the eyes. He laughs, turns his face towards me, and looks me in the eyes.

"Yeah, that belongs to your mother. I'm drained and didn't have to drive all the way down here. I could've called a cab for you and your mom."

"Whatever," I say, getting out of the car and closing the door behind me. He puts Tracy in the back seat. We get in his truck, and he starts driving. There's an awkward silence, but he finally breaks the ice.

"So, do you go to school?" he asks me.

"Yeah, sometimes." I roll my eyes.

"What do you mean sometimes? Why aren't you going all the time?"

"Because I don't feel like it."

"That's not a good reason."

"It is — when you don't learn shit, and your mother used to fuck your principal, and he keeps on calling you to his office asking why she won't call him. That man suspended me for bullshit reasons because of her. I got tired of that crap. I've missed so much school, I'm way behind now, and that's why I've stopped going," I explain to him in a fuck-you asshole kind of way for being too damn nosey.

"Did you tell Tracy?"

"Nope."

"Why not?"

"Because she doesn't give a fuck. Any other questions?"

"Look, I know Tracy is messed up on drugs, and she probably has a lot of men in her life. But I love your mother dearly and plan to spend the rest of my life with her. I hope you'll soon understand and accept me into your life too," he says.

"Doesn't look like I have much of a choice," I reply, being snarky.

"Hopefully, we can become friends while your mother is away in rehab," he says with what appears to be sincerity.

The poor guy seems to love her, and for reasons I don't know, I'll find out soon enough. How can anyone love a drug addict who is a prostitute and gets high in front of her daughter? I guess the real question is, why do I still love her after all the shit I've been through, and all because of her, I think to myself.

It was another two hours before we pulled up to his mansion. The place is jaw-dropping. Steve Sandino's house is bigger than most malls. Well, maybe that's a stretch, but his home is enormous. It's white with tons of palm trees and sits right above the ocean. We unload the truck and go inside with Tracy still passed out and Steve carrying her in his arms. "Wow," I gasp, walking in and looking up at the ceiling and all around. The mansion is mostly glass and, I swear, has the best ocean view in the world. The stairs are curved and U-shaped; you can go up or down on either side. The floors are marble, squeaky clean, and shiny. To my ten-year-old eyes, this place looks like a castle.

"Do you like it?" Steve asks, smiling.

"No. I love it! It's the most beautiful place I've ever seen in my life."

"Would you like me to show you your room?" he asks. I jump up and down, surprised and giggly with tears.

"What? I have a room?"

"Yeah, and it's all yours. I hope you don't mind."

"No, of course, I don't mind! I've never had a room before that's all mine," I tell him.

He walks me up the stairs to the room further down the hall. He opens two French doors to the most breathtaking bedroom I've ever seen. The wall is a huge window, giving amazing ocean views, and there's a King-size bed with clean white sheets, a big fluffy white cover, and pillows. The bedroom floor is also marble. I have my own bathroom with a Jacuzzi tub, a walk-in shower, and two toilets, an American and European one with a bidet. There's even a balcony and a walk-in closet that catches my eye. I'm overjoyed; tears trickle down my cheeks. Tracy hit the jackpot this time, I think to myself. She finally picked the right one.

"I hope you like it," Steve says, interrupting my little moment.

"I love it. I've never had my own room. Heck, I've never had a bed. I used to sleep on the couch. I just don't get it," I'm still in disbelief.

"Get what?" Steve responds.

"Why are you doing this for me? You love Tracy, but that doesn't mean you have to be nice or love me too. You could've left me back in Long Beach, but you didn't. Why?" I ask him, really wanting to know his reasons.

"Because Dawn, we're more connected than you think, and not only by Tracy," Steve says.

"I'm starting to think you want two for the price of one." I snap back, wondering what he means by "we're more connected" and not just by Tracy. Is this another Earl? His eyes get big, and he jerks his head back.

"No! Not at all. You're ten and haven't even gone through puberty yet, and I'd never mess with a child."

"Good, because I won't do it willingly."

"Okay… this is getting weird," he says, again uncomfortable with my mature, smart mouth and self-protective stance. He quickly changes the subject, "Well, Dawn, I didn't paint or decorate the room because I thought you might want to do that yourself. We can go to the mall whenever you're ready and get you some new clothes. Oh, and by the way, my nephew Scott will be coming down soon for the summer and possibly staying longer. He'll be at the other end of the hall; he's fifteen. And, one last thing, your mother is leaving tomorrow for rehab. If you need or want anything, use this intercom. Here, this is your cell phone," he sticks out his hand with a phone in it.

"A what?" I ask, a little shocked by the things he's giving me.

"Cell phone."

"Why do I need a cell phone?"

"So… we can stay in touch. I thought you'd be more grateful."

"Don't get me wrong, I am. I'm just confused about why you'd do all this for me?"

"Why not?"

"Because you don't know me."

"I know more than you think."

"From who? Tracy? Heck, she doesn't even know me."

"Then, hopefully, you will give me a chance to know you," he says, smiling. He tosses the iPhone over to me; I catch it in my hands. "Well, I'll let you get situated," he says, and leaves the room.

I throw myself on the bed, drowning myself in the covers. I find a remote control and start pressing buttons. The one that says "blinds" makes my window turn all black, blocking the sunlight. Next, I click the TV button, curious what would happen since I didn't see one. Suddenly, the window transforms into a TV. Amazed by everything, I think, why the hell is he doing all this?

Everything is over the top, and he's acting like it's no big deal. He loves Tracy, but she's a total mess. What is he planning to do with me when she leaves? Is he going to take advantage of me like Earl did? I know Earl was one of Tracy's johns and not her boyfriend, but let's face it, she was having sex with him like she has with Steve. His nephew, Scott, who is he really? Is he also nice like Steve or an asshole like Earl? I guess I'll find out when I meet him next week. Steve seems like a nice guy, and I can tell he loves Tracy deeply, but looks can be deceiving.

A week later, I meet Scott. He's a sexy guy with a tan. His hair is black and is cut military style and pushed up into a low mohawk. He has an Irish accent and a few tattoos, and his clothes fit him perfectly. He comes off like a cool person, offers to drive me to school, and asks me if I want to go to the movies. But going to the movies with him is too private for me. I don't want him trying to have his way with me. He's nice, but I still can't let that fool me. Besides, he just got his driver's permit a few months ago. How can he drive without an adult when he's only fifteen? You have to be at least sixteen to drive without an adult.

According to Scott, his parents are very relaxed and let him drive without them all the time. He started driving a year ago, even before he had a permit. Although Steve is much stricter than Scott's parents, he still lets him drive without an adult, even living under his roof with only a permit.

Chapter 3

PRESENTLY

It's morning time; I get out of the bathtub and start drying off. My door opens suddenly, startling me. I jump to wrap the bath towel back around me, anxious to cover my back where Earl branded me. I turn around and look over to the doorway. It's Steve. He stands there in shock; he drops the breakfast tray he has for me on the floor. His face shifts from shock to pain as we lock eyes.

"What the fuck, Steve! Knock!" I yell, no longer looking him in the eyes.

"What the hell is that!" he yells, disturbed by my slaughtered back.

"Nothing! Get the fuck out!"

"The hell it is! Who did that?" he demands.

"Steve, I'm trying to get fucking dressed. Please leave!" I beg, crying.

"Okay, but when you're done, I want you downstairs so we can talk."

He leaves my room. I hear him stomping down every single step back downstairs. He's really pissed, I think to myself. He never stomps, and he never cusses, but he did today. "That poor girl," I hear him repeating over and over.

I continue getting ready for the day and begin thinking about my birthday. It's in two days, and I'm turning twelve. Also, Tracy is out of rehab and back at Steve's. I can't believe she completed the program. She's up and out and always shopping. Hey, what can you say? Steve is loaded, and Tracy knows how to spend his money. Living with Steve is not as bad as I thought it would be. He hasn't tried to make a move on me, and neither has his nephew, Scott.

We go to Steve's parents' house every weekend for their big family dinners. His family treats me like I'm one of them. I feel safe in my new environment and with my new family, but I'm not letting my guard down anytime soon. Feelings can be tricky, and that's how you get got. Not me — won't be me.

Finally, I'm dressed. I take a deep breath; it's time to head downstairs. Thank God Scott is out with his friends right now. Steve and I are the only ones home. There's no way of getting around the subject with Steve. By the tone of his voice, I knew he was serious and wanted the truth about my back. I go downstairs, and feel my face turning red and my heart pounding a mile a minute. My stomach is sitting at the bottom of my gut. I feel like a criminal on their way to trial, but I'm the victim.

Steve is sitting on one of the kitchen island stools facing the kitchen entrance. When I walk in, he looks directly at me. "I know I'm not your father, but Dawn, I want you to know I care for you deeply. You're like my daughter, and I'll do anything for you. You can also speak to me about anything. So please, Dawn, tell me who did that to you?" he says to me calmly, his face stricken with sadness.

My eyes become glossy, and tears trickle down, "Like, you really care what happens to me?" I reply.

"Open your eyes, Dawn. If I truly didn't care, I wouldn't have done any of this for you."

"How do I know you're not just pretending to be nice so you can get in my pants? You're faking this nice guy act, so I won't fight back. I'm not stupid."

"Is that what you think?" Steve responds, shaking his head in disbelief at the words spewing from my mouth.

"I don't know what to think anymore," I tell him.

"The bastard that did this to you has really fucked you up internally, Dawn. This is sad, sweetheart. You can't see it when someone sincerely cares about you. I think of you as my daughter, and please believe I'd never ever do anything to hurt you like that son of a bitch has. I swear, I'll never do anything to hurt you." Steve speaks from the bottom of his heart.

Steve's protective and fatherly nature strikes a chord; my tears flow nonstop. I walk over to him, remove my shirt, and show my back to him. He reads it. Steve is quiet; it's a lot to take in. I start to put my shirt back on, and as I turn around, Scott is standing there. Steve is so hurt by what he's seen he falls out of his seat, overtaken by the grossness of what someone has done to me.

"What the hell is going on here!" Scott yells at Steve, believing something inappropriate has occurred between Steve and me. He starts to approach Steve, enraged and ready to beat the hell out of him. I stop Scott. He looks me in the eyes sternly, "What is he doing to you?"

"Nothing!" I turn around to Scott and reveal my sex slave imprinted back to him. I know I have a hell of a lot of explaining to do. I hurry up and finish putting my shirt back on. I don't need Tracy to come in and see this too. Scott helps Steve get up from the floor, and they sit on the stools. They wait silently for me to start talking. I tell them everything.

I feel like a huge weight has been lifted from my shoulders. I even tell them about how I'm triggered by what Earl has done to me and my nightmares that won't go away. "It's like it's still happening. I wake up in the middle of the night. I'm always drenched in sweat, crying, and screaming. The only reason you never hear me is because I tie a cloth around my mouth. I don't want to scare anyone." I let them know.

Steve and Scott don't yell, criticize, or accuse me of lying. They sit there and listen. They comfort me in my moment of vulnerability and let me cry and get it all out without interruptions. Steve was right. Earl did fuck me up mentally. I hate and distrust all men, even the good ones like them that do things for me and never hurt me. I was taking all my anger and hatred out on them for all the months I've been living here. I was mean and nasty. I never thank them for anything and question everything they do for me. They were doing nice things for me out of the kindness of their heart and for no other reason. Honestly, they love me, but I've never been able to realize that until now.

Steve's parents and family treat me like I'm part of their family. They take me places and always give me things. They even planned a huge birthday party for me, including presents. I've been too blind to see that they genuinely care about me. I realize how much of an asshole I've been towards them, and they've never been anything but kind to me. This family has not abandoned me like my father did, nor has anyone raped me or carved anything into my back.

For the first time, I feel like Steve is my father. So, from this day onward, it'll be the last day I call him Steve. Also, Scotty has become my best friend. I decide to put my guard down with them because I feel safe. At the next family dinner at Steve's parents' home, I'll make it known that Steve is my father and that I accept the Sandino family as my own, as they have accepted me.

"Uncle Steve, is taking Dawnie to the movies okay?" Scotty asks Dad.

"Yeah, if it's okay with her," he says. They both turn and look at me.

"Yes, it's okay. Let me change my clothes for the movies. Thanks, Dad and Scotty, for listening," I say to them. I look over to Dad to see his reaction. He looks at me joyfully, his eyes watery.

"No problem," they both reply.

"Oh, and kids, don't forget about the family dinner at my parents' house tonight," Dad reminds us as I go up to change clothes in my room. I get up to my room and throw a nicer pair of jeans and a top on. Scotty and I are hanging out together, and it's nothing new. We always hang out together. We've become best friends. I must admit, I do have a slight crush on him. Although I'm very mature for my age, I doubt anything will happen between us because he's a few years older. I like being around Scotty; he's funny and my first real friend.

"We'll meet you at Grandpa and Grandma's house," I say to Dad as I come back down the steps.

"Ready?" I ask Scotty, who's waiting by the front door. I can sense Scotty and Dad's hesitation; they're registering that I referred to Dad's parents as Grandpa and Grandma.

Scotty finally speaks, "Yeah." He opens the door, and we hop into the car. He blasts music like always. We start singing our favorite song that's playing, "Gotta Live Like We Dying" by Kris Allen. We watch *The Fighter*, then go to Ruby Tuesday to eat. I order my usual steak, cooked medium-rare with green beans. Ever since Dad made me one that way, I crave medium-rare steaks. Scotty gets something different each time we come here.

"You know, I always wonder why you get the same thing every time we come here," he says.

"And I always wonder why you always get something new every time we come here," I reply, laughing.

"I like trying new things," he says.

"Well, I don't. I'd rather stick to what I'm use to."

"Playing it safe, I see." Scotty chuckles.

"No," I laugh.

"I can tell a lot about girls from the way they look and what they eat."

"Oh yeah? So, what does my eating say about me?" I ask him.

"That you're afraid to try something new because you're unsure if you'll like it. You're afraid of change, Dawn, because of what the outcome might be. You're what you put off being, but deep inside, I know a part of you wants to come out and be free," he says, glaring at me.

"Oh yeah, well, I think you choose something different all the time because you swear you're spontaneous, and you're a hard ass. You like to put on this 'don't fuck with me or I'll break your face' persona. But you're really a sensitive, scared, and lonely little boy crying for help… you like to hide it, though, by sleeping around and fighting people. You can't hide your feelings from me, though, Scotty. I can see right through you. I see you." I say with an attitude, glaring back.

The waitress arrives with our food, but we stare at each other in shock over what we've revealed about our thoughts on each other. I have no idea how he noticed that about me, and I bet he's thinking the same. We break our stare and eat in silence. It's such an awkward moment. After we finish, we head to the car.

"No one has ever said that to me before," he says.

"Same here, and I'm not sorry for telling you, but I am sorry for insulting you," I say softly.

"You didn't insult me, but you did surprise me. No one gets me like you get me. You understand me without me telling you," Scotty replies. He leans in and touches my face gently; Scotty kisses me. I kiss him back. I pull away, wondering if he thinks he's made a big mistake and ruined our friendship by kissing me. "Sorry, Dawn. I don't know what came over me. I swear, please don't be mad."

"I'm not mad, and I don't regret it. I've been waiting for what seems like forever for you to kiss me." I say coyly.

"Then, why pull back?" he asks.

"Because I don't want you to wake up tomorrow regretting it and ending our friendship." He starts the car and looks at me before pulling off.

"That would never happen." He kisses me again, and I don't pull back as quickly this time.

We must get to our grandparents' house; we're already running late. He pulls off and drives us for about five minutes; our grandparents live nearby. He parks in their long driveway, and we go in. Of course, Tracy is nowhere in sight — she's not even here, and Dad is in the living room with his brothers, cousins, and father having a drink. All the women are in the sunroom having cocktails. Whelp, we're really late, I see. The family always does this after dinner.

My grandparents have the entire family over for dinner twice a week, Saturdays and Sundays. We gather at a huge table and eat for what always seems like forever because everyone is always talking and mingling. Afterward, everyone retreats and socializes. We go to the backyard, swim, and play. I always find it to be quite enjoyable. Right before it's time to leave, the men go to the living room, the women go to the sunroom, and everyone my age and Scotty's go down to the basement and hang out while the younger children remain outside and play. Today is no different. We're just late.

When my dad started bringing me, I used to stick with him or Scotty. They were the only ones I knew. However, I've become close to my dad's family. They refer to me as their granddaughter, niece, and cousin. Scotty and I walk over to greet the men. I kiss Dad on the cheek and sit beside him on the sofa. Scotty sits on the floor between us.

"How was the movie — Denny and Scott?" Grandpa asks, often calling me by his deceased daughter's name.

Grandpa's name is Arthur. His hair is salt and pepper, and he stands slightly shorter than Dad. Dad looks just like his father, too. At first, I used to get annoyed when he called me by her name, but Dad told me his father is old and doesn't mean any harm and that I reminded him of her, but he knows I'm not her.

"Good, Grandpa. Sorry, I missed dinner," I answer.

For a moment, the room becomes silent. The family, surprised. I've been here for almost a year, and they have been trying to get me to call them grandpa, grandma, aunt, uncle, and cousin. Grandpa gives me a huge grin and other family members' faces lit up in the room. A little later, I hear people in the kitchen. By their voices, I know it's Uncle Brian and his wife.

Uncle Brian and his wife, Aileen, live in Ireland. Aileen's daughter, who's around my age, also lives with them, as do Uncle Brian's three sons. They take their private jet here every weekend. It's not a secret that Uncle Brian and his wife have severe problems in their marriage. The family doesn't like Aileen. Even Aileen's own daughter has a problem with her. I feel bad for Aileen since she's the most hated person in the family. Everyone blames her for her and Uncle Brian's marital problems. She's alone in this family. No one likes her around and talks bad about her right in front of her face.

"Hey, Uncle Brian and Aunt Aileen," I say, hugging them both. They're stunned by how I address them. I've never called them uncle or aunt.

Grandma walks in with an empty wine glass. "You call that an aunt? More like a mistake."

"Grandma!" I say, displeasure heard in my voice because of her meanness towards Aunt Aileen.

"Mom. Really?" Uncle Brian chimes in.

"Just when I thought you couldn't go any lower," Aunt Aileen snaps back.

"Bitch. You're in my house." Grandma blurts.

"Aednat!" Grandpa says, exiting his armchair and walking towards the open kitchen. We know Grandpa is mad when he calls someone by their real name and not by the nickname he gave them.

"Yeah. Not for long or by choice. I'm ready to go now!" Aunt Aileen says, storming out of the kitchen and escaping her mother-in-law.

"What?" Grandma roars.

While tempers flare, I slip out the back door to check on Aunt Aileen, but she's not in the backyard. She's made her way to the front and is walking down the long driveway. I run to catch up with her. "Auntie, wait up!" I yell from a distance. She turns around, and boy, is she pissed off.

"Hey sweetheart, how are you," forcing a sweet tone.

"Well, better than you are right now," I reply, catching up to her.

She laughs a little, "Oh, that was nothing compared to what she always says and does. You should see her when she comes to Ireland."

"After seeing that, I believe you. I mean no offense, but it's no secret the Sandino family has something against you," I say, putting two fingers up and moving them up and down to quote "the Sandino family."

"Sweetie, I know it's no secret, and your grandma makes it no secret either. The whole family hates me, and I think your uncle does too."

"Then, why stay? Why even put up with all of this?" I ask her.

"Well, at first, it was because of Brian. I love him so much."

"And now?"

"Now, I sadly have no choice."

"What do you mean?"

"You know that saying, 'You chose the life you live'?"

"Yes, I hear it all the time," I mention.

"Well, one day, when you get older, you will learn that is a bunch of bullshit."

"Wow! Aileen Sandino. Did you curse?" I gasp. This woman never curses even when she should cuss Grandma out for things like what happened in the kitchen.

She musters a chuckle, "Yes, I believe I did. But really, it's bullshit. Not everyone chooses the life they live. Some of us are forced to live a life we no longer want."

"Is that what's happening to you?" I ask her.

"Yes, sadly. My life was chosen for me ages ago. One day, you'll know what I mean."

Alarmed by Aunt Ailee's coded messaging, I ask, "What do you mean 'one day'?" We're interrupted by a truck pulling up and blowing the horn. We see Uncle Brian driving. The windows are rolled down halfway, and all their kids were in the back. Auntie hugs me and kisses me on the cheek.

"Like I said, one day, your life is a written book unlike the rest of us. You be safe, my girl." She hops in the black truck. Uncle Brian lowers Aunt Aileen's tinted window and leans over her.

"Hey, when are you coming to Ireland to visit us?" he asks me.

"I can come to Ireland?"

They laugh, "Yes, you can come — use the family jet."

"Family jet?" I say, my face scrunched up.

"Wow, I'll speak to your father; he'll set it up. Come over here and give me a hug. I'll see you next weekend, hopefully," he says. I walk over to his side, give him a hug, and kiss him goodbye.

"See you, Uncle Brian, bye Auntie, and bye guys," I say to Aunt Aileen's daughter, Elizabeth, and Uncle Brian's boys.

"See you, sweetheart. I love you." Uncle Brian says.

"Love you too."

Chapter 4

SCOTTY

After the incident at my grandparents', everyone leaves. When we get home, Dad is tired and tells us goodnight before retreating to his bedroom. Again, Tracy is not home. She tends to stay out late and leave home early. How Dad is still in love with her is beyond me. I start going upstairs; I turn around, and Scotty's right behind me, halfway up. He catches up to me; I kiss him goodnight. The kiss is excellent. He wraps his arms around me and holds me close. It's like a dream come true. I don't want this moment to end, but I know it must. I pull away from him, and we reach the top of the stairs. Scotty expects me to kiss him again, but I don't. Instead, I head to my room. "Thanks for tonight. I had a nice time," I whisper to him, still walking to my room.

"No more kisses?" he whispers back.

I blow him one last kiss and go into my room. Kissing Scotty tonight was the first real kiss that I've had and liked. Well, technically, nasty Earl kissed me first, but that doesn't count because I didn't want him to. I can't stop thinking about Scotty. I've always liked him more than just friends, but I never thought we'd kiss, especially considering our age difference. Then, by surprise, my thoughts are interrupted. Scotty opens my bedroom door and whispers my name.

"Come in," I say.

Scotty enters and closes the door behind him. He walks over and sits at the end of my bed. I sit up and turn on my lamp. We squint at each other. My eyes take a few seconds to transition from the darkness to the bright light.

"Can you turn that off? It's hurting my eyes. Please?" he asks me, moving closer to me.

"Yeah, sure." I turn off the lamp, and glimpses of the moon peek through my blinds, turning us into silhouette figures. "What's up? Why did you come in here?" I ask him.

"Well, I was in my room alone and could not stop thinking about you. I know what you're going to say. I'm too old for you, and this will never work, but if you forget about how old I am and how old you are and think about our emotional connection, we're the same age. Dawn, you're so mature for your age, me and you work." He pauses and waits for me to respond. I say nothing. He continues, "What I'm trying to say, Dawnie, is I can't get you out of my mind. I've always liked you but never had the guts to tell you, but after tonight, I was hoping you felt the…" I lean in, reach for his face, and pull him towards me, interrupting him with a kiss. He pauses between our kisses and continues with his last word, "…same."

"That answers your question?" I ask.

"Yeah, it does. Can I see your remote?"

"My what?"

"Remote. I want to show you something." I feel for the remote on my bed and hand it to him. He turns off the blinds, and they retract to the ceiling. I see the moon and stars fully, shining above the ocean.

"Wow, that's really beautiful."

"I know, it reminds me of you. Can we look at it together and cuddle?" Scotty asks while scooting me over and hopping in.

"Yeah, sure." My heart pounds. We look at the moon and stars reflecting on the ocean. I feel so safe. Nothing can hurt me. I feel loved, wanted, and needed. It's the best feeling in the world. Is this what it feels like to be in love? Is this the same feeling that makes people want to marry? I become so comfortable and relaxed in my blissful thoughts that I fight my sleep. I don't want to have nightmares in front of him; they will only ruin the moment, especially if I pull out my cloth from under my pillow and tie it around my mouth to muffle my screams.

I become more tired. My eyes grow heavy, and I feel it. I decide to rest my eyes. It's a moment of serenity. Laying in Scotty's arms brings me such contentment. I fall into a deep sleep without the cloth. When we wake up, I'm still in his arms. "You've got to go before Dad and Tracy see us together," I say, coming to my morning senses. I begin to drift in my thoughts and reflect on last night. I can't believe I slept so well last night. No cloths, no nightmares, no sweats, no screams. I slept like a baby, even better than when I used to sleep in that box in the alley. But then again, my back was bleeding at the time; it was dirty and very uncomfortable. I was free from Earl in that hiding place, and that's the only reason I could sleep then.

"Don't worry about it. Uncle Steve and Tracy think I'm in my room; they never go in there. Besides, as always, Tracy is probably not even here, and Uncle Steve is downstairs. I heard them go down there hours ago making breakfast. Uncle Steve knows we're best friends and has seen us in each other's rooms before, remember?" he says reassuringly.

"Yeah, I know."

"We should spend the day together," Scotty suggests.

"Don't we do that already?"

"Yeah, but then we split and go our separate ways."

"Okay, let me cancel with Brittany; I'm all yours," I say eagerly.

"I like the sound of that. See you downstairs," he says, kisses me, gets up, and leaves.

I look at my phone. I have ten missed calls and two voicemails from Brittany, my best friend. We became friends when I moved here and started going to school. We hit it off from the start because we liked the same things. Brittany's hair is long; her complexion is a little lighter than mine; her nails are always done; she's very high maintenance, wears high heels only, and, unfortunately, can't dress that well. She's fat and swears she's the shit. Her voice is high-pitched and annoying, like someone from the movie *Mean Girls*. She sounds so fake. It's not her real voice, but she wants it to be. I call her back.

The phone barely rings once, and she answers, "What the fuck, Dawnie?"

"Sorry, I overslept and wanted to know if we could chill tomorrow.

"What? Why?" she whines.

"Because I have to go somewhere with Scotty."

"Go where?"

"I don't know, Britt. I was told to get dressed and that I have to go with him somewhere."

"Fine."

"Sorry."

"It's okay, call me later."

"Okay, I will. Bye, girl." I hang up.

"Dawnie, come and eat!" Dad yells.

"Okay, coming!" I shout back. He doesn't call Scotty's name, though. Scotty must be downstairs already, and I am right. I sit at the kitchen counter to eat my breakfast. My phone vibrates on the counter. It's Scotty texting me from the other side of the kitchen, telling me to remind Dad and Tracy that I'm hanging out with Brittany today and that Scotty will drop me off at her house.

"Dad, I'm going to go to Brittany's house today, and Scotty said he will drop me off. Is that okay?"

"Yup. Take your phone and call me if you need anything," Dad says. I look around, waiting to hear Tracy's voice, but again, she's not there, which is not surprising.

"Tracy didn't come home last night again?" I ask loudly.

"I don't believe so," Dad replies.

"What a shock," I say sarcastically.

"Do you know where Tracy is?"

"Not at all. You know how your mother is. She likes to keep her business private." Dad says, blindly defending her as usual.

"She sure does. Well, I got to get ready," I say, jetting back upstairs to get dressed. I'm excited and nervous about hanging out with Scotty. We've hung out so many times before, but this time will be different. We've never taken things further than being friends, but now we've kissed, sat under the stars in my room, and cuddled. This time will be different. I want to wear something cute and sexy, but I don't want to be like all the other girls Scotty dates.

I have a hard time narrowing down my outfit. When we first moved in with Dad, he took me shopping. When Tracy came out of rehab, he took her too. I have a huge wardrobe now. I have all name-brand clothes; my walk-in closet is full. I finally settle on wearing shorts, a plaid shirt thrown over a white tank top, and Gucci flip-flops.

Scotty knocks on my door and comes in as I look at myself in the mirror and brush my hair. "You know you don't have to dress up for me," he grins.

I look at him with a snippy stare, "Who said I was dressing up for you?"

"Umm, maybe because we're spending the day together," he replies, chuckling. He stands behind me, holds my waist, and kisses my neck. We both look into the mirror, stare at each other and smile. "I'll be downstairs," he says.

"Okay, I'll be down in a minute."

When Scotty leaves my room, I run to the bathroom and spray my favorite perfume, Victoria's Secret's Pink Fresh & Clean, all over me. I hurry downstairs. Scotty is already outside in the car waiting for me. Dad is in his office, and Tracy is still not here. She's probably at the mall on a shopping spree with the credit cards Dad gave her. Another thing is Dad gave Tracy and me credit cards with no set limits. I have no doubt Tracy takes advantage of that.

I get in the car, and Scotty zooms off. "Where are we going?" I ask.

"You'll see," he says, looking straight ahead. We drive for about ten minutes and arrive at a beautiful lake — a hidden gem. He parks the car, and we get out. He opens the trunk and pulls out a basket.

"A picnic?" I say, in my guessing voice.

"Yeah, Uncle Steve thinks I'm going with someone else; that's the only way I could make this day work."

We find a good spot by the water. He spreads the blanket out, and we lie down on it. A few minutes later, Scotty starts to take his clothes off. What is he doing? Does he really think I'm going to sleep with him? Scotty knows what I've been through! I drop what's in my hand and walk away from him.

"Where are you going?"

"Far away from you!"

"Why?"

"Because I'm not another one of your slutty, whorish girlfriends who sleeps with you in a blink of an eye!"

"I didn't say you were," he says, running after me.

"Then, why would you undress in front of me?"

"Because I'm about to swim in the lake and don't want to get my clothes wet. I didn't think you'd mind; you've seen me in my boxers before!" he says, trying to reason with me.

I stop and look at him, "Oh, my bad. Sorry, I thought…"

"That I was a pervert and was going to have my way with you?" he exclaims.

"Yeah."

"No offense. You're a lovely girl, Dawnie, but I don't want to do that with you… yet. You're not that kind of girl. That's why I like you more than these other girls. I want to swim, eat, and talk. I hope you'll join me." He holds his hand out to me. Feeling so dumb, I grab his hand. I thought Scotty was trying to make a move on me, but I was wrong. I apologize to him, and we walk back to our picnic. I keep my tank top on when we get into the lake. I don't want Scotty to see the scars on my back again. I want the rest of this day to go perfectly.

"You never struck me as the picnic type," I say to Scotty while floating on my back in the water.

"That's because I'm not. I normally come here by myself to swim. It's quiet, peaceful, and helps me clear my mind and think."

"So, why did you bring me for a picnic if it's not something you like to do?"

"Because, for some reason, you're different, Dawn."

"Well, you've never lived in the same home with the other girls," I reply.

"Yeah, true, but it's not because we live together. It's because I can be myself around you. I never could do that before. Somehow, you understand me better than I understand myself. Like that time at Ruby Tuesday when you said I'm like a little boy hiding and screaming for help. How did you know that about me? How can you see who I am deep down inside before I can see it for myself?"

"I don't know, maybe because you try so hard to be something you're not. You start to forget the real person inside of you. When I look at you, I can tell you're unhappy, and you always put on this fake smile in front of people." I say, standing up in the water and feeling small rocks under my feet.

He places his hands on my hips, pulls me towards him, and kisses my lips softly. "Come on, let's go eat," he says, quickly changing the subject. Scotty has sandwiches for us with extra Miracle Whip and chips. He also has Sprite and my favorite candy, Swedish Fish. We act like fat asses and eat away. Being greedy together is one of the best things we like about each other. We laugh and play around for hours. The sun is slowly setting, so we put our clothes on. When we leave, my underwear and tank top are completely dry.

We drive two hours away to San Diego because no one knows us there. We can be a couple without it getting back to Dad and Tracy. Scotty pays for everything I point out that I like. We go to the movies but don't pay attention because we're too busy making out. It's late when we get home. Thankfully, Dad and Tracy are not home. I go to my room to shower and change into my night clothes. Scotty does the same. I climb into my bed and think about everything happening between us. I like Scotty so much, even though we live in the same house; I don't like it when I'm not beside him. Is this love I'm feeling for Scotty? Because it's not lust. Lust is just people having a lot of sex with no real feelings involved.

Scotty and I are not even on that page. I'm not ready, and he said he's not either. This is my first real relationship by choice, and Scotty makes me feel safe. No one can hurt me, not even Earl. There's a knock at my door; I'm sure it's Dad. I pretend to be asleep. Seconds later, I feel lips touch my face. It's Scotty. I return the kiss when he reaches my lips.

"Thought you were sleeping," he whispers.

"And I thought you were Dad," I say with a giggle.

Scotty hops in the bed with me. While we lie there, a random thought pops in my head. I want to find Alex. I want to find him and meet him and his family, too. I'm clueless to why I'm having these thoughts because I've never had them before, nor did I care about my biological father's whereabouts. Right now, all I know is that I want to meet him. Maybe Dad can help me. "Hey Scotty…"

"Yes?"

"I want to meet Alex."

Chapter 5

IRELAND

I'm asleep in my room when Dad and Scotty barge in. Scotty jumps on my bed, all excited. "Happy birthday! Happy birthday! Pack your bags! We're going to Ireland, where we will stay for a while!" Scotty sings while jumping up and down on my bed. Dad sits down next to me and laughs.

"What? Where are we going?" I ask as I sit up.

"Belfast, Ireland! Going to Uncle Brian's house, birthday girl, for your birthday, so get your shit, and put it in a suitcase so we can leave!" he says, plumping his butt down on the bed.

"Wait! What? When?"

"Happy birthday, sweetheart! We're going today. Get some clothes on. Your Uncle Brian said you two were talking about it that night at the last family dinner," Dad replies.

"Are you serious?" I scream, jumping out of bed, too excited for my own good, and trip over my feet. We're laughing and I notice something on the other side of my bed. I get up, and see lovely brown Gucci luggage. I've never had any luggage or Gucci at that, but Britt has tons of Gucci. I remember looking at one of the price tags. It was over a thousand dollars. "Wow! Gucci! Dad, seriously?" I say while picking up one of the bags of luggage that is way too heavy to be empty.

"That's not all, look inside!" he grins.

I look over to Scotty; he's smiling, too. I open the bag, and it has Gucci clothes inside. One thing about my dad and Scotty is they know exactly what I like. They can go shopping for me without me even having to be there, but on the other hand, Tracy can't. We have different tastes. She buys things, and I hate them.

"You guys are the best!" I scream and jump on my dad to hug him and Scotty.

"I'm glad you like it. Now get dressed and ready so we can go. We can have breakfast on the plane," Dad says.

"Wait. I don't know what to wear."

"Put on something warm. It's cold as ice down there. Trust me, the hottest it gets is nineteen degrees around this time of the year," says Scotty.

"Woah, are you serious? I've lived in Cali my whole life. All I have is spring and summer clothes." I reply worriedly.

"Open your suitcases and look in your closet. I'm sure you will find something. Plus, your Uncle Brian will send Elizabeth and you shopping," Dad answers.

Sure enough, there are winter clothes in my suitcase and closet. I know Dad and Scotty put them there. "Yes! Thanks guys, you're the best."

"No problem. But hurry up so we can go! I love you. Happy birthday!" Dad cheers again. He hugs me and kisses my forehead; he and Scotty leave the room so I can get ready.

I'm not surprised Tracy never came to my room this morning. She always forgets my birthday. I don't think Tracy even knows how old I am. She'd probably forget I existed if she didn't have to feed or deal with me before we lived here. Tracy was always like that. Fuck birthdays and holidays unless it meant presents for her or giving her attention. One of the reasons Fawn left home was she become tired and short-tempered with Tracy. Fawn was always mean to Tracy, but the month before she left home, she acted weirdly for some reason.

I see a few pairs of Uggs in multicolor, white, baby blue, and black. The multicolor ones combine violet, brown, and dark blue. I grab them and put them in a bag with jeans, long-sleeve shirts, and a red peacoat. It's too hot here to wear that stuff, so I'll change on the plane, I think to myself — I can do that. This is going to be my first time on a plane.

There's a knock on my door; Dad is seeing if I'm ready to go. "I'm ready! I need help with my bags," I tell him while throwing one of my bags over my shoulder. Scotty and Dad take my bags, and we drive to the airport. Little did I know, the plane we're getting on is our own private plane. I knew Dad was wealthy, but I never knew he could afford a private plane! Dad's last name is on it, along with everything else. We get inside the plane, and it takes my breath away. I stop dead in my tracks, and my mouth opens wide in astonishment like a dummy. I look all around the plane. The seats are white couches with seat belts attached, a bar, white carpet, a kitchen, a hot tub, a bedroom, a bathroom, a huge widescreen TV, and more. Everything on the plane is stitched and etched with the capital letter "S" in red.

"Wow!" I gasp.

"You like it?" Dad asks.

"No, I love it," I say.

"Me too," says Scotty.

"I didn't know you had this, Dad."

"You never asked," he replies.

"I'm not supposed to. You're just supposed to tell me." I say back.

"Okay. Hey, Dawnie."

"Yes?"

"By the way, I own a private plane," he laughs.

"Ha, ha. Very funny, Dad. Uncle Brian said there was a family jet, but he never told me you had your own one, too!" I sit down to buckle up. Scotty sits beside me, and Dad sits across from us; they buckle up. We take off.

"There's a family jet, too, but I had to get my own with work because I was traveling a lot. Other family members needed to go places but couldn't because I'd be using it. So, I decided to get my own," Dad explains. A few minutes pass, and Scotty removes his seat belt and goes to the bedroom. I stare at Dad crazily. "Why the face, Dawnie?" Dad laughs.

"Scotty took off his seat belt and got up like we aren't moving. Is he crazy? We're in the air!"

They both start laughing, "This is not a car. You're allowed to move around on a plane once we're up in the air, hence the hot tub and bed," Dad says.

"Oh, I had no idea!" I say, feeling embarrassed and turning red.

"It's okay, Dawnie. I thought the same thing my first time here, too." Scotty chimes in and throws me bikini bottoms and a white shirt. "Coming in the hot tub?" he nudges.

"You know it. Just let me throw this on."

"You kids have fun. I'm going to do some work in my office. If you need anything, just let me know." Dad tells us while walking to the back.

"Okay, Dad, thanks."

"Yeah, thanks, Uncle Steve."

"No problem."

We get in the hot tub. It's big, more like a swimming pool. Dad spends at least an hour in his room before he returns to hang out with us. I'm having so much fun on the plane. We try to watch a movie, but it's an epic fail. So, we decide to keep playing. We play Marco Polo blindfolded, and before I know it, we're landing in Ireland. The captain lets us know it's below thirty degrees outside, so we change into our winter clothes before leaving the plane. Uncle Brian is waiting in his truck outside when we deboard.

"Happy Birthday!" Uncle Brian cheers and hands me a bouquet of flowers.

"Thank you, Uncle Brian!" I say. I hug him and plant a kiss on his cheek. He opens the truck door for me, and we all get in. We drive for two hours and arrive at a castle. Not a house, not a mansion, but a castle! The castle is in the middle of nowhere. Nothing is around but a lake, woods, a little barn, and acres of land. There's a little house next to the castle; we pull up to it. "Wow, this house is beautiful." Uncle Brian chuckles, but no one says anything. I peep at the smirks on their faces. We walk inside; the house is empty. "Where is everyone?" I ask.

"Oh... they're somewhere. Why don't you three get settled and dressed so we can go? Oh, and Dawnie, in that room, there's a special dress for you to wear," Uncle Brian mentions, then sits down on the couch in the great room to watch TV.

"Okay," I reply and head to the room with the dress.

There's a white dress bag labeled Cache on the bed. I open it and see the most beautiful dress my eyes have ever seen. It resembles a wedding dress minus a husband. It's white with rhinestones, but the rhinestones are not cheap-looking; they look real. They're diamonds! It's peplum princess style, and the bottom is beautifully draped to the floor. The dress takes my breath away. Tears stream down my eyes. I'm speechless, "Wow." I whisper.

"Do you like it?" asks Uncle Brian.

I turn around and see all of them standing there looking at me, waiting for an answer. I'm so amazed by the dress; I didn't even hear them come in. "I love it. I've never had anything so lovely. What's this dress for?"

"You'll see, just get ready. Your bath is drawn, and your stylist will be here when you come out. It's your big day, and you have several surprises." Uncle Brian says to me. They close the door.

I look around the room. I was so focused on the big white bag and amazed by the beautiful dress inside that I had overlooked the room. The room is gigantic, with a big fluffy canopy bed. It has large windows that give a grand view of a charming lake. The bathroom has candles and a warm bubble bath that awaits me. Living with Dad and being part of his family has spoiled me. I get into the bathtub. The water is still hot as if someone just ran the water for me.

More than an hour passes, I finally get out of the tub. My stylist is set up and waiting for me. She puts my hair in a Roman style. She gives me loose curls, one medium-sized braid on each side of my hair, pulls it back, braids them together, and curls the ends. She crowns me with a tiara; my hair is divine. Next, she does my makeup perfectly to go with my dress, helps me get into it, and zips me up. I put on white flats that match the dress. "Why am I wearing flats with such a lovely dress?" I question out loud.

The stylist laughs with a heavy accent, "You're such a funny girl. Soon, you'll be a lady and will wear heels, but not any sooner."

"Okay…" I say, a little lost while thinking about the poor optics of wearing flats with this lovely dress. These flats make everything look horrible. I leave the room and go to the great room.

The guys are in nice tuxedos, patiently waiting for me. They all stop looking at the TV and stare at me like a stranger. "Hey, how do I look?" I say, turning red and feeling embarrassed.

"Beautiful," they reply collectively.

"Really? Because these flats look horrible with this dress."

Uncle Brian laughs. "Trust me, you will be out of those flats sooner than you know it. Come on, time to go." We go outside and get into Uncle Brian's truck again. We head straight for the castle, leaving me confused.

"Where are we going Uncle Brian?" I ask for the second time today.

"Dawn, you sure ask many questions," he keeps laughing. He pulls up in front of the castle, and a man in a suit opens the door. We leave and walk towards two enormous doors that slowly open for us. We don't even have to touch them. Two butlers take our jackets. We go upstairs to a hallway, and another flight of stairs meets us, but then we stop. Dad, Uncle Brian, and Scotty look at me and smile. I'm still confused. I have no idea what's going on. Scotty gestures towards Dad and me as if introducing us to someone.

"Surprise! Happy birthday!" is all I hear in the commotion of the crowd before my eyes. Everyone is formally dressed like us. It's like it's a beautiful ball or high school prom. I walk into the huge room. There are calla lilies and orchards of all colors everywhere, servers holding trays of champagne with hors d'oeuvres on them, white color marble stairs, huge crystal lights hanging from the ceiling, an enormous chocolate fountain, a sushi bar, and more than I can even wrap my mind around.

"Ladies and gentlemen, I want to introduce Scott McLoughlin..." Scotty smiles and cockily walks down the stairs to all the people, leaving me standing there with Dad and Uncle Brian. "... and last but not least, the birthday girl, Dawn Trieger, and father, Steve Sandino." Dad and I start walking down the stairs. I look around in amazement. I've never seen anything like this before. Walking down, I notice familiar faces, I see Grandma, Grandpa, Uncle Brian's kids, Aunt Aileen, and the rest of my family. No one has ever remembered my birthday or cared enough to throw me such a grand party in secret and make me feel like Cinderella without the wicked stepmother and evil sisters. "... look and witness her as she walks down the stairway to her destiny and into her womanhood," the announcer continues.

I can't help but cry. For once, I finally understand the meaning of family. Dad and his family have taught me the true meaning of family and what it means to love and be loved. Tears of happiness stream down my face as we meet Scotty at the bottom of the stairs. Scotty is holding high heels that match my dress. "Dawn Trieger, will you accept the next step into womanhood?" Scotty asks me.

The room goes quiet. I look around and take everything in. I realize something. Although I'm part of the Sandino family, my last name remains Trieger. I've never had anything to do with Alex or met him. He left before I could even say "Dada." Here, a man and his family go above and beyond to make me feel like one of their own.

"Wait!" I interrupt. The guests begin to look taken aback, even Scotty and Dad.

"Honey, it's usually a 'yes' or 'no.' Most girls say, 'yes' in case you were wondering," whispers Dad.

I ignore him and run back up the stairs to the announcer. "Sir, you called me by the last name, Trieger, and so did Scotty at the bottom when he asked me to put on these heels." I hold one of the heels up for him to see.

"Isn't that your last name?" someone shouts from the crowd below.

"Yes, it is. But I call Steve 'Dad' for a reason. He and his family have shown me what a family is and what it means to be loved by one. They knew I never knew what a family was before I met them. I'm trying to say that the only way I'll accept the next step into womanhood is if, from this moment forward, everyone accepts and calls me Dawn Sandino instead of Dawn Trieger," I respond to the crowd, then turn towards Dad to see his reaction. I see the happiness on his face and the gloss in his eyes he's trying to hide. The room is pleasantly surprised, and Scotty, still bending his knee with the other shoe, is shocked.

Uncle Brian makes his way back up the stairs, takes my hand, and walks me down, breaking the chitter-chatter, "Ladies and gentlemen, we now present Dawn Sandino and her father, Steve Sandino! Look, see, watch, and witness her take her next step into womanhood!"

"Dawn Sandino, will you accept the next step into becoming a woman?" Scotty asks me again.

"Yes, I do accept." The room erupts in applause.

"Ladies and gentlemen, I present to you now and forever Dawn Sandino, who has accepted the first step into womanhood, and her father, Steve Sandino!" Uncle Brian announces to the roaring crowd.

Dad and I walk into the crowd to join the family. So many people come up to congratulate me and wish me a happy birthday. I look over to the corner where Scotty is with our cousins. They're all laughing at me because I'm being bombarded from being the center of attention. Scotty and my cousins escape the ballroom through a back door that leads to the backyard. I follow but can't quite make my way through the crowd because I can't get away from everyone.

"Excuse me, sir, pardon us; I have to show my cousin something," Aengus cuts in, grabs my arm, and weaves me through the herd. I've never been so happy to see him in my life. Aengus is two or three years older than me, and we call him Gus for short. He has short black hair, a muscular frame, and a face that is too square-shaped. Aengus also has dimples, is a little taller than Scotty, and is strikingly sexy.

"Oh, thank God, where is everyone?" I ask, relieved that he's rescued me from all those people. We make it to the same door Scotty and the others left out of.

"They're at our hangout, away from everyone. Come on, I'm here saving you from everyone. Time to go," says Gus. I hold on to his arm, and we walk out the door into the cold.

"Holy shit, it's freezing!" I screech.

"I forgot, being from Cali and all, you're not used to the cold weather. Here, take my jacket," he laughs and hands it to me.

"How far is this hangout?"

"Not far at all. Remember the house you were getting ready in?"

"Yes."

"That's the hangout."

"I thought you lived there."

"Hell no, the house you were just in is where we live, silly," he laughs.

"You mean the castle we just left?"

"I guess if you call it that." Gus chuckles.

We arrive at the hangout and go inside. I run towards the fireplace to get heated. My cousins laugh at me. "Good god, it's fucking freezing outside." I blurt.

"It's not that cold," Elizabeth says. Elizabeth is Aunt Aileen's daughter. She has the same complexion as me; her body figure and stature are identical to mine.

"The hell it is. You're used to it." I remind her.

"So, Dawn Sandino, how are you today?" they say jokingly.

They aren't laughing to tease me or be assholes. They're laughing lightheartedly like friends do in funny situations. "Oh God, honestly, I have no idea where all that came from. I just opened my mouth, and it all started coming out. Thanks for the fucking heads-up, guys. What's up with this big ass ball? So, no one could've clued me in? I thought this family was simple. I would've settled with regular clothes and some music and the immediate family around, believe it or not," I say, laughing.

"Hey, we were going to do that, but your mother insisted we do all this. She said it's your first step into womanhood. She was supposed to come. She said the only way she would come is if we had the ball," says Aedan. Aedan is another one of Uncle Brian's sons. He looks like his brother, Aengus, but nowhere as muscular. Aedan is way more serious than Aengus. Aengus is all about his looks, working out, and girls, but Aedan needs to be more confident; he sticks to his studies. He's super book smart, rarely makes jokes, and when he does, it catches everyone off guard. Even Uncle Brian says he needs to lighten up a little.

"Yeah, but Tracy's still M-I-A," I tell them.

"Yup," they say.

"Why did she want this?" I inquire.

"Who knows. Tracy even told me what to say before I gave you your shoes," Scotty says.

"What do you mean?"

"At home, back in Cali, before we got on the plane, she told me in person what to say. When we got here and was going down the stairs, I saw her with a wine glass in her hand and she reminded me," he says.

I sit on the couch next to him. "What? She's here?"

"Yeah, she's in the room with everyone."

"First time I've seen her at a family function," Gus butts in.

"Yeah," they all agree.

Aedan enters the room with a bottle of red wine, "Anyone cares for a drink?"

"Where did you get that?" I ask curiously.

"Wine cellar downstairs where we keep all our wine," he replies, looking at me like I'm stupid.

"Dawnie, we have one back at home. Uncle Steve locks it up," says Scotty.

Aedan pops the wine bottle open, and we all get a glass. We sit down, talk, and hang out. Scotty puts his arm around me. I become nervous. What if Elizabeth and the other boys see us and tell Dad? I move away, putting a little space in between us. They all break out in laughter. "What's so funny?" I ask while starting to feel dizzy-headed.

"Dawnie, you don't have to hide it from us. We already know you and Scotty are a thing," Aedan says, taking another gulp of wine.

"What?" My face turns red in fear.

"Dawnie, it's okay. They know. I already told them. Look around you. Gus and Elizabeth are also together; we're the only ones who know."

I look at Gus and Elizabeth, realizing they're too close. "I didn't know until now," I say, giggling.

"Yes, we've been for a while. We're just extra careful with it so we won't get caught," Elizabeth says, moving closer to Gus. He kisses her on the cheek, and the way they look at each other makes me think they're deeply in love.

Scotty's phone rings, and he answers, "Hey, Uncle Steve." We wait while Dad is saying something on the other end. "Okay, coming now," Scotty hangs up.

"What did he want?" I ask.

"For you to come and open your gifts."

"I got gifts?"

My cousins start laughing again. "Umm, yeah… it's part of

birthdays."

We leave the hangout, return to the castle, and find Dad. I hear someone's fork clanking glass. Everyone turns towards the noise. It's Tracy standing there smiling. "If I can have everyone's attention, please." The room becomes quiet.

Grandma mumbles, "Ahh, shit." There's a shared feeling of uncomfortableness amongst some of the guests as we all turn towards Tracy's announcement. The room is silent out of fear, not because they're inclined to listen. She tries to stand on a chair but stumbles off and continues talking like nothing happened.

"I'm Tracy Doyle, and that's my daughter, Dawn. I'm so happy she made it to fifteen and is alive and well. I want to thank everyone for coming out here tonight."

I whisper to Dad, "What is she doing here? No one updated her on my real age?"

"Beats the hell out of me," he whispers back in shock.

"Dawn, sweetheart, come stand next to me please while I say what I have to say," she looks over to me, sniffing like she has a cold. Her nose is extra red, dry, and peeling — like when she was on drugs. I don't understand why she looks like this, especially since she just got out of rehab.

"I'm not going up there without you," I say to Dad, pulling him with me. I stand next to her shyly and take my dad's hand. She snatches me away from him. I look back at him with a "what the hell" expression.

"I've known Dawn her whole life. I was so excited when she was born. I raised her into a lovely, fully developed young lady." She turns me around like I'm for sale or something. "She has brains, bravery, a nice slim body with lovely hips, and a to-die-for ass," and she walks around me. I feel like she's auctioning me off. My face turns red. My eyes search the room for help while giving a fake smile. Somebody, save me — now, please, God.

My eyes catch several men making perverted smiles towards me — like they want to eat me for dinner. I lock eyes on Aunt Aileen, and she sees me screaming on the inside for someone to save me. She quickly snatches the microphone out of Tracy's hand and bumps her out of the way. "Okay, and thank you for that lovely and odd introduction, Tracy. We will keep all that in mind when Dawnie turns fifteen, but for now, she's twelve and very anxious to open her presents," Aunt Aileen says, redirecting the crowd from Tracy's odd behavior.

Tracy becomes highly upset. Uncle Brian and a few other men quickly rush her out of the room while she blurts obscenities, "You, stupid bitch! No one cuts me off. Get the fuck off me assholes!"

"Thank you so much, Auntie. That was very scary. What the hell was that about?"

"You know how Tracy can be. She's an attention seeker." She plays it off, kisses my forehead, and reassures me not to worry.

"Yeah, she sure is," I reply. I turn towards the crowd; the perverted-looking men are gone.

"Dawnie, baby, what's wrong?" Dad asks.

"I thought I saw something in the crowd."

"Saw what?"

"I saw some weird-looking men but don't see them now. It's probably nothing. I'm not feeling well, and my mind is playing tricks on me." I force a smile.

"Let's open the presents," says Dad, reminding me of the original reason we walked back over from the hangout.

I open my presents. Good god, there's a lot of them. We cut the cake, eat, dance, and socialize. I meet more of Dad's extended family, tasted sushi for the first time, and love it. I love salmon, tuna, shrimp tempura, and eel sushi. Sushi is the only thing I can't stop eating. I barely even eat my cake. I take two bites and go back to the sushi. After a while, the dizziness goes away. I walk to the DJ and tell him to announce a Father-Daughter dance. He cuts the music. People look nervous; they hold their breath, wondering if Tracy is about to pop up again.

"Hello, everyone. I'm Dawn Sandino, and I want to thank you for coming out. I also want to thank my family for doing all this for me." I say teary-eyed. Some of the guests say, 'Aww.' "I also want to give a special thanks to my dad and Scotty, who taught me what it's like to have a family and not be alone. And — Daddy, I'd love to have this next dance be a Father-Daughter dance."

Dad smiles ear to ear while holding back tears. "I gladly accept," he replies, kissing my cheek and giving me a big hug. I take his hand, and we dance. The music continues to play, and other fathers and daughters join us. Elizabeth dances with Uncle Brian while they talk and smile at each other. The dance ends, and Uncle Brian asks everyone to go outside. "It's freezing outside, though," I whisper to Dad. He smiles. We go outside, and an oversized trailer-looking thing is parked out front. They have me open the trailer doors, and a lovely white horse is inside.

"Oh my god! She's beautiful, Uncle Brian! Thank you so much! Can I ride her now?" I ask while giving him a hug and a peck on the cheek. Next, I try to get on the horse, but my dress stops me.

"You're welcome, sweetheart; hold your horses; your dress won't fit over it. Wait until the party is done, and you can ride her," he chuckles.

"Okay," I say, giving him another kiss on the cheek. Everyone heads back inside. After about another hour or so, the ball is over. I run to the hangout where my stuff is so I can put something on to ride in. However, I discover my belongings are missing. I start to panic. I run to Dad; he's talking to Uncle Brian. I'm breathless and can barely speak.

"Woah, kiddo, what's wrong?" they both ask, looking completely worried.

"We've been robbed! I went to the house we were at to put something on so I could ride the horse, but all my stuff is gone!"

Uncle Brian bursts out laughing so hard that it turns into crying laughter. "Dawnie, that's a guest house. Heck, barely even that because we don't have guests that stay over; it's just family. The children use that house as a hangout to get away from us grown-ups," Uncle Brian explains as he leads me up some stairs. Dad follows.

"Oh, I knew that..."

"Sure, you did, kid. Anyways, here is your room where your stolen things are." Uncle Brian says, still chuckling.

"Wow!" Again, I'm breathless. I have no idea why Dad's family keeps surprising me with all their money. The room is like I stepped into Italy or something. It's huge, bigger than our house. There is a canopy bed and light brownish granite flooring that warms up every time I step on it. A fireplace, a gigantic flat-screen TV, and a pair of clothes — not mine from home — are lying on the bed. "Whose clothes are these?"

"They're yours, Dawnie. Those are the clothes you wear when riding a horse," says Uncle Brian.

I grab the clothes and quickly run into the bathroom. "Thanks, Uncle Brian, for the riding clothes. I love them!"

He and Dad both laugh, "No problem."

Chapter 6

MEARA

Uncle Brian tells me my horse is in the barn waiting for me. I run to the barn as fast as I can. Sure enough, she's waiting right there for me. I look at the eyes, which are light blue. They remind me of the ocean when it's calm, innocent, and pure. I run my hand over her back and feel something. It's a scar of some sort. For some reason, she reminded me of the ocean, and at that moment, I pull out my iPhone and began to google names. I was looking for something that meant ocean, but instead, the name Meara caught my eye. Meara means sea, and this is why I name her Meara.

Something about her reminds me of the sea. I don't know what it is, but it's certainly something. I climb on the step stool beside her and hop onto my new, beautiful horse. I've never ridden or seen a horse in person, but everything comes naturally when I get on Meara. If anyone saw me, they'd think I'd ridden horses a million times before. Being on a horse is an amazing feeling. I feel free, safe, adventurous, and invincible like nothing can harm me ever again.

My mind goes blank, and all I do and know is riding and the feeling it gives me. It makes me forget everything that is wrong in life. The uncomfortable speech Tracy made at my party, Earl raping me all those times, the engravings from my back, the perverted men at the party, just everything slips my mind, and I'm free. Free to ride and be me.

Meara starts picking up speed on Uncle Brian's field; motion lights turn on when we pass them to see where we're going. She jumps over mini fences set up for her, then I bring her to a stop, and that's when I notice I'm laughing with joy. I pet her neck and say, "That's a girl, Meara. Did you like that girl? It was fun, wasn't it?"

"I thought you never rode a horse before," Dad says, stepping in from the shadows. I jump at his voice; I thought Meara and I were alone.

"Oh, Dad, you scared me," I laugh.

"Sorry, I wasn't trying to. I saw you out here riding, and I wanted to see you since I thought it was your first time, but it's not," Dad says with a chuckle.

"But it is my first time. I don't know what it is. I only know that when I hopped on Meara, riding her just came to me. It's beyond amazing, and the feeling it gives me makes me feel like I'm out of this world. I have no idea how I survived this long without a horse," I say, catching my breath and feeling happy.

"You named her?"

"Yes, Meara. It means sea! I was looking for a name that means ocean, but instead, my eyes came across the sea, and bam! I had to have it," I say, laughing, excitedly.

"You were looking for a name that 'meant' ocean." Dad corrects me.

"Sorry, English teacher," I joke while still on top of Meara and Dad walking us back to the barn.

"You said you just got on her, and it all just came to you?" Dad asks strangely.

"Yeah, why the face?"

"Did it come to you like a memory, or was it out of nowhere?"

"Out of nowhere," I reply hesitantly, realizing I don't know if it was a memory. At least, I don't think it's a memory. How can something come to me so quickly? I start to think back to before I met Dad. My memory won't go further than nine years old; I never remember riding a horse.

Dad sees the confusion on my face and helps me off the horse.

"What's wrong?" he asks.

"I don't know."

"You don't know what's wrong?"

"No, I don't know if it was a memory."

"What do you mean you don't know? Just think back to when you were younger."

"That's the problem, I did, then it gets fuzzy."

"Fuzzy?"

"For some reason, I can't remember anything from before I was nine."

"What do you mean?" Dad asks, his full attention is on me.

"I can't remember anything before I was nine years old. It's like eight and lower has been erased from my head."

"How is that possible?"

"Don't know, you're the grown-up here, not me. I thought you were supposed to have answers."

"Yeah, but not for that. Tell you what, I'll look into it for you. Don't you worry about it?"

"Okay," I say, and we walk back to the castle in the freezing cold. I was so distracted by Meara and how I felt riding her that I forgot it was freezing. Dad laughs and puts me under his arm.

"The weather here is totally different from Cali, huh?"

"Oh yeah, totally," I say, laughing.

We go inside, and I head to my room to get changed. I walk into the bathroom and fall in love with it. Everything is granite, and another fireplace is directly in front of the Jacuzzi bathtub. There is a massive mirror above the sink. The sink is white, with one cabinet and a marble countertop. There is a stand-up shower separate from the tub. There are two other doors. One is a closet with towels and washcloths, and the toilet is behind the door of the other.

I don't hear when someone opens my bedroom door, but I always know it's Scotty whenever he does. When it comes to Dad and Scotty, I can sense when they enter a room without even looking. It's like I can feel their presence or something. Come to think of it, it's like that with all of Dad's family. I know when they enter a room or when they're around. It's not a scary feeling; it's a comforting feeling.

Scotty puts his hand on my arm. "Hey, sweetie, we're watching a movie at the hangout; come on."

"Okay, be right there. I want to change out of these clothes."

"I'll meet you there." He walks out of the room, and I finish getting dressed. I leave my room and see an open door with light coming from it. I hear Uncle Brian's voice and walk closer to listen, but not too close to stay hidden.

"She doesn't remember anything from when she was eight and under?" he asks. He must be talking to Dad.

"No, she doesn't, and how she rode that horse was not her first time. Something had to happen to her when she was nine to have her forget everything," says Dad.

"Well, when she came to your house, and you took her to those doctors, what did they say about her head?"

"Never took her to a Neurologist."

"Why the hell not, Stevie?"

"She's never shown any symptoms or reason for me to take her to one."

"Memory loss of her whole childhood isn't a sign?"

"She never discloses any information about her childhood or anything."

"You never found that to be abnormal?"

"No, not for Dawnie. She's not the type to disclose anything. It was nearly impossible to get her to feel comfortable with us. You know how she is."

"True. You don't think... you know?"

"It might be possible they've made her forget so many years," Dad says.

"Holy shit! That poor girl. That's trillion shades of fucked up!" Uncle Brian replies.

"Trillion what?"

"Something I got from Elizabeth. I liked it, so it stuck to me."

"Hmm, don't use it again," Dad says humorously, but his voice turns serious quickly. "Might have something to do with that barbaric speech Tracy gave today."

"You mean that auction she was doing? Now we know why she wanted a ball instead of a regular birthday party we were originally going to throw. Holy shit Stevie!"

"What? Why didn't this occur to me before?"

"What?"

"The book…"

"You don't think that's about her, do you?"

"It would make sense."

"But that book was written so many years ago."

"The book was written before the person it was about was born. It would make sense with everything that happened today and her memory loss, brother."

"She said she saw some men in the crowd. Did you notice anyone strange?"

"Some men I've never seen before, but they said you invited them, so I kept it moving. I had a lot going on with the surprise party and everything."

"Strange men that are my friends — and you never met them? Think about that, Brian. What friends do I have that you don't know?"

"Fuck me, you don't think that…"

"Oh, I know now that you confirmed it."

"That bitch! Her own daughter. How could she?"

"She's Tracy."

"What are you going to do?"

"I have to continue acting like nothing has happened, or she'll take Dawnie away. Who knows what will happen to her then? I can't chance that. She's my daughter, and I love her."

"True, which won't be hard since Tracy doesn't live with you anymore anyway," Uncle Brian says.

"Yeah, maybe this all to get back at me for kicking her out."

Wait a second, Tracy doesn't live with Daddy anymore? How? When did that happen? Why didn't anyone tell me? How did I not know? Why did she get kicked out and not me? What the hell was happening? Out of everything they just said, the only thing that sticks in my head is that Tracy no longer lives with Dad. When I hear that, I forget everything else they say.

I should be more worried about the other things they're talking about, like my memory loss and a damn book. However, the only thing I'm stuck on is that Tracy no longer lives with us. The door opens while this runs through my mind, and Dad stands there with Uncle Brian. I was so caught up about Tracy not living with us that I don't hear them getting up to leave, and now I'm stuck standing there looking at them with the same fuck-my-life look.

"Fuck me." Uncle Brian says.

"Dawnie, what are you doing standing out here? Thought you were outside," says Dad while forcing a fake smile.

"Cut the bullshit, Dad. Tracy doesn't live with us anymore?" I ask and walk into the office with a cherry-red face that matches theirs.

"It's not polite to eavesdrop," says Uncle Brian.

"It's not polite to lie, keep secrets, or talk behind people's backs. But what do you know? Here you two are whispering away."

"How much did you hear?" Dad asks.

"Enough to know she's not living with us."

"Sit down, and we'll explain," Dad says, pointing to a couch in Uncle Brian's office. I sit down, Uncle Brian sits on the corner of his desk, and Dad sits beside me. "Your mother and I are having some differences, and usually, when that happens between adults, we take a break."

"They break up," I say flatly.

"You sure cut to the chase, kid." Uncle Brian chimes in.

"What happened, and when did she stop living with us?"

"We grew apart, and she moved out."

"You mean you kicked her out. And why am I still staying with you?"

"Because you're my daughter, and I want you to stay and hope you want to stay too, but I understand if you think differently. I want you to know that I love you very much, no matter your choice."

Uncle Brian butts in, "Look, sweetheart, what he's trying to say is you are family, not a stranger. Just because he and Tracy are done doesn't change how we feel about you. Just think about all the things we've done for you. The big ball we threw, the Christmas you had, the family dinners, Meara, and everything we do for and with you. We do it because you're our family and love you wholeheartedly. It doesn't matter that you're Tracy's daughter because, to us, you're Stevie's daughter, my niece, our parents' grandchild, and more. We love you with all our heart. You're one of us, a Sandino, and will always be, no matter what."

I sit there crying silently in Dad's arms while listening to Uncle Brian. I'm crying because this family keeps surprising me with their love for me. Tracy never says these kinds of things to me. Fawn left me, and my biological father, Alex, abandoned me. "How do I know you won't get tired and abandon me like Tracy, Fawn, and Alex?"

"Because we wouldn't be here saying all this and have done all we've done for you with the ball, the holidays, and more if we were going to abandon you. Tracy has never lived with us. When she got out of rehab, she slept over at her friends' houses, and the next thing I know, Tracy was walking out the door, saying she's leaving. I begged her not to take you with her. I couldn't lose you because you're my baby girl. I can't imagine this world without you. You're the reason I wake up every day," says Dad.

After about an hour, we finish talking. I go outside over to the hangout. I can't help but think that someone is watching and following me as I make my way over. When I get there, they're watching an action movie; Elizabeth is knocked out in Gus's arms, Aedan is alone, and Scotty is on the other couch with a blanket. I go to where Scotty is, lift the blanket, and sit under it with him. I lay my head on his chest and hug him, smiling.

"Hey, it's about time. You took forever," Scotty complains.

"I know I'm sorry. I was talking to Dad and Uncle Brian. And it felt like someone was watching or following me outside."

"They probably were."

"Why would someone be watching me?"

"Because guards are covering every inch of this place."

"I didn't see any at the party or afterwards."

"They stay hidden and blend in, so no one sees them. Now hush and watch the movie," says Scotty.

I wasn't paying too much attention to the movie. I'm way too tired after everything going on. I look around and see what Uncle Brian means. I'm their family, and they're my family. I feel safe with them, and they comfort me when needed.

I fall asleep on Scotty, and he takes me to my room. The housekeepers wake me in the morning and tell me breakfast is ready.

The rest of the stay is great. I hang out with my cousins and go to this corner store for snacks. There are many bikes with men on and around them wearing biker jackets with the words "Out Laws" on them. Gus says the Out Laws are our family, and our dads were in it when they were younger; someday, we will be in it.

I tell Dad about seeing the Out Laws, and he says he never wants to hear that we've joined them. He goes on to say that it was a mistake they made when they were young, and when they realized what a fuck up it was, it was too late. Somehow, they managed to get out. Well, at least my dad did. Uncle Brian is still in it, though. He doesn't dress in biker clothes or ride a bike anymore.

Regardless of their mistake in joining them, I always feel safe around them and our family. Uncle Brian tells me they're also in San Diego, and if something ever were to happen to him and Dad, Scotty and I need to go there, and we would be safe. Dad agrees but makes us promise we will never join them. He says they're called "Out Laws" for a reason, and not a good one.

After two weeks in Ireland, it's sadly time to return to Cali.

Chapter 7

FINDING THE TRIEGER FAMILY

Finding Alex Trieger is a challenging task. Instead, we find his family. Tracy is not happy with the idea because he left her with two children and never paid child support. All I want is to see where I came from on his side. I don't want to grow up and accidentally marry my cousin or half-brother. Then again, I'm marrying Scotty — so that won't happen anyway. Scotty hasn't asked me to marry him yet, but I know he will.

Dad finds Alex's family and says I can meet them if I don't tell Tracy. I've kept secrets from Tracy all my life, and this one won't be hard to keep from her. Dad has already spoken to Alex's dad, Sal, about me, and they expect to meet me. They live in Beverly Hills. I assume not only are they rich but are probably the snobbiest people ever — even Scotty thinks that. I can't believe Scotty and I have been together for almost a year. The car ride there is two hours long, and I'm nervous to meet them.

"What's wrong, kiddo?" Dad asks.

"Nothing." I lie.

"Lie." Scotty interrupts from the front seat.

"Sorry, kiddo, but you can't lie; we know you all too well now. Spill the beans," says Dad.

"It's nothing. I'm just a little nervous, that's all." Dad looks at me from the rearview mirror, and Scotty turns to face me.

"What if they don't like or accept me like you guys do?"

"Then, they're assholes, and we should burn their house down with them in it." Scotty laughs.

"Scotty, I'm serious."

"Look, Dawnie, you're a sweet and intelligent girl, and they will love you just as you are. You make straight A's in all your classes and are very mature for your age, sometimes too mature and smart. But that's what makes you so special," Dad says, still looking at me in the mirror.

"And if they don't?" I ask him again.

"Then they're insane, and we'll burn their house down with them in it like Scotty says," he replies, smirking. We laugh, and Scotty turns the radio on. I fall asleep. "Wake up, kiddo, we're here," Dad says, turning the car off. I open my eyes and am blown away from the mansion before us. It's enormous, almost bigger than Dad's, but not entirely.

A man walks out the front door towards us as we're getting out of the truck. He's wearing a suit and looks like he belongs in *The Godfather*. His skin is tan, his short black hair is neatly styled, and his face is clean-shaven. He has rings on both his ring fingers and is sporting a diamond watch.

"Hey, how was the drive?" he asks.

"Long," Dad replies while I hide under his arm. The guy sees me and can't take his eyes off me, making me even more nervous.

"Is that her?"

"Yes, she's nervous and just woke up from a nap," Dad says.

"Hi, I'm Alex's father, Sal, and your grandpa. I must say you look just like your father. Let's go inside and get something to eat; David should be here shortly," he says to me pleasantly.

"David?" I ask.

"David is your father's identical twin brother. I told him about you, and he wants to meet you, too. Alex doesn't talk to us much."

"Why not?"

"A falling out we had a few years back, and we just haven't gotten over it quite yet."

The house is breathtaking. It's elegant, and you can tell a woman rather than a man decorated it. The foyer has marble floors, and the living room we walk into has a huge flat-screen TV on the wall and a white carpet that matches the white couches. They also have a beach view like Dad's, but Dad's is way better. I sit down between Scotty and Dad; their butler brings us sodas.

A skinny woman comes in with long black hair and tanned skin. Her breasts are big like mine. She's nicely dressed, and her fingernails and toenails are French manicured. She's beautiful. "Hey, I'm your father's mom, Andrea. You must be Dawn. You look just like your father," she says with an accent that I can't tell if it's Irish or Scottish. She hugs me; I try to hide the uneasy look on my face every time they call Alex my father. I don't know him. Being a sperm donor and a father are two different things.

"Steve tells me your favorite food is pizza, sushi, and cannoli," Sal says, trying to warm me up.

I look at Dad and smile, "Yeah, they're my favorite. I'd eat them all the time if I could. What's your favorite food?"

"I'm a bit greedy, and I can't decide on my favorite because I like too many of them," he chuckles.

Dad's phone starts to ring, and he steps outside to answer it. I look at Scotty with a face that says you better not leave. He nods his head in agreement and stays next to me.

"So, Dawn, how old are you?" Andrea asks.

"Twelve."

"You look older," she says with a smile.

"Yeah, that's what everyone tells me."

Dad walks back in and smiles at me. I know he's about to say something I don't want to hear. "What is it?" I ask bluntly.

"I have to make a quick run." I stand up to let him know I'm leaving too because I don't want to stay here alone; I just met these people.

"Dawnie, stay here. I'll come back once I'm done," Dad says.

"Or we can just leave together and come back together," I reply with a big fake smile.

"Please, Dawn, stay. You just got here, and we haven't had dinner yet," says Sal.

Scotty gets up and stands next to me. "Dawnie, if it makes you feel better, I'll stay here with you while Uncle Steve goes and handles his business."

I look at Scotty and smile at him. "Yes, I would feel much better."

"Okay, I'll be back. You two have my phone number if you need anything. Don't hesitate to call." Dad kisses me on the forehead, and I hug him. He gives Scotty a hug and heads to the door. I look at Scotty with relief that he's staying with me. We sit back on the couch.

"You two must be close," Andrea says.

"Yeah, we've become best friends since she moved in," Scotty tells her. I hear the front door open and hope it's Dad coming back, saying he doesn't have to make that run anymore.

"Hey, Mom and Dad, sorry I'm late. I ran into traffic," says a voice from the foyer.

"Who's that?" I ask.

"Your Uncle David, sweetheart," Andrea says.

They don't notice the discomfort on my face when they call themselves my uncle, grandma, grandpa, and Alex, my father. I know they mean well, but damn, I just fucking met them.

A guy walks in. He has curly black hair, a muscular build, tan skin, and an average height, with a shaven face that gives him a look like he's in the mob. "Hey, how are you? I'm your Uncle David. Your father looks just like me — and so do you," he says with a puzzled look and half smile.

"Told you she was his. You didn't believe it, but I did when I saw her come out of the truck," Sal says.

"Yeah, but why didn't he tell me she was alive, Dad?"

"For pity and most likely money, that son of a..."

"Okay, I think it's time for dinner, dear," Andrea cuts Sal off.

"Wait. What do you mean Alex didn't tell you I was alive? What? Am I supposed to be dead?" I ask, confused. The three of them look at me with a face that screams, 'Oh shit.' "Umm, hello, I'm waiting for an answer," I say, raising my voice in irritation.

"Umm, no." David quickly replies.

"Then why haven't you ever contacted me? Don't lie because I've had enough lies in one lifetime."

"We found out you were alive when Steve called me," says Sal.

"What do you mean about alive?"

"Alex told us you were dead," he frowns.

"So, you lied to me in front of my face?" I say to David, looking him straight in the eyes. Scotty stands up and puts his hand on my shoulder; everyone stares at me. Without looking at anyone, I grab my purse and walk out. I tell Scotty to call Dad. I'm ready to go home. I sit on the steps outside and cry while waiting for Scotty to come out. How could Alex tell his family I was dead, and how could David lie to me in front of my face? The door opens, and I quickly wipe my tears away. It's not Scotty. It's Sal.

"Hey," he says and sits down next to me.

"Where's Scott?"

"Inside talking to David and Andrea. Is it okay if I sit here with you?"

"It's your steps, not mine."

"Yeah, that's true, but I like to be considerate. We didn't mean to upset you, and David didn't want to hurt your feelings."

"Talking about me like I'm not right here in front of you isn't being considerate. It's not watching out for my feelings either," I snap.

"I know. We're shocked by the fact that Alex lied to us like that. I mean your father."

"He isn't my father, you're not my grandpa, Andrea's not my grandma, and David is not my uncle. My only family is Steve, Scotty, and Steve's family. Steve is my father, not Alex — someone who's never been there and tells people I'm dead."

"I know, and I'm sorry. How old did you say you were again?" Sal asks curiously.

"Twelve."

"You're very wise for your age, and you look older than twelve. You must have been through a lot."

"Yeah, I guess you can say that."

"Can we start this whole thing over and go in and have dinner, please? We really want to get to know you more."

"Why should I?"

"Because we won't lie to you anymore or speak about you like you aren't in the room. I promise."

"Is Alex coming?"

"No."

"Why not!" I demand furiously.

"Because we don't speak anymore."

"Why not?"

"We had a falling out a while ago and never got over it... now we learn Alex has a kid that he told us was dead."

"He has two, but Fawn left long ago with some guy she met."

"Wow, are you serious?"

"Yeah."

"You have his temper."

"I have my own temper."

"I know my son is messed up, but this is fucked up to the fullest."

"Story of my life," I scoff.

"Maybe you can share your life with me," Sal replies.

We sit there for at least an hour talking. We joke around and tell each other stories from when we were younger. I don't tell Sal about Earl. Only Scotty and Dad can know about that. We go inside. Scotty walks towards me and hugs me.

"You, okay?"

"Yeah, Scotty, I'm fine."

"Still want me to call Uncle Steve?"

"No, not yet."

"Food is ready," the chef says.

We make our way to the dining room, and there's sushi, pizza, potatoes, cabbage, steak, and stuffing. It's like Thanksgiving but a different day. I look at Scotty, and he looks at me. We're psyched about all the food. We sit next to each other. For a moment, there is silence, and everyone gets seated.

"Dawn, what do you like to do?" David asks.

"Hang out with friends, go to the movies, and eat. What do you like to do?" I ask back.

He laughs. "I travel a lot, and I enjoy hiking and boxing."

"So, you beat the hell out of people for fun?"

He laughs again. "Yeah, I guess you can put it that way."

"Do you have any kids?" I ask.

"No, I don't. My fiancé, Julia, has a lot of nieces and nephews.

She has a lot of siblings that have kids, but one of her nieces and nephews is around your age. Maybe you can meet them one day."

"Yeah, that would be nice," I reply.

"We got pizza and sushi since it's your favorite and David's favorite, too," Andrea says, smiling.

"Thank you, Andrea, it's delicious," I say with a mouthful of sushi.

"Wait until dessert; she's got cannoli," David sings.

I laugh; I can't believe a grown man is more excited about cannoli than I am. We finish eating and work our way through dessert. It's great. I almost forget Dad has been gone for hours. I excuse myself to call him. The phone rings and rings. No one answers. This is weird because Dad always answers on the second ring whenever I call him. Now, I'm worried. I go back inside, sit in the living room next to Scotty, and text him that Dad didn't answer his phone. He texts back:

I'm sure he's okay. He had something important to do.

Two hours later, Dad finally texts me back and tells me David will take us home. I look at Scotty and know something is wrong. Scotty will not look me in the eye. Dad always picks us up and won't leave us somewhere unless it's very important, especially when we're two hours away.

David is a fast driver, way faster than Dad, which is a little scary. Scotty enjoys the quick ride, but I want to get home and see if Dad is okay. We arrive home. There are cop cars everywhere. I run inside with Scotty trailing after me. I forget to thank David for the ride home. "DAD!" I yell. He's speaking to a police officer.

He looks at me with tears in his eyes, "Tracy is gone, and they think she's dead."

Chapter 8

TRACY GONE

"What do you mean? How? And don't lie to me!" I demand, my eyes fill with tears. He moves closer to me and puts his arms around me. My knees give out completely, and he holds me up.

"They found her car on the expressway, and it was all banged up."

"So, she was in an accident? She might still be alive!" I say.

"Dawn, do you remember Earl's last name?" he asks without looking me in the face.

"No, just his first. Mom never told me last names," I reply without thinking.

"Okay, Scott, can you please take her upstairs while I speak to the police?"

Scotty and I turn around to go upstairs and see David standing inside our home. We go into my room, and Scotty holds me, I cry in his arms. Tracy has to be alive. She can't be dead, I keep thinking to myself. Scotty goes downstairs to get me a glass of water. Something tells me to sit next to the wall by the steps. I overhear the cops talking to each other.

"We have a lead, no last name, only a first," one cop says.

"Who?"

"Some guy named Earl. The mother used to have a john. He used to abuse the little girl upstairs and carved something in her upper back."

"Let me guess. *'YOUR MINE'* in capital letters, just like the door on the car. You think he carved it on the mother, too?"

"It would explain all the blood."

My entire body freezes. I stare into space. No wonder Dad wanted to know Earl's last name. Earl found us and went after Tracy because I told Dad and Scotty. He's going to kill her if I don't stop him, and it's all my fault. I notice the cops leave the room, and no one is in the foyer. Without thinking, I tiptoe down the stairs and reach the door. Scotty will be back up with my drink any minute. I hurry and make my way out without being spotted. I walk out the door and jump in the bushes next to the door so no one will see me.

I see David's car. He's being nosey inside, trying to find out what happened. The two cops walk to their vehicle. With pity in their voices, they continue to talk about Tracy and me. Their backs are turned to the house. They don't see me run behind David's car. They both throw their heads back and turn around to head back inside; they must have forgotten something. No one is outside but me. I make a run for it before anyone comes back outside.

I have to get to Long Beach and am trying to figure out how. I'll stop for directions somewhere or buy a map. All I know is that I must get to Long Beach and go alone. I only have a short amount of time to make it to the gate to get out of here before Dad and Scotty send police cars after me. I'm almost at the gate. I look behind me to make sure no one is following me, especially Scotty. I know he will follow me if he knows I'm out here. I make it to the gate, but the patrol guy is there. He opens the gate for a vehicle. This is my only chance. I have to do it now.

The patrolman's attention is away from the gate while he's speaking to the driver, trying to gain entry. Without him noticing, I slip out of the gate. I run for at least ten minutes until I can no longer see my residential area. I make it to a safe zone, stop running, and start walking to catch my breath. I'm safe now; no one will spot me. Suddenly, a car approaches slowly from behind, its headlights blinding me. Fuck! I've been spotted, and I think it's Scotty. To make matters worse, the car gets closer and closer to me, and who do I see? David! He's in the driver's seat, following me.

"What the hell are you doing, David!" I yell at him frantically, and annoyed that he's following me.

"I can ask you the same question since it's past your bedtime, and Steve and Scott are about to have a heart attack when they find out you're not in your room," he says.

"I have to run to the store."

"At midnight?"

"Yes."

"What store?"

I think hard, but I don't have an answer. I just look at him. "Look, I don't have time for your questions."

"If I didn't know any better, I think you were off to look for your mother. I can help you."

"Don't need your help. I need you to get away from me."

"Why not?"

"Because it's too dangerous for you," I respond. David chuckles and pulls his car over. I keep walking, knowing he's going to follow me on foot.

"More of a reason to go with you. If it's too dangerous for me, it's too dangerous for you."

"Isn't Julia going to be looking for you?"

"No, she knows where I am, and I have a cell phone if she needs me."

"I overheard the police talking," he says. I stop walking and stand in place.

"Talking about what?" I ask, trying to play it off, hoping he'll tell me more.

"About Earl, and I know what he's done to your back."

His words upset me. I become angry. My face starts to get hot and turns red. "How dare you spoon on a conversation like that about me? Who do you think you are?"

"Your uncle," he replies sharply.

"Well, you're not, and you might never be, so get over yourself."

"Ouch, that hurts. I'm sorry, but it's hard not to overhear something, especially when it concerns someone in my family."

"You just met me today, and not only met me but found out I was still alive, and lied to my face. So, how can I be your family? To me, you're just another man with a dick that is making me mad. It's not like you or your piece of shit brother were there when I needed you before, and I damn sure don't need you now, so be gone."

I try to wipe my tears away before he sees them, but I know I did it too late. I start walking faster, hoping he will get tired and return to his car, but he doesn't. He hugs me from behind, and I lose it. I punch and kick at him. I take all my anger out on him, knowing none of this is his fault.

"Get off me!" I yell, but he doesn't; he squeezes me tighter.

"I'm sorry I wasn't there before, but I'm here now."

"I don't need you now." I cry. I continue punching him until I get tired.

"Shh, it's okay. I'm here."

I yank myself from his arms and get up. "I have to do this alone, or Tracy has no way of living."

"That's only if she's still alive, Dawn. What are you going to do about money and food? Do you even know how to get to Long Beach? Do you know how far it is?"

"My dad gave me credit cards, so I have more than enough, and I know Long Beach is two hours away."

"Steve can track you by the credit cards and have a police officer pick you up, and Long Beach is two hours away when driving, not by foot."

"I'll hike."

"What if a psycho comes and tries to kidnap you? Not to mention that hitchhiking is illegal."

"What do you want from me?"

"I want to go with you."

"You'll get hurt," I say to him.

"And so will you."

"No offense, but this guy has already hurt me in the most unimaginable ways, so whatever he has in store for me now, I can handle it as long as Tracy is okay," I explain.

I realize he will not leave me alone and that I need someone with a car. Some company would be nice, but it's risky. For some reason, I doubt David will let me go alone without him, and I think he would tell the police. I can't risk it.

"You're not going to let me go alone, are you?" I ask, already knowing the answer.

"Nope, not at all," he says firmly.

I'm wide awake, sitting in David's passenger seat. David's mumbling about something, but I'm too worried about Tracy to listen to what he's saying. How the hell am I going to get Tracy back? I know Earl will kill her if the police show up. I hope to God we get there before the police do.

"Dawn, Dawn…"

"Yeah…" I reply while snapping out of my thoughts. I stare at him.

"Help me out here. We're in Long Beach, but I don't know where we're going," says David.

I notice that we're around the corner from my old house. "Earl and Tracy are at my old house, which is around the corner from…" David slams on the brakes and pulls his car to the side of the road.

"What the fuck is your problem!" I yell at the top of my lungs, scared as shit for my life.

"We've got to walk the rest of the way so he doesn't see the car. We can sneak into your house and grab Tracy and go," he suggests.

"We?"

"No way in hell you're going in there by yourself."

"I have to."

"No, you don't."

"If I don't, he will kill Tracy."

"And if you do, he will kill you and Tracy."

"Maybe."

"Not on my watch," he says.

"If I need you, I'll call or scream for you," I say, hoping to change his mind.

"What if he sneaks up on you from behind and covers your mouth," he says.

"Shit, then look in the window or something, I don't know. You can't go inside with me; you're not supposed to be here."

"Okay, I'll look in the window."

We get out of the car. I go to the door, and David goes to the side window where the bushes are. I knock on the front door. It's open. I enter my old home. The lights are on. "Tracy, you in here?" I whisper, hoping she will answer or appear out of thin air, but there is no answer. I walk into the room, and the door closes behind me. I jump. I sigh in relief when I see Earl is not behind the door.

"Don't you look sexier than before?" I jump at the voice. It's Earl!

"Where's Tracy?"

"Well, hello to you too."

"Hello, and where's Tracy?"

"She's a little busy at the moment. You can check on her later, though." Earl says snidely.

"What did you do to her?"

"Gave her what she always wants, what else, drugs."

"Fuck, Earl, she just became clean!"

He laughs and looks me in the eyes. "Since when?"

"Since she got out of rehab a few months ago."

"She came to me a few months ago for drugs, probably when she got out of rehab," he says.

"Bullshit! Where is she?"

"I missed you. Did you miss me?"

"Tracy!" I yell, still no answer.

"Why did you leave me?"

I start to cry. Something tells me I'm too late. "You killed Tracy, didn't you?"

"Ain't answering the question," Earl grumbles.

"Answer what?"

"Why did you leave me?"

"Tracy got a new boyfriend, and we moved in with him. Now, please tell me where Tracy is," I beg.

"In the room," he replies.

I rush to the room, but it's empty. Standing in the middle, I glance around and hear the TV. I walk slowly back into the living room, the TV sound growing louder. Suddenly, I hear screaming — I know it's Tracy. I look at the TV screen, and Tracy is sitting in a chair all tied-up. Her mascara smears all over her face while she cries; her forehead is bleeding. She's been hit with something hard! There's a rope tied around her mouth to shut her up. She starts shaking her head from side to side, saying no, and a gun appears directly in her face.

It only shows someone's hand holding the gun, not their face, but I'm not stupid. I know it's Earl. He puts the barrel of the gun in her face and moves it around in a circular motion, brings it to her nose, then to her forehead again. Then, boom! The gun goes off, and a dirty ol' voice whisper, "*YOUR MINE.*"

I can no longer hold it anymore. I start screaming to the top of my lungs and fall to the floor, still looking at the TV, at Tracy's head, blown off. I feel hands grab me. I jump and throw punches until I realize it's David. I look around and notice Earl is no longer in the room. "Where is he?"

"I don't know. I think Earl ran out of the house when you came in."

"What you mean you don't know? Weren't you watching outside?" I ask angrily.

"I was watching you. I saw you run into a room and I came in to follow you. By the time I got back to the living room, Earl was gone, and the door was open and..." he says, pausing to look at the TV. "What the hell is that?" he asks.

"Tracy..." I bellow quietly.

"Oh my," he says, turns off the TV, and runs to me. He holds me and calls 911. I'm so out of it I sit there and let him hold me. What's going to happen to me now that Tracy is dead? What am I going to do? Dad and Scotty will hate me and throw me out of the house.

Tracy is dead because of me, and when they find out, they're going to regret making me part of their family. I have no one, not even Tracy anymore. God knows where Fawn is; Tracy's family hasn't talked to her in years. How am I supposed to tell everyone she's dead? That she's never coming back because her head got blown off by a man who raped me and is mad at me for leaving. It's all my fault. I should've made Tracy stay here instead of running with her to Dad's to escape Earl. I left him, and he killed her to get back at me. Now I'm alone forever, and Dad and Scotty will want nothing to do with me because of it.

I sit there crying and stare off into space. I imagine a lonely future awaiting me, unaware David is still holding me. The police come in, and David puts me on the couch.

"You, okay?" One of the police officers asks. I shake my head no.

"What happened?" he asks.

I don't say anything. I point to the TV. He walks towards it, and David sees him about to turn it on. He takes me outside and goes back in to speak to them. I hear the boom again and collapse on the front steps, staring into space. An officer comes and sits next to me. "I saw the tape. I'm sorry for your loss, but I have some questions. Is that okay?" the officer says. I nod my head. "I must wait to ask them when your dad meets me at the station. Since you're underage, I can't question you without your parent or guardian present."

I nod my head yes again and feel something weird in my stomach. My mouth gets watery, and my stomach is killing me. Next, I see the sushi and pizza I ate at Sal's and the cannoli. I threw up everything I had eaten earlier. David comes out of the house, gives me a handkerchief to wipe my mouth and nose, and walks me to the police car. We sit in the back seat and wait for the officer.

"No one, especially someone your age, should see or go through something like that," he says.

"I shouldn't see or go through many things, but I do. I've gotten used to it."

"No, you shouldn't get used to it."

"Well, it doesn't matter now anyway."

"Why not?"

"Because I know I have a hell of a future ahead of me."

He puts his arms on my shoulder and pulls my head on his chest, and I start to cry. Still in shock, I didn't care; probably the last time I'll see him. We arrive at the police station and wait for Dad and Scotty. They finally arrive and run up to me. I began crying harder, and they ask me what happened.

"I'm so sorry. I swear I didn't want any of this to happen," I say to Dad.

"What happened, Dawn? Where is Tracy?" he asks.

"Tracy's gone."

Chapter 9

NOW WHAT?

I tell the police everything that happened, and they record me. They ask me the same questions repeatedly. Dad is trying hard not to cry, but this situation is challenging. He loved Tracy more than anyone; now she's gone and never returning. The cop finally stops asking questions and says he will investigate Earl further. We all walk to the truck in silence. Scotty drives while Dad and I sit in the back seat.

I lay on Dad's chest and fall asleep, not even waking up when we get home. Scotty must've carried me to my room because he's next to me when I wake up the next morning. I see if Dad is okay, but he's not in his room. I go downstairs, but he's not there either. He's nowhere to be found. I check my phone and see seven missed calls. Two from David, two from Sal, and three from Brittany. Brittany is my friend, but I don't want to talk to anyone now. I don't even care to check voicemails.

"Dawn!" Scotty calls my name.

"Down here in the kitchen!" I shout.

He walks in the kitchen with his bedhead, pajama pants, and chest out. "How are you doing?" he asks, puts his arms around my waist, and kisses me.

"Been better. Still a little in shock. Do you know where Dad is?"

"No, I thought you might know," he replies.

"No, when I woke up, he was already gone."

"I'm sure he'll be back soon. He needs some time to himself."

"Yeah," I say to him with a worried face.

"What happened last night was horrifying. He lost someone he loves dearly."

"I know; I lost Tracy, too. She was my mother, remember?"

"Yeah, I know. I'm just saying..."

"Saying what"

"If I lost you like Uncle Steve just lost Tracy, I'd probably feel how he does right now."

"Probably?"

"Yeah, probably."

"Saying it like you're not sure," I say to him and walk to my room.

"Dawn, wait, I didn't mean it."

"I know what you meant," I reply, closing my door.

"You're upset. You just need time alone for a while."

The last thing I need is to be alone. Can't Scotty see that I need someone to hold and love me? But he can't see that and thinks I need to be alone. Dad is probably looking for a home to send me to. I pack my things, getting ready for Dad to throw me out. Without Tracy, there is no reason to keep me here anymore. There's a knock on my door, I'm sure it's Scotty. "Go away, Scott."

"It's not Scott. It's me, Dad."

"Oh, come in."

He walks in and sees my bags with clothes on the floor. "Going somewhere?" he asks with a confused look on his face.

"Umm, yeah."

"Where?"

"Wherever you send me off to," I say to him, getting irritated by his good acting.

"Send you off?"

"Look, Dad, you don't have to put on this show. I know it's my fault Tracy died, and the only reason you put up with me is because you didn't want her to leave you. Now she's dead, and there's no reason for you to keep me. I'm not yours and..." he puts his hand up and cuts me off. I stand there trying to stop crying, but it's useless.

"Yes, it's true. I first took you in because of Tracy, but as time has passed, I got to know you, Dawnie. I grew to love you like you're my own daughter. Heck, I forgot that you aren't my biological daughter because you've been my daughter ever since you walked in that door. I love you, and you will always be my daughter, even if you don't think so. And remember, Tracy moved out, and you still stayed here with me because I begged her," he says with tears in his eyes.

"Really?"

"Yes, and I came in here to see if you were okay, not to kick you—." Before he finishes his sentence, I run and hug him.

"No one has ever told me that before. You're the only one that tells me that. I love you too, Dad."

"I see. Now, let's get some breakfast, and you can unpack later. I knew something was up when you said Scott and not Scotty," he says chuckling.

I look up at him, confused. "When you're mad at him or something serious, he goes from Scotty to Scott quickly." This time, we both laugh. I hadn't noticed that I did that until he brought it to my attention. We go downstairs to the kitchen, and Scotty is there eating cereal. He looks at me, and I know he's sorry about what happened earlier. I force a smile at him and sit next to him. Although Tracy is gone, and I should be sad, I'm happy, not because she's dead, but for the first time, I have a father and Scotty, two people I care about and love. I call Steve, Dad, and he thinks of me like a daughter. Before, we carried on like father and daughter because of Tracy, or at least I thought that's why we did.

Tracy's death confirmed that we're close. The only reason we ever met was because of her. I know now that a father is more than just having sex and giving sperm to the egg; it's being there every day through hard times. Dad wasn't there when Earl used to rape me, but he's here now, and he's been here since I moved here with Tracy; I just never accepted it.

Dad and Scotty know everything about me, and I don't have to act like something I'm not. I can be myself, and they accept me for me. For the first time, I feel like I belong. I'm part of a family now; I can call my own. I have no idea how things with Alex's family will turn out, but if it's not good, then I know at least I have my own family, The Sandino's.

Chapter 10

THE MEMORIAL

They never find Tracy's body, but today is her memorial. Tracy had no friends, just drug dealers and johns. They were obviously not invited to the memorial. Only Dad's friends, family, and Brittany are here. Brittany was here for a while, but left, and had her driver take her somewhere because she hates being around sad-looking people. After the memorial, Dad has a repast at the house. Dad's brother, Jimmy, rides with us in the car to the house. Uncle Jimmy is shorter than Dad but dresses and acts like him. He speaks with an Irish accent. Uncle Jimmy and Dad aren't as close as Uncle Brian and him, but they're still close. When we get to the house, I go upstairs to my room, and Jimmy comes in.

"Hey, Dawnie."

"Yeah, Uncle Jimmy…"

"I just wanted to make sure you're okay."

"I'm not going to do anything crazy if that's what you mean."

"Ha, I think the whole situation is kind of crazy."

"Who are you telling?"

"Yeah, hey, if there's anything you need or want, don't hesitate to call me, especially if you're in trouble. You're my niece, and I want you to know you can count on me for anything."

"Thanks, Uncle Jimmy; I know I can count on you for anything!"

He gives me a hug and a kiss on the forehead. We walk downstairs; our family and friends start to arrive. They come up to me, hug me, and give their condolences. I don't feel like being bothered by anyone, so I go outside. I put my feet in the pool, hoping to be left alone, but that doesn't last long. Dad comes out and sits next to me quietly. For a while, he doesn't speak. "Hell of a day," he finally says.

"Yeah, tell me about it."

"Dawnie, has anything happened since you've been here?"

"What do you mean?"

"Anything out of the ordinary?"

"Like what?"

"Letters or someone following you?"

"No, why do you ask?"

"Just making sure. You'd tell me if there were any, right?"

"Yes," I say a little hesitantly.

"Dawnie, I know when you're lying and something is wrong. You're my daughter, and it's my job to protect you. I have a feeling things are going to change greatly after today. The past is catching up with us."

"Okay, I'll tell you," I say, hoping to ease his mind.

"You have to promise."

"As long as it doesn't put you in danger."

"Don't worry about me; I can take care of myself," he says, and we walk into the house. I stop in my tracks and see Fawn walking in the door.

"Dawnie, what is it? Why'd you stop?" Dad asks.

"That's Fawn."

Fawn has a pale complexion, raven-black greasy hair, and skinny, frail, and unhealthy-looking skin. Her nails are overgrown, dirty, and unkempt. She's wearing a black crop top, an old leather jacket, and jeans with beat-up sneakers.

"Aww hell, this is going to be a heck of a memorial with the oldest daughter. I can't deal with all this shit right now," Dad says, throwing his head back.

"Who you telling?"

Fawn spots me and walks towards me. Dad stands next to me. "Hey, Fawn, this is Steve. He was Tracy's boy..."

"I know what he was," she replies.

"Hey, how are you? It's a pleasure to finally meet you," Dad says to her.

"You don't have to lie, Steve, because I'm not going to—"

"Okay, I'm going to let you two catch up," Dad cuts her off mid-sentence.

"Okay, Dad, thanks."

"Okay, Fawn, sorry, but I must ask. What are you doing here?" I question her.

Fawn looks at me strangely, "Even though I hate the bitch for all she's done, I still have to pay my respects. And why did you call him dad? He's not Alex."

"How did you know she died? And Alex is not my dad. He's my sperm donor who's done nothing for me but leave me." I remind her.

"Tracy's parents told me; he's still not your dad."

"Yes, he is, since I moved in… and who?"

"Tracy's parents dummy," she says.

"Oh, I know what you said. You just caught me by surprise; I thought Tracy's parents were dead."

"Yeah, so did I until I did my research."

"Wow, you doing research? I guess there is a first for everything."

"Don't be smart, bitch."

"They told you she died?"

"Of course they did. I live with them."

"Why didn't they come?"

"They did, and they're here somewhere."

"Oh really? Where?"

"Just said somewhere."

I change the subject quickly. "Oh, how's that boy you left with?"

"Obviously, we're over if I'm living with Tracy's parents, dumbass."

"You don't have to act like that. I was just asking a question, geez."

"Then, stop asking them."

"Okay, why weren't you at the memorial?"

"Don't worry about it. I had some business to tend to."

"Well, you're kind of late."

"Not in Tracy's world. Besides, it's not like she's complaining. She's lucky I even came to this shit."

"Okay, Fawn, well, nice seeing you, but I have something to do with my dad."

"I've barely been here for five minutes, and you're trying to run already."

"I'm not really in the mood," I tell her and walk off quickly to go to Dad.

"What in the hell was that about?" he asks me.

"Oh, that's just the way Fawn is."

"I see why she and Tracy didn't get along." We laugh, and one of his co-workers comes up to us, offers condolences, and starts conversing with him. I tell Dad I'm going to my room for a nap, and he's fine. I go to my room and close the door. I walk over to my balcony to look at the ocean.

"Boo!"

"What the hell, Fawn? You scared me!"

She laughs and stands beside me, "Wow, Tracy really hit the jackpot. Is this your room? Talk about moneyyyyy."

"Tracy loved Dad. It had nothing to do with his money."

"Tracy is incapable of such a thing," she says, touring my room.

"How did you get in here?"

"Walked up the steps like you did," she replies snarkily.

"I mean, what are you doing up here?"

"Came to check on you."

"Thanks, but I'm fine. You can leave now," I say as Scott walks in.

"Hey, Dawnie, everything okay?"

"Yeah, Scotty, this is Fawn, and Fawn, this is Scott."

"Hmm, no one told me about you," Fawn tells Scotty.

"This is my dad's nephew."

"Nice to meet you, Fawn."

"Pleasure is all mine," Fawn says, practically throwing herself at him. Her bulky pockets catch my eye. I grab her arm and turn her towards me. I shove my hands into her bulky pockets. Fawn is back to her old tricks of stealing and pickpocketing. I see money and jewelry that I know belongs to my dad and some other stuff that I have no clue who it belongs to.

Fawn looks at me with a red angry face, "You fucking bitch! You really had to embarrass me like that in public, didn't you."

"Embarrass you? You're stealing at a repast for our mother and mad at me for catching you?" I say back, pissed off because she stole from my family. Scotty is standing next to me in shock.

"It's not like he will miss it. Look at this place. He can get tons more."

"That's not the point. Since you arrived, you've been extremely rude to my family, and now you're stealing from them. That is not okay."

"Family? What family bitch?! I'm your family, not them."

"No, you're not. You left me. It's time to go."

"You're just going to kick me out? How dare you on the day of our mother's memorial? I'm sorry." Fawn looks down at the floor and starts to cry. I feel sorry for her.

"Fine, you can stay, but don't steal from my family again." She looks up; her face is dehydrated, and there is not a tear in sight. She looks over at Scotty and walks to him. I look at Scotty to see his reaction; he laughs, makes a weird face, and looks at me. "Okay, Fawn, I think it's time for you to go downstairs. I really don't feel like dealing with you right now."

"Would you like to join me, Scott?" she asks, sticking her upper chest out to make it a little bigger.

"Not a chance in hell," I say and slam the door in her face before she can respond. I turn and look at Scotty. I wait for him to say something like he wants to show her downstairs or around the premises.

"Wow, that's your sister?"

"Yeah, and what's the 'wow' for? Something you like? Of course, it's because she's slutty and sleazy like the others and way prettier than me — you can have her."

"Hey, hey, take it easy. I was saying 'wow' badly. I don't like slutty and sleazy; that's why the others didn't last. I cheated on them. You two act so different from each other, and I was surprised. You're like another virgin of the virgin Mary, and she's the devil's bitch on the side. No offense. She makes me love you more and more. Eww, how could you think I could possibly..."

"Yeah, I know, I'm sorry. Fawn has always been the beautiful one everyone goes for, and I'm the one who becomes the best friend or girl they know."

"That's because the boys that go for her are nasty and want one thing. I've already had all that from other girls, plus she looks like she hasn't washed in years. Did you see her hair? Are you blind?" I start laughing, and Scotty looks at me in question.

"Why are you laughing?" he asks.

"You sound like a dumb blonde. Did you see her hair?" I say, mocking him. He laughs, too.

"Well, did you? It was so greasy?"

"Yeah, I saw it. I didn't pay any attention to it."

"Well, I did."

"Obliviously. What were you saying earlier?"

He walks towards me, puts his arms around me, and kisses me. "It's nice to hear you laugh, see you smile, and for you to speak to me again," he says while kissing me in between words.

"Same here."

We hug each other, lie on my bed, and fell asleep, leaving Dad downstairs with everyone. I wake up hearing Dad tell everyone goodbye downstairs. "Shit, shit, Scotty, get up! We fell asleep and left Dad by himself."

"Lay back down, Dawnie, he's a grown man. I think he can deal with them," he says, his eyes still closed. He rolls over and continues to sleep. I look at him and nudge him. I go downstairs. Dad is closing the front door. He turns around and forces a smile.

"Hell of a day, huh?" he says.

"Which part? The reunion between my long-lost sister or the memorial in general?" I joke.

"Both." he laughs.

"Sorry, Scotty and I left you downstairs..."

"Hey, it's okay. You had a hell of a day with the unexpected visitor." he laughs.

"Well, that's good to hear."

"The doorbell rings, and we look at each other. Whenever we answer the door, it's news reporters or people saying how sorry they're for our loss."

"I'll get it," Dad says.

"No, I will. Let me make it up to you for leaving you downstairs alone." I open the door to two men dressed in business clothes.

"Hello, I'm Detective Smith, and this is my partner, Detective Reed."

"Hi, please come in," I say to them.

"Hello, detectives, how are you?" Dad says, walking up behind me.

"Good, sir. I'm sorry for your loss, and I know this is not a good time, but..."

Dad interrupts."Say no more. I know you two are trying to do your job, and it can't be easy."

"Thank you for understanding the position we're in."

"No problem, gentlemen. What can we do for you today?"

"We're here to take you and Dawn to the station and ask her some questions."

I butt in, "They asked me questions the night of the murder already."

"Yes, we know, but we have to ask them again. I'm sorry," Reed says.

"Okay, let us get our coats, and we can meet you there," Dad tells them.

"We can wait in the car and follow you there," replies Reed.

"Okay, just let us get our coats."

"Want me to get Scotty?" I ask Dad, thinking he's going to say yes.

"No, let him sleep. We'll leave him a note."

We get in the car and drive to the station. They take us to a room and make us sit for what feels like forever. They finally come into the room with what appears to be sincerity written on their faces. They smile, and one of them places a recorder on the table.

"Dawn, can you tell us where you were on the day of the murder?" Reed questions.

"I went to Sal's house with Dad and Scotty."

"About what time was that?"

"We left the house at noon," Dad answers.

Reed looks at Dad and says, "Mr. Sandino, these questions are for Dawn right now, but don't worry, we'll ask you some when we're done with her."

"You already questioned me," Dad says.

"Well, we have to do it again." Reed returns his attention to me and asks me another question, "What did you do there?"

"We ate dinner."

"That's it?" Smith says curiously.

"Yes."

"Mr. Trieger told me you left at 10 p.m. Why did you take so long to eat?"

"Oh, we talked and got to know each other."

"I thought you only ate there."

"I did."

"Well, you're now saying you talked and got to know each other. Which one is it?"

"Both."

"Why didn't you tell us that?"

"I don't know. I didn't think it was important."

"We're investigating a murder, Ms. Sandino. Everything is important."

"Why does this feel like my daughter is being interrogated?" Dad interjects.

"I'm sorry, Mr. Sandino. I'm just trying to get the facts."

"Well, ask differently because you're making it seem like she did something wrong."

"We didn't say she did anything wrong. This is how I ask my questions. What did you guys talk about?"

"Everything."

"Everything like what? Be specific, Dawn."

"I don't know my favorite color, food, or hobbies."

"That's all?"

"Yes."

"Mr. Trieger said you two got into an argument of some sort."

Dad looks at me. I know he wants to know why he hadn't heard this before.

"Yes."

"What was the argument about?"

"They kept calling Alex my dad and... "

"Who is Alex?" asks Smith.

"My sperm donor."

"Your biological father?"

"Yeah, but he's not my father."

"And what else?"

"They kept calling themselves my grandparents and uncle."

"And that made you mad because?" Smith inquires.

"Because they aren't," Reed answers for me.

"No, they're not," I say.

"Then, what are they?" Smith asks.

"People I know for now."

"Why?"

"Because grandparents and uncles are always there, and they've never been."

"Our report says that you left that night to go to your old house in Long Beach."

"Yes."

"Why?"

"I knew Earl was there, but I thought Tracy was with him."

"Why did you think Earl was with Tracy?"

"Because the car had the words *'YOUR MINE!'* on it.

"Who told you it said that?"

"No one, I heard the police talking."

"What does *'YOUR MINE'* mean to you?" I look at Dad and the detectives.

Dad quickly butts in, "If you read your report, you will see what it means."

"I read the report. We have to ask Dawn for ourselves, sir."

"It's okay, Dad, I can answer it."

"Before Tracy and I moved in with Dad, she was a prostitute. Earl was one of her johns." I explain to the detectives, giving them the backstory about Earl, my eyes tearing up. "Earl was also Tracy's, umm... drug dealer and would come over every night." My face heats up and my mouth waters. I feel sick to my stomach and very lightheaded. I try to continue, but I'll throw up all over the them if I do. They look at me and become worried; I fall silent.

"Are you okay, Dawn," I hear everyone repeating, but I can't answer them. I spot a trashcan in the corner of the room and run to it. I puke everything inside of me. I feel Dad next to me. He holds my hair from behind to keep it out of the way.

"I think she's had enough for today," Dad tells them..

"We think so too. We will question Dawn again tomorrow."

"About something else, I hope," says Dad, sternly.

"Yes, but we still need her to answer that question."

"Are you serious? Look how it hurts her to talk about it."

"I know, sir, but we still have to. I hope you understand we're just doing our job," Smith says. I put my back against the wall and cry. My breathing gets heavy.

"Yeah, didn't know your job is to torture the hell out of little girls," Dad retorts.

"Like you said, we'll question her tomorrow."

We get back in the car, and I say to Dad, "I'm sorry." he tells me not to apologize and that it's the detectives' fault. I always feel sick to my stomach at the near thought of Earl, but it's never been this bad. This is the first time this has happened. It's probably because of everything that has transpired. My stomach can't handle what that sicko did to Tracy and me. I can't figure it out yet, but I'm convinced he's responsible for her death.

We arrive home. I quietly go straight to my room. Scotty is not in there. He must be downstairs eating. I lie down on my bed and cry myself to sleep. The nightmares resurface. Earl is raping me again. Things flip to Tracy. The video replays her being shot in the head. I wake up in a frantic, drenched in sweat.

Chapter 11

ARE THEY REALLY THAT DANGEROUS?

"Hey, Dad?"

"Yes, sweetheart"

"Umm, I have to ask you a question."

"Go ahead."

"Why didn't you tell me Tracy's parents came yesterday?"

Dad's face changes from a smile to a pissed-off one, "What do you mean?"

"Well, Fawn told me they were here. They came with her."

"Did you see them?" he asks worriedly.

"No, but I wanted to."

"Did anyone come up to you?"

"A lot of people did."

"Anyone you didn't know at all, someone out of the ordinary?"

"No, I don't know all your friends that came up to me, and I don't know all your co-workers."

"Dawn, if they spoke to you, you must tell me."

"Dad, what's the big deal?"

"Shit, I knew this would happen sooner or later."

"What would happen? What's going on?"

"The past catching up to us."

"It's Tracy's parents..."

"There's a reason Tracy ran from them."

"She ran?"

"Yes, and now it's my job to protect you."

"From what?"

"Them."

"How?"

"When you get older, you will understand more of what's happening. When you leave school, we'll talk about what will happen. I need to get a few things in order first. Your world is going to change now."

"It's already changed."

"Not like this. Remember, there is a reason for everything."

"I don't want Tracy's past becoming your future."

"Dad, you're not making sense."

"I won't be for now, but in time, I will be," he says, and goes upstairs, leaving me in the kitchen.

What the hell is going on? Why is Dad acting like this? What does he mean about all of this? Are Tracy's parents really that bad? Dad isn't telling me something is happening, and I want to know what. All in time, I'll understand, but in how much time?

Dad sits Scotty and me down the following day, and you can tell he's been up all night because of the dark circles and bags under his eyes. So much for waiting until after school, I'm thinking to myself. Scotty and I are super confused. Scotty's confused because he has no idea why we're having this meeting. However, I know exactly why we're having the meeting but just confused about why Tracy's parents are so damn scary for Dad.

"Kids, I want you to know, recently, I had to increase the security around here,"

"What do you mean?" I ask, completely confused.

"He's got more guards stalking us," Scotty says.

"Wait, we were being watched before?"

"Yeah, genius. You haven't noticed or felt like someone is watching you?"

"No, I haven't. Will the guards stand beside us everywhere we go like the Secret Service?"

"No, they will still be undercover. We have a few of my old friends trying to get to Dawn and you, that's all."

"You mean Tracy's parents?"

He takes a sip of his coffee before answering me, like he's trying to control his reaction, "Yeah, that's what I mean. They aren't safe, Dawn."

"Are they really that dangerous?"

"No, they're worse."

"Then my sister must be warned."

"It's too late for her; besides, Fawn and you are different. You're not safe around them, but she is."

"How am I different than her, Dad? We're from the same parents. She might be a bitch, but she's still my blood."

"Dawnie, baby, please, I beg you to trust me on this. I have never lied to you, and you know I don't ever do anything without a good reason," he says while looking me in the eyes, not breaking contact. I know he's very serious and right. He doesn't lie to me and always has a good reason for his actions.

"Okay, fine," I agree.

"Thank you. You won't see the security team, but they'll be around, and if anything happens out of the ordinary, they will know. Do you understand me?" Scotty and I both nod our heads in agreement. "Nodding your head yes isn't good enough for me. I need words out of you two."

"Yes," we both say.

"Okay, good. This is the best way to stay normal at school without being bothered or standing out. Now, let's get ready for school and work," he says, kissing me on the forehead.

Chapter 12

BACK TO SCHOOL

On the way to school, Scotty tries to start a conversation, but it doesn't go far. I answer him quickly and keep it very brief, then look out the window. We finally get to school. I hop out of the car and head for the school doors. They treat me like a celebrity visiting the school when I walk in. All eyes are on me. They've all heard what happened to Tracy. I had no idea middle school kids watch the news. I only watch it because Dad use to make me, but then I got used to it.

Everybody is whispering and pointing at me. They won't take their eyes off me while rushing pass them to class. I sit in the back of the class, hoping people don't notice me, but I'm wrong. My classmates' eyes land on me while they walk into the classroom.

Brittany walks in and has a big smile on her face, "O-M-G, you're finally back! I missed you so freaking much!" she says, hugging me.

"Yeah, same here."

"How are you? I've been calling, but someone has been ignoring me."

"I know. I'm sorry. I needed some time alone."

"No, you needed someone with you by your side."

"Dad and Scotty were there and still are."

"Yeah, but I'm your best friend. I should be there too."

"Well, it's not too late. I'm still going through it. Just look around the room."

"Wow, all eyes on me. I must be looking good today," Brittany jokes.

"Yeah, I wish they were on you," I say as students find their seats. I get out of my seat and go to the board. Turning around with a long ruler in my hand as if I'm about to teach the class, I announce, "Okay, everyone, I know it's going to be hard, but can you please stop looking at me like I'm from another country? Not only is it annoying, but it's extremely rude. Gather your manners and focus on the board — this is your first lesson of the day." I proceed to write on the board, 'DO NOT STARE AT DAWN!!!' "In case you forget, just read the fucking board!" I finish and walk to my seat next to Brittany.

"Wow!" Brittany says, completely shocked.

"Sorry, but it's getting annoying."

"Yeah, I see that."

The teacher finally walks in and looks at the board. He turns his head to me and starts laughing. "I guess we've had our first lesson for today."

A guy walks in and sits next to me. "Good one, D. Looks like you're our next teacher."

"Not in this lifetime," I say, turning my head to look at him.

"Everyone is a teacher in their own way," he says, taking out his notebook.

I've never seen this kid before in my life. I write a note to Brittany:

> who is this new guy next to me?

> LOL! No, silly. He's been sitting next to you for the whole school year. You even let him copy off your homework once.

> Really?

> Yeah, that's Damien Shranagan, a.k.a. Loup. All the girls love him. He's one of the best boxers

ever. How can you not notice him?

I rip up the note and place it on the corner of my desk to get it out of the way. The teacher is saying something, but I'm not paying attention. Dad already taught me everything he's teaching anyway. Dad is strict when it comes to academics. When I moved in, he noticed I was way behind everyone in my class. He sat me down and reviewed everything I was supposed to learn and know. He taught me past my grade level, then I was moved to all honor classes, but I still know it all. I usually answer questions and participate, but I'm not in the mood today. Instead, I doodle in my notebook for the entire class. Before I know it, the bell rings, and I hurry to my locker to escape all the eyes glued to me.

"Are you okay?" Damien asks.

"Yes, why do you ask?"

"It's just that you didn't take notes or answer any questions in science."

"What does that have to do with anything?"

"Well, science is your favorite other than history."

I look at him surprised, "And you know that because?"

"I heard you say it to Brittany one day."

Wow, this boy makes me feel so bad. I don't remember him, but he knows my favorite class, and that I usually participate. "I'm fine. I have a lot on my mind."

"Well, if you need to talk, I'm here. I know we aren't that close or anything, well, not close at all, but sometimes it helps to speak to someone other than yourself for a change."

"Yeah, I'll remember that. Thanks, Damien."

"Anytime," he replies and walks away.

"O-M-G, you were talking to Loup! How was it, and what was it about?" gasps Brittany.

"He was just asking me if I was okay. That's all, Britt. It's no big deal."

"No big deal? Are you serious? He's the hottest guy in school. You just noticed he was alive today, and you two exchanged words with each other, and you say no big deal?"

"Shut up, and let's go to class," I say, rolling my eyes.

The whole day is a blur. The bell rings again, and it's time to go home. I put a few things back in my locker, and when I turn around, I bump into Damien.

"Oops, sorry," I say.

"Don't be sorry because I'm not," he says, smiling. He goes to his locker. It's right next to mine. This guy sits next to me in class and his locker next to mine. Dang, I feel bad.

"Hey, Dawn," Brittany calls my name, interrupting my thoughts.

"Hey, ready to go? Scott should be here already." I reply.

Scotty or Dad usually picks us up from school and takes us home, and today is Scotty's turn, but he's not here yet. We sit on the bench waiting for him, then Britt gets a call.

"Hey, Mom, what's up? Okay, all right, I'll tell her. Yeah, okay, see you in a bit, bye." She hangs up the phone.

"Hey, my mom is having a car pick me up. Want to catch a ride?"

"No, it's okay. Scotty should be here soon."

"Yeah, sure, he will, but it's been ten minutes, and he's not here yet."

"But he will come. He always does."

"Okay, fine," she says. Her driver pulls up. Britt gets in the car, puts the window down, and asks me again if I want a ride. I look at my phone. It's 2:20 p.m., and Scotty is only ten minutes late. I text him just in case:

Hey, where are you?

Stuck in traffic, I'll be there in a second.

K.

The buses are leaving, and I'm sitting alone on the bench. It reminds me of when I was sleeping outside after Earl engraved my back and how peaceful it was. I lie on the bench and close my eyes while waiting for Scotty. I listen to the sound of cars driving by and birds chirping. I feel a nice, warm breeze against my face. I fall asleep, and the nightmare about Tracy's murder returns. I get to the part when Tracy is shot. I jump out of my sleep from the loud pop and see Damien staring at me.

"Bad dream?" He smirks.

"You know it's not nice to stare at people," I say, sitting up. I grab my phone to see what time it is. It's 3:00 p.m.

"Not that I was staring, but I think that only applies when the person is awake."

"I wasn't sleeping," I reply, irritated that Scott still hasn't picked me up. I call Scott, and it goes straight to voicemail.

"Are you okay?" Damien asks, a little more seriously this time.

"Yup, my ride is running late."

"What time was it supposed to be here?" he asks.

"When school got out."

"Oh, wow, that's more than late. That means your ride is not coming. I just got done wrestling, and it's still not here."

"Yeah, I know. I have to find another one."

"Where do you live?"

"Barnaby Road."

"That's not too far. I'm walking home, and if you want, I can drop you off on the way."

"Nope, that's okay."

"Okay, I'll sit and wait with you until your ride is here."

"No, you can go home."

"Why are you being so mean? All I'm trying to be is nice?"

"I don't need your pity, Damien."

"Pity?"

"Yeah, pity."

"I'm not giving you my pity. This is just how I am. Look, just let me walk you home. That way, I know you're safe. I'd never forgive myself if I left here and something happened." I give him a serious look, and he looks at me.

"We can stop for ice cream on the way."

"I don't know, I'm not big on being alone with guys," I tell him.

"Who said we'll be alone? We're outside with everyone watching us." I look around and notice he's right.

"Okay," I say, giving in and standing up. We start walking, and Damien takes my book bag.

"I can carry my bag, Damien."

"Yeah, I know. I'd rather carry it for you."

"I hope you don't think this walk means anything."

"I hope it means we can be friends."

"Yeah, only friends, nothing more."

"Truce," he says, putting his pinky up so we can make a promise. I must say the walk with Damien is nice. He makes me laugh. We stop at the ice cream place before he walks me home.

"Bubble gum burst, please," I say to the worker behind the counter in the ice cream shop. Damien laughs at me.

"Bubble gum burst?" he repeats.

"Yeah, what's wrong with that?"

"Nothing, I just took you as the strawberry shortcake type of girl, that's all."

"Oh, really? What are you going to order?"

"Vanilla soft served with rainbow jimmies, please," he tells the ice cream lady. I giggle.

"Vanilla with rainbow jimmies?" I repeat.

"Yeah, what's wrong with that?" he asks.

"I took you as the vanilla-only type of guy."

"Ha-ha, funny," he says; the lady tells us our total. I dig in the side pocket of my book bag on his back for money, but he pushes my hand away and pays for it.

"Damien, you don't have to do that. I can get it."

"I know, but I want to. That's what friends do sometimes."

"Yeah, sometimes. I'll get the next one."

"Ha, we'll see."

For some reason, I feel comfortable walking with him. Not only because people were watching us and because he took me for ice cream, but for how he made me feel. It's a funny feeling, and I can't call it yet. I do not feel this way with Scotty, so I know it's not love. We continue walking and playing around. Damien puts ice cream on my face jokingly and wipes it off. Next, Scotty pulls up with some blonde girl in the front seat with a super push-up bra on. She has makeup that can last for years and clothes that look so revealing like she has nothing on.

"Hey, Dawnie, what are you doing over here?"

"Walking home because my ride never showed up or answered his phone."

"Your ride is here now."

"Kind of too late? Don't you think?"

"Don't be a smart ass, get in."

"Okay," I say to Scott.

I turn to Damien. "Thanks for everything. I had a nice time."

"Yeah, me too. Hopefully, we can do it again, D."

"Yeah, definitely," I say, hugging him, and taking my bag.

Anger spikes on Scott's face, but I don't care because I'm pissed at the blonde hoe in the front seat. I get in the car and close the door. Scott speeds off, not saying anything. The blonde turns around and starts cheesing at me. "Hi, I'm Jane. Scott told me all about you," she says, smacking and popping her gum while still cheesing. I give her a mean-ass stare. She puts her hand out for me to shake it. I roll my eyes at her and look out the window. I can feel Scott's eyes on me as he watches me from his rearview mirror.

"Don't mind her. She's not the talkative type," says Scott.

"It's okay. I was protective over my older brother when I was her age. She's so cute."

"Yeah, wish I could say the same for you too, Barbie," I say with a fake smile and turn towards the window. She shuts up quickly and looks at Scott. He continues to look at me through the rearview mirror. We drop her off, and she kisses him on the lips. It pisses me off. I stay in the back instead of sitting beside him like always.

"Sit in the front," he says.

"Fuck you."

"Wow! Language, little girl!" He drives off until he finds a place on the side of the road.

"Wasn't little before," I snap back.

"Who was that dude? And get your ass in the front."

"A friend, and who was that?" I snap again.

"She introduced herself, but if you weren't such a bitch…"

"And you weren't when I was with my friend?"

"Bullshit, he's not only a friend…"

"And neither is she. Friends don't fucking kiss!"

"Yes, they do."

"Bullshit, then I'll kiss my friend."

"Fuck you will."

"Why not?"

"Because he wants to be more than your friend."

"How do you know?"

"Holding your bag, walking you home, giving you a nickname and a hug, I bet he even bought that fucking ice cream. Now get in the fucking front seat!"

"Fuck you, asshole! And friends buy friends stuff, come up with nicknames, and do stuff like that."

"Yeah, when they're the same sex," he yells and speeds off.

"You would not know that since every friend from the opposite sex is fucking you."

"Not true."

"Oh yeah? Well, what's up with the blonde bitch with her tits and ass all in your face?"

"That's how she dresses."

"And so will I."

"You wouldn't dare."

"Try me," I say.

Scott pulls the car to the side of the road again. He turns towards me and snatches his glasses off. "Dawnie, baby, I'm sorry."

"Fuck you, asshole, you're not sorry. You called me a bitch!"

"I didn't mean it. I was hurt when I saw that boy walking you home."

"You never came and didn't answer your phone, and when you finally show up, you have some blonde whore in your front seat."

"Something came up, and I lost my phone. She needed a ride home. I felt bad letting her walk all the way home — she had very high heels on... may you please come sit next to me?" he asks, climbing in the back seat with me and trying to kiss me, but I move my head. He laughs. "I see how you're going to be. Come on, stop acting like that, please." He makes a sad face, nudges me with his nose, and kisses my neck. I smile and look at him, and he places a soft kiss on my lips. "Sit in the front, please."

"Okay."

"Thank you," he says, kissing me again, but this kiss is harder and more aggressive. I should like it because I like it every other time, but I don't. I play along with it. He pulls away, exits the car, and moves to the driver's seat. I do the same but in the passenger's seat. He plays our favorite song, and we drive home. Dad's car is not home, which is normal. He isn't home until eight at night on weekdays. My phone goes off when we walk in, notifying me of a text message. I look at the number to see who it's from. I don't recognize the number. I open it and read it. It says:

Hey, it's Damien.

Hey, how did you get my number?

Brittany gave it to me. I hope you don't mind.

No, it's okay, I'm sorry about earlier.

Earlier?

Sorry for the way Scott was acting earlier.

I didn't even notice.

Did you get home okay?

Yeah, I got home fine. I was just wondering something.

Wondering what?

I don't have practice tomorrow and wondered if I could walk you home again.

Why?

Because I like hanging out with you. You're fun and funny.

LOL, thanks. You're fun and funny, too.

I want to hang out with him, but Scotty will not like it. Scotty is my boyfriend, so I can't hang out with Damien like that. I don't want to lead him on or anything:

IDK if that's a good idea, Damien.

Please, D, just as friends.

Okay.

Thanks. Meet at the same place?

Yeah.

I lock my phone's screen when I hear Scotty coming.

Chapter 13

SECURITY

S cotty and I hear the front door slam shut downstairs; we jump. "What the fuck was that?" says Scotty. We go to the steps and see Dad.

"Uncle Steve, you scared the shit out of us," yells Scotty.

"Why?" says Dad.

"Maybe because you slammed the door hard," Scotty replies sarcastically.

"Oh, I'm sorry. I had a few things on my mind hiring this extra security and going through the hiring process with them."

"Hiring process?"

"Background checks and all."

"Damn, shit is real, Uncle Steve."

"How dangerous are Tracy's parents? Are they really that bad? Maybe they won't try anything. They haven't tried anything for long as I've been living. Why would they try something now?" I persist.

"Because they never knew about you before. You and Fawn were hidden, but Fawn screwed all that up. She went to them, and now they know. They were never supposed to know about you two, especially you."

"Why not?"

"I told you, when you get old enough, and when you're ready,

I'll tell you. But right now, I don't think you are. The only thing I do know is that you have to trust me, that's all. Do you trust me, Dawnie?"

"Yes."

He looks at Scotty, and Scotty nods his head yes. "Good," says Dad.

Dad makes dinner, and I retreat to my room to search for answers. I have a laptop; I can google them. Maybe there's something I might be able to find. I type "Doyle" into the search bar, but nothing comes up — the site is blocked! Dad must've known I'd look them up and blocked the site. He doesn't want me to know about them yet. It's killing me. I want to know why the hell they're so dangerous.

Chapter 14

WAY TOO MUCH

I tell Scotty that Brittany is dropping me off, and I tell Brittany that Scotty is picking me up to take me somewhere, and we can't give her a ride home today. Then, not looking, I accidentally bump into someone while retrieving stuff from my locker. I turn around, and it's Damien. "Oh, it's you. Hey, what's up?" I say to him.

"Nothing. You ready to go?" he asks.

"Yeah, are you?"

"Yeah," he says and reaches for my bag. I'm about to let him take it when I remember what Scotty noted yesterday about him holding my bag, so I pull it away and start walking away, acting like I didn't notice him trying to get it.

"Hey, D, let me hold your bag," he smirks.

"No, it's okay; I feel like holding it today because it goes with my outfit," coming up with a quick lie. But it's true. It does go with my outfit.

"Okay," he replies and holds the door open for me. I glance at the bench where Britt and I usually sit where we wait for our rides, and I'm relieved she's not there to see me walk off with Damien. We stop at the ice cream place again and sit at one of the tables outside. "So, what's wrong, D? Did I do something wrong?" he asks worriedly.

"No, why do you ask?"

"Because you've acted strange around me since we left your locker. Are you embarrassed to be seen by me or something?"

"No."

"Then what is it?"

"I don't know, it's just that…" I pause and take a deep breath.

"Just what?"

"I don't want to lead you on or make you think this is something it isn't."

"So, we're not friends?"

"Yes, but that's all we are."

"And that is all I think we are unless you want…"

I quickly cut him off, "Unless — nothing. That is all we are, and there is nothing else."

"Okay, fine, you don't have to be so cruel about it, geez," says Damien.

"I didn't mean to be."

"Sure, you didn't. Come on, it's going to be dark soon, so we should start going," Damien says, throwing away his barely-touched ice cream. I look at the sky and notice it's not even near nighttime.

"If I knew you were going to be a poop-head, I wouldn't have ever walked home with you. I still have time not to. Good-bye, and thanks for the ice cream."

"Me? A poop-head? Are you kidding me right now? Look at the way you're acting towards me. You're like Brittany," he says.

I can tell I've really hurt him. "Wow, I'm sorry for being a bitch, and I didn't mean to be like that, I swear."

"It's okay. I shouldn't have overreacted like that. I like being around you. You help me forget about the bad in the world," Damien says. He takes my bag and starts walking. We share my ice cream since he threw his away. Damien making fun of my ice cream flavor quickly changes when he tries it himself. He really likes my ice cream flavor, maybe more than me. We're having so much fun we don't realize we've arrived at my house. I ask him if he wants to comes inside since no one's home.

"Looks nice!" says Damien.

"Yeah, that's what I said the first time I came here."

"What do you mean?"

"My dad was Tracy's boyfriend, and when I met him, I called him "Steve," but then we became very close, and I started calling him Dad," I turn away to the fridge and ask him if he wants something to drink, hiding my tears as I wipe them from my face.

"D, what's wrong?"

"Nothing," I reply.

He places his hand on my shoulder; I turn towards him, continuing to look down. He takes his hand, lifts my face, and says, "Then why am I sensing something is wrong with you?"

"It's just... I get sad when I talk about Tracy."

"Why?"

"Because I feel it was my fault. Well, not feel — I know it was my fault, Tracy, umm..." My face grows hot, and tears stream down. I desperately try to wipe them away, hoping he won't notice, but I fail miserably.

"Your fault... that?"

"That she died," I cry, and he holds me.

"Shh, it's okay. It's not your fault, D."

"Yes, it is. He even said it was."

"Who?" he asks.

I notice before I answer his question what I'm revealing to him. I feel so comfortable around him. I tell him things I don't mean to say to him. I fearfully push him away and tell him he should go home. He stares at me and removes his shirt. Shocked by his actions and not knowing what he's about to do, I yell at him, "What are you doing? I thought we were only..."

He cuts me off when I see all the bruises on his body, "You're not alone, and you can tell me anything. I went and still go through hell just like you. My dad hurts me, too." he cries, holding his arms out to me.

"I didn't know. I'm sorry."

"I know. How could you know, D? You don't have to hide anything from me because we both have gone through hell and still go through it." I look at him and realize why I feel so comfortable telling him stuff.

I sensed something had happened to him before without realizing it myself. I haven't ever known anyone who has gone through hell just like me. He's the first. It feels good to talk to someone who knows exactly what I'm going through and how it feels. I take a few steps and hug him, careful not to hurt him.

"It's okay, D. I think you're the only person in the world who can't hurt me," he says, tightening his hug.

I look at him and surprise myself with what I do next. I kiss him and love it, but I don't think I mean to. He kisses me back, and instead of pulling away, I keep kissing him. In that kiss, my gut tells me that I can trust him, and it's okay to care for him. Scotty is nothing compared to him. My gut is my mind, heart, and, at this very moment, my actions. I forget about Scotty and Dad and everything else around me. It's only Damien and me. I don't dare think about anyone or anything else. We pull away and look at each other, smiling.

"Wow," he says with a huge grin.

"Yeah," I say, and look at the ground, cursing at myself. Damien puts his shirt back on, and we stand there looking breathless at each other. Suddenly, we're startled by the doorbell ringing.

"Who is it?" I ask.

"Detectives Smith and Reed."

I open the door to tell them my dad is not here.

"That's okay. We want to show you something, and only you."

Confused and curious, I invite them in since Damien is here; it's not like they will hurt me. "What is it, detectives?" I ask.

"We said alone." Detective Reed says.

"Whatever you have to tell me, he can hear it too," I let them know, keeping a straight face.

They both look at each other weirdly and shrug. "Dawn, where is Steve?"

"My dad's at work."

"Are you sure?"

"Yeah, why?"

Reed pulls out an envelope and tells me to open it. I look inside and see photos of Dad and a woman who is not Tracy all over him. They were kissing and holding hands. I cry and look at Damien. He puts his arms around me and holds me.

"I think you should come with us to the station," Reed says.

Damien comes with me and sits in the waiting room while I enter the interrogation room.

"So, Dawn, what do you have to say?"

"Nothing, but what does this have to do with Tracy's murder?"

"A lot."

"No, it doesn't because I already told you what happened and who did it."

"How did you know to go to Long Beach?"

"I don't know. It was a gut feeling, I guess."

"You sure no one told you she would be there?"

"No one told me anything; besides, she wasn't there, only Earl and a video."

"Oh, come on with that bullshit, Dawn. You hated Tracy and still do. She was a junkie and a whore who let some guy rape you over and over!"

"I don't hate her, and she was unconscious from drugs when I got raped."

"She brought Earl into your house, and when Steve found out about your back, he got pissed at Tracy."

"He got pissed, but that doesn't mean anything!" I scream at Reed, who's asking all the questions.

"Something tells me Steve killed Tracy and wants to frame Earl but needed your help. That's why you and David left for Long Beach that night, so you could cry wolf and act like Earl was there and pretend you were just a victim, but you're not! Are you Dawn? Are you?" he screams in my ear.

"That's not what happened! Earl was there, and he killed Tracy! I swear he did it! I saw him!"

"No, what you saw was a video of Tracy getting her brains blown out by someone!" Reed screams.

"He did it to her because I left!"

"Left what?"

"Left him when Tracy and I went to move in with Dad!"

Detective Smith looks at Reed, puts his hand up for him to stop, and says to me, "Dawn, I know this is hard, but is there any way that maybe Steve could've had Tracy killed and made you believe it was Earl?"

"No, Earl was there. Even David saw him and heard me speak to him, I swear," I plead, bawling my eyes out. "The car even… even…"

"Even what?"

"It said, *'YOUR MINE!'*"

"What does that have to do with anything?"

I drop my hands from my face and fold my arms. I look Detective Smith in the eye with an evil stare, "You know damn well what that has to do with this. I heard the police talking that night. They already know about my back!"

"She's underage, and you're not supposed to interrogate her without an adult present, you bastards!" Dad screams from the hall.

The Lieutenant steps into the room and lets Dad inside. Dad sees how distraught I am. "That's it, we're done here. We will not be answering any of your questions anymore. Wait until my lawyer hears about this. We're going to have your ass," he says, grabbing me and my stuff, and heading for the door.

I stop Dad. He's baffled. I tell the Lieutenant to close the door because I've had enough of this bullshit. "You sick fucks want to see what *'YOUR MINE'* means to me? You want to know the reason why I break down every time you bring it up? Fuck this! No more telling you, I'll show you!" I yell in rage while looking Detective Reed directly in his face with nothing but pain. I pull up my shirt, and Dad stops me.

"Dawn, baby, no. You don't have to do this."

"No, Dad, I do. They have to see who and what we're dealing with. I'm done with them attacking and blaming you all because they don't feel like doing their fucking jobs!" I snatch off my shirt and turn my back to them. I hear someone's breath caught in their throat.

"Bloody hell!" Detective Reed gasps.

"Oh, my!" Detective Smith says while losing his composure from the grotesque of it all.

"That is what Earl carved on my fucking back when I decided to fight back after not being able to let him rape me anymore." I turn around and face the room with my shirt still in my hand, "Now do us a favor and do your fucking job! Find this man and take him off the street so maybe, just maybe, I might be able to sleep without having nightmares. I'm tired of having to tie something around my mouth so my dad and cousin won't hear me scream in the middle of the night!" I walk towards the door.

Dad stops me. "Dawnie, baby, put your shirt on first. Please," he says with a sad, wet face.

"Oh, yeah, my bad." I quickly put on my shirt, and we walk out the door.

I haven't tied anything over my mouth since Scotty started sleeping in my bed to comfort me, but they don't need to know that. I wanted to make a point and have them stop questioning us and do their jobs. "Wait. My friend, Damien, came with me. We have to give him a ride home," I tell Dad. He gives me an odd look and tells me to get him.

Damien is on the bench where the detectives and I left him. He looks at me, gets up, rushes, hugs, and kisses me on the forehead, which I need right now. I hope Dad didn't see because I don't want Scott hearing about it. Dad, Damien, and I get in the car. Dad is so mad he doesn't say anything. We take Damien home, but he's still silent.

"Dad?"

"Yeah."

"You wouldn't lie to me, right?"

"Of course not. Why do you ask such a thing?"

"They showed me something at the house before we went to the station."

"What was it?"

"A picture… of you and another woman."

Dad hits the steering wheel with his hand, swivels the car to the side of the road. He presses on the brakes so hard, I would've hit the dashboard if I hadn't been wearing my seatbelt.

"Those sons of bitches," he yells.

"Is it true, Dad?"

"Yes, but let me explain."

I keep talking, "Earl told me about Tracy still using. Is that true?"

"Tracy went back to drugs and doing her own thing, and there was nothing I could do anymore."

"You knew Tracy was a junkie when you met her."

"Yes, that's true, but she said she was going to get clean and stay that way," he cries. "The drugs changed her. I didn't want to leave her though because I knew she would try and take you, and like I said before, you're my daughter — I couldn't have that."

"So, you stayed with her because of me even though she made you unhappy?"

"Yes."

"They think you had someone kill Tracy because of the other girl you're with and that you made me help you."

"I know. The detectives interrogated me yesterday."

We sit there in silence until Dad decides to drive us home again. We stay silent all the way home. When we arrive, I'm relieved that Scotty is still not here.

"Where the hell is Scott? I told him I don't want him coming home this late anymore," Dad says, looking at the clock.

"Who knows? Probably hanging with friends like always."

I'm honestly glad he isn't here. Especially after tonight, I don't feel like being bothered by him right now. I'm confused about us with Damien coming into the picture. I'm totally in love with Scotty, or so I thought, and here comes Damien, who I never knew existed until the other day. We're supposed to be friends, but something tells me that our kiss and hug at the house before the detectives came make our friendship more than just a friendship.

Scotty is not only my best friend but also the first boyfriend I've ever had, even though he's older by some years. Scotty is sweet, and I care about him, but he's been acting strange since Tracy died. He's been picking me up late from school, having sluts in the front seat of his car, calling me a bitch, and rarely home.

Damien, on the other hand, can relate to what I'm going through, and he makes me feel comfortable around him, and he's my age. He walks me home and holds my bag. Scotty never holds my bag for me and probably never will. He thinks it's too girly or something. I know I cheated on Scotty by kissing Damien, but it felt so right, although it was so wrong. I wonder if Dad felt this every time he was with that other woman and not with Tracy. Shit! Dad knows about Damien. I hope he doesn't tell Scotty.

While all these things spin away in my mind, I fall asleep. I dream of Damien, which is unusual because I've never dreamed of Scotty. Then suddenly, my dream turns into a nightmare. I'm in my old house in Long Beach and watching the video of Tracy again. When I stare at Tracy's terrified face, I see the gun and hear the words, '*YOUR MINE*,' and then a gunshot, and I wake up instantly covered in sweat. I glance at my phone in the charging holster on my nightstand to see what time it is. I notice a text notification from Damien on the screen. I feel Scotty lying next to me. Careful not to wake him, I move slowly towards my nightstand, grab my phone, and open it to read Damien's text:

Hey, you up?

Yeah.

Can I call you? I hate texting.

Relieved by his texts, I run downstairs so Scotty can't hear me talking and get jealous like last time. I text Damien back:

Yeah.

Two seconds later, my phone vibrates. It's him. "Hey," I say in a low voice.

"Hey, how are you? You looked pretty upset when we left the police station."

"Fine."

"Dawn, this is me you're talking to, so you don't have to lie."

"I'm not."

"Yes, you are. It's okay to feel pain and…"

"I know, I just don't want to talk about it, okay," I whisper.

"Okay, fine." A long second of silence passes by. He's going to bring up the kiss; I know it.

"So… about yesterday, the kiss…"

"Yeah, what about it?"

"What does it mean?"

"I don't know what it means."

"I really liked it," he emphasizes.

"Yeah, so did I," I say, yawning.

"I'm going to let you get some sleep because you've had a hell of a day. I'll see you tomorrow."

"I'm not going to school tomorrow," I say.

"Oh, okay. Is Steve taking you somewhere?"

"No, he's going to work. I'm staying home alone. I'm not telling my dad or Scotty because I don't want them worrying."

"Oh, okay. Well, I'll see you when I see you. Good night, D."

"Night, Damien. Thanks for checking on me, even though you didn't have to."

"No problem."

I hang up the phone and feel bad. Not bad about having feelings for Damien, but for having feelings for him when I'm supposed to be in love with Scotty. Scotty has always been there for me and is my best friend, or should I say he was, until he started acting crazy. I didn't even know Damien existed until three weeks ago, but I have more feelings for him than for Scotty. This is very stressful and is giving me a headache. I'll have to sleep on it and try and figure it out tomorrow.

Chapter 15

DAMIEN

Sleeping is an epic fail. I toss and turn all night and only get about an hour or two of sleep. Looking in the mirror, I see bags under my eyes and a light tint of dark circles around them. "You look tired," says Dad.

"Yeah, I didn't get much sleep yesterday at all."

"Yeah, me neither, and something tells me that yesterday is just the start of a bad beginning," he says. I look at his face and see he isn't lying at all.

"Want to stay home, and I'll call out, and we can have the day all to ourselves?" Dad asks me.

I don't want to tell Dad I'm already staying home because I need time alone, but I also don't want to hurt his feelings. "It's okay, Dad. I got to go to school and catch up on the work I keep missing."

"Okay, if you change your mind, you can text me, and I'll pick you up."

Scotty comes down and looks all refreshed; he grabs a cereal box. "You look like shit Dawnie."

"Thanks, I feel like it," I reply sarcastically.

"Where were you last night?" Dad asks Scotty sternly.

"At Drew's."

"You must've forgotten I told you to return home early last night."

"I didn't think it mattered."

"Well, it does."

"Sorry, I won't…"

"Don't say sorry! You've got to start taking things seriously; not everything is a joke!" he yells.

"What's your problem, Uncle Steve!" Scotty blurts out. I'm surprised, too. Dad never yells, and he yelled last night and today.

"Nothing. Come on. I don't want you to be late, Dawnie," he says, walking out.

"Brittany is driving me to school, so you two don't have to."

"You sure?" Dad asks.

"Yeah, thanks anyway."

"Okay, call me if things change," Scotty cuts in.

"Yeah, and me too," Dad says. He gives me a kiss and leaves for work.

"Something is going on with Dad. This is the second time he's yelled," I tell Scotty.

"What do you mean yelled?"

"He yelled at the detectives yesterday for questioning me without an adult."

"Yeah, that is unusual. What is it that makes Tracy's parents bad?"

"I don't know, but you should have seen him after I told him about them coming to her memorial, he snapped."

"Snapped like what?"

"Like this."

"Wow, you're right. We got to look into it." Scotty says.

"I can't."

"Why not?"

"He blocked their last name."

"No way. Tracy never said anything about them?"

"Nope. Tracy never talked about them; I thought they were dead."

"What do they look like?"

"I don't know."

"How do you know they came to the memorial?"

"Fawn lives with them."

"Shit, ask her."

"Can't."

"Why not?"

"Don't have her number."

"Damn, we have to start snooping."

Something catches my eye briefly, and I notice a fingerprint lock. "Why does Dad have everything on lock around here?"

"I know."

"Pick the lock," I say, wanting to know more.

"Can't, fingerprint only."

"Are you serious?"

"Yeah, go look at it."

He goes to the fingerprint lock. "How didn't we notice that?"

"I don't know," I reply.

"Well, this lock here goes to the wine cellar. Uncle Steve knows I picked his other locks."

"Are you serious!"

"What? I like my wine." he laughs.

I look at Scotty. Something catches my eye. My eyes zoom in closer to him and notice something on his neck. It's almost like a bruise, then it hits me — it's a hickey, and I know I didn't put it there.

"What the fuck is that?" I yell.

"What is what?" he replies, confused.

"On your neck."

He makes that face people make when they know they've been caught red-handed with something. "Oh, I was fighting, and I got hit in the neck. Now, back to the…"

"Fuck that look, Scott. I feel like we're drifting further and further apart. You're acting very different lately, and it doesn't look like a bruise."

"Don't start with that shit."

"Excuse me?"

"You heard me. Don't start with that. All you're trying to do is break up with me in a nice way. Don't bullshit me. Just say it, Dawn."

"I'm not trying to break up with you. I'm just bringing up our problems. We barely hang out anymore because you're always with your friends and probably that blonde whore."

"Oh my god, are you trying to bring her up again? She's just a friend, and now I can't hang out with my friends anymore. Do I have to hang out with you all the time? I'm young, Dawn, and I need to hang out with my friends, not spend every waking minute with you."

"A friend doesn't kiss you on the mouth and hangs all over you... and you can hang out with your friends, but heaven forbid I have someone walk me home."

"I know you're not talking about 'Armstrong' walking you home and buying you ice cream!"

"First of all, his name is Damien."

"I don't give a shit. I don't like Damien or want you hanging out with him."

"Oh, but you can hang out with blondie?"

"She's a friend."

"So is he."

"If I see you with him again, we're done."

"Oh, so I can see you with blondie, and be okay with it?"

"Yeah."

"No, I don't want you hanging out with her, or we're done."

"Fine, I'll cut her off. Just cut Damien off."

"Fine, I will."

Scott kisses me, has his hands all over me, and throws me on the counter. I don't know what it is, but ever since I started hanging out with Damien and kissing him, I feel disgusted when Scott touches or kisses me. I begin to push him off, but he ignores it and moves closer. I finally get my lips from his, but he moves to my neck.

"Scott, stop."

"I want you so bad, Dawnie."

"No, Scott, not now, stop."

"Come on, Dawnie, I love you, and you love me," he says between kisses.

"I said stop, Scott, and I mean it!"

He notices the pitch in my voice and pulls away. "What's wrong with you? We've been together for a few years, and you don't want to touch me."

"No, Scott, it's not true. I just..."

"Forget it. I got to go. I'm going to be late for school." He grabs his bags and slams the door shut. I know I should feel bad, but I feel relieved he's off me and has left for school. I don't know what's going on with me, but I have to figure it out quickly because I don't want to keep hurting Scotty anymore. I go to my room and lie in bed, still exhausted. I get a piece of paper to weigh the pros and cons between Damien and Scott.

Damien is a perfect, lovely, bad boy with a sensitive side; he can relate to what I'm going through. I can hang out with him without sneaking around, but all the girls at school like him; then again, everyone likes Scotty, too. I hate liking boys everyone else likes for some reason, but I've known Scotty for longer, and he knows everything about me. He knows about Earl and what he did to me, and Damien doesn't. However, I can tell Damien about it and probably more.

Damien doesn't seem like the type that will let some blonde bitch kiss him all over the mouth right in front of me, even if we're together in secret. I can't throw away two years with Scotty for just three weeks with Damien, even though they've been an amazing three weeks and helped get my mind off what's been happening with Tracy. These last three weeks feel like it's been three years. I've never felt like this with Scotty. While sorting through Damien and Scotty's pros and cons, the phone rings. I look at the caller ID and see it's the front gate. Out of curiosity, I answer it. I'm not expecting anyone, and neither is Scotty or Dad because they're not here. "Hello," I say.

"Hello, Ms. Sandino. We have a visitor for you. His name is Damien Shranagan."

Surprised that Damien is at the gate, I tell them to let him in. Thank God I already have my clothes on. I wanted Dad and Scotty to think I was going to school. Getting ready for school at my normal time was the only way to make them think I was going. I look in the mirror to check my hair; I pause for a second. I have to stop seeing Damien because I'm with Scotty. Damien and I are supposed to be just friends, and we're turning out to be much more than that.

I have to tell Damien this when he gets here — my hair

doesn't need to look good to do that. It would make things more complicated for me. So, instead of fixing it, I mess it up and run to throw on some pajama pants or something. The phone rings again; I don't look at the caller ID because I know it's the front gate again calling for Damien.

"Hey, I said to let…"

"YOUR MINE, BITCH!" is all I hear on the other end; I freeze in terror. Earl is the person on the other end, using a voice changer. I hear the doorbell; my heart nearly stops. I hang up the phone and tiptoe downstairs to the door in fear what might be on the other side. I look out the window, and no one is there but a box. I open the door slowly, making sure no one is going to pop out of the bushes or anywhere else and kidnap me. I make it outside to the box, open it, and see a shirt, but it's not just any shirt. It's the shirt I wore the first time Earl raped me!

I'm in complete shock. I stand there, paralyzed, not noticing Damien approach and call my name until he's standing next to me, wondering what's happening. He grabs the box and reads it. It says, *'YOUR NEXT!'* I'm so shocked about the shirt, I didn't even notice the message on the box. I snap out of it and start pushing Damien inside. "Get inside, hurry. He still might be out here."

"Who, D? What's wrong?" he continues to ask while I lock the doors in a hurry.

"Oh my god, he's found out where I live."

"Who, D?"

I run to the kitchen to get a knife before I check the rest of the doors. "Did you see anyone out there before you got here?"

"No, only you outside standing there in shock." I pace back and forth, and Damien grabs my hands, "What's wrong? Who is he?"

"The guy that killed Tracy,"

I look him in the eyes and start to cry. He holds me tightly. We sit on the floor.

"We've got to call the police," says Damien.

"Yeah, you're right." I walk over to the phone, but I'm distracted again before I can get to it. Once again, I stop dead in my tracks. On the window, written in red, is *'NO CALLING THEM OR ELSE!'*

"What the fuck!" Damien shouts.

"I suggest you go. It's obviously not safe here."

"And leave you here? Hell, no!"

"I got to stay here. I have to wash the window."

"I can help."

"No, Damien. It's not safe."

"And you think it is for you? You can talk until you're blue, but I'm not leaving you here alone."

"Okay, fine, but stay here until I clean the window."

He laughs frustratingly, "I'm not doing that either."

"Fine, come on," I say, breathing hard. I clean the window, and Damien helps me. We keep looking around to ensure no one is trying to sneak up on us. Luckily, no one does. It's just us; we return and sit in the kitchen. I throw my face in my hands and start hyperventilating. Damien comes to my side and holds me. I find him to be quite calming.

"So, what are you going to do?" he asks.

"Stay quiet, and not tell anyone what was on that window."

"You can't do that, Dawn. You must tell someone."

"No, I can't, or they'll hurt someone I care about."

"But D…"

"But nothing, you don't know what he's capable of, and I do. You can't say anything, Damien. Promise me you won't."

"Okay, okay, I won't, D."

"You swear?"

"I swear," he says and gives me another hug.

"What are you doing here anyway?"

"I didn't want you to be alone after all that happened yesterday and now after whats happened today. Thank God I came."

"Thanks. That means a lot to me," I say to him with a smile. He goes to his bag and pulls two turkey and cheese sandwiches and two water bottles out of his backpack.

"I thought you might be hungry, so I decided to bring you breakfast," he says with a huge smile. He sits down at the counter and winces like he's in pain.

"What's wrong?" I say, becoming worried.

"Nothing, just something my dad and I disagreed on."

"So, he beat you?"

"Yeah, but it's okay, really."

"Let me see."

"No, let's just eat, D, please."

"At least let me look at it to see if you need ice or something, Damien."

"I don't need ice. Stop, you've been through enough today, D."

"I'll be the judge of that." He looks at me, and I make a sad face.

"Please," I beg.

"Fine, but don't touch it." He pulls up his shirt, and I see a huge bruise over his rib cage.

"What didn't you two agree on, Damien?"

"I don't want to talk about it now."

"But…"

"Please, D, I'm sure you understand."

"Okay, we don't have to talk about it."

"Thanks," he says, looking at me, touching my face, pulling it closer to his, and kissing me. He isn't forceful with his kisses. They're light and innocent. Something I've never had before, not even in the two years with Scotty. It was all sex with Scotty, but with Damien, it's more, and I can feel it. I haven't had sex with Scotty yet, but whenever he kisses me, his hands roam all over my body, and it feels like all he wants is sex.

Honestly, I can't see myself ever having sex with Scotty. I also know that Earl raping me means I'm technically not a virgin, but I didn't choose him. If I had to pick anyone, it would be Damien. I told Scotty I'd stay away from Damien, but deep in my heart, I can't even if I tried. I care about Damien more than Scotty, which is crazy because I've known Scotty for longer, but with Damien, I enjoy kissing him. I know it's early, but my gut tells me I wouldn't mind losing my virginity to him, either. I feel incredibly comfortable with him, which is not good at all. I pull away from Damien, back away, and walk to the couch to turn the TV on.

"Sorry, I didn't mean to scare you, D, I swear." I look at him and see his eyes are remorseful and glossy, like he's about to cry.

"No, don't be sorry, I wanted to see. But why are you about to cry?"

"Because I know we just started being friends, and I don't want to lose you because I can be myself around you."

I grab his hands, pull him to the couch, and sit him beside me. "As long as you don't push me away, I promise you won't lose me, Damien."

"I won't push you away."

"Good, bring them sandwiches here, and let's find something on TV." He smiles and gets the sandwiches. I lie on the right side of his chest, watch *The Three Stooges*, and fall asleep in his arms. While asleep in his arms, I don't dream at all — I sleep. When I wake up, I feel refreshed, as if I had slept for days, and I'm still in his arms. I notice he's sleeping, too, and he looks so peaceful. I can't help myself. I kiss him on the cheek.

"Have a nice nap, D?" he says with a smile.

"Yeah, sorry, I didn't mean to wake you."

"It's okay. I was about to wake up anyway." I look at my phone to see if I missed any calls or texts.

"What time is it, D?"

"Little after 1:30 p.m."

"How did we both fall asleep for so long?"

"I know you went to sleep first because I heard you snoring," he laughs.

"Hey, I do not snore."

"I know, I'm just playing with you. Besides, you looked tired, I thought I'd let you sleep, then I fell asleep," he chuckles.

"Thanks, I needed it. I couldn't sleep at all last night."

"I didn't think you could after everything, and you confirmed it when you opened the door."

"Hey," I giggle and punch him lightly, careful not to touch his bruise.

He laughs back at me, puts his arms around me, and says, "You look nice. You always do... but I could tell you hadn't slept in days. Besides, we both needed it and I haven't slept in who knows how long?"

"Yeah, tell me about it." I reply, then changing the subject. "What do we do now?" I ask him.

"Get dressed. I want to take you somewhere."

"Where?"

"Surprise."

"Hate surprises."

"You'll like this one."

I run upstairs and find shorts, a grey American Eagle shirt, a white tank top, and white flip-flops. I brush my hair, run downstairs, and see Damien at the bottom of the steps. "You might want to put on some sneakers, D."

"Okay," I say, turning around and grabbing my grey sneakers.

"You look lovely."

"Thank you."

"Let's go."

We walk over to his bike, and he puts me on his handlebars. We ride away to the beach. He locks his bike up, takes my hand, and walks me to the woods near the beach. "Where are we going, and why are you taking me to the woods?"

"You'll see, come on." I see a small mountain, and we climb it. Standing at the top, I see a lovely view.

"Oh my god, it's beautiful."

"I knew you'd like it."

"No, I don't like it."

"Wait, what?"

"I love it."

He smiles. "Yeah, I come here often to think and clear my mind."

"Thank you for bringing me here."

"You look like you needed to clear your mind," he says.

"It's clear when I'm with you," I say, grabbing his hand.

"That's good to know," he says, kissing my lips.

While we stand on the mountaintop looking over at the beach, I decide between Scotty and Damien. I choose Damien and always will. Damien gets me before I get me. I can sleep without any trouble with him. I need Damien; he's the best thing in the world compared to Scotty. He makes me forget about all my problems and makes me so happy. My gut tells me choosing Damien over Scotty is the right thing to do. My only issue is figuring out how to tell Scotty we're over.

Chapter 16

HELL OF A BREAKUP

Damien takes me home. When we arrive, I see Scotty's car and worry that Scotty might see Damien and me. I tell Damien goodbye and promise to call him later. When I walk into the house, I notice two pairs of shoes. One pair is Scotty's, and the other belongs to a girl, but the girl isn't me.

"Hey, Scotty," I call out, and no one answers. I begin to walk up the stairs. Scotty's door is cracked open, there's moaning and heavy breathing. Still not sure what's going on, I peep into the crack of the door and see Scotty and that blonde bitch fucking. I'm so pissed because he's cheating on me. I don't stop to think. I bust the door open. "What the fuck, Scott!" They're startled when I barge in, and they jump up.

"Oh, it's only you," says the blonde bitch.

"Shit! Dawn, I can…"

"No, don't. You can't because there is no explanation for this," I say to Scott with glossy eyes. I turn and run out of the room. I grab my phone and purse and dial Damien's number. He instantly picks up.

"Hello."

"Damien," I say, trying to hide that I'm crying, but fail.

"What's wrong?"

"I need to see you now."

"I'm on my way," he says and hangs up.

Scott runs out of the room with a sheet around his waist and catches me out the door. "Dawn, wait, please."

"No, stay away from me. I can't believe you right now."

"It's just sex. It means nothing, I swear."

"Then go finish because we're done for good."

"No, please."

"You wanted me to stay away from Damien while you fuck blondie-go lucky," I fuss. Then, Damien catches my eye. He's riding up on his bike. I start walking to him. Scott grabs my arm. I quickly turn around and smack him hard in the face; his head turns to the side. He's so shocked; he releases my arm.

"If you leave with him, we're done forever, and I'll go up there and finish what I started," he says.

"Is that a promise?" I scowl, shaking off his hand and walking right up to Damien as he brings his bike to a stop. I grab his face, make his lips meet mine, and kiss him like I've never kissed anyone before. I do it to get back at Scott, but when my lips meet Damien's, that changes, I'm doing it because I want to. I forget about Scott and what I just saw. I only want to kiss Damien. He pulls away slowly and looks me in the eyes, smiling.

"Wow," he says.

"Take me away from here right now, please."

"I thought you'd never ask. Hop on."

I turn around to ride on Damien's handlebars and see Scott in the distance in disbelief and speechless; he's mad, and storms back into the house. As pissed off as I was a second ago, I'm happy that I'm with Damien now. I knew I'd eventually break up with Scott, but I never expected it to be like this. We'll never recover from this, and I'm not talking about recovering as a couple but even as friends — if we ever did, it would be tough. How can he say that and do that to me? 'Leave with him, and we're finished?' Fuck him. He can go back to his blonde bitch. Damien takes me to the beach again, and we sit and watch the ocean's waves.

"D?"

"Yes?"

"What happened?"

"With what?"

"I saw you slap your brother."

"He's not my brother. He's my dad's nephew. My dad *was* Tracy's boyfriend — no relation at all," I reply sternly, emphasizing my words.

"I'm sorry, but anyways, I saw you slap him."

"I don't want to talk about it."

"Okay, you don't have to if you don't want to, but I just want you to know you can talk to me if you want to."

I realize I'm taking my anger out on him, and all he's trying to do is help me. "It's okay, Damien. I'm sorry for going off on you like that. I don't want to talk about anything else when I'm with you. You make me forget the bad things, so I love being around you."

He smiles and plants a kiss on my lips. "It's okay, and you don't have to apologize. I know how you feel."

"Thank you, Damien." My phone starts ringing, I look at it, it's Dad.

"Hey, Daddy, what's up?"

"Nothing, where are you?"

"With Brittany, we're looking at the sunset at the beach."

"Okay, well, be safe and call me when you leave there. Do you need any money?"

"No, I'm good — but thanks, though."

"Okay, just be home by 8:00 p.m."

"Okay, Dad."

"Okay, I love you; see you in a bit."

"Love you too, bye."

"Daddy checking up on you?" Damien teases.

"Shut up. It's getting late; I think we should get going."

"Okay. I have a fight tomorrow, and I was wondering if you could come."

"Of course, wouldn't miss it for the world."

He takes me home. Before we get there, we go around the corner where no one can see us. I hop off the bike and kiss him — catching him off guard again. He gets off his bike and kisses me passionately, the most I've ever felt. He picks me up from my butt and leans me against the tree, and we have the most intense make-out session anyone can imagine. His hands are all over me, and I love it. For the first time in my life, I actually want to have sex. I creep my hands up under his shirt and whisper in his ear, "I want you." He pulls away and looks into my eyes.

"Not here and not now, D."

"What?" I step back, insulted by him turning me down. I push him and walk fast towards the house. He's cringing in pain. I realize I accidentally touched his bruise. I yell 'sorry' and run until he catches me by the waist; he pulls me towards him.

"What's wrong? Why are you running from me, D?"

"Nothing."

"Lie."

"Why don't you want me like I want you," I ask, looking at the ground.

"I do want you, D. I just don't want you outside on a tree where everyone can see. I want it to be romantic and mean something. Having you now would only mean sex, and you're more than that to me, especially if you're going to be my first."

"I'm sorry I brushed up against your bruise when I ran off — I didn't mean to."

"It's okay, it didn't hurt."

"Now, look who's lying."

He laughs, "You know me way too well."

"I can say the same about you." I give him a smile

"Let's go. I got to get you home safe."

We grab his bike and walk the rest of the way to my house. I only see Scott's car. Dad is not home. I give Damien a kiss and go to the door. It hits me. I don't know what time he's fighting tomorrow. "Hey, Damien, what time is your fight tomorrow?"

"2:00 p.m. and I'll pick you up at twelve."

"And I'll be waiting." I blow him a kiss.

He catches it in his hand, puts it in his pocket, and says, "I'll cherish it forever."

"You're so corny," I laugh.

"Only when it comes to you." he laughs back.

When I walk inside, a light comes on in the kitchen. I don't have to turn around to see that it's Scott. "Still up," I say sarcastically and continue to walk towards the stairs.

"Where were you?"

"Don't worry about it."

"I'll tell Uncle Steve then."

"Go ahead; he already knows about Damien."

"Bullshit."

"He drove him home when he picked us up from the police station."

"He never told me," Scott growls.

I give him an evil smile and walk towards him slowly, "Beeecaaauuusseee, it's none — of — your — business!" I shout while momentarily staring him in the eyes before heading towards my room again. He grabs my arm and yanks me to him. He catches me off guard. I'm clueless about what's going on at first.

The next thing I know, Scott's tongue is damn near down my throat. "Is this how he kissed you?" Scott yells.

"Get off me! Don't you ever touch me again!"

"Not until you stop acting like his whore!"

"How dare you call me that!"

"I didn't call you that! I said, you're acting like it!"

"Coming from the one person who can't keep his dick to himself!"

"Well, maybe if you were putting out for me and not everyone else, I wouldn't have to!"

I pause in the middle of the steps and turn to swing at him. But this time, I miss, and my hand hits the wall. I move towards and hit him continuously, saying, "How dare you say that to me! You know what I've been through! I've never given myself to anyone, not even you, and I loved you with every piece of me!" I hit him one last time and run to my room.

"Dawnie, wait, I'm sorry. I didn't mean…" I slam the door in his face. I turn the music on and lie in my bed and cry. My phone rings; I look at it and see it's Dad. I answer it, trying to hide my cry.

"Hey, Dad."

"Hey, you okay?"

"Yeah," I lie.

"I'm on my way home; we can discuss your problem when I arrive."

"Dad, I'm okay. I don't have a problem." I say. The phone beeps, it's Damien on the other line. I ignore the call and continue speaking to Dad.

"You're lying, my little one. I hear the tears in your voice you're trying to hide."

"See you when you get here, Dad."

"Okay, sweetie, be there in a bit."

I hang up the phone and go on the balcony to look at the ocean. I always look at the sea, but only really like its beauty. It's crazy and calm at the same time. I look far into the ocean and see how peaceful and relaxing it is. Looking at the rocks, I see the waves smashing against them hard as if trying to break them. I look at how it touches the shore. It's also calm. The ocean has split personalities, but acts on them simultaneously. My phone rings again. I go to answer it, already knowing it's Damien.

"Hey."

"Hey, you okay?"

"Yeah, why?"

"I feel like there is something wrong."

"Nothing is wrong."

"Why didn't you answer your phone earlier?"

"Because I was talking to my dad."

"Oh, okay, I miss you."

"You just left." I laugh.

"I know, and I miss you already, isn't that something?"

We both laugh, and I hear a knock on the door. Thinking it's Scott. I yell, "Fuck off!"

"Wow, D, what's going on?" Damien says.

"Dawnie?"

"Shit, I got to go, Damien," I tell him, realizing I accidentally just cussed out Dad.

"Come in, Dad." He opens the door and stares at me skeptically. I know he's about to address me for cussing at him.

"Interesting language there."

"Yeah, sorry, I thought you were Scott."

"Oh, I see. What's going on with you two?"

"Nothing, that's how we play around."

"Oh, really?"

"Yeah, so what's up?"

"You tell me."

"Tell you what?"

"How's everything going with you? I haven't spoken to you in a while."

"Dad, I spoke to you this morning." I giggle.

"Yeah, but it was quick. We haven't hung out in a while. Get your bag and meet Scott and me downstairs. We're going to hang out tonight."

"Okay," I say, knowing I don't want to be anywhere near Scott. But I don't want Dad to know that, so I play along. We walk down; Scott's waiting for us.

"Hey, Uncle Steve, is it okay if I stay home? I'm not feeling well," he lies.

"I haven't spent time with you two in a while. We can stay here and watch a movie if you'd like."

"Yeah, I know, but we always spend time together, and I'm not going anywhere. I can join you two another time."

"He's not feeling good, Dad. Let him stay here, and we can bring him some movie popcorn back." I say with a sarcastic smile, only for Scott to see.

"Okay, fine, we can do that. Won't be the same without you, though."

Dad and I leave and see *The Hangover Part II*. It's way funnier than the first one. We eat at Applebee's afterward. During dinner, I feel Dad's going to ask me about Damien. I don't want him to ask me about Damien, so I try talking about everything else. Whenever I feel he's about to hit me with the topic, I bring up something else, like his work. I ask him how he got interested in his field, where he grew up, and anything else to keep us from discussing Damien. I know he'll get to Damien eventually, but I'm trying to avoid it for as long as possible.

"You've never asked these questions before, Dawnie. Why now?"

"I don't know. I never really thought of asking about it before. Since we're alone, I thought this would be the best time to ask." He makes a face and smiles at me, puts a fry in his mouth and takes a gulp of his Coke. "What… Why are you making that face?"

"Dawnie, if I didn't know any better, you're trying to stay off the subject of something you think I'll bring up. Am I right?"

"Maybe."

"Maybe?" He chuckles. "Hmm, so the question you know I'm going to ask is about that boy."

"Hmm, what boy?" I laugh, trying to play dumb, but I know it's not working.

"Dawnie?"

"Okay — his name is Damien, and he's my best friend."

"I thought Brittany and Scott were your best friends?"

"Yeah, me too, but Damien has been through what I've been through. He can relate, you know?"

"Yeah, I know, but what do you mean been through? Like, the back and stuff?"

"No, not that, other stuff."

"Like?"

"Like stuff."

"He wants me to go to his fight tomorrow."

"Huh?"

"He's a boxer and invited me to his fight, and I want to go."

"Okay, you can go, but I want to meet him and whoever else you'll be around tomorrow. Including the person driving."

"Okay, thanks, Dad. Oh, and by the way, Damien's dad is picking me up and taking us.

"Yeah, okay… hey, Dawnie."

"Yeah?"

"I don't have to give you the talk yet? Right?" his tone now serious.

I laugh and say, "No."

We finish our food and go back home.

Dad is determined to get us running with him when we get home. Scott and I finally give in. I'm mad about many things, but the anger begins to leave me as I run longer and harder. I don't become tired, I keep the same pace. Scott is next to me and is about to pass out. Dad and I are beside each other almost the entire run until he has to keep slowing down for Scott. Then Dad says we have to go back to the house.

For the first time during our run, I complain and ask to run longer. Surprised and happy, he says 'no' because I must save my strength. We get to the house, and I get something to drink and jump on the couch. Scott falls on the floor and lies there. Dad sits next to me and smiles.

"What, Dad?"

"Nothing, I'm just proud of you. You knocked out that run today and still wanted to keep going. I know you were a little mad when I said no."

I laugh. "Yeah, I kind of did."

"What's wrong, Dawnie?"

"Nothing."

"I hate when you lie to me."

"I hate when you say that, Dad."

"Then don't hide anything from me. You don't think I can tell something is going on with you two? I felt the tension between you and Scott before we left to go out today."

"I'm not hiding; I just don't want to discuss it. It's nothing; it'll blow over before you know it."

"I hope so because we're family and must stick together. We're all we have."

"I know, Dad, and it's not that serious. We'll talk later. I just don't want to get into it right now."

"Okay, then. When you're ready to talk, I'm ready to listen."

"Good, and for now, let's watch *The Three Stooges* on TV."

We call it a night, and I go to my room and look at my phone, seeing two missed calls and three texts from Damien. I call back, a little worried because I feel something may be wrong since he called and texted so many times, saying he needed to talk to me.

"Hello," he answers. I can hear a car driving past him in the background.

"Where are you? Are you okay?" I ask in a hurry.

"Yeah, I just fought with my dad and left."

I quickly think of how I can help him, I can let him in downstairs, and my Dad will never know. He'll think it's Scott and me, and Scott will think it's Dad and me. I can sneak him out in the morning before anyone notices. No one will walk in on us if I lock the door. "Come to my house. Don't let the security guard at the gate see you. Text me when you're outside, and I'll let you in." I whisper.

"I don't want to get you in trouble or involved, D."

"Shut up and do what I just said. Besides, I got involved when we kissed at my house today."

He laughs sarcastically, "Sorry about that, I didn't mean to…"

"Don't be because I'm not."

"Okay, be there in a bit."

We hang up, and I wait for him to text me. Twenty minutes later, I feel my phone vibrating. I know it's Damien. I don't answer. Instead, I go to the door, but no one is there. Leaving the door open, I walk outside and whisper his name. Noises come from the bushes, and my heart stops. I walk closer to the bushes, praying it's Damien, and whisper his name again. He comes out of the bushes. He's in pain. "Oh my god, what the fuck happened to you?"

"My dad."

"Okay, come on."

"Wait."

"What is it?"

"Your dad, D?"

"He's asleep."

"Scott?"

"He's sleeping too. We can go in my room, I'll lock the door, and we'll be safe."

"Okay," he says and begins walking with me again. We get to my room, and I lock the door. I lay him down on the bed and go downstairs to get some ice for his bruise. I place it on his ribcage. He gasps in pain.

"Want to talk about it?"

"No, I'm tired. I just want to sleep and hope it doesn't hurt tomorrow by the time of my fight."

"You're still going to fight?"

"Of course."

"You're in no condition to fight tomorrow."

"I have to, or things will get worse. This is nothing. D, my dad has done worse. Now let's get some sleep, and I'll be better tomorrow," he says, conjuring a smile.

"First it's you hope, and now it's you will; which one is it, Damien? Why do I feel you're just talking out your ass?"

"Because, for the most part, I am. I have no choice but to fight tomorrow, and win that match. What you see now will be like a paper cut compared to what my dad will do to me tomorrow. You know how it is, D."

"Yeah, I know."

"Come here so I can hold you. I missed you."

I laugh. "We've only been apart for a few hours today."

"I miss you even if it's just a minute away from you."

"I feel the same way."

I smile at him and kiss his lips. We fall asleep, and again, like earlier today, I sleep peacefully like nothing can hurt me. After Tracy's death, I always have nightmares of her dying again and again. But being in Damien's arms makes me sleep soothingly and not dream at all. We both wake up with a knock at the door. "Coming," I say, quickly shoving Damien into the bathroom, where I put my clean towels.

I open the door and see Scott. "What do you want?" I ask, my face stern.

"Uncle Steve just cooked breakfast, and I, uh…"

"Spit it out, Scott, I don't have all day."

"I'm sorry about yesterday. I didn't mean anything by it, Dawnie. I was just upset and…"

I cut him off before Damien hears him say something I don't want him to hear, "It's okay, just don't let it happen again."

"I'm about to go to the beach. Do you want to go?"

"I can't. Damien has a fight today."

"Oh, okay, maybe next time."

"Yeah, maybe next time," I repeat, and he turns around to go downstairs. "Hey, Scott, who's here?"

"Me and Uncle Steve."

"Where is he?"

"In the kitchen, he wanted me to get you so you can come and eat with us. Why do you ask?"

"No reason; I thought I heard more voices downstairs. It must be the TV."

"Yeah, it must be," he says. I close the door and go to Damien, hoping he hasn't heard anything.

"Morning," I say to Damien.

"Morning," he says, grabbing and kissing me by the waist.

"Someone's feeling better."

"I'm only better when I'm around you."

I pull away and run to the clock. "Shit, it's ten o'clock. We only have two hours. I can sneak you out while everyone is in the kitchen."

He laughs. "I don't have to pick you up at twelve. I just said that so I can spend some time with you. Since I slept over, I can give you an extra hour. But I do have to get going. My dad will be looking for me." He grabs his stuff, and we go downstairs quietly, ensuring no one sees us. We make it to the door, and I give him one last kiss, and we say see you later to each other. I go into the kitchen and see Dad and Scott waiting for me.

"Morning," I say with a huge smile on my face.

"Someone looks happy and like they slept great," Dad smirks.

"Yeah, sure did."

"Hmm, so when is that boy picking you up again?"

"I asked him to pick me up at one in the afternoon instead." Scott stops eating and looks at us in confusion.

"Wait, what?"

"Oh, yeah, Dawnie will see one of her friends fight today. His name is Damien. He and his dad are picking her up today."

"That should be nice," Scott says, putting his head down and eating.

Chapter 17

THE FIGHT

The doorbell rings, and I know it's Damien and his dad. My dad gets the door and invites them in. We all go into the kitchen. Damien's dad and my dad are in the front, and Damien and I are following them from behind. Damien wears red basketball shorts, a black tank top, and black Under Armour basketball sneakers. Mitch has blonde hair, is muscular, has blue eyes, and is slightly taller than my dad. He has on Khakis and a baby blue Polo shirt that brings out the color in his eyes.

"Hi, my name is Mitch."

"And I'm Steve, and you must be Damien. Nice to meet you again. I hear you have a fight today."

"Yes, and Dad, this is D — I mean Dawn from school," Damien says, smiling.

"I heard a lot about you, Dawn; glad to finally meet you."

"Thank you, and I heard a lot about you," I say to him, and he hugs me.

"Well, I hope it's good things," he says.

"Yeah, they're good," I reply, totally lying.

"When can I expect her back home?" Dad asks.

"Around eight or nine."

"Okay, Dawnie. You have your phone. Call me if you need anything. Good luck with your fight today, Damien. I hope you win."

"Thanks, I hope I win too," Damien says.

"Aww, he'll win. He's the best fighter anyone has ever seen," Mitch butts in with a smile on his face.

"Alright, we should be going now so you can get warmed up. It was nice meeting you, Steve."

"Nice meeting you too, Mitch."

We all go outside, and I see a brand-new black Mercedes-Benz truck. Damien opens the door for me, and I hop inside, and he sits beside me. Mitch and Dad are still talking. "That's your Dad?" I say in a low voice to Damien.

"Yup."

"He doesn't seem like he would do…"

"They never do, D."

"But he seems so nice."

"They all seem that way."

"He doesn't even look like an abuser."

"And what does an abuser look like, D?"

"I don't know, mean probably." He looks at me, and we both laugh.

"They look mean; I guess they do when they're mad." we agree.

"Yeah, oh, and heads up. My dad calls me Loup, not Damien," he laughs.

"Huh?"

"It's my boxing name and nickname he calls me, and everyone calls me. You'll see."

"Okay."

Mitch finally gets done talking to Dad and gets in the car. "You two got your seatbelts on?" he asks.

"Yes, Dad," answers Damien.

He starts up the car and plays the radio. He sings along with songs that come on and occasionally asks questions like where I'm from, who is my real dad, how's school, whether I liked living with Steve, and what sports I like. We finally arrive at the gym, and Damien goes to warm up, leaving me with Mitch. We sit on the bench on the front row where we can see Damien, and he can see us. The match starts in half an hour, and Damien is the first fight. Damien's fighting name is Loup, and he's fighting against someone named Snake.

"Why did he pick the name Loup?" I ask Mitch.

"Because it's French for wolf."

"Okay, why the name wolf?"

"Because a wolf is sneaky and deadly like Loup's punches."

"But he's not killing them."

He laughs, "Of course not, but when he knocks them down, they lie unconscious, as if dead. They never stick to the same routine when they kill their prey. Loup can't stick to the same routine, or his opponent will know what he will do next. Remember, a wolf is always in a pack and is loyal to them. Fighters must stay loyal to the people they work with."

"Did you ever box, Mitch?"

"Yeah, when I was younger, I loved it and still do."

"Why'd you stop if you loved it so much?"

"I had to grow up and get a job. I didn't have the time, and before I knew it, it was too late to suit up and get back in the ol' boxing ring."

"It's never too late to do something you love. You can do it now, and they can call you the Big Loup." When I say Big Loup, he starts laughing so hard he spits it out the water he's drinking.

"Yeah, I guess they can call me 'Big Loup,'" he says proudly.

"Since Damien is called Loup already, you're his dad."

"I think I can get another name. Loup didn't tell me you were a funny girl," he says, still laughing.

Damien is in the back, ready for the fight to start. The sound of a howling wolf comes over the loudspeakers. Damien walks out with three men behind him. His robe is red with a black lining, he's wearing black boxing shoes, and his boxing shorts have 'LOUP' in big capital letters on the back. Damien runs around the ring, throws his hands up, and smiles. He looks my way and blows a cocky kiss at me. I blush, and Mitch says, "Aww, how cute."

The music stops playing, the hard metal starts pounding the sound system, and a boy appears wearing a black robe, shorts, and boxing shoes. The only thing with color on him is the capital letters saying 'SNAKE.' He does the same thing as Damien, except for blowing me a kiss. They take off their robes and pound gloves together; a sign goes up that says round one. "If you watch Loup closely, you'll see why I gave him the name," says Mitch excitedly.

Damien focuses only on Snake. Snake throws a punch at Damien, but he blocks it. Snake throws another punch. Damien blocks it again, but this time, he punches Snake in the ribs and repeatedly hits him. Snake hits the floor and tries to get back up. He finally gets back up, but you can tell he needs to gather himself. The referee counts to ten, and Snake is still stumbling but standing. Damien wins the round.

In the next three rounds, Damien continues to knock him on the ground like before but doesn't even have to punch his ribs. Snake doesn't give up, though. In the fourth round, Damien's had enough because as soon as the bell rings, Damien knocks him out, delivering to Snake a TKO and howls like a wolf. Mitch and I jump up and start screaming Damien's name with many other Loup fans.

"How the hell did he do that like that?" Mitch screams and cheers for his son and gives me a hug. We both clap. Damien blows a kiss at me with one hand. The referee has his other hand in the air. We go back to see Damien, and they try to ice his body, but he tells them he doesn't need it. Mitch runs over to him and gives him a big hug. Damien hugs him back, seemingly trying to figure his Dad out.

"Dad, are you okay?"

"How did you take that boy out like that? And that quick? You didn't break a sweat."

"I don't know how Dad. He just wasn't that much of a challenge, I guess."

"Loup, you fought him last time and won, but he put up a hell of a fight today."

"Well, you always said to keep the fans entertained," Damien says to Mitch while keeping his eyes on me. He puts his arm on me, and I kiss him.

"Yeah, I did. Anyway, you got one more fight left," Mitch says.

"Yeah? Against who?" Damien asks.

"I don't know yet," replies Mitch.

"Yes, you do, you always do," Damien says confidently.

"No, I always have an idea," Mitch says, arms folded.

"That's always right, Dad," Damien says.

"Well, I don't have one just yet. I'm going back out there to see now. These boys are different and are hard to read. They're not like the others." Mitch says. "Oh, Dawn came up with an idea and a crazy name for me," Mitch says, laughing.

"Oh yeah, and what is it?" Damien asks, looking at me.

"I told him he should box again."

He laughs. "You got to tell him the nickname."

"Big Loup," I say, and we all start laughing.

"You should come back to fighting again, Dad. It would be like father and son, The Undefeatables."

"Oh yeah, I'll think about it." Mitch chuckles.

"I wouldn't be what I am today without you," Damien tells his dad. Mitch looks at Damien, grins, and starts heading back up front.

"I'll leave you two love birds; I'll be back in a bit." Damien takes a towel and throws it at him, and we all laugh.

"You two look like you're getting along nicely. Your dad told me he used to box, too," I tell him.

"Yeah, but he quit when he started working."

"Yeah, he told me."

"The only time we really get along is on days like this. It's like boxing brings us closer together, and I'm not his punching bag for a while — I like calling him Dad on fight days. How was it sitting with him throughout the fight?"

"Good. Your dad's really nice. He seems like he really cares about you. I'd never think he does what he does to you."

"Let's forget about that and focus on us right now," he says. I kiss him. He picks me up and straddles my legs around him.

"I don't want to hurt you."

"The only way you can hurt me is if you leave me."

"Then, don't push me away." I say to him. He laughs, and we kiss again. We sit there and cuddle and talk until he has to get ready for his last fight.

"Hey, D."

"Yes?" He goes to his bag to get something, but hides it behind his back.

"I was wondering something."

"Wondering what and what's that you're hiding?" He looks at me and stands behind me, kissing me on the cheek.

"Well, I've been hiding this…" he says, pulling out a lovely diamond necklace with the letter' D.' He puts the necklace around my neck. "And what I'm wondering is if you will be my girl?" he says, blushing.

I know I just broke up with Scott, but something about Damien makes me want to be in a relationship with him. We have such a strong connection that jumping into a relationship with him seems to be okay. I have this gut feeling about Damien, which I've never had with Scott. I give him a big smile, turn around in his arms, stare into his eyes, and, without hesitation, say, "Yes."

"Yes! Yes?" He picks me up and spins me around while giving me a huge kiss.

"I've got to put my gloves on before my dad comes in, or he'll say you're a distraction."

"Would he be lying?"

"Nope, not one bit."

Mitch returns, and Damien sits with me, I try wrapping his hands. Mitch laughs, "I'll do it, D, and I can show you how. Looks like she's not a distraction after all."

"Told you," he smiles back.

"So, who am I fighting against?"

Mitch cracks up so hard he nearly falls out of his seat and looks Damien in the eyes. "Terminator." We laugh with him.

"What?"

"Terminator?"

"That's a stupid name. How does he look?" Damien asks.

"He's bigger than you and will be a challenge."

"But?"

"But nothing."

"I'll beat him, Dad, don't worry. I have a gut feeling that it'll be a winning-filled day."

"Gut feeling, huh?" Mitch replies with uncertainty.

"Yeah, Dad, like I said, don't worry."

"I'm not. Come on, D, we got to get up front," says, Mitch

"You okay, Mitch?" I ask him.

"Yeah, just a little nervous for him, that's all."

"He'll beat him, Mitch. Just watch." I say encouragingly.

"Yeah, I hope so because this is the fight."

"What do you mean?"

"All the other ones are just for practice, but I know this will be challenging. This fight depends on whether Loup is growing as a boxer, taking it seriously, or taking all he learns and throwing it down the drain. When we practice, it seems like he's paying attention and is focused, but is he really? Damien's never had a competition like this before. Terminator is the real deal, and I hope Loup sees that when he comes out. I didn't want to make him nervous by telling him, that's why I let it go," he says, then goes silent.

I can tell Damien's dad is on edge about something else other than the fight. My gut tells me it still has something to do with Damien, but it's just a little more than he tells me. "Damien takes everything seriously, especially boxing because he knows how much it means to you."

"He shouldn't do it because it means so much to me, but if it means something to him."

"It means a lot to him too. If it didn't, he wouldn't be as good. It also brings you two closer together. He loves that." I say cheerfully.

"I hope so," says Mitch.

The howling of a wolf plays again, and Damien walks out. He does the same thing he did before. The music begins to play from Disturbed, one of my favorite heavy metal bands. I already know it's the Terminator walking out. I look at him, and Mitch wasn't lying when he said he was bigger than Damien. Damien looks like an elf compared to that boy. I wonder if Terminator belongs in the Heavyweight division of boxing versus the Lightweight, like Damien. Is this a fair match? But Damien doesn't look scared or threatened. He looks determined. The bell rings, and they pound their gloves together and fight.

Terminator is fighting hard and dirty. He busts Damien's lip in the first round, then his eye in the second. Mitch and I are so worried in our seats. Mitch doesn't even move. He puts his cherry-red face in his hands. Damien stands there and lets the boy punch him but makes sure he's blocking his ribs. I can tell Terminator is getting exhausted because he takes longer to punch and backs up too much.

Then it happens, Loup starts to get tired of losing. Suddenly, Terminator moves in closer to punch Loup, but Loup punches him in the face hard and quickly. Terminator hurries to block his face, forgetting about his ribs. Loup goes all out, harder and faster, then plants one right in the middle of his stomach, making Terminator go forward and gasping for oxygen. Loup punches him on the left side of his face, then on the right. He finishes him with the biggest uppercut, making the Terminator fall flat on the floor like he's dead. The crowd goes wild, and Mitch and I are in complete shock.

"He did it! He did it!" We yell.

"I knew he could do it," I shout at Mitch.

"He sure did. I started to lose hope for a second, but I'll never do that again," he says.

Damien blows a kiss my way again and looks at Mitch while taking off his gloves. "I told you, Dad, I'd win."

"Yes, you did, yes, you did," Mitch says, tears coming down his eyes. We run back to see Damien. Mitch gives him the biggest hug. "Wow, you did good, son. I'm very proud of you. I thought for a second…"

"You thought I was going to lose, but that was my plan the whole time, or should I say it was yours."

"What do you mean mine?" Mitch asks curiously.

"Your grandma gave me your old boxing videos. I watch them all the time and practice your moves. You fought a big guy like that once. You tired him out — just like I did — you knocked him out cold, Dad."

"I sure did. I forgot about that fight." Mitch says astonishingly.

"I didn't because it was the best fight I've seen you in. Caught everyone by surprise, kind of like I did today." Damien replies.

"Yeah, you sure did," Mitch says.

"Well, you know what you always say…"

"Keep the fans entertained," they say together, laughing.

Mitch takes us out to eat, then drops me off back home. Dad and Scott aren't there, but I'm not surprised.

Chapter 18

THE PROMISE

Things are going great for Damien and me. I really love him. I used to love Scotty like this, but I realize my love for Scotty was different and not like my love for Damien. The good thing is that Scotty and I are back to being friends; he doesn't hate Damien anymore, and I'm relieved. What's better is since Damien's fight against the Terminator, he and Mitch are getting along well, too. Damien still sneaks over at night. It helps us both sleep, but when he doesn't, my nights are sleepless and rough.

Brittany is always mad that I never invite her for sleepovers at my house, but I don't care. Damien and I hang out all the time. I can't believe it's been two years, and we're still going strong. I even met his dad's girlfriend; she's charming. She has light brown hair and keeps her nails clean and trimmed but doesn't get them done at a salon. She only gets pedicures, and her eyebrows shaped. She's down-to-earth, wears boho clothing, and is really into spirituality — she meditates, practices yoga, and always goes on spiritual retreats. We even go shopping together, which Damien finds bizarre, but what does he know? He's a guy.

Mitch and my dad are best friends, which works in our favor because that's how we mostly hang out. The detectives never solve Tracy's case but are still investigating it. I don't know why, but they don't believe me about Earl. David and Sal keep in touch with me.

I even meet David's girlfriend, Julia. She's charming and very pretty. Her long blonde hair accentuates her slim model-type body figure and French mani and pedi. She's a classy woman.

David wants me to meet Julia's niece, who is about my age, which I will when I have the time. I've become very comfortable with Alex's family and have been visiting them. It's always lovely to see David and Sal. Dad and Scotty no longer have to come when I go over there. I never meet Alex because he's too busy, and they don't speak to him either. It bothers me occasionally but also doesn't because I've gotten to know everyone else. I already have a great father, Steve Sandino. If it wasn't for him, I wouldn't have met Damien and wouldn't be getting ready to go to the movies. Everything in my life is going perfectly, and I'm thrilled. For the first time in years, I enjoy the freedoms of being a kid — well, a young teen — just not a grown-up, and it feels so good.

"Dawnie, Damien's here!"

"Okay, coming!" I yell back to Dad. I go downstairs to meet Damien. He's in the kitchen with Dad. They're talking about Damien's upcoming fight he's preparing for.

"Hey, gorgeous."

"Hey, you ready?"

"Yeah, just waiting on you."

"Alright, Dad, I'm out."

"Okay, let me walk you two out. Do you have your cell?"

"Yes," I reply, jumping into the backseat of Mitch's truck. Dad comes over. He and Mitch talk, then Dad goes back in.

"Hey Mitch," I say, greeting him.

"Hey, sweetheart, how're you?"

"Good. How're you?"

"Great, just getting Loup ready for this fight. Are you coming again?"

"Of course, I wouldn't miss it for the world."

Mitch drops us off at the movies, and we go to get the tickets. When I take my card out to pay for the tickets, Damien snatches it out of my hand, puts it in his pocket, and gives his card to the cashier. "Hey, not fair," I say to him, trying to get it back, but he grabs me by the waist with one hand and pulls me to his other side so I can't snatch it back.

"Hey, what kind of guy would I be if I let you pay for anything?"

"A fair one."

"Umm, life's not fair," he whispers in my ear, kissing me on the cheek.

"When can I get my card back?"

"After I get the snacks."

"You know me too well."

"Yeah, I know," he laughs.

We watch the movie *Transformers: Dark of the Moon*, and it was great. I like it better than the other ones. Damien and I zone in and out of the movie because we're too busy making out the whole time. We're seated in the back where no one can see us, even though the theatre isn't full anyway. Damien pulls away and looks at me.

"What's wrong, Damien?"

"We don't sit and watch movies anymore."

"Yes, we do; what do you think we're doing now?"

"Making out, barely paying attention to the movie."

"We're doing both."

"Oh yeah, then tell me what's happened so far."

I sit there without a comeback. He's right; we don't sit and watch movies like we used to. We're always making out. I sigh, "You're right. I didn't know it bothered you."

"It doesn't. I don't want us to only be about sex."

"But we don't have sex."

"But making out leads to it. You mean more to me than that, and I hope the feeling is mutual. I don't want us to be two horny teens. I want us to be able to watch a movie and cuddle."

"Okay, you're right, and I don't want that either," I say to him. He opens his arms and wraps them around me. We both watch the movie, and it's hilarious.

Mitch picks us up, and we go back to my house. Mitch and Dad talk in Dad's office while Damien and I go to my room. Dad doesn't mind Damien being in my room because he trusts me. Dad's rule is my door must stay open.

We're in my room, and Damien is watching me; he smiles at me. However, worry is written all over his face. "What's wrong,

Damien?"

"What do you mean?" he replies, my question clearly catching him off guard.

"Why did you smile like that?"

"Smile like what?"

"You gave me your worried smile."

"I have a worried smile?" he raises his left eyebrow, still caught off guard.

"Yes, you have a few smiles."

"Wow, sometimes I feel like you know me better than I know myself, D."

"What's wrong? You know you can talk to me about anything."

"Yeah, I know; I don't want to worry you about my problems, especially when you have problems to deal with."

"Hey, not fair; when I have problems, I tell you about them. It should be the same way for you. Can you please tell me what's bothering you?"

"I know, it's just the problems I have, I want to forget them and not worry about them. When I'm with you, they slip my mind because my world revolves around yours. It's kind of corny, but that's how I feel."

"No, it's not because I feel the same way. Holding all your problems on the inside starts to eat away at you; trust me, I know. I'm all yours and ready to listen — spill the beans."

He laughs and says, "I like that."

"Like what?"

"You're all mine."

"Well, of course, how did you not know that?"

"I don't know, but having something all mine for once is nice."

"Is that the problem? You feel like you don't have anything of your own?"

"No, D, it's not that. It's my dad and his girl and my sisters and brothers being apart."

"Wait? What? You're not an only child?"

"No, I have a twin and a trillion brothers and sisters."

"Why?"

"Because my dad has a lot of kids, I guess."

"No, why didn't you tell me this?"

"Because it's hard talking about it when I never see them. We barely talk; when we do, it's only for seconds."

"What's going on with your dad and his girl?"

"They're arguing a lot, and I think — never mind."

"Think what, Damien?"

"I think that something is going on that shouldn't be. Whatever it is, it's not good and will get my dad in trouble. Do you know my dad has a gun?"

"No, I had no idea."

"Me neither. I saw it in his office when I was looking around like I normally do. It scared the shit out of me. I'm always in his office, and I've never seen it. He stays fidgety and yells like crazy at Martha. I think he even hits her now."

"What!"

"I know it sounds crazy, but that's what's going on."

"I thought everything was going well with your dad?"

"It was — and still is between me and him — but he's losing it with everything and everyone else. I notice he only relaxes when he comes here, and that's it. He's left home for long periods, and the last time he returned, he was in bad shape. Someone beat him up pretty badly. It scares me because if something happens to him, I don't know what will happen to me. Which means we could be torn apart. I really can't handle that. It sounds crazy because we're so young, but I love you like crazy. If you were ever taken away from me, I don't know what I'd do."

"It doesn't sound crazy. I feel the same way about you, too," I tell him.

"I hate that something always happens to take away whenever I'm happy."

"It's going to be okay, Damien."

"And if it's not?"

"Then we try hard to fix it."

"If we get torn apart?"

"Then we find each other and get back together no matter what."

"You promise?"

I place my hand on his chest where his heart is, "I promise you,

Damien Shranagan, that if anything tears us apart, I will not rest, and I won't ever be happy with any other guy until I find you. You're the only guy I ever want to be with."

He places his hand on my chest where my heart is and says, "And I promise you, Dawn Sandino, that if anything tears us apart, I will not rest, nor will I ever be happy with any other girl until I find you. You're the only girl I ever want to be with. I love you, Dawn Sandino."

"And I love you, Damien Shranagan." We stare each other in the eyes and kiss. The kiss is passionate and sweet. Damien holds me in his arms, and we look at the moon. A little while later, Mitch calls Damien to come down so they can go home. We go downstairs, and Mitch and Dad are at the door talking and laughing.

"Alright, kiddo, are you ready?" Mitch asks Damien.

"Yeah," says Damien.

They get in their truck and drive off. I feel good about the promises we made to each other. I trust that we will both keep our word. I know we're young and still have a lot of living to do, but there is something about Damien that makes me want to be with him forever. There's nothing that can come between us. If it ever did, we would find each other again. We're unbreakable no matter what.

Chapter 19

DAY AT DAMIEN'S

I'm over at Damien's; we're in his room. Damien's dad is an architect and has money like my dad. Damien's room is huge for a guy. He doesn't have a balcony or bathroom, but he does have a big window. Instead of an ocean view, he has a tree view. His room is painted grey and is filled with trophies, medals, and posters. I sit on his bed, and he runs to the kitchen for snacks. We have a picnic in his bed and watch movies. We don't bring up the conversation we had a week ago. I put on his gloves and start play punching him.

"Hey, you got a good form going on there," he says.

"I learn it from the best," I say, throwing another playful punch. We're play-boxing each other and fall on the floor laughing. We glance at one another, both out of breath and smiling. I kiss him, and he kisses me back romantically. I throw my gloves off and run my hands in his hair, wanting more and more from him. He pulls himself away fast and stands up. We're both breathing hard. He walks back and forth, running his fingers through his hair, trying to control himself.

"Ah, D, you make it so hard for me to resist you, I swear."

"Why do you want to resist me?"

"Because I don't want you to regret it."

"Why would I regret it?"

"I don't know, maybe because you think you're ready, but you aren't."

"Is that what you think? That one day, I'll wake up and regret being with you?"

"Yeah, and I can't have that."

I walk over to him, put his hands around my waist, and kiss him once again, "Damien, I'd never do that, and I could never hate you. I love you too much to ever hate you. I want to be with you. You're the only one I want to be with in every way."

"I love you too," he says, and we kiss again.

He picks me up by my waist and walks me over to the bed without breaking the kiss. He removes his shirt, realizing he will try to take mine off. Damien doesn't know about my back or anything about Earl yet. Yes, Damien knows that Earl killed my mom and now torments me here and there, but he doesn't know about the rape or engravings. He knows something horrific happened between Earl and me, but I never told him everything, and thankfully, he never asked.

I want to have sex with Damien, but I wasn't expecting him to take my shirt off or at least hoping he wouldn't. He works his hands up my back, almost touching the engraved part. I quickly put his hands back on my waist, hoping he won't notice my surprise, but he does. He breaks the kiss and looks at me in confusion. "What is that, D?"

"What is what?"

"You quickly moved my hands."

"Nothing, I just want to leave my shirt on, that's all."

"D, when will you learn you can't keep anything from me? I know when you're lying."

"What?" I say, trying to laugh and hide my fear of him seeing my back.

He looks at me, then up at the ceiling, "I knew you weren't ready, but I was too selfish to stop myself. I'm so sorry, D; please don't hate me. I didn't mean to hurt you, so please forgive me."

I study his eyes and see so much pain and hurt. He's hating himself because he thinks I've changed my mind about wanting to be with him. He says I'll regret giving myself to him. "Damien, that's not it, I swear."

"Then, what is it?"

"I just want to keep my shirt on," My eyes become glossy.

"It's not only that, D. I can hear it in your voice and see it in your face."

"No, it's not that, I swear."

"D, it's okay. I'm not mad at you, I swear. I don't want to mess up what we have."

"But you're not! Damien, we haven't had a serious talk about my past. You only know about Tracy, but there's more. Trust me, I want to make love to you so bad; it's just my shirt hides a part of me that I don't want you to know...," I say, crying.

"D, I know what's on your back."

"What! How?"

"D, I've felt what's on your back before. You have profound scars." I begin sobbing uncontrollably. I can't believe he knows. He holds me in his arms, "Shh, it's okay, D. You don't have to hide anything from me or explain anything to me now."

"No, Damien, I want to tell you," I say, thinking how we're close now, and how we tell each other everything. I'm not being honest with Damien if I keep hiding this from him or never tell him. I take a deep breath, sit in his arms, and tell him everything about Earl. He listens and holds me closely. We cry together. "I told you; it wasn't you. I didn't want to take my shirt off, then have to tell you all of this."

"Understandable, I'm sorry. I jumped to conclusions and forced you to tell me," Damien admits.

"No, it's okay. I'm actually glad you did this. It strengthens our relationship, and now we have nothing hidden between us."

He laughs, "Listen to us. We sound like a married couple."

I giggle, "We're like a married couple. We're always together. We spend almost every waking hour together. I go to all your fights, I hang out with Martha and our families get along well. You know, we even sleep in the same bed together almost every night, but the one thing is, we've never had sex."

"Yeah, you're right. Funny how things work out."

"Damien."

"Yes?"

"I really do want to have sex with you."

"I know, D, but we can do it another time. It wouldn't be just sex; it would be us making love. When the time is right, we will. Hopefully, I won't screw it up again," Damien replies.

"No, I want to have it now," I say to him and straddle my legs around him.

"D, c'mon — we don't have to do this now. We can do it another time. We have all the time in the world."

"No. Now. Damien."

"Is now the right time for you?"

"When it's the right one, it's always the right time," I say, looking him in the eyes and leaning in for a kiss. He returns the kiss and touches the side of my face lightly.

He pulls away and says, "Are you sure?"

"Never been so sure in my life. I have a good feeling in my gut about this."

He kisses me and gently slides his hands up my back to unfasten my bra. He looks at me to see if it's okay. I give him a nod. He unbuckles his belt and unzips his pants. Before we know it, we're in our underwear and under his covers. He reaches over into his top drawer and pulls out a condom. "Looks like you're prepared," I laugh.

"Yeah, well, my friends gave it to me a while ago as a joke, and I decided to keep it just in case."

"Good, I'm glad you did."

He kisses me and gets on top of me. It hurts a little when he tries to put it in, but not too bad. It starts to feel good when he finally gets it all the way in and works it up and down. Real good. We smile at each other between kisses, and I get on top of him. I have no idea what to do, but I realize he doesn't either. He's just going with the flow, like me. I start to rotate my hips while he moans in pleasure. I must be doing something right. He moves upwardly and begins to kiss my breasts and puts his hands on my hips, moving them in a circular rotation, and it feels good. We finish the first round quickly and lie next to each other, our breaths panting heavily.

"Sorry, I've never done this before," he says.

"It's okay, I haven't either. Well, anyways, not consensually."

He turns his body, lays on his side, and gently holds my face, "Nonconsensual doesn't count, baby. So, I'm your first. We can stop if you want." He plants a light kiss on my lips.

"You have another condom?" I say, desirably.

"Yes."

"Let's keep going then," I smile.

"I love you so much, D."

"I love you too, Damien."

We give it another go, it's even better than the first time. I feel comfortable being with him and know he feels the same way. We don't have sex, we make love just like he said. Making love with him makes me love him even more. When we finish, we lay in his bed and cuddle. "Did it hurt?" he asks, sounding worried.

"Not really; I thought it would hurt way more."

"Sorry."

"No, don't be. I wanted to be with you, remember?"

"Yeah, but I still could've said no."

"And you still would've given in, but by the way, you were great."

"I was horrible. I had no idea what I was doing," Damien chuckles.

"Me neither."

"You sure tricked me."

"Look who's talking."

He laughs, kisses me again, and says, "We better get dressed before my dad and Martha get home."

"Yeah, you're right."

We finish getting dressed and go downstairs to his game room. A door slams. We hear Mitch and Martha yelling. I don't know what they're arguing about, but it sounds serious. Damien closes the door and turns on the radio to drown them out, and it works. I tell by his movement he's pissed. I touch his hand gently and give him a hug. "Sorry you have to hear this."

"Heard worse."

The door opens, and Mitch barges in, looking beyond upset. "What are you two doing in here?"

"Playing games and drowning you and Martha out."

"Oh, sorry about that. Come on, let's get out of here."

Mitch takes us out to eat, but he's acting very jumpy. He picks up his phone every two seconds, checking it to see if anyone has called or texted. Mitch looks around quickly and keeps going to the bathroom. He doesn't ask us how our day was or make fun of us being close. He goes to the bathroom again, and I look at Damien and say, "Is this what you mean?"

"Yeah, and it's getting worse. My dad can't even sleep at night. It's annoying."

"Are you serious?"

"Sadly."

"For how long?"

"The last month or so."

"And you just told me last week? What the fuck Damien!"

"Hey, I told you why."

"Do you think it's about your sister?"

"I don't know. My dad won't let me call Jen."

"How did you two get split up like this?"

"My dad and mom can only handle one kid. Jen and I see each other sometimes but haven't seen each other lately. My dad wanted a boy, and what do you know, my mom wanted a girl."

"How do you feel about all of this?"

"I don't know. I try not to think about it too much. I wish Jen and I lived in the same home, but I know it'll never happen, so why bother with something I can't change?"

"True. Hey Damien..."

"Yeah?"

"You said he hasn't been sleeping, right?"

"Yeah, he comes in my room all the time."

"How do you leave your house and get to mine at night without him noticing?"

"Pillow and a wig," he replies nonchalantly.

I giggle, "What?"

"What do you mean, what? He never goes to my bed and looks at my face. He sees something like a body in a bed and some brown hair. He doesn't think I'm that smart, so I get away with it," he laughs. Mitch returns to the table, and we leave to drop me off at home.

Chapter 20

BRITTANY

"Hey Dawnie, oh, and hey — Damien," says Brittany. Brittany says my name like she typically does but says Damien's like she's annoyed. She sounds like someone punched her in the face.

"Hey, Britt," I reply.

"Brittany," Damien says, nodding instead of saying hello.

The three of us have lunch together. Brittany doesn't really like Damien, which I can understand. I spend most of my time, well, all my time with him and not her. Britt and I stopped hanging out after school and on weekends. Every time she sees me, I'm with Damien. Next, I feel my phone vibrate. It's a text from Damien saying:

Ask her to hang out tomorrow so she can stop being a jerk to me. It'll only be YOU TWO.

He puts 'you two' in all caps.

I laugh at the text and look at Brittany.

"What's so funny," Brittany asks with a confused face.

"Nothing; I was wondering if you want to chill tomorrow after school?"

"Who? Me?" she says, surprised like someone just threw water in her face.

"No, thank you. I always feel lonely when I'm around you two."

"Damien won't be there. It'll only be us girls."

"Oh, then okay, I'd love to. What do you want to do?"

"Don't know, but I'm sure we can figure something out."

Brittany is so excited about us hanging out tomorrow that she talks about it whenever she sees me. When we're not together, she texts me about it. I'm starting to regret hanging out with her, but I know I'd feel bad if I canceled on her. Damien's friends were excited because he also decided to hang out with them. Damien and I never totally blocked out our friends; we hang out with them occasionally — way less than we used to before we met, though. Even when I went out with Scotty, Brittany and I would still hang out with each other a lot. Damien and I can't be away from one another that long. If we were, we would be texting or calling the whole time, mostly texting.

The next day, Brittany's mom picks us up from school. Her mom has dirty blonde hair and sunglasses on, as usual. I don't even know what her actual face looks like without them. She talks with her hands, smokes a lot of cigarettes, and uses Botox to hide her wrinkles. Her Botox is horrible, her voice is dramatic, and when she speaks, you can tell right away it's not her real voice. Her smoker's voice is starting to really kick in. She tries to hide it to sound sexier, and she uses way too much expensive perfume to cover the smell of her cigarettes and booze.

"Hey, Dawn, how are you?"

"Hello, Mrs. Smith, I'm good. How are you?"

"Wonderful darling, I haven't seen you in a while."

"Yeah, I've been busy lately."

"Oh, okay, well, you shouldn't put too many things on your plate. These are your best years. You will never get them back. Trust me on that one."

We finally arrive at Brittany's house and go to her room. Brittany's parents are directors, so they have loads of money. Brittany's room is way bigger than mine; it's like a loft or something. She has her own sunroom with a Jacuzzi in it. Her room is pink with cheetah print all over. She's such a Hollywood cliché, almost like that girl from *Mean Girls* who's the head of The Plastics before Lindsay Lohan took over.

"We can hang out in the Jacuzzi, then go to the movies. Do you want to sleep over, too?" Brittany says with an enormous smile on her face. I don't want to hurt her feelings, but I don't want to sleep over anyone's house since Damien comes over to mine at night. I don't sleep well at night without him there.

"Yeah, we can do that, but I can't sleep over because my dad is having a family meeting in the morning," I lie to her.

"Uhh, a family meeting. Thank God we never have those."

Brittany doesn't have family meetings because her parents don't care about her or her brothers. They buy them stuff so they can avoid them. They even have a driver for all of them. I was surprised her mom picked us up today. "Yeah, they suck," I lie again.

"Brittany, I'm leaving now, and I won't be here for dinner," says Mrs. Smith.

"Okay, Mom," Brittany says back and gives me a slick grin as if she's up to something.

"What?" I say to her, wondering what she has up her sleeve.

"I got an idea," she picks up her cell phone and walks out of the room.

I put on the bikini bottom, take one of her tank tops that covers my upper back and get ready to hop in the Jacuzzi when Brittany walks in with her brother, Zach, and his friend, Dan. Zach is a few years older than us. He's muscular, tan, tall, and sexy. He's also the football captain and runs through girls like a NASCAR track — he's one of the racers. He's always had a crush on me, but I was with Scotty and now Damien, so I never really gave him a chance.

Dan is tan but less tanned than Zach. He's muscular but not too muscular, has high cheekbones, and is sexy too. Dan is also on the football team and is Zach's best friend but more like a groupie. Whatever Zach does, he does, but to another extent so that the attention can be on him instead of Zach. "Dawnie, what's up, girl?" Zach says, hugging me and rocking us side to side.

"Hey Zach," I say, pulling out of the hug and giving Britt a look, but she's too busy flirting with Dan to notice. I walk over to the Jacuzzi, totally pissed at Britt for doing this, but make sure not to show it on my face.

"I haven't seen you in forever," says Zach, trying to start a conversation.

"Yeah, I know. I've been busy, that's all.

"I hear you go out with that kid, Loup."

"Yeah, for two years now."

"Oh wow, don't you think you two are too young to be in such a long-term relationship?"

"Why would I think that?"

"Well, you haven't seen the world or even met anyone new, and you two are already ready to settle down. I don't want you to miss out on something good — like me, for example," he says smiling. He gets close to me, touches my thigh, and starts to slide it up with his hand. It doesn't take a rocket scientist to notice what he's doing. I know he's trying to get in my bikini.

"Wow, no, I don't think that, and you're too close," I say to him, taking his hand off me.

"C'mon, I won't bite…" he says; Britt and Dan come in with a bottle of vodka and beer and cut him off.

"Hey, you two, look what we got," Britt says, dancing like she's hit the jackpot.

I don't like drinking, but I also don't want to be square. Brittany starts pouring shots and giving out beers as a chaser. After four shots, I feel the buzz and barely can stand up to go to the bathroom. Zach shoves another drink in my hand, and I chug it down with another beer. He gets closer and puts his hands all over me, but I can't stop him. I have no idea what's going on. The room is spinning. We're all laughing for no reason. The more drinks come my way, the more I drink.

I hear my cell phone buzzing, and I tumble towards it, still laughing. Zach has his hands on my waist, picks me up, and leans in for a kiss, but I can't move my head away. I look at my phone and see a missed call from Scotty. I call him back, and he answers.

"Hey, Dawnie."

Unable to control my laughter, I answer, "Hey, Sssssscooooooottttttyyyyyy…"

"Are you okay? You sound a little off."

"Of course, I am." I laugh harder, thinking Scotty can probably hear everyone else in the background.

"Dawnie, have you been drinking?"

"Umm, no…, yes… I think so."

"What the fuck, Dawnie?"

"I didn't mean to get drunk. I was only taking sips, but now I'm like this."

"Who's there?"

"Zach, me, Dan, and Britt."

"I'm picking you up now!"

"Wait, Scott, don't tell Dad!"

"Of course I won't, Dawn."

I hang up the phone, turn around, and stumble into Zach. He catches me, and we both laugh. "Careful there, sweetie; I don't want you to hurt yourself."

"Sorry," I say, trying to get up and go to the kitchen to get a drink of water.

"Don't be. Where are you going?"

"The kitchen."

"You can't go down stairs like that."

"Like what?"

"Drunk."

"I'm not drunk." I trip again, and he catches me making a told-you-so face.

"How about I go downstairs with you so you won't hurt yourself."

Something in my head tells me to say no, but my mouth spits the word, "Okay."

Zach is getting very touchy-feely, but I'm too drunk to remove his hands off me. I keep tripping over my feet. He's the only thing keeping me from hitting the ground. We go into the kitchen, I try opening the refrigerator but Zach closes it, puts his hands on my waist, and turns me around. We're face-to-face. Without warning, he kisses me. I pull away, still dizzy from the alcohol. "Woah, what are you doing?"

"What does it look like I'm doing?"

"I go out with Damien Shranagan!"

"So what? What he doesn't know won't hurt him, and you might not want him anymore after me."

"But it'll hurt me. I'll always want Damien because I love him, something you'll never know about."

He laughs and moves closer. I try to push him away, but he's too strong. It reminds me of Earl. Suddenly, I have flashbacks of Earl lounging at me on the couch and grabbing my hands. I'm unable to fight him off because I'm way too weak. "Stop, Zach!" The flashbacks continue. Earl forcing a kiss, pushing his disgusting tongue down my throat. I bite Zach's tongue, and he smacks me. "C'mon, stop fighting it."

More flashbacks of Earl assaulting me consume me in full force. "Zach!" I yell. My heart drops. Zach's not going to stop. I'm too drunk to make him. Then again, would I've been strong enough to stop him even if I were sober? I was sober when Earl raped me, but also weak, like right now. I'll always be weak and helpless, I cry, realizing this. I try again, hoping he'll stop before it goes too far. The next thing I know, Zach is flying back. His head hits the counter, knocking him out. I go into shock and nearly scream, but Scotty covers my mouth.

"It's okay, it's me. Are you okay?" Scotty asks, while I continue to cry. Zach just tried to force himself on me. I'm crying uncontrollably because Zach reminded me of when Earl raped me when I was younger — I had no one to save me. Scotty showing up and saving me means so much to me. I fall into Scotty's arms and bawl. "Shh, it's okay, it's okay, Dawnie. Let's just go home, okay?"

As we're getting up, Dan and Britt come downstairs and see me crying in Scotty's arms. Zach is still on the ground, whimpering in pain, trying his best to get up, but still kind of out of it. "What the fuck!" Dan yells and runs up to Scotty, throwing a punch. Scotty ducks and swings back, knocking him right in the face. He flies to the ground.

Britt screams, "Get out, both of you!"

"Happily!" shouts Scotty, disgusted by what just took place. He picks me up, and I continue to cry and shake. He puts me in the car. We don't say anything. The drive home is silent. I'm completely in shock. Dad's still at work when we get home. Scotty takes me to my room and gives me pajamas because I'm still in Britt's bikini bottom and tank top, which are now damp. I look at my phone and see ten missed calls from Damien and Britt. I'm out of it because I never heard my phone go off.

I check my voicemail, and the first one is from Britt yelling, "You, bitch! How dare you come over to my house and drink up all my alcohol and try to fuck my brother? Then get Scotty to beat him and Dan up! You're no longer my friend; you're done in this town. I swear on my life!"

Wait! I wasn't trying to fuck her brother! He was trying to fuck me! He's the one who was pushing up on me and wouldn't stop! That was the only reason Scotty beat the shit out of him. Now, I'm pissed. I'm upset that Zach tried it with me, but I'm angrier at Brittany for threatening me. I know she's about to start rumors. I call her back, and she answers right away. I tell her in the coldest voice ever, "Listen here, you fucking nasty rodent, don't you ever threaten me. And I didn't try to fuck your brother; he was trying to fuck me! Would've probably raped me if Scotty didn't push him off me! I'm going to tell you once, and only once, and if I hear one rumor about me, not only will I tell the whole school about how Scotty whipped both Zach and Dan's ass, but I'll destroy you and everything around you. Do you understand me?"

She's a sitting, raging bull. She breathes heavier and heavier in shock, fear, and anger. She's shocked because she didn't expect me to say all of that, but I didn't expect to either. She fears me because she knows I can destroy her, and I will if she spreads rumors about me, and she's angry because she knows there is nothing she can do for revenge that I won't do to her ten times worse. She finally responds stuttering, "Yes, I understand."

"Good, and oh, Britt..."

"Yes."

"You were right about one thing."

"What?"

"We're done being friends." I hang up the phone and throw it on my bed, and try to regain my composure. I take a deep breath.

My bedroom door opens, and Scotty asks, "Wow, who was that?"

"Britt."

"Oh, then good," he says, and we both look at my phone because it starts to buzz. I answer it before looking at it, thinking it's Britt calling me back.

"What!" I yell.

"Oh, wow, must've called you at a bad time."

"Shit, sorry, Damien, I thought you were Britt."

"The last time I checked, I thought you were with her. What's wrong?"

"Long story."

"Okay, I'll be over..."

I cut him off, already knowing what he's about to say. "No, it's okay. I'm hanging out with Scotty." My phone beeps, and Dad is calling on the other line. "Hold on, Damien. My dad's on the other line." I click over, "Hello."

"There better be a good reason why you haven't been answering any of my calls," Dad says, raising his voice.

"Trust me, Dad, there is."

"Where are you?"

"At home, with Scotty."

"Why? What's wrong? I thought you were going over to Brittany's house?"

"I did, left early."

"What's wrong?"

"Nothing."

"Liar, I'll be there in a second; I'm leaving my office."

"I'm okay, Dad, really. I'm with Scotty."

"I'm still coming home."

"Okay."

"I love you."

"Love you too, bye." I click over to Damien, who is very silent. "Hello..." I say, wondering if he's still there.

"Hey," he says.

"I'm hanging out with Scotty, but I'll talk to you later."

"Okay. I love you."

"I love you too." I hang up the phone and look at Scotty lying beside me on my bed.

"So, what just happened," he asks, looking at me.

"At Britt's or on the phone?" I say, already knowing the answer.

"Both."

"Where do you want me to start?"

"Britt's."

I tell him about the Jacuzzi, the drinking, going downstairs to the kitchen to get water, and how Zach kept pushing himself on me. Then that's when he showed up and saved the day.

"And on the phone?" he asks.

"Britt threatened me, and I just lost it."

"You, okay?"

"Yeah, I'm just shocked, and umm..." tears run down my face.

"Hey, it's okay. You're safe now."

"Yeah, I know, and that's the thing. When Zach wouldn't get off me, it reminded me of how Earl used to..."

"You don't have to say it. I know what he did." Scotty replies gently.

"Yeah, but I always prayed and wished someone would save or help me somehow. Tracy was always way too passed out on her drugs to help, but tonight, when you beat Zach and Dan up, that meant so much to me, you don't even know. No one has ever done that for me. I was always alone, and tonight, for once, I wasn't. Who knows what Zach would've done if you didn't arrive in time?" I cry, barely catching my breath. Scotty takes me in his arms, and I lie on him. He holds me; it's nothing more than brotherly love.

"Shh, Dawnie, it's okay. You're not alone anymore. You got me, Uncle Steve, and Damien; we love you very much."

"I love you guys too."

"Hey, how about we go to diner and the movies like old times?"

"Now? I look like crap."

"C'mon, get dressed," says Scotty.

I get dressed and meet him downstairs. A day with Scotty is exactly what I need. When Damien and I started going out, Scotty and I had made peace but didn't hang out at Ruby Tuesday or catch movies anymore. Hanging out with Scotty made me forget about the whole thing that happened at Brittany's today and the fact I'm not her friend anymore.

"Thanks, Scotty, I really needed this."

"Yeah, you and me both." When we return home, Damien texts and calls me off the hook. I go to my room and call him back. He says he's here waiting to get in. I leave my room and see Scotty in his room. I quietly and quickly go downstairs to the door, get Damien, and we go to my room.

"What's wrong with you?" Damien asks.

"What do you mean?"

"I mean…, what I said. I can sense something is wrong with you, especially when we talked on the phone and you don't answer my calls or texts until you get home."

"I was with Scotty, and we were catching up on stuff. Sorry, and Brittany and I are done as friends."

"Why?"

I tell Damien what happened; he's pissed. It takes me two hours to calm him down, but he still wasn't calm.

Chapter 21

EARRING

amien and I walk to every class like always. I see Brittany, but we don't say anything to each other. At lunch, she picks another seat, which is good because I don't want to move. I'm popular at school and have a lot of friends. I made even more friends when Damien and I started going out.

We're sitting at the lunch table when I sense someone watching me. I look around but only see other students like me talking and eating their lunch. "What's wrong?" asks Damien.

"Umm, nothing."

"Lie," replies Damien.

"No, it's just I think someone is watching me."

"What do you mean?"

"I feel someone staring at me."

He looks around the lunchroom and doesn't see anything. "I don't see anyone, but you're the most beautiful girl in the school. I wouldn't be surprised if someone is watching you."

"Damien…" I playfully punch his arm.

"What? — you are, though."

"I'm serious."

"And so am I. No one can get in here and watch you without us spotting them, especially an older person. You're still slightly riled up from Friday… which is perfectly understandable."

"You're right."

"I know I am," he puts his arms around my waist and places a kiss on my lips.

"Hey, I got to go to the bathroom, okay. I'll be right back."

"Okay, I'll walk you over there," he says.

"No, it's okay, just sit. I can walk over there by myself."

"Okay, you sure, D?" he asks.

"Yeah, it's only right there," I tell him, pointing over to it.

I give him a kiss and head to the bathroom. While I walk to the bathroom, a tall shadow appears. I turn around. It's a guy. I can't see his face because he runs in the opposite direction at full speed. Not thinking, I run after him, but he's going so fast, I lose him. I find myself in front of my locker. There's a piece of paper sticking out of it. I hesitate and look around. I'm the only one in the hallway; no one else is around. I grab the paper and read it:

I THOUGHT YOU MIGHT LIKE THIS BACK!

The note has Brittany's name written all over it. It's got to be her. We're no longer friends, but I know how she is; she must've left something in my locker. I open my locker and see a small box. It's Tracy's earring! I become fearful and quickly close the box and shut my locker. Who put this in my locker? I look around, but still, no one's in sight. The bell rings. That's right — Damien is supposed to meet me next to the bathroom. I beeline back to the bathroom to beat him there. I don't want to lie to him, but he cannot know about this. He'll be concerned about this and tell Dad. I can't let him jeopardize our family.

I'm too late. He's standing there with Snake, the guy he boxes with. Snake is his best friend. Their friendship is not superficial like Brittany's and mine. They're close, like brothers. Brittany and I, never. Snake has black hair and has the same muscular build as Damien. Snake is a class clown and is always joking around. Besides that, he and Damien are the same when it comes to personalities, but Damien can be more serious. He always wears this winter hat, even when it's hot out. He says it brings out his character more, but he doesn't wear it when he's boxing because it's prohibited. I walk up to Damien and put my arm around him.

"Hey, there you are. I thought you were going to the bathroom?"

"I was, but I had to go to my locker too."

"Went to your locker for what?"

"Umm, forgot something in there."

"Forgot what?"

"Umm, hairspray."

Damien gives me a look. He's confused but lets it go. Whew! We always sit beside each other in chemistry class, but he doesn't speak to me. I sense him tensing up. I look at him, wondering what's wrong. He returns my stare with a half-smile. I tear a piece of paper from my notebook and write:

What's wrong?

Damien reads my note, crumbles it, purposely ignoring me. I reach over and grab his notebook and write:

Liar!

He scribbles it out and returns his focus on the teacher while they write on the board. This is unusual coming from Damien. He's never been mad at me like this before. We never fight or argue — what's this about? It's really getting to me. The bell finally rings, and I'm relieved. It's been a long day. I grab my book bag and storm out of the room. I decide not to go back to my locker after what happened earlier. Instead, I go outside and look for my cell phone. I reach deep down in my book bag to retrieve it. I need to get Scotty or Dad to come pick me up. For some odd reason, Damien's tripping, and I don't want to be around him right now, especially if he's not going to talk to me. Next, out of nowhere, Damien comes up behind me and says, "Thanks for waiting."

"Didn't think you noticed I left," I say back.

"Of course I did. I always do."

"Yeah, well, you're sure not acting like it today," finally finding my phone and scrolling my contacts looking for Scotty's number.

"D, what are you doing?"

"Calling Scotty to pick me up."

"Are you serious?"

"What? You're the one being mean." I remind him.

"Well, maybe because you keep lying to me, D."

"What are you talking about? I didn't lie to you."

"Whatever reason you went to your locker is not for the reason you told me. I know something happened because you were jumpy."

I stop scrolling my phone and throw my head back, "That's what you're mad about?"

"Yup."

"Damien, I didn't know how to tell you because I feared your reaction."

"Tell me what?"

"The real reason I went to my locker. But I swear, Damien, I was going to the bathroom." My eyes become watery, and tears take over. Damien hugs me and tells me I can tell him what happened on the way to my house. We stop to get ice cream and sit on one of the benches where no one is around. I tell him everything, and like I thought, he's pissed.

"Why didn't you tell me, D?"

"Because of how you'd react. You'd punch anyone left and right. You know how you are."

"Yeah, but—"

"But what, Damien? If you get in a fight because of my situation, boxing is over for you, and that's your life. Mitch would not be happy at all, neither would I."

"You're wrong about one thing, D."

"And what's that?"

"You're my life, not boxing," he says, kissing me on the lips.

I smile, "You're so corny, but I'm being very serious."

"So am I," he replies.

I look around us, "Damien, we need to start going."

"D, if I wasn't serious, then why would I risk going to your house every night, especially with my dad acting the way he does?"

"I don't know."

"Because I love you, and you're my life. I can't sleep without you or spend more than ten minutes without you. We tell each other everything, and I know you feel the same way."

"I do, but…"

"But what?"

"I'm…"

"Scared?"

"Yeah," I say hesitantly.

"So am I, but I'd rather face my fear with you than not at all."

I kiss him, "We must get to my house and room right now." He laughs, and we throw away our trash. We barge into my room and take off our clothes. Damien picks me up and throws me on the bed. We make love like never before. Our first time was good, but this time, it's magical. It's like we've learned what to do and how to do it in our sleep. We finish, and I lie in his arms. We pant heavily like we just ran a marathon. "Wow!" I gasp. I'm completely mesmerized by our lovemaking session.

We laugh, and Damien agrees, "Oh yeah."

"That was…"

"Amazing!" he finishes my words.

"I didn't know you could do that with your tongue."

"Yeah, me neither, but D, I'm blown away by you. You really know how to please me — you did your thing."

"Nice words." I giggle.

"When is your dad coming home?"

"Not until after six."

"Good." he kisses me again.

"Are you hungry?" I ask him.

"I think — I already ate," he laughs. I pause for a second; we both start laughing.

"I'm serious, Damien."

"I know, I know. Yes, I'm a little hungry." We put our clothes on and go downstairs to find something to eat. When we make it down, a piece of paper on the back door catches my eye. I hesitate to read it because I know it's from Earl. I open it, just like I thought, it's from him. It reads:

HOPE YOU LIKE YOUR PRESENT BECAUSE I DID!

Dad and Scotty cannot see this.

Chapter 22

THE SURPRISE

My phone starts ringing. I look at Damien in fear. He checks the caller ID for me; it turns out to be Dad. He hands it to me. "Hey, Dad," I say, adjusting my voice to sound normal.

"Hey, sweetheart, how are you?"

"Umm, good."

"Liar. I'm on my way home. Is there anything you need before I come home?"

"No, I'm okay."

"Alright, we're having a family meeting when I get home. I have some great news for you. Damien may need to go home because it has to do with your back."

"No, it's okay. Damien can stay. He knows about it."

"He does?" By the sound of his voice, I know he's surprised.

"Yeah, we don't have secrets."

"Oh, okay, we'll see you in a second."

"K, bye."

"Bye, love you."

"Love you too."

Dad makes it home and darts inside with Scotty — they can't wait to tell me something. They both have big smiles, like a baby getting candy for the first time. Dad gives me a big bear hug. Damien and I look at each other, wondering what's happening.

"Hey, you guys, what's going on?" I ask, still confused.

"Dawnie, I have been talking to one of my friends about you and your situation," Dad says.

"What situation?"

"Your back."

"What! How could you? I trusted you! That is only supposed to be between us, not for the whole world. Do you know how embarrassing this is!" I shout from the top of my lungs. I feel so deceived that they would tell someone about my back when I could barely tell them. Shit, I just told Damien what happened to me, and I love him with all my heart. I get up and run off, but Dad grabs my arm and tries to bring me back to the couch. I'm so mad. I punch, kick, and scream, "Get the fuck off of me!"

But then he screams, which is not normal for Dad to do, "They can fix it!" He yells. I stop my tantrum to register what he's saying.

"They can what?" I say.

"I have an old friend who is a plastic surgeon, and he said to bring you in, and they will fix it. I didn't tell them what your back said or how it got the way it did. I just said you have something carved in your back and want it removed. He's one of the top plastic surgeons in the country, and he's doing me a favor," Dad says, his tense demeanor becoming more relaxed.

Following his words, I began to calm down, too. Without realizing it, tears surface and trickle down my face. Dad warmly embraces me with a hug, wipes my tears, and calms me down even more.

"Why?" I say, confused by why he would do this for me.

"Why, what?" Dad says back.

"Why would you get my back fixed for me?"

"How many times do I have to keep telling you, Dawnie, that you're my daughter before you start believing it?" he says, hugging me still.

"All the time. I guess... I love the sound of it," I laugh between tears.

"Well, you have an appointment tomorrow to see him. He will have a look at your back to see how he's going to fix it. You don't have to tell him or his medical team anything if you don't want to. But they will have to examine your back. They will draw on your back with markers to mark where they'll need to cut during your surgery. Do you understand me, Dawnie?"

"Yes, Dad, but..."

"But what? What's wrong?"

"Can you come with me?"

He chuckles, "Of course, I'll come with you."

I must admit, I'm happy to be getting this off my back. When I get this off my back, I won't be Earl's anymore; I'll finally belong to me, myself, and I. The thought of it all makes my heart jump for joy. I look at Damien, and he looks at me; we smile at each other. Dad takes us all out to dinner to celebrate. Afterward, we drop Damien off and go straight home to get settled for the evening. We first do our family run, then take it down for the night. My doctor's appointment for my back is early tomorrow morning, and I don't want to be late.

I lie down in bed and start to think about tomorrow. I hope they can do everything at the doctor's tomorrow; I want this to end. I want to avoid coming back and forth for visits. My phone buzzes. It's a text message from Damien that says:

I'm on the way.

Okay.

I wait downstairs in the family room by the door. Scotty comes down and sits next to me.

"Hey, how are you?" Scotty asks me.

"I'm excited about tomorrow."

"Yeah, I knew you'd be."

"My back will be normal, and I'll belong to myself."

"Yeah, your back will be normal, but Dawnie..."

"Yes, Scotty?"

"You were never his. Your back just said that you were. You've proved differently. You've always belonged to yourself."

"Thanks, Scotty," I give him a hug.

"You're welcome, sweetie." He hugs me back and kisses my forehead. He holds me for ten minutes, then goes back upstairs. A few minutes later, Damien texts me to let me know he's here. I let him in. We go to my room, hop in bed, and cuddle.

"So, are you excited for tomorrow?" Damien asks.

"Yes, but I'm just a little nervous."

"Why?"

"I don't know. What if something goes wrong and they can't do the surgery, or something worse? Like, they mess it up more than it already is, making me uglier than I already am, or what if I die?" I rapidly spit out all these thoughts while they run through my mind.

Damien places his hands on my face and makes me look him in the eyes, "Calm down, take a deep breath, and stop worrying so much or you'll get wrinkles. You're not going to die. Nothing is going to go wrong. There is no way in hell someone can make you ugly because you're the most beautiful and loveliest girl in the whole world."

"But Damien, how do you know?"

"Because I know you. You can never be ugly, nor will you die. I feel everything is going to go great tomorrow." he says, boosting my confidence. We look each other in the eyes. I kiss Damien intently. Surprised, he pulls back, "Wow, I wasn't expecting that."

"Gotta keep the fans entertained," I reply, kissing him again.

We laugh, and he starts returning my kisses. We both know where this is heading. We make love and fall asleep in each other's arms. I don't know what it is about Damien; he makes everything feel right. I love making love to him, and I want to again and again.

Chapter 23

D LOVES D

We wake up the following day, and I feel something on my neck. I touch my neck and see a lovely necklace. The charm has two D's with a heart in the middle, going diagonally. I look at Damien, who is play-sleeping. I can tell he's trying to hide his smile but failing horribly. I kiss him softly, and he finally stops trying to hide his smile.

"I take it you found the present I left on your neck," he says, kissing me.

"Yes! I love it very much. Thank you!"

"Good, because I love you very much too."

Dad knocks on the door, "Wake up, Dawnie, we're leaving soon."

"Okay, Dad. Shit! Damien, they will both be around the door waiting for me."

Damien laughs, "I knew that would happen; that's why I brought my change of clothes. We'll act like I rode my bike over here."

"Good plan."

"I know. Hey, D…"

"Yes."

"I gave you the necklace because I want you to know I'll always be with you… even if I'm not beside you. It symbolizes us. It's you and me together and how we will forever be."

I kiss him again, "This means more than the world to me."

"I hope not more than me."

"It's you, remember."

He smiles. "Yeah, I remember."

We get ready, and I open the door to ensure no one is around so I can sneak Damien downstairs. Dad is in his room, but I need to figure out Scotty. We get to the bottom of the steps and bump into Scotty. "Scotty!" I blurt out, trying to mask the shock in my voice.

"What the fuck is going on?" Scotty questions us as if he's caught us.

"What do you mean?"

"I mean, he was in your room overnight, that's what I mean."

"No, he wasn't."

"Bullshit. I just saw you!"

"Yeah, seen us come out of my room because he wanted to speak to me privately. That doesn't mean he slept over."

"How and when did he come over? I never heard the doorbell."

"A little while ago. I rode my bike and texted D when I was outside," Damien cuts in.

"Uh-huh, sure," says Scotty, not buying our story. I take Damien's hand and lead him to the kitchen before Scotty can say or ask anything else.

"Do you think he bought it, D?" asks Damien.

"Not sure, but he has no room to talk."

"Should we be worried?"

"No, of course not."

"Alright, gang, are you all ready?" Dad asks eagerly, coming down, filled with energy and excitement.

"Yeah," we reply.

"Oh, hey, Damien, didn't know you were coming," says Dad.

"Yeah, I wouldn't miss this for the world."

We drive to Stasinski's Beauty Clinic, about half an hour to an hour away from home. Dad introduces me to Dr. Stasinski, and he seems nice. He was one of Dad's college buddies. Dr. Stasinski is clean-cut with dark brown hair, has a corporate beard, trimmed and clean fingernails, and is semi-muscular — but not too much muscle. You can tell he takes care of himself. He's a high-maintenance kind of guy, yet he's very manly.

He examines my back and takes pictures. He tells me the risks are delayed healing, skin sensitivity, and damaged nerves and veins. He asked about my medical history, which I have no idea about. However, since living with Dad, he's ensured I have regular checkups and that I'm up to date with my vaccinations. Tracy never cared about that stuff, especially since it cost money. We didn't have insurance until she met Dad and moved us here. Dad hands a folder to Dr. Stasinski, letting him know it's my medical records. Dad tells us to go to the waiting room. We wait for three hours before he calls me back into his office.

"Okay, Dawnie, I went over everything," says Dr. Stasinski.

"And... how does it look?"

"Well, the scars are deep, but not that deep. I can do the surgery. Since I have nothing scheduled for the rest of the day, I can do it today."

"Is that possible?" I ask.

"Of course it is. I own this clinic — no one else does. Besides, Steve is a close friend, and you're his daughter. I have no choice," he chuckles.

"Yeah, you're right, you don't," Dad says, laughing with Dr. Stasinski.

"Anne will take you to a room where you can change into one of our gowns. When you're done, we'll start the procedure."

"Okay, thank you, Dr. Stasinski."

"Please call me Bill."

"Okay, thanks, Bill."

I follow Anne, the anesthesiologist, and change into a gown. I go into the procedure room and lie face down on my stomach on the hospital bed. She gives me an oxygen mask and tells me to count backward from one hundred. I fall sound asleep. I don't dream, but I have a glimpse of Damien that lasts a few seconds, and it all goes blank. When I wake up from the surgery, I only can see the floor and shoes. I can tell Damien, Dad, and Scotty are standing in the room. I try to get up, but it hurts like hell. "Ouch!"

"Hey, how are you feeling, sweetheart?" asks Dad.

"Like a truck ran over my back," I reply, in heaviness and pain.

"Sounds painful," Scotty says.

"Yeah, try feeling it," I laugh.

Damien lies on the floor under the hospital bed so we can see each other face to face. "How are you doing, beautiful?"

"Been better."

"He told you it would be sensitive," mentions Dad.

"Sensitive and painful are two different things," I reply, still a little drugged up from the anesthesia.

"I thought the painful part was common sense," says Bill, walking in. "I came to check your back." He pulls off the bandage and looks at my back. "Looks like things went well. Just have to give it time to heal."

"When can I go home?" I ask him.

"Today. Your Dad finished all the paperwork; he has your release papers."

"That's fast."

"You didn't get heart surgery, Dawnie. You had a scar tissue removal procedure," he chuckles.

"Yeah, but it's still surgery," I wince in pain, slowly sitting up.

"True, but not the overnight hospitalization kind. I want you to come back in two weeks so I can make sure your back is healing as expected," says Bill, handing something to Dad in a tube. He begins telling Dad something, and they have a short conversation walking out of the room together.

Damien sits beside me, holding my hand while Scotty grabs my bags. "Ready?" Scotty asks. I nod yes; Damien helps me get into a wheelchair and wheels me into the SUV. We finally make it home, and Dad, Scotty, and Damien help me up to my room. My back is killing me, but not as bad as it did the day Earl engraved me. It still hurts like a bitch from hell. However, the best part is that I'm no longer reminded about being his property. Yes, I'll have the memories of what he did to me, but now I can wear a bikini, halter tops, and anything else that shows my back. I love that it'll be normal and beautiful after my back heals.

"Hey, Dawnie," Dad says, interrupting my thoughts.

"Yes," I reply.

He throws the tube Bill gave him at the clinic on my bed. "In an hour, I have to put that on you. It helps with the pain and makes the healing go faster."

"Okay, thank you, Dad."

"No problem, kiddo," he says, and he and Scotty go downstairs.

I sit on the bed and try to lie down, but it's a total epic fail. I'm tired of lying on my stomach, and sitting up is starting to hurt. Dad comes back up and gives me some pills that begin to make me tired. Damien turns the TV on, and I lie on his chest. He holds me, and I fall asleep. Whatever it is, it's strong because when Dad returned to apply the cream to my back, I sleep right through it. I moan in relief because it feels so good The burning goes away briefly.

When I wake up, Dad is holding me. He took over Damien's place when Damien had to leave and go home. Also, Damien and Dad have different scents — I sensed while sleeping. I feel Scotty on the other side of me. I wish I had them back then, when Earl was around. I would've never been alone.

Dad and Scotty know me more than anyone other than Damien. They know when I lie and when something is wrong. They also know when I don't want to be alone. Scotty used to be oblivious to my not wanting to be alone, but he's getting better. That's why I think of them as family; they treat me as such. If I hadn't known I wasn't their biological family when I moved here, I might never have realized I wasn't part of their family. Honestly, I don't think they would've ever mentioned it. They love me so much, and it doesn't matter to them.

Chapter 24

NEW BACK

My back is finally good enough to be exposed to the world. I bought a halter top a week after the surgery. I'm so excited to let my back show; I can't stop smiling. I walk in class; my hair has loose curls falling on my back but not covering it. I want to be extra sexy today for Damien. Damien sees me and stops talking to Snake. Snake looks at me and says, "Whoa," in front of Damien. I laugh and go straight to Damien, kissing him.

"Hey guys," I say to them.

"You look… Wow!" Damien says.

"Yeah, you do," Snake agrees while Damien gives him a "stop looking at my girl" stare.

"Thanks, Snake," I reply, feeling all giddy inside, then I look over to Damien, "Thanks, Damien. I wanted to look even better for you today," I give him a flirtatious wink and smile.

The noisiness in class catches my attention. I turn around and see Britt staring at me in amazement. Everybody at school comes up to me and compliments me on how I look. When I moved here, everyone hung out with me because I hung out with Brittany. Brittany always threw the best parties at her house. Her parents were never and still aren't ever home. They let her and Zach throw parties and give them money instead of the time they should spend with them. I never had a party because Brittany had so many; there was no point in me having one. When her friends got to know me better and hung out with me, I became very popular on my own very quickly. I sometimes feel they like me more than Brittany because I memorized their names and listen to them when they speak. When I started going out with Damien, more and more people began to talk to me because they were his friends.

"Isn't your birthday coming up," Damien whispers in my ear.

"Yeah, that's right, it is. I almost forgot," laughing at the thought.

"Well, I didn't," he responds.

"Didn't what?" Snake butts in.

"D's birthday is next week," Damien says.

"Hells yeah, party!" Snake says, grinning extra hard.

"No party, Snake, just my birthday."

Snake is shocked by my response. He folds his arms, tilts his head slightly to the right, and looks at me like I'm crazy, "D, you have more friends than Damien and I put together, and you're not having a party?"

"I never had a party before. Britt always had enough for both of us."

"What? Are you serious?"

"She sure is," Damien says, holding my waist from behind.

"Well, you and Britt aren't friends anymore. So, it would be good if you had a party for yourself this time," Snake insists.

"My first party. I don't know if my dad will let me."

"It's a first time for everything, D," says Snake; the bell rings. We get our books and go to our next class.

"I want a party, but what if no one shows up, especially since Britt and I are no longer friends? Or what if Britt throws a party on the same day as mine? I'll be publicly embarrassed and feel totally played — hey, Damien…"

"Yes."

"Do you think people will come if I have a party?"

"Of course, why wouldn't they?"

"I don't know. It's just that I think I only have friends because of you and Brittany. " He stops and pulls me to the side out of the student hallway traffic.

He holds my face in his hands, "Hey, you have friends because of who you are, D."

"No one would even look at me when I moved here, only Britt did, and everyone noticed that. They started to hang out with me because of her, and when I met you, the same thing happened again — but with even more people, adding on to the ones I already had," I explain.

"You met people because of Brittany and me, but they stayed your friends because of the person you are. If you weren't a nice and cool person to hang out with, they would've only talked to you when we were around. So, don't worry, D, they will come."

"And, if they don't?"

"Then, they aren't your friends and never were. Think of it as telling the real from the fake." He kisses me on the lips and takes us to our next class. I think about what Damien says all day, and when the bell finally rings, I make up my mind and decide to ask Dad about a party. We get out of class, and Brittany comes up to me.

"Hey girl, what's up?"

Damien and I look at each other, surprised, and roll our eyes. "What do you want, Britt?" I reply.

"Nothing, just want to catch up. We haven't spoken to each other in forever."

"Maybe because after what happened at your house, I told you to fuck off." I snippily remind her.

"Wow, language, Dawnie. I see you're like new and improved now, wearing sexy clothes and all," she points to my halter top.

"It's a halter top, and it's not that sexy," I say while starting to walk away with Damien.

She grabs my arm, "Wait!"

"What?"

"I miss you, and I forgive you, and we can be friends again," she smiles.

Surprised by the words coming out of my ex-bestie's mouth, my head snaps back in disbelief, and my response rolls casually off my tongue. "Fuck you, Britt. I don't want to be your friend, and I should be the one forgiving you, not you, forgiving me."

I walk away and loop my arm in Damien's. He cracks up while we walk away and continues until we're halfway home. Damien cackles so hard that he trips himself up for so long, almost falling to the ground. I grab his arm, breaking his fall, "What's wrong with you?" I ask him.

"I've never seen you act or say something like that. Hell, I honestly didn't think you had it in you. I never liked her ugly ass. Seeing her have her ass handed to her by you made my life."

"I know, it's like since my new back, the part of me that I was afraid to show disappeared. I feel like I can finally let the real me out."

"You always let the real you out around me."

"Yeah, but only you, Dad, and Scotty. I always did what Brittany wanted, and everyone else wanted. I even got drunk at her house. Deep down, I knew that's what she wanted. My new back gives me the courage I never had."

"That's where you're wrong, D."

"Wrong?"

"It's your new back, giving you the courage you always had inside. You weren't born with those engravings. That bastard, Earl, did that to you."

"How do you always know the right thing to say?"

"Because I know you, and I know how you think," he replies, kissing me softly on the lips. We get ice cream like always, and he takes me home. We go swimming, and I wear a bikini for the first time. It feels so good to wear.

"Damien, how do you throw a party?"

"You don't know how to throw a party?"

"I told you, I never had one."

"Yeah, but didn't you help Britt plan all of hers?" I begin laughing uncontrollably.

"What's so funny?" Damien asks, really wanting to know.

"Britt never planned her parties; she has a party planner. She doesn't even pick her clothes out for them. She has a stylist, and they do that for her, too."

"Are you serious?" he starts laughing.

"Yes, I can't believe you thought she planned them herself."

"She told me she did."

"She also tells you she's skinny. Do you believe that?"

"I know, right..."

"Hey, you two, what's so funny," Dad cuts in.

"Oh, nothing. Damien thought Britt planned her parties," I answer, letting him in on the joke.

"That's a good one, Damien," Dad bursts out laughing.

"Hey, Dad."

"Yes."

"Can I have a..."

"Yes, you can have a party. Tell me what day and the food you want, and you're good to go."

"How did you know I was going to ask that?"

"Fatherly instincts," he replies, kissing my forehead and returning inside.

Damien smiles and sings while doing a little dance, "Party! Party!" I laugh at his antics and join in on the singing and dancing.

Chapter 25

PARTY PLANNING

Damien calls Snake to tell him about the party and how we need his help. Snake and Damien are experts in party planning — they've had many parties. After school, we head to my house, but as usual, we stop to get ice cream first. Scotty is another party expert, so he chips in, too. They're more excited than I am about the party. Don't get me wrong, I'm excited but nervous. I keep thinking about all the things that will go wrong.

"Okay, I can get Jimmy to be your DJ," Scotty says.

"Jimmy, can DJ?" I asks, kind of surprised.

"He's the king of turntables. Who do you think does mine?"

"I don't know, a radio?"

"Hell no! I go all out — that's why I'm the king of parties." He does a little dance. I laugh and shift my focus to Damien and Snake. They're writing a long list.

"What are you doing?"

"Guest list."

"How do you know who I want to invite?"

"I know everyone you know. I know all your friends and haters — I got this," Damien replies, implying I should trust him.

"Same here. I'm always around y'all at school," Snake chimes in. They let me see the list. They're right — everyone on the list can be invited.

"Guys, what theme should I pick?" The room goes silent, and all three begin snickering.

"Theme?" They ask, confused and laughing.

"Doesn't every party have a theme?"

"No, they might have decorations, but this is a high school party, not kindergarten," Scotty says, and they laugh again, me included. "There are party stores all over if you want decorations," Scotty adds.

"What food do you want?" asks Snake.

"I don't know. I haven't thought about it yet."

"Sushi, cannoli, and pizza are already on the list, but I have to add more," says Damien.

"You two can make the food list. Damien knows what I like."

"When do you want your party?" Scotty asks.

"Lordy, I didn't know planning would be this hard. That's why I have you three — to help me, remember… and not ask me a million and one questions — because you know I don't know."

"We don't want you thinking we're trying to take over your party," mentions Snake.

"Yeah, that's why we're asking you," says Scotty.

"You three know me. You know what I like and what I don't like. Just make the list and show it to me later. I know I'll like it." I tell them. The three of them nod in agreement, and we continue party planning. After my little speech, everything goes smoothly; the guys and I are finally vibing. We schedule the party for two weeks from today. Snake creates some cool party flyers, which we pass around to everyone at school — except Brittany. Every person we hand a flyer to says they're coming.

While Damien, Snake, and I are talking during lunch, Brittany approaches and asks to speak with me privately. I glance at the guys, and they give me a "that's on you" look. Annoyed by Brittany's request and ready to get this over with, I walk over to the side with her.

"Hey, Dawnie."

"Hey Britt, what do you want?"

"Well, don't you have to ask me something?" she says with a stupid smirk.

I look at her long and hard, thinking about what I should ask her. "Nope, don't think so." I start walking back to the guys. Britt grabs my hand. I stop dead in my tracks. I feel all eyes on us in the lunchroom. I turn around slowly, trying to stay calm. Damien and Snake begin walking over to me — sensing something is about to happen.

"Dawnie, don't be like that. How dare you have a party and not invite me — of all people? Did you forget I'm the one who made you!" she fusses. I snatch my arm out of her hand. By this time, Damien and Snake are next to me.

"Come on, D — she's not worth it," Damien says.

Ignoring the guys, I give Britt the evilest look, "Don't you ever put your hands on me again — you rodent bitch! You didn't make me; I made myself. You were not invited to my party because I don't like you. You and your brother better not show up. Got it!" I walk back to the lunch table. Damien and Snake follow me back to the table in shock. They start cracking up nonstop. The entire lunchroom is watching to see what may transpire next between Brittany and me. Brittany storms out of the lunchroom, and everyone returns to eating lunch. Britt and I are now everyone's hot topic.

"Dawnie, I had no idea you were like that," says Snake.

"She grabbed my arm and pissed me off," I quickly remind him.

"You and Damien are the perfect couple with the exact same temper. Damn!" he says, laughing. He dabs up Damien, and they continue laughing and replaying the scene.

"You two are a mess," I say.

"Hey, I told you I hate the bitch," Damien says.

"Same here." Snake weighs in. The bell rings, and we go to class. Britt walks in, standing in front of the class, and clears her throat so everyone will look at her — and they do.

"Sit the hell down!" I yell at her. Everyone starts to laugh and agree.

"Excuse me, everyone, I have something to say," she says. The class sits and listens as she announces she's having a party on the same day as mine. Becoming furious, I jump out of my seat and approach her. I get in her face and am seconds from smacking the bitch, but Damien catches my wrist mid-air while Snake grabs me by the waist, pulling me back.

"Let me at her!" I yell.

Britt jumps back, scared her face is about to get smacked up or smashed in. She realizes Damien and Snake are not letting me go and starts pretending she's tough. "What's the matter, Dawnie," she taunts with a dumb smirk.

"Watch it, you fat bitch, or we will let her go!" Snake threatens. Damien and Snake pull me out of the classroom. Britt gasps in surprise and walks to her seat.

The class shouts in excitement, "Fight, fight, fight!" Damien and Snake will not let me go.

"Get off of me!" I yell.

"And have you beat the shit out of her, so Steve won't let you have your party? Hell no!"

"It's not going to be one now! Everyone is going to hers!"

"No, they're not. No one likes Brittany; they like you," Snake assures.

"How do you know?"

"Because I know everyone. They only chill with Brittany because of her money."

"Really?"

"Yes, trust me. If you don't believe me, ask Loup, and he will back me up." Damien nods his head, agreeing with Snake. I realize I'm doing too much.

"Sorry guys, I guess I'm overreacting a little."

They chuckle, "A little? We had to pull you out of the classroom, or you'd probably have killed her! You're lucky the teacher isn't here yet," Damien adds.

"Not like anyone would blame you — Brittany had it coming, but we couldn't let it go down, D," says Snake.

"Yeah, tell me about it," says Damien.

The teacher walks past us and goes into the classroom. "You're going to be late if you don't get in now," he warns.

The guys make sure I'm calm before heading to our desks. All eyes are on me. Britt is on the far side of the classroom, almost hiding in her seat. I scoff, smirk, and give her a wink before taking my seat.

Class is a blur. I barely pay attention because I'm too worried about people attending my party. I hope Snake's right about our classmates disliking Britt.

Chapter 26

PARTY

It's finally the day of my party, and I'm very excited about it. I've never had a party — I've only gone to them. Jimmy is the DJ; Scotty followed through on that. Jimmy is skinny, with a slinky-like figure. He's pale with black hair to his ear. He loves music and is always beat-boxing and silently singing to a song.

The party is starting soon, and I'm wearing a super cute new outfit that accentuates and gives a sizable peek at my lovely new back. I'm dressed in stone-washed denim mini-shorts with frayed lace trim, black strappy-wedged sandals, and an eye-appealing black sleeveless crop top. Damien is wearing plaid shorts and a polo shirt. Everyone is starting to arrive. There are way more people than I invited. They come in, say, "Hi," and I lead them to my backyard.

"Told you they would come," Damien whispers in my ear.

"Yeah, you sure did," I whisper back.

"Hey, Dawnie, I'm going to be upstairs if you need me," says Dad.

"Why? You don't want to stay down?" I ask, kind of hoping he would.

Dad chuckles, "And cramp your style?"

"No matter how much you try, Dad, trust me — you can't. Believe me."

"No, it's okay, sweetheart. I have a lot of work to catch up on," he tells me, kissing me on the forehead and retreating upstairs.

The party is partying! Some are in the pool swimming and playing while others are dancing. Damien and I have been dancing for a while and are ready to enter the pool. I tell Damien I'll be back down shortly. I run upstairs to put on my bikini and discover it's on my bed. This is weird. I didn't put it there earlier. Maybe Dad or Scotty did so I wouldn't have to spend time looking for it. I grab the bikini, but first, I need to pee. I run to my bathroom — I hate keeping Damien waiting.

When I come out, laying on my bed, spread out is a dress. I can't believe my eyes, it's not just a dress, it's "the dress" — the one Earl always used to make me wear! I look around my room in fear. Whoever put it there might still be here. Shocked that it's in my room, I grab the dress and stuff it under my bed. How the hell did Earl get upstairs in the house without anyone seeing him? There's a noise inside my room; I run to the stairs. I don't know where it's coming from, but I'm not staying around to find out. I haul ass down the stairs and jump down the last few — slamming right into someone. We both fall to the ground. Not noticing who it is, I enter defense mode and begin punching and kicking to escape.

"D, it's me."

I instantly realize it's Damien because he's the only one who calls me "D."

"Damien!" I screech, raising my voice but ensuring no one hears me. I throw myself in his arms and cry.

"What did he leave this time?"

"How did you know?"

"Because he's the only one that can get you this worked up," he says. We quickly get up from the floor before anyone sees us.

"He left the dress."

"He left a dress?"

"Not just any dress, "the dress" Damien!"

"Tracy's?"

"No, a dress he used to make me wear before he... he..." I start explaining frantically while going back down memory lane.

"You don't have to say it, D, I know." Damien holds me in his arms, calming me down for the most part. We go to my room to check if Earl is still here, but he's nowhere to be found.

"D, do you want to tell yet?"

"No, we can't."

"Then, what do you want to do? Your dad and Scotty will ask questions if we stay up here any longer."

"I know, we got to act like nothing happened."

"How?"

"We get in the pool as planned and act normal like before."

Damien gives me a 'you've got to be kidding me' look but agrees with the plan to act normal. We get in the pool. He stays next to me like glue the entire time, his hands on my waist. Snake comes up and asks us if we're okay, and we say, "Yes."

"D, we got to loosen up a little more because Snake can feel something's off with us."

"I know, I'm trying."

Damien kisses me softly on the lips and tells me to breathe. I listen to him, wrap my arms around his neck, and look into his eyes. It helps me loosen up, and I can feel him loosening up. Whenever something bad happens, or I feel scared, things become much better if Damien is around. Like the kiss he just gave me, it relaxed me despite one of the scariest things happening. I feel very safe that he's here with me.

The rest of my birthday party is going well. I almost forget about the Earl situation this evening in my room. I believe Damien has, too. If not, he's doing a good job hiding it. After the party, Damien, Snake, and I start cleaning up, but Dad tells us to stop because he's hired a cleaning company. We pretend Damien is leaving with Snake to avoid Dad offering him a ride home, but Damien sneaks into my room for the night.

Chapter 27

THANK YOU DADDY

I want to thank Dad for everything he's done for me. I go into his room, but he's not there. But I know where to find him when he's not in his room — he's in his office. There he is, burying his face in a heap of paperwork.

"Hello, sweetheart."

"Hey, Daddy."

"Why the long face? The party wasn't what you expected?"

"No, it was better!"

"Then, why am I sensing something is wrong with you?" he asks, putting down his papers and assessing me with concern.

"I have a lot on my mind, that's all."

"Oh yeah, like what? All my attention is on you." He swivels in his chair towards my direction and gives me his undivided attention.

"Like, everything that has been going on," I say, walking over and sitting on his lap.

"Everything? Like with Tracy and your back?"

"Yeah. Hey Daddy…"

"Yes, Dawnie?"

"I know I've asked you "why" a hundred times, but I've never really told you thank you and how grateful I am for everything you've done for me."

"You don't have to. It's not only my duty, but also my job, that I love to do."

"A job?"

"Yeah, it's not always easy, and I may not be perfect at this dad thing, but I try."

"You do a great job. Tracy never did anything for me. She never helped me with Earl... then again, she didn't know about him, but if she weren't always high, it wouldn't have even happened, and now she's dead. Fawn left me with her, and Alex left before I got to know him. Before coming here to live with you, I hated everyone, even Tracy — even though she was the only thing I had. Night after night, Earl raped me; it took a piece of my soul every time. I've spent my life protecting her because if I'd told her, he would've killed her, and not once did she ever do anything to protect me. She moved in with you because she loved you and your money and not because it was right for me. She even left me by myself with you. At first, I was pissed, but then, I got to know you." I explain.

Dad listens to everything I have to say and chuckles at the part when I mention being pissed when we moved in with him. "You sure were pissed. I remember the day I picked you up," he jokes.

"Yeah, I was an asshole."

"No, you were just being alert and had a level of awareness about yourself. After everything you've been through with Earl and Tracy, there's no doubt in my mind you're grateful. You don't have to tell me."

"But I do. Look how much you've done for me. Even my back! I cursed you out, punched, and kicked you. I'm so embarrassed."

He laughs again, "Don't be. Like I said before, this lifestyle is all new to you, and as a child, you were thrust into it. Unfortunately, betrayal and abuse were normal to you, and that should've never been. I would've probably acted the same way, but you're safe now. No one can hurt you as long as I'm here." He kisses my forehead, and I hug him.

"Thanks, Daddy, I hope you're always here."

"You're welcome, and I always will be. You know there is a way you can make it up to me."

"What?"

"Go to school and earn your degree. Be an independent woman

when you grow up and be strong. Don't be like Tracy or Fawn. Make the right decisions and make me proud. It means the world to me to see you succeed in life. It's the best thing you can do for me."

"Deal. Oh, hey, Daddy."

"Yes?"

"I was thinking, this girl you're seeing…"

"Woman, not a girl. You're a girl."

"Sorry, woman, you're seeing, I've never met her, or at least I don't think I have. Why don't you have her over so we can meet?"

He pauses for a moment. He's surprised by what I'm saying. "Are you sure, Dawnie?"

"Yeah, why wouldn't I be? If she's lasted this long with a guy like you, she must be worth something special if you're still together. Dad, anything special to you is special to me."

"Thanks, Dawnie. I'll invite her over for dinner." Dad says, hugging me.

"Good." I head towards the door when I think, "Oh, Daddy, did you leave my bikini on my bed?"

"No, I didn't. Why?"

"No reason, just asking; it must have been Scotty."

"No, Scotty doesn't go in your room like that or mess with your things, and definitely not your bikinis."

"Oh, I must've laid it out and forgot." I conclude — it was Earl. However, I still haven't asked Damien; he's my last hope.

Chapter 28

MY ROOM

I go into my room and whisper Damien's name. He leaves the bathroom and asks, "Hey, D, what took you so long?"

"Having a heart-to-heart with my daddy," I reply.

"How did that go?"

"Great. Better than I thought."

"Did you tell him?"

"Of course not."

"D, he knows there's something up."

"Yeah, but he thinks it's Tracy, not this."

"I don't know, D. He's smarter than that."

"I know, but I hope he's not today. Besides, we need to figure out how Earl got in here," I stress.

"Already did. Earl got in through the balcony. There are little stubs on the building that anyone can climb up," Damien explains.

"Shit, are you serious?"

"Yeah," he says.

"Hey, Damien?"

"Yeah, D?"

"Did you take out my bikini and put it on my bed?"

"No, why?" Shocked and not thinking, I snatch off my bikini like there's a big bug on it. I cry hysterically. Damien is confused as ever.

"He picked it out for me. He wanted to see me in it. Ol' nasty Earl is disgusting — just sickening. I'm scared, Damien."

"Oh my gosh, D, I'm sorry." Damien holds me. He's seen me naked before, so I'm not worried about being fully exposed in front of him. I let him keep holding me. He places me on the bed and tells me he's turning on the shower. I get in the shower and scrub the heck out of my skin. When I step out, my skin is beat red. Damien is sitting on the bed waiting for me. "How are you feeling?" he asks as I sit down on his lap. He holds me.

"When I'm in your arms, I feel great," I say, kissing him.

"Ready to go to sleep?" says Damien.

"Yeah."

We lie down; I make sure I'm still in his arms. I fall fast asleep right in his arms.

Chapter 29

DAD'S GIRLFRIEND

Today is the day I finally get to meet Dad's girlfriend. She's coming over any minute for dinner, and if I like her, we'll go to the movies. Of course, Damien and Scotty are here too. I hope I like her; I have a gut feeling I will. Dad usually has good judgment about people. The doorbell rings; it's her. "I'll get it!" I yell before Dad can even blink. I open the door and see a beautiful woman with long brown hair and light caramel skin. She has the perfect figure and is in her mid-thirties or younger.

"Hello, you must be Dawnie," she says, with a strong Irish accent.

"You must be my Dad's girlfriend," I reply.

She giggles, "Yes, the name is Victoria Jennozi."

"Nice to meet you, Victoria."

"Same. I've heard so much about you." We walk to the kitchen. She has a box in one hand and wine in the other.

"Do you need help with that?"

"If you don't mind."

"Not at all," I say, taking the box. We go into the kitchen, and Dad sees us and smiles.

"I see you two met already," he says.

"Yes, we did. Want to watch TV while my dad makes dinner?" I ask her.

She looks at Dad in surprise, "Do you need my help, Steve?"

"No, not at all. Go and watch TV with Dawnie. Get better acquainted."

"Okay." We walk into the living room and sit down.

"So, you're from Ireland," I say.

"Yes, I guess my accent gives it away, huh?"

"Yeah, but I like it," I say, giving her a smile.

Damien and Scotty meet us in the living room and introduce themselves. We sit down and talk for half an hour before Dad tells us dinner is ready. I determine she's good for Dad during the short time we speak. The box she brought with her is filled with cannoli. Of course, this gives her major brownie points with me. She was born in Ireland and moved to the US when she was ten. Victoria and Dad met at a Starbucks when she was getting her morning coffee one day. Her dad owned a company that did plumbing for casinos and big corporations. When he died, everything was left to her, including a ton of money. Mystery solved — she definitely wasn't with Dad for his money, another plus in my book. She's very independent, has her master's, and is working on her PhD in business administration.

"How long have you two been going out?" I curiously inquire.

"Two and a half years," she replies, hesitant in her response.

They were scared to admit it because Dad was with Tracy around then, so there was an overlap. "It's okay. I already know you two were together when he was with Tracy. My dad deserved better than Tracy. He only put up with her because of me," I tell her. I should be upset, but I'm honestly not. Tracy was a bitch to Dad. Seeing my Dad and Victoria together, I know what happiness is. I'm only fifteen and happy with Damien; why can't Dad be happy, too? They smile, relieved I'm not upset. "Hey, Victoria, do you want to go to the movies later?"

Surprised by my invitation, Victoria says, "Yes, I'd love that Dawnie, thanks."

I look at Dad, and he smiles at me and mouths," Thank you."

"No problem. Anyone special to Dad is special to me, too," I tell Victoria. We finish dinner. Dad and I start to wash dishes, and everyone else clears the table.

"I assume you like her since you invited her to the movies?" Dad mentions.

"Yeah, I like her and the way she makes you smile. She makes you happy, and after everything, you deserve it. But, if she hurts you, I'll beat the shit out of her," I say slickly with a sheepish smile.

He laughs and says, "Okay, deal, and you won't get punished either." We burst out laughing. Victoria walks into the kitchen to ask if we need help.

"No," we say. Dad goes upstairs to get something, leaving us alone in the kitchen — the perfect opportunity to give Victoria a pep talk.

"Hey, Victoria."

"Yes?"

"My dad is a very nice man and means a lot to me. Scotty, Damien, and him are the only ones I have. He's been through a lot, and even though he looks strong, I don't know how much more he can take. Please don't hurt him. He's been through more than enough. I love him and I'll do almost anything for my dad." She sits on the stool, listening to everything — at least, she looks like she's listening.

"I understand, Dawnie. I won't hurt him. Do you want to know a secret?"

"Sure, why not?"

"I'm in love with your father."

"That's perfectly understandable," I reply; we both start giggling. Dad walks in on us, laughing, "What's perfectly understandable?"

Victoria and I look at each other and reply, "Nothing." We go to the movies and watch *Colombiana.*

Chapter 30

DAD'S ANNOUNCEMENT

Dad tells Scotty and me to come home right after school today because he has an announcement. Scotty and I have yet to learn what it is. We think he's announcing that he and Victoria are engaged, but we doubt it because we just met her. She's nice, and I like her, but I don't want her and Dad to get married yet. Scotty picks Damien and me up from school on time — for once. Scotty's too eager to find out what Dad has to tell us.

"Do you have a clue of what it might be?" Scotty asks for the second time in a row.

"No, I don't think he and Victoria are announcing an engagement," I answer.

"Yeah, I doubt it's that because Victoria would be there too, and he didn't mention her being at the house," says Scotty.

"Yeah, you're right. Maybe the police found Earl and finally convicted him."

"Maybe, or maybe, we're moving." Scotty guesses.

"Bullshit!" Damien and I shout.

Scotty looks at us, "I said, maybe, not a definite."

"He knows how much we love California; he wouldn't do that to us," I remind Scotty.

"Yeah, you're right. Then what is it? He never says he has

something important to tell us before we go to school, and then he doesn't tell us. It's been killing me all day."

"Yeah, me too," I say, agreeing. We arrive at the house, and Dad's car is in the driveway, which is weird because he's never been home before us. We jump out of the car and race to the house.

"Dad!" I yell.

"In here!" he yells back from the living room. We walk in, and Victoria is right next to him. She's holding his hand, and Dad greets us with a huge grin. I nudge Scotty in the back — no one sees me do it but Damien. We know what the announcement is going to be. The three of us sit on the couch. Things go silent. I break the silence.

"What's the announcement?"

"Oh, yeah, I have to visit France for two weeks this summer. I've never spent two weeks away from you kids, so I made it a family vacation," Dad says, smiling.

Scotty and I sigh in relief. We're happy and giddy. Scotty mentions something about a passport. I'm clueless about what he's talking about. "What's a passport?"

"It's something you must have when leaving the country. Don't worry, Dawnie, I got yours when we went to Ireland," Dad informs me.

"Oh, okay, is this all you have to tell us, Dad?"

"Umm, kind of. I also want to ask if Victoria can come?"

Scotty and I chuckle, "Of course, she can come. You don't have to ask us that."

They sigh in relief. "Okay, good. We were worried for a second there." Damien and I go to my room while Dad and Victoria go out. Damien looks sad and has been quiet.

"What's wrong?" I ask.

"Don't get me wrong, D, I'm excited for you, but I can't spend a day away from you. You're telling me I have to spend two weeks away from you? I don't know how I'll make it without you here," he says, becoming emotional.

"I know what you mean. I didn't think about it like that." I reply.

"I've never been anywhere. I don't know how I'm going to sleep at night. How're you going to sleep?" he mumbles, looking defeated.

I kiss him. "Absence makes the heart grow fonder. I'll miss you and call you all the time. I promise I'll be with you as soon as we get back," I say, soothingly, trying to make him feel better.

I remember I'm wearing the necklace Damien gave me. It reminds me to think of him when we're apart. But he doesn't have anything from me — nothing I've given him that symbolizes me. I go to my bathroom and look through my cabinets and drawers until I find a pair of scissors. I return to the bedroom, cut a piece of my hair, and hand it to him. "I know it's not fancy jewelry, but the best I can do on such short notice. You gave me this necklace so you can always be with me, but what do you have? Nothing. It's only fair you have a piece of me, so I can always be with you too," I tell him, kissing him on the lips.

"This, D, is better than anything fancy. It means more to me than any jewelry ever will. Thank you, babe."

I begin kissing him harder. I press my body close to his, letting him know I want more than a kiss. He picks me up and lays me on the bed. We make love once again. We channel our frustration about being away from each other for two weeks into making sweet love. It makes the situation much better. Thankfully, no one is home but us because it's hard for me to stay quiet. We finish and cuddle.

"Summer starts in two weeks, D."

"We have two weeks together before I go, so let's make the best of it." I say back. So, for the next two weeks, Damien and I spend every waking minute together. Instead of me letting him in by the front door, he comes in and out by the balcony now.

Chapter 31

FRANCE

It's the night before I leave for France with my family. Although I'm super excited, I'm bummed I'll be away from Damien for two whole weeks. Something in my gut tells me something will go wrong, but I ignore the feeling. My gut is always right — well, maybe this one time it's wrong — I hope. As usual, Damien comes to my house to spend the night — but this is the last night before we leave for France in the morning. Something is bothering him — it's showing more and more as the time closes in on our takeoff.

"What's wrong?" I ask.

"Nothing."

I give him the "stop lying" stare.

He takes a deep breath and says, "Things are getting worse with my dad. He won't let me speak to Jen or my mother at all. Hell, he won't even allow me to talk to them on the phone."

"Damien, I can stay if you want. I'll go to France another time."

"No, D. That's why I didn't want to tell you. I knew you'd try this. How would you be able to stay home anyway?" I run to the bathroom, close the door, and lock it. I make puking sounds. It's very convincing because Damien bangs on the door, demanding I open it. He's very worried. I mess up my hair and makeup, pat water on my face, and open the door, trying to look as miserable as possible. He rushes over, picks me up, and places me on the bed.

"Are you okay, D?" he asks worriedly.

I stop the antics and smile. "And that's how I can stay home." We look at each other and start cracking up.

"I must say, D, that… was pretty convincing," giving me an applause and kissing me. "I still don't want you missing your family trip to France because of me. We can spend all the time in the world together when you get back," says Damien.

"Okay," I say, giving in. Suddenly, I feel like something is punching me in the gut. It's also happening to Damien because we simultaneously have the same jerk reaction. We look at each other, holding our guts, "Did you feel what I just felt?" I ask him. He nods his head yes.

"Something tells me you going to France — is not a good thing." Damien blurts.

"Yeah, me too."

"But, you have to."

"No, I don't. I can stay and be with you."

"Did you see Steve's face when he told you he wants you and Scotty to go with him, and when you both said yes? That's all he's been talking about. Even my dad says that's all Steve talks about lately."

"Yeah, you're right. Well then, shit, what are we going to do?"

"You'll go to France and call every chance you get. You're not to be alone at all. Do you understand me?"

"But.." I sigh, beginning to cry.

"But nothing. Unless you want to tell your dad everything that has happened?" I look him in the eyes. He's right. I must go to France with my family or tell Dad about Earl. I'd rather go to France and face whatever is there than tell my father about the crazy presents Earl has been leaving for me and the sick mind games he's been playing. I nod my head yes. He holds me in his arms.

"I won't be alone, I promise." Damien kisses me on the lips. We cry ourselves to sleep.

We wake up the next morning to sunlight hitting our faces. I hop in the shower first and Damien afterward. While I finish getting dressed, I hear a knock on my door; I know it's Dad — I know the sound of his knock.

"Be down in a second!" I announce loudly.

"Okay, try to hurry. I don't want to miss the flight," says Dad.

I look at Damien. He's just as scared as me and what might happen while in France. We hug, followed by a long, passionate kiss. Neither of us wants to say it, but deep inside, we know this might be the last time we'll see each other — at least for a while. We wipe each other's tears, and he climbs out my window. I grab my things and go downstairs, where Victoria, Scotty, and Dad are waiting for me. We get in the limo, and the driver drops us off at the airport. I try my best to act normal — like nothing's wrong. Besides, nothing is wrong right now.

The eerie feeling I have won't shake. My gut is telling me something is going to go wrong. I can't hide it anymore. Worry is written all over my face. When Victoria goes to the bathroom, Dad and Scotty ask me what's wrong. They can sense something, too — they just don't know what it is. "Nothing's wrong," I reply. They don't buy it one bit and tell me to fess up. "I just have a funny feeling that something will go wrong on this trip — terribly wrong." They look at me with great concern and worry.

Dad comforts me, "It's okay to be afraid of flying on a plane. Trust me, I've flown on planes my whole life, and nothing has happened yet. You'll be okay, Dawnie. You're with me and Scotty. We won't let anything happen to you. You've flown on our private plane before and were always safe."

Scotty nods his head in agreement. I force a smile and say, "Okay."

I'm not worried about the plane. I'm concerned about France and what's going to happen there. It's a gut feeling about France I can't shake. Something horrifying is about to transpire in France — I sense it. I don't want to mess up the trip for Dad and Scotty. I decide to let it go. Victoria returns from the bathroom, and it's time to board the plane. Scotty sits next to me in first class; we buckle up and prepare for takeoff.

When we arrive at Paris Charles de Gaulle airport in France, a limo picks us up. Dad booked a penthouse suite with butler service. The view is fantastic. We can see everything from our penthouse, even the Eiffel Tower. We have two queen beds with white fluffy pillows and covers, a huge bathroom with a stand-up shower and Jacuzzi tub, marble floors, and floor-to-ceiling mirrors everywhere. The elevator and stairs in the penthouse are an added touch, giving it the feel of an apartment but way bigger and way more beautiful. Dad and Victoria's master bedroom is upstairs. Their room has a little sitting area with lovely large windows, and a cozy fireplace.

"Wow, this is beautiful," I say to Scotty.

"Yeah, Uncle Steve definitely has a way of going all out," Scotty adds.

"Yeah, you think?"

"Let's unpack and go explore the city," he laughs. We unpack and dress up nicely. Dad and Victoria come downstairs, and we dine at a five-star restaurant called Le Jules Verne in the Eiffel Tower. Our dinner table is positioned right next to the window. The view is stunning, even better than the view at the penthouse. Dad and Victoria read and translate the food selections on the menu for us because Scotty and I don't know French. The food is excellent. We eat pasta and cannoli for dessert.

After dinner, we walk around the streets of Paris and take pictures. Most museums are already closed for the day or near closing, so we go back to the penthouse to relax for the rest of the night.

Chapter 32

SCOTT'S PAST

All the channels are in French — ugh — so watching TV is out of the question for Scotty and me. We end up sitting and talking for the rest of the evening. I know nothing about Scotty's parents or siblings. I know Uncle Brian, Uncle Jimmy, and his grandparents, but that's because our grandparents always have Sunday dinners, and those uncles are always there along with a few other family members, except Scotty's parents. He never seems to care that they never show up. He doesn't speak about his parents or siblings. You'd think he didn't have any. I'm sure most believe my dad is his dad. "Hey Scotty"

"Yeah."

"Can I ask you a personal question?"

"Umm, sure, not too personal, though," he says playfully.

"Why don't you live with your parents? Are they drug addicts like mine?"

"Umm, no, they umm… died," he says, looking away.

Right away, I felt sorry for asking him. "I'm so sorry, Scotty. I didn't know."

"It's okay, Dawnie, I know you didn't know. How could you? I never talk about them."

"Do you have any brothers or sisters?"

"Yeah, but umm…. he's different since our parents died. I really don't speak to him ."

"Do you miss him?"

"Yeah, of course."

"How did they die, if you don't mind me asking?"

"My dad died in a car accident."

"How old were you?"

"I was nine years old."

"How old was your brother?"

"Five."

"What's his name?"

"Jesse."

"Do you ever speak to him? Like… call him on the phone?"

"No."

"Why not?"

"Do you speak to Fawn?" he jabs back.

"You know I don't."

"Why not?"

"Because we're different, and I don't like her ways."

"Well, there you go."

"Wow… this whole time we've known each other, I never knew your background."

"I don't like talking about it; no one ever actually cares enough to ask anyway — but Christina knows."

"Who?"

"Someone I grew up with and care deeply about."

"I haven't met her yet."

He lets out a small laugh under his breath. "Don't worry, Dawnie, you will. She's been with me through thick and thin."

"You said you two grew up together. How?"

"My father used to own a club before he was killed. I always hung out with my father when I was younger; she was one of the club members' daughters. First, we started as friends, and then we grew to like each other more than that. When my dad died, I moved in with Uncle Steve. She lives with her mom, and we've always stayed in contact."

"What kind of club did your dad have?"

"Biker's club. Uncle Steve was in it."

"The one in Ireland?"

"Yeah — that one. Uncle Steve was my dad's right-hand man. They did everything together. They traveled a lot to Belfast, Ireland. That's where the club originated — the corner store in Ireland we went to."

"Dad's Irish?"

"Umm... yeah, you can't really tell though," replies Scotty.

"Then, what's up with his last name?" I ask, trying to figure things out in my head.

"What about it?"

"Sandino sounds Italian."

"Hmm, I don't know. I've never thought of it like that," he says.

"Looks like there are family secrets — more than meets the eye."

"Yeah," Scotty agrees, his face puzzled. He turns off the light for us to go to sleep. I try to sleep but can't. Damien isn't here with me — so getting a good night's sleep while on this trip is out of the question. I still can't budge the feeling that something terrible will happen here. I hop into Scotty's bed to see if it'll help me sleep. It helps a little, but not much. I fall asleep, but I do not like my dreams. I dream I'm in a small, dark place. There are two dead bodies. I take their gun and go upstairs with someone behind me, but I can't see their faces. Then, I end up in someone's kitchen, looking at a window full of light. I hear a gunshot.

The nightmares are so bad that I wake up in a panic, breathing hard and loudly gasping for air. I hear the shower running. I look next to me and see an empty bed. Scotty turns off the shower and comes rushing into the room with a towel around his waist. My phone rings, it's Damien.

"Dawnie, what's wrong?" Scotty asks.

"Nothing," I say, quickly answering the phone.

"What's wrong?" Damien asks, sensing the intensity in my breathless voice when I answer the phone.

"Nothing, why are you two..." I cut him off mid-sentence. The room door swings open, and Dad comes running in.

"What's wrong?" Dad asks frantically.

"Nothing. Why are you three asking me what's wrong?"

"I don't know, I just got a feeling something was wrong with you, Dawnie," says Dad.

"Me too," Scotty adds.

"Me three," says Damien on the phone.

"It was a nightmare, that's all," I tell all three of them.

"Who's on the phone?" Dad asks.

"Damien… Who else?" I reply, irritated that he asked.

"Oh, tell him we said, 'hi,'" says Dad, plopping down on the bed.

"Tell them I said, 'hi too.'" replies Damien.

"Damien says, 'Hi too.'"

"Do you want to talk about your nightmare?" Damien offers.

"Yes, but not at the moment."

"You, sure?"

"Yeah, I'll call you later when we can speak privately."

"Okay, I love you, but be careful. Make sure you're not alone," Damien reminds me.

"Okay, love you too, see you soon." The words, "See you soon," I say to Damien, are lies. I don't want them to be — but that's what it feels like.

"You look like a baby who just had her toy stolen. What's wrong?" Dad inquires.

"Nothing, Dad. My nightmare seemed so real," I tell him.

"What was it about?" he asks, becoming very curious.

"I don't know. All I remember is being in some small, dark place, holding a gun with someone behind me. I went up the stairs and saw some light from the window. Then, all of a sudden, I heard a gunshot, and woke up to you guys checking on me."

"That's pretty dynamic," says Dad. I start cracking up.

"What's so funny?" Scotty asks.

"Dad came up with a new word." I giggle some more.

"What is it?"

"Dynamic."

"Wow, Uncle Steve, you sure have… become a corny old man." Scotty laughs.

"Hey, watch. You two will both be saying it soon enough, too," Dad chuckles.

"Mmm hmm. Yep, sure we will," I say sarcastically.

Chapter 33

SEEING FRANCE

I get up, get my things, and kick Scotty out of the bathroom to shower. It's a standing shower with marble everywhere and a glass window. When I flick on a switch, the windows turn foggy so no one can see through them. The showerhead also comes off, reminding me of my shower at home. When I finish getting dressed, we all go for a walk. We see and visit the L'Aquarium de Paris, Musee de I'Hommeé, and the Palais de Chaillot. Later, we take a fifteen-minute train to the Palace of Versailles, which is by far my favorite place we visit.

I fall in love with the artwork. My favorite room is the Salon d'Hercule. This room is filled with portraits on the ceiling and wall, except for the floor and windows. The border around the portraits is a golden trim. The beauty of the Palace of Versailles is unmatched. I love that kings used to live in it, but it bothers me. Unfortunately, no royal family currently exists here in France. We finish the day by eating dinner at another five-star restaurant, and Dad and Victoria order dinner for Scotty and me again.

"You really love the Salon d'Hercule's room — huh, Dawnie?" Dad asks.

"Of course I did, Dad. Did you see that ceiling?"

"Yeah, I saw it," he says with splendor.

"I want my ceiling just like that," I reply.

"You would want something whack like that," Scotty laughs.

"What can I say? It was so 'dynamic,'" I say back, and we start cracking up. Dad looks at us, trying to hold his laugh, but fails miserably.

"I see the kids took your new word," Victoria says to Dad, laughing too.

"What can I say? I'm quite compelling." We sit there, laughing and talking, and suddenly, I feel that someone is watching me. I try my best to stay calm because somehow, every time I'm scared, confused, or just uneasy, Scotty, Dad, and Damien can tell. I don't want to ruin the amazing dinner we're having. I get up to go to the bathroom, but Scotty and Dad catch on to it anyway. I feel my phone vibrating. I don't have to look at it to know it's Damien.

"What's wrong, Dawnie?" Scotty and Dad ask.

"Nothing, I just have to go to the bathroom." I know they're not buying it by the look on their faces, but I grab my purse and hurry off to the bathroom with their eyes following me. Victoria is totally oblivious to Dad and Scotty's intuition and tense demeanor. I walk to the bathroom; no one I see in the restaurant seems too interested as I make my way. I still feel like someone is watching me besides Scotty and Dad.

The bathroom is lovely with marble everywhere, golden faucets, so much detail in the mirrors, and a lovely painting with two people. It's a woman and a man in the painting. They have something that looks like a white sheet on them and sandals that wrap around their legs. I glare at the painting and hear the bathroom door close. I quickly turn around to see the bathroom empty, just as it was when l entered it.

I look out the door and see no one standing by or walking away, but I do see Dad and Scotty looking in my direction, right at me. I look back at them and force a smile the best I can. I return to the table and continue trying to eat my meal. Dad offers to order me dessert, but I don't have a taste for any today. We finish dinner, return to our penthouse, and I go to my room. Victoria tells us, "Good night," Dad tells her he'll see her in their room in a minute, and comes to make sure we have everything we need. This is strange because Dad knows we already have everything we need.

"Is everything okay, Dad?"

"You tell me," he says back.

"What do you mean?"

"At dinner, something happened. I could sense it."

"So could I," Scotty butts in.

"What happened?" Dad persists.

"Nothing," I say nonchalantly.

"Liar. If nothing happened, Dawnie, why didn't you order dessert? You always order dessert, especially when chocolate or cannoli are on the menu. Now fess up." Dad says sternly.

"Nothing to fess up."

"When will you stop these lies, Dawnie, and start trusting us?"

"I do. I trust you both."

"If you trusted us, you wouldn't lie to us."

"I'm not lying."

"Maybe not about trusting us, but you're definitely hiding something. Has Earl been in contact with you in some way?" Dad asks, trying to get the truth out of me. I freeze, stunned that he hit it on the nail, but I return to my senses before he notices, and he catches on to me.

"No, of course not."

"Would you tell us if he was trying to?"

"Yes, of course."

"Okay," he says and looks at Scotty. He kisses me on the forehead.

"Goodnight. I'll see you tomorrow." He walks to the door and stops before leaving my room, "Hey Dawnie..."

"Yes, Dad."

"Remember when I said I can tell when you're lying?"

"Yes."

"Well, that still hasn't changed," he says, leaving the room.

Chapter 34

TELLING THEM THE TRUTH

My heart drops all the way to hell and will not return to my chest. How much does he know or sense something is happening? Does he expect me to tell him everything tomorrow morning? Is his life in danger now that he knows Earl has contacted me? I look at Scotty in silence, unaware that tears are running down my eyes. He approaches me and tries to wipe them away, but they keep coming. "How long?" I ask Scotty.

"How long what?" he replies, caught off guard.

"Don't play dumb with me. How long have you known?" I demand.

"I've known since we went to Ruby Tuesday's, after, you know, the thing with Zach…"

"And Dad?"

"No clue. I didn't even know Uncle Steve suspected anything until now."

"How long has he been contacting you, Dawnie?"

"Since Tracy died. He will kill you two if he knows you both know, Scotty!" I remind him.

My tears downpour, and I can barely breathe. Scotty puts his arms around me and tries to calm me down. I cry myself to sleep. I wake up to Scotty and Dad standing in front of me. They had ordered room service because the cart in my room is filled with food.

"What happened, kiddo? Tell me." Dad says.

"I can't, Dad, or he'll…"

"He'll what? Kill me and Scotty, here? Highly unlikely. Now spill it," Dad says, not backing down.

"Dad, what do you mean? It's highly unlikely. Did you not see Tracy's tape? He's been to my school locker and has snuck into our gated community, even though it's supposed to be secure like Fort Knox. Oh, and not to mention, he's been in our residence, Dad, in my room!"

"He's what!" Dad shouts.

"Been in my room," I whisper, a little frightened because Dad is not the one who really snaps, but it's not pretty when he does.

"And you're just telling me this?" He shakes his head in disbelief.

"Dad, I told you both, if anything were to ever happen to you, I'd…"

"Nothing will," Dad cuts me off.

"I don't know that. I know how Earl is, and he's ruthless and soulless." I spit out.

"Wait a second, how do you know he was at your locker?" I pause and look at Dad,

"He left something in there."

"Which was?"

"Tracy's earring, the one she was wearing the day she died," I say, crying.

"And how do you know he was in your room and our residential area?" Scotty asks.

I lift my head and look at them both, knowing I must tell them everything; I no longer have a choice. It has to be the truth, too. It's not like I can keep this away from them anymore because if I do, they'll know. I ask Dad and Scotty to sit down. I tell them everything that has happened, from the blood on the screen door to the bikini and dress on my bed the night of the party. I even reveal to them that Damien knows all about this and was there when it happened. He knows everything, from when I found the shirt in the shoe box to the notes he wrote and left for me, with all his so-called gifts, and the feeling of someone following me at school and the restaurant.

Dad is crushed that I've been keeping all this to myself, and Scotty is furious that there's nothing he can do to change it. Dad and Scotty both have their own ways of expressing their anger. Dad doesn't outwardly show his anger like Scotty. He's skilled at concealing it and is very unassuming, but in knowing Dad, he will handle it.

"A father's job is to protect their child, and I've failed you on so many levels. I'm so sorry, and I hope you'll forgive me. You're so used to being alone and dealing with something not even most adults go through. You're so mature, Dawnie, that you keep trying to protect me, even though it's not your job to do so. All of this is too much for you, and it's obvious that it hurts you to endure it, but I'm the parent, not you. You need to tell me these things so I can and will take the proper precautions. How can I protect you if you don't keep it a buck with me? I need to know what's going on, and if you had told me the first time this happened, it would've been the last time." Dad lectures very calmly.

"But Dad, you don't understand. I really wanted to, but I was so scared that I was going to lose you and Scotty. I couldn't bear it if anything ever happened to either of you." Dad gets up and goes to the door in silence. I sit there crying, Scotty holding me. Dad returns briefly with several men in suits, looking like the mob. "Who are they?" I ask him.

"These men are your guards."

"Is this really necessary, Dad?"

"Very. It's my job to protect you and Scott, and from the looks of it, I haven't been doing so."

"Dad, you have been doing a great job protecting us."

"If I had been Dawnie, none of this would've happened. Now, I'm going to make sure it never happens again," Dad says, his tone serious and firm.

"If you do this, Dad, he will kill you and Scotty, and I told you I can't have that."

"Not with us here, ma'am," one of the guards interrupts with a strong Irish accent.

"And who are you?" I ask, slightly irritated.

"David."

Dad butts in and points to each guard, naming them, "Their names are Joseph, Patrick, Benny, and David — the guy who already introduced himself. These men are going to be your main guards. They will be close to you and around you at all times. The rest will stay distant, constantly scanning the surroundings for potential threats."

"But Dad…" I whine.

"It's this, or we end the vacation early and put you in self-defense training, Dawnie."

Scotty nudges me, and I look at him. I don't want to ruin the trip for him any more than I already have. I let out a long breath of air and nod my head up and down, giving them their way. "Victoria and I have a meeting in town. We will be back in a bit. Remember, wherever you go, they go. Understood?" Dad's tone is firm and fatherly.

"Yes, Dad," I say, and Scotty nods in agreement.

He leaves the room, leaving the guards with us. I'm so mad. I run to the closet and shut the door behind me, crying like a baby. I ruined the family trip to France. Our vacation is messed up now, and it's all my fault. They'll hate me for it. Scotty will be more distant than ever because we have to have a trillion and one bodyguards, like the queen of England always did. I hear a knock on the door and know it's Scotty. "Go away," I cry.

"What's wrong?" he asks.

"France is now ruined because of me!"

"No, it's not. Open the door so we can talk."

"No, I don't want to see anyone; I want to be alone. I never should've told Dad anything."

"Technically, you didn't. We found out, and you're a terrible liar anyway." I finally give in and crack open the door for him to come in. He comes in and sits next to me on the floor.

"Sorry."

"Sorry for what, Dawnie?"

"If I wasn't here and you didn't know me, you wouldn't be cooped up on vacation in a hotel with bodyguards. Because of me, we can't leave."

"Uncle Steve didn't say we have to stay in the hotel; he said if we go anywhere, the guards must come with us."

"Scotty, I know you. You're too proud to go anywhere with a guard. You'd rather be dead than be babysat."

He laughs. "Well, I don't think of it as being babysat. I think of it as an extra company."

"Extra company?" I say, letting out a little giggle.

"Yeah, I like to hang with a crowd, and guards are the best thing. They make me feel important. Uncle Steve isn't trying to ruin your vacation or make you feel that way. He's trying to protect you and keep you safe. Uncle Steve and I love you so much, Dawnie, and if anything ever happens to you, we'll go crazy."

"Really," I say.

"Really, can we please get out of this closet?"

I laugh and say, "Yeah." We get out of the closet, and the guards are standing around the room. One is at the window, scanning the outside.

"Are you men hungry?" Scotty asks.

The guards look at each other and hesitate before answering. "No, thank you."

"I'll tell you what, how about I order some room service just in case you change your mind."

"That would be great, sir. Thank you," says David.

"No problem at all," Scotty replies.

David is a short, stocky man with salt-and-pepper hair cut in a military style. He's well-kept, and judging by his hands, he gets manicures. David is freshly shaven and has a few scars on his face, nothing scary. Honestly, his facial scars are barely noticeable. I wouldn't have seen them if I wasn't too focused on his face. He's the kind of person you look at and can instantly sense he's lived a life that's not been easy. You can't help but wonder how he's managed to endure; it's written all over him.

Scotty and I get dressed and go out for the day. Scotty is right; bodyguards are cool, especially when they have fashion sense. Everything is calm — we're enjoying ourselves — but I still can't shake the feeling that someone is watching me, even though I can't see them.

"Still feel like someone is watching?" Scotty asks.

"Yes."

"Well, remember, you're a beautiful young lady. That's a great reason why people may be staring at you. They're probably mesmerized by your beauty," he laughs.

"Ha-ha, not funny. I'm serious, Scotty; I feel someone is watching."

"So am I. Look at it like this, they can look at you as long as they want, but you're protected. No one can get close to you without writing their death sentence."

"I hope you're right," I tell him.

"I'm right. Just trust me. We've been through this before," Scotty replies reassuringly. My phone starts buzzing, and I know it's Dad.

"Hey, Dad."

"Hey, how are you and the guys?"

"Good, just shopping."

"That's good. Well, Victoria and I are almost done here. Just wrapping some things up."

"Okay, see you in a bit. Love you."

"Love you, too."

"What did Uncle Steve say?" Scotty asks.

"Nothing. Uncle Steve's just checking on us and telling me he'll be done in a few."

We call it a day and head back to the penthouse. Dad and Victoria are waiting for us in their room. I drop my things off in my room and notice a box on my bed. Not thinking, I go to it and open it, and inside is Tracy's other earring. Without thinking, I scream because this means he knows I've told Dad and Scotty. I have no doubt their lives are in jeopardy because of me.

They all hear me scream, as does the guards. They barge into my room. Dad is ahead of them, Scotty is behind, and there is a note like always. It wouldn't be Earl if there weren't one. I open it and read it, my hands shaking:

THEY CAN'T KEEP ME AWAY FROM YOU! WE WILL BE TOGETHER SOON. I PROMISE.

"I told you this isn't going to stop him!" I yell at them.

"How did he get in without anyone seeing!" Dad demands,

completely dumbfounded by security and very concerned.

"It's Earl! He can do anything. Nothing is impossible for him! All this pisses him the fuck off and only draws him out more. Dad, he's sinister! I'm as good as dead, and so are you guys."

"Watch your mouth. Earl won't get to you or us." Dad says sternly.

"None of the guards stayed at the penthouse when the two went shopping. All of them went with us. We thought the more the guards, the safer they'll be," explains David.

"I understand, but next time, leave some behind so this won't happen again," Dad instructs.

"Yes, sir, I have my men checking the security cameras as we speak."

"Thank you, David. May you please leave us for a while?"

Victoria is taken aback by everything going on. She has yet to really be filled in about Earl. Dad comes to me while I'm crying my heart out in Scotty's arms. He hugs me and shushes me, trying to calm me down. After a while, it works, and I lie on the bed with an ice pack on my head. All my crying gave me a headache. We stay in and order room service, trying to make the best of the situation.

Watching TV is a total epic fail for me and Scotty since we don't know a lick of French. Scotty hops on the computer. I excuse myself and walk out onto the balcony. I have a ton of missed calls and voicemails, all from Damien, around the time I discovered Tracy's earring in my room. I call him because I need to hear his voice. The phone doesn't even complete the first ring before he picks up, "What the fuck, D!"

"Sorry, I couldn't answer the phone, something happened," I tell him.

"I know; that's why I've been calling you like crazy. What happened? Are you okay?" Damien asks frantically.

"Yeah, just spooked a little. I have bodyguards now."

"What! Bodyguards? It's Earl, isn't it?"

"Yes."

"What happened?"

"They know."

"What do you mean? I thought you didn't want them to know because it would cost them their lives?"

"They found out, asked me questions, and knew I was lying."

"What they say?" he insists.

"Well, this morning, I woke up to them both standing in front of me. They asked questions, and I told them the truth. Dad leaves my room and, seconds later, comes back with bodyguards."

"And what did you say?"

"I was mad initially, but they're not that bad."

"What else happened?" he keeps asking.

"Well, umm, remember when I found one of Tracy's earrings in my locker?"

"Oh hell, you found the other one, didn't you?"

"Yeah, in my room, here. I just started screaming, and Dad, Scotty, Victoria, and the bodyguards came running. They're checking security cameras and everything right now. We're staying put because Dad is not letting us go anywhere. He's not saying we can't leave, but he doesn't have to say it."

"Damn, never thought he would get guards," says Damien, shocked by everything I'm telling him.

"Yeah, me neither, and worse, I've been having nightmares every night here."

"Nightmares, your entire trip?"

Damien and I talk for hours about everything. He catches me up on everything in Cali, and I catch him up on everything over here. We haven't talked in ages — at least, that's what it feels like, although we've been texting my entire time here in France. While we're talking, Dad comes out to the balcony. I tell Damien I have to go, and we hang up.

Chapter 35

RUN!

ey, Dad, what's up?"

"Seeing how you're holding up?"

"Okay… I guess. Hell of a day," he says.

"Yeah, well — trust me, I've had worse," I remind him.

"Yeah, I know, and for that, I'm sorry," he says.

"It's okay. I'm starting to get used to it."

"Yeah, but you shouldn't be; you're only fifteen."

"Yes, I am, but others always tell me I look older," I say, smiling.

"And it's no wonder — with everything you've gone through. Hell, most people live to their eighties or nineties and haven't been through as much as you have," he sighs with a light chuckle. I look at him and notice he's acting weird.

"You have a great way of putting things, but what's wrong, Dad?"

"What makes you think something's up?" he responds, raising his right eyebrow.

"The way you're acting, I can sense it."

Instead of looking at me, he turns to the city. "Put to the test to succeed, so all can follow. No one chooses their life or the one that loves them. The life chooses you, and destiny chooses your love. The job is — to accept it." Tears stream down the side of his face.

"Dad, what are you talking about?"

"Don't worry about it. Hopefully, you won't ever find out."

"Won't find out what?"

"The very thing I'm trying to protect you from."

"Who? Earl?"

"Like I said, don't worry about it. Go to sleep. We have a long day ahead of us. You start training again."

"Training again?"

"Yes," he says and kisses me on the forehead. He leaves the balcony, gets Victoria, and they go to their room. When I walk back inside, Scotty is still on the computer.

"Hey, there you are," Scotty says.

"Yeah, I was out here speaking to Damien, then Dad came out to talk to me."

"Oh yeah, and how was that?" he inquires, all interested and wanting to know details.

"Good — until the end, then it became weird."

"Weird? That's a first," Scotty says, looking up from his laptop and removing it from his lap. "How was it weird?"

"Something he said… about the life chooses you and being put to the test to succeed."

"Put to the test? Hmm, sounds like advice, Dawnie," he laughs dismissively.

"Yeah, but not the way he said it."

"Maybe you're overthinking into it. Uncle Steve probably doesn't mean it in any kind of way," he says, trying to make reason out of what I'm telling him.

"I don't know, maybe it wasn't anything." I say to him, thinking aloud.

"Let's sleep on it. I'm tired after today," Scotty says, turning the light off. We fall asleep. I have the same dream again. It happens in the exact same order, but after I open a door and hear the first gunshot, I start running and shooting a gun. Why am I shooting a gun? This is not like me at all. I'm not screaming or scared but full of revenge and anger. Someone is still next to me, but I can't see their face. I'm wearing only a bra and underwear, and so is the other person. Out of nowhere, I discover a door. The person next to me opens it, and I see the light. I wake up from my reoccurring dream to gunfire and shouting. Our room door busts open. The guards are standing at their posts, shooting.

"Run, get her out of here!" someone yells.

Masked men are everywhere — in black combat — private forces style. One of them looks me in the eye. In the middle of all fucking hell, it's like everything goes into slow motion, and our eyes meet. It's not like I found my soul mate. It's an 'I know you from somewhere' slow-motion type moment. The man grins, and someone snatches me and throws me in the closet. I scream at the top of my lungs; Scotty puts his hand over my mouth and tells me to hush.

We get in the back corner of the closet and try to hide behind hanging clothes, but it's not really helping. He holds me, and we cry, crouched down, hoping no one finds us. Scotty tells me it'll be okay, and the guards will protect us, but something tells me they will fail this mission. Still hearing gunshots and screaming, we see several bullets come through the closet door. I jump, and he holds me tighter. "Scotty!" I screech.

"Yes?" he whispers.

"If any..."

"No! Don't even think to say that — nothing's going to happen," he interrupts.

"Okay, okay — I still have to tell you, you're the best brother in the world. You make a way better brother than a boyfriend. After we broke up, I thought of you as my brother. I just want to say... I love you, bro."

"I love you too, sis," he whispers back, tears in his eyes.

Suddenly, the closet door is kicked in, and two masked men enter. Right away, they see us both. My body freezes, too scared to move. Scotty tackles one of the men and wrestles him for his gun. Boom! Scotty drops to the floor. He's been shot. Scotty turns to me, gasping for air, and whispers, "Run!"

I scream, "No!"

Immediately, the other man comes towards me. Without thinking, I do what Scotty says. I run as fast as possible to escape the closet, but someone pulls my hair. I quickly spin around and knee him as hard as I can in the balls. Falling to his knees, he releases my hair to grab his nuts. I charge out of the closet. Gunfire won't stop. Blood and dead men are everywhere. David and Dad are yelling, telling me to run for my life. I run — I run straight into the arms of the enemy. He seizes me with one arm. "Daddy! Scotty!" I kick and scream. Dad sees me, I see him — he's devastated. He starts fighting like hell — like I've never seen before. Dad executes these deadly fighting moves, like in the movies. He's angry and full of revenge, breaking necks and on a stabbing spree.

"Dawnie! Dawnie!" he yells, but it's too late. My capturer thrusts me into the elevator, still gripping my arm with all intensity. He smashes a white cloth over my nose to take me out and put me to sleep, but I bite his hand as hard as I can, tasting his blood. He throws me down to the floor, releasing my arm. He takes his gun and pistol whips me until I black out.

Chapter 36

WAKING UP TO HELL!

I wake up with a bad headache in a dark place. For some reason, it feels like I've been here before. A faucet is dripping, and I hear crying. I listen closely; the crying comes from girls. I look around for signs — where the hell am I? There's nothing but a window — a small one. A basement window! I get up, and a heavy chain is tied to my ankle. I pull it to detach it from whatever else I'm attached to.

"Ouch, what the fuck, dude!" someone yells.

"Who the fuck are you? Where am I?" I yell back.

"You must be a newcomer."

"What? A newcomer to what?"

"This hell!" she shouts back.

"Why are we in hell?" I ask, scared and worried.

"Getting sold."

"What! How is that possible?"

"Shh, lower your voice, or they will beat us. They kidnap us and sell us for sex. We're nothing but their sex slaves."

"Sex slaves?"

"Yeah, they get paid for every man we have sex with."

"But I'm only fifteen!" I reply frantically.

"So am I. The younger — the better. They own us now."

A door opens and slams shut. Someone is speaking in French about something. "Shh, they're coming. Don't speak to them or ask any questions. Don't look them in the eyes, and don't cry," the voice says. I nod my head, as if she could see me.

The light turns on, momentarily blinding us. Men yank us up by our arms and line us up. The blaring light shines on us girls only. The rest of the room remains dark. I notice someone coming from the stairs, but the light near the stairs is very dim. I eye him briefly before he disappears into the darkness. I face the ground quickly before anyone catches me watching.

A man with ear-length black hair, blue eyes, and smooth skin wears Levi's jeans, a white graffiti T-shirt, and a black leather jacket. He gazes at the girls, runs his hands over them, inhales their scent, and smiles as they cry. Speaking softly in French, he inspects them with a disturbing fascination.

He makes his way to me and looks me in the eyes. I look away. He lifts my head slowly and rips my shirt off. He brings his hand up to my face and shows me his bite mark; it has pierced through his smooth skin. This is the guy that grabbed me and put me in the elevator; he's the one I bit and the one that hit me. He sees my necklace, which Damien gave me, and snatches it from my neck. I scream, "No!" The girls gasp in fear of what's going to happen next.

"Please, anything but that!" I get on my knees and take his hand, letting him know I'm begging and not trying to tell him what to do. "Please take anything but that, I beg you," I plead over and over — tears streaming down my face. He yanks me up with his right arm and says something else in French. The girl I'm chained to says something back to him in French in my defense — I think. Men come to us and blindfold us and drag us upstairs. They throw us in a room that looks like an office. We're alone and scared.

"What the fuck were you thinking speaking to him like that?" she asks me.

"Like what? I just want my necklace back," I say, sobbing.

"Is a stupid necklace really that important that you risk your life for it?" she asks while pacing back and forth — wondering what's to come. She's in nothing but her bra and underwear. I pause — thinking really hard before I answer her. But I already know my answer — I always knew the answer to that question. I don't have to think.

"Yes," I reply.

"Yes, what?" she says, forgetting she asked the question.

"Yes! It's important. Someone very special gave it to me."

"I doubt that special someone wants you to kill yourself for it. Who knows what's going to happen to us because of this shit!"

I'm speechless. I feel bad that I've put someone else's life in danger. I think about it more, she didn't have to speak up back there — she could've kept quiet. Why did she say something? Hell, what did she say? She spoke in French. She said something I didn't understand because I don't know French. "What did you say in there?"

"You were there. Didn't you hear?"

"I don't speak French."

"You better learn it if you want to survive in here."

"What did you say?"

"I told him you didn't mean any harm. I asked him to spare your life and begged him to give you the necklace back. I told him it was a special gift from your father before he died, and it's the only thing you have left of him."

"Why?"

"Why, what?"

"Why say that?"

"I don't know, something inside me made me feel like I needed to help you. You're the first person I've spoken to since I was taken. I don't want to be alone."

"How long have you been here?"

"I don't know, lost count," she says.

"My name is Dawn. My family calls me Dawnie."

"Jennifer..." a door opens, interrupting her.

The guy who took my necklace walks in with two other men. My necklace is in his hand — his smile is devilish. He sits at the desk chair, says something in French, and points his finger at the chain linking Jen and me. They cut the chain and remove her from the room. From the doorway, she resists them and screams in French. She shouts, "No!"

I attempt to go after her but am stopped immediately by one of the men. They slam me to the ground. The guy holding Jen puts his hand over her mouth and closes the door. She's gone. My heart drops, and I fear for my life. I stay on the floor and don't move, sobbing nonstop.

"Leave us!"

I don't have to look up to know who's speaking.

Chapter 37

BEING ALONE WITH HIM

He walks up to me slowly, crouches down, and raises my face with one hand. He goes to kiss me, but I move my head away. He laughs and pulls me up by my left arm.

"You speak English?" I ask, still not taking my eyes from the floor.

"I speak a lot of things. English is just one of them," he replies.

"Where did you take her? Please don't hurt her. It's my fault. She was trying to help me. All I…," he puts his hand in the air to silence me.

"We aren't going to hurt her. I just want to be alone with you." I'm scared that the only reason he wants to be alone with me is to teach me a lesson.

"I'm sorry if I made you mad. I really wanted my necklace back — and still do."

Someone walks in and hands him something in a bag. They leave the room. He throws it at my feet. "Open it." Scared to disobey him, I open it and hate what I see — it's lingerie.

"Like it?" he asks.

"Little too old for me, don't you think?" I reply.

"No, not at all."

"Why am I here?" He walks up to me and touches my hair.

"You're a beautiful girl."

"Is that why I'm here?"

"Part of it. Put this on. I want to see it on you."

"Then, will I get my necklace?"

"Maybe. Walk straight that way, and you'll see a bedroom. There is a bathroom; you can change in there and shower." He points to a further part of the room I hadn't noticed.

"Please don't," I beg.

"Don't what?"

"Make me do this."

"Aww, sweetheart, but I haven't even done anything yet. Go do what I just said; I really hate repeating myself." I walk slowly toward where he's pointing; he becomes impatient, grabs me by the arm, and drags me to the bathroom. "I really don't have time for your scary ass right now." He throws me in the bathroom. "Ten minutes and nothing more." I fall to the floor in disbelief. I sit there for several minutes before removing my half-ripped shirt and pajama shorts. The bathroom door opens wide, startling me.

"Ten minutes already?" I ask, shaking from him barging in.

"No, not quite. I hate hearing you cry. Hurry up," he says, handing me a towel and rag.

"I need more than ten…"

He cuts me off, "Fine. But don't take too long; you don't want me getting angry again, do you?"

"No. I don't."

I turn on the shower, and the water runs. I step in, and the water hits me; with soap on the rag, I scrub every part of my body. I get out and put on the lingerie. It's black lace, something nasty ol' Earl would've made me wear when he used to rape me. The door slams open; I don't have to look to see who it is — it's him.

"Come, now!" he demands. He grabs my wrist and yanks me out of the bathroom, looking me up and down. "You're even more beautiful in this." He examines me, from head to toe, for what feels like an eternity. He runs his hand over almost every part of my body. "Tell me how bad you want this necklace back."

"Really bad," I answer, knowing this is the only way to feel closer to Damien.

"Bad enough that you'll do anything for it?"

"For the necklace… yes," knowing what he already wants. He doesn't even have to say it. If my stomach weren't so empty right now, I'd throw up all over. I kiss him on the lips, feeling disgusted.

"Mean it," he says, smirking. He takes off his jacket and shoes and lies on the bed. I walk over to him on the side and get on top of him, giving him another kiss. Catching me off guard, he puts his tongue in my mouth. Eww, gross, it tastes like Earl's filthy mouth, but not as bad. He laughs. He moves me off him and goes to his dresser, where there's liquor. "Here, drink this; trust me, it will help."

"Trust you? That's a hell of a lot coming from someone like you." I say, taking the glass out of his hand, about to drink it. He grabs my hand before it touches my lips. "What?" I ask.

"What's that supposed to mean?" he asks aggressively.

"You killed the only family I know! Don't think I'm clueless about your right hand, and I know you're about to sell me off to the highest bidder," I say, drinking from the cup. It burns going down. I start coughing and hand him the cup.

"Something you'll have to get used to — I guess," he puts the glass back on the dresser. He begins kissing me again, and I sickly return them. "Remember, I said enjoy it — or the deal's off." He gets on top of me, but not inside me yet. He keeps kissing me and rotating his hips. I can feel his manhood getting bigger. He slips on a condom. He's trying to put it in me but is having trouble.

"Ouch, what are you doing!" I yell.

"Trying to put it in. You need to get a little wet for me, sweetheart."

"What?"

"Wet." He looks at me and sees I'm green — clueless and naive. "Never mind, forget it. I know what to do."

"Yeah, sure you do," I say under my breath.

He puts his sordid fingers inside me and moves them around. That's what he means about being wet. Not only am I feeling his gross fingers move around inside me, but I'm also feeling the side effects of the liquor he made me drink. He goes in and out of me twice and won't shut up. He moans loudly. "Oh yeah, you like that," he keeps repeating.

"Oh yeah," I say, repeating it and praying this is soon over.

Time goes by, and he collapses on top of me, breathing heavily. He falls asleep. I have a feeling I'm not allowed to get up. I lie there still — very still, in disgust. I feel like I've cheated on Damien — the only person I want to be with. I want my necklace back; Damien gave me that — it's mine. It's the only way I can feel him with me in this hellhole.

Either way, this guy's going to have me. He's going to get what he wants from me — by force or by choice — his choice, I can tell by how he's acting. He turns over on his side and puts his arm around me. I lie there quietly crying, sickened, and violated by this piece of shit. How can men be like this? Sell girls like they're nothing. There are tons of ways to make money. This is how they choose to make it. The worst! Why don't they sell their own damn selves instead? They love having sex, anyway, so they might as well.

He pulls me in closer, and I feel his nauseating breath on my neck. He kisses my neck and holds me; his body expression tells me he relishes the moment. He snores away. Hours later, he wakes up, yawns loudly, and stretches in bed — taking up all the room. "Sleep well?" he pokes.

"Not at all," I reply.

"C'mon, it couldn't be that bad. You look like you were enjoying it."

"You said to act. Necklace, please." I say, and he throws me the necklace. I catch it, but he takes it out of my hand. I look at him — shocked. "What was that for? I did what you wanted!"

"And — I did what you wanted. I never said you could keep it," he replies; his smile, sinister.

"What do you mean? I said I wanted it back!"

"I don't care what you meant; I did as you asked."

"The hell you did, this is not fair!" I reply, careful not to curse or upset him.

"Sorry to break it to you, but life's not fair," he says manipulatively.

"Please let me keep it. What use is it to you?"

"Tell you what, give yourself to me anytime I want, and I can let you keep your necklace."

"That wasn't the deal," I whine, becoming madder.

"It's the best one you're going to get. Regardless, I'll have you. At least this way, you'll be getting something out of it. Take it or leave it — doesn't matter much to me," he taunts. Tears fill my eyes, and shame fills my body, "Deal."

"That a girl." He throws the necklace back at me. "Get dressed; we both have a long day ahead of us."

We get dressed while this stupid smirk of his never leaves his face. He's holding a bag and something else in the other. I know what they're for; he makes me snort something. It burns like hell. I run over to the trashcan and vomit, and become tired. He puts the bag over my head and sends his men to take me back to where I was before. They chain me. When they leave, I call for Jennifer. I'm so tired. I try to fight the side effects and figure out what's going on with me, but I can't keep my eyes open any longer.

The drug is making me feel so good. I've never felt this good before. Now I know why Tracy became a drug addict. Was this the drug she was on? I get it now. I fall fast asleep. I dream of Damien having a breakdown — mentally and emotionally because I'm not there. He's all alone. I hate this for him. I wake up to Jen nudging me and calling my name. "Jen?" I call out.

"Are you okay?" she answers. I can tell she's worried.

"Yeah, but I feel funny."

"What happened?"

"He made me have sex with him and snort something. I threw up and then became very sleepy."

"Who, Mark?" she says.

"Is that his name?" I ask.

"The guy that ripped your shirt off — yeah, that's Mark... but he's never had sex with any of us before."

"Well, maybe no one you know of down here, but I'm sure he did — they're probably too embarrassed to admit it. What did he give me?"

"No, all the girls talk down here. We whisper to each other and keep each other informed. He must've given you heroin. Every girl down here is on it — including me. They give us meth sometimes too — to keep us awake... and other drugs, but usually heroin and meth."

"First time for everything — I guess. It felt so good," I admit.

"It's weird he only slept with you, Dawn. I mean, I know his brother sleeps with girls here and mostly me — but Mark sleeping with you — there's a reason why."

"Yeah, all for my necklace," I answer.

"Okay, I got to ask. What's up with that necklace?" Jen says, wanting to know more.

"Someone very special gave it to me."

"Can't you get another one?"

"Yeah, but it won't mean anything."

"Did you get it back?"

"Yes, I got it back, but the only way I get to keep it is by fucking him whenever he wants and pretending I enjoy it."

"That's a really messed up deal."

"Tell me about it." I sigh.

"We have to get out of here, Jen."

"Yeah, but how? The only one who can really give us the answer to that is Mark.

"What do you mean?" I ask, leaning in, and wanting to know how.

"Well, watch him. I think he's the leader or something down here."

"So, what you're saying is if we want anything, we'll have to go through him to get it?"

"Exactly," she says.

"I know you hate him and don't want to sleep with him, but you must take one for the team."

"Woo-hoo — lucky me," I say sarcastically.

"Yeah, sorry"

"Jen, did you eat? I'm hungry."

"No, I haven't eaten anything in a few days — they starve us here."

"I hope this works, Jen, because I hate this place, and I hate fucking him. The only person I ever want to be with is Damien. I feel like I've betrayed him."

"Dawn, here, we have no choice. They'll take it from us if we don't do what they say. Believe me, rape is worse than anything."

"If anyone knows — I know. I've been violently raped before, and this is rape too — another sick form of it."

"I agree, same here," Jen replies.

She reaches for my hand to hold, and I reach my hand to meet hers; we hold hands. I don't know what it is about Jen, but I feel connected to her — like she's my sister. Maybe it's because she's a victim, too, or could it be for something else? I'm glad we've met — even in these circumstances. Something tells me I can call her my sister and friend.

We lie down but quickly sit up when the door creaks open. A flashlight shines directly in my face, blinding me. The person holding it steps closer, then switches it off. Crouching down, they hand me some bread and water before leaving without a word. I break the bread and share it with Jen, taking the smaller piece because I know she's been without food longer than I have.

"Thank you," says Jen.

"No problem. We have to stay together, remember."

"Yeah, we do."

Chapter 38

NEW GIRL

I have no idea how long it's been since my kidnapping; it's hard to tell down here. I used to count the number of times I saw sunlight through the small basement window, but they kept giving me heroin. It knocks me out; it controls me, and it leaves me in a state of confusion. I never know if it's the same day whenever they wake me up. They drag us to closed-off rooms to have sex with men and barely feed us — making sure we're too weak to fight back. They mistreat and beat us like animals. I've come to despise men so much from being trapped down here. My heart grows colder and darker.

Every now and again, that bastard, Mark, comes for me to fuck me. He doesn't last long. It takes him two strokes, and he's done. He always wants to cuddle afterward — weird ass, dude. I force myself to pretend to like him only to get information from him when we cuddle. I ask him questions about himself. He answers some questions but is still suspicious and careful about what he tells me. I tell him I'd like to know something about the person I'm sleeping with everyday.

When he sleeps, I lie there and look at the ceiling, daydreaming of home and the day I'll see Damien, Dad, Scotty, Uncle David, Grandpa Sal, and the whole family again. I miss them so much; it hurts. Jen is right. We must find a way out of here. If I steal Mark's heart, will it be the key to our freedom? I never give myself to him entirely during sex. I wonder if he knows I'm faking it. Every time he touches me, I want to regurgitate.

I'll never be able to make love to someone who isn't Damien, but maybe picturing Damien's face on him will work. His touch won't feel like Damien's, but I can fantasize like it is. I miss Damien so much; I can't stand it anymore. I have no idea what to do — I must do something — and quickly if I ever want to leave this place.

I get on top of Mark and start kissing him. I catch him off guard; he opens his eyes, mushes my face back with his hands, and pushes me off him. "What are you doing?" he asks, stunned by my actions — they're out of character for me.

"Whatever I want," I kiss him again, getting back on top of him. He kisses me back, smiling. This is the first time I let him really kiss me. He puts his arms around me, yanks me off of him, and gets on top of me. He shoves himself inside me and starts stroking away. I hate it. I want to beat him until he can't move anymore. But to be free, I must act like I like it. It's the only way I can gain his trust to get out of this shithole. I try hard to imagine Damien's face on Mark's, but it's impossible.

How can I imagine he's Damien? Mark is incapable of ever making love to me. His touch is rough and painful. Damien's touch is gentle and a little rough from boxing and wrestling — but I like that about him. Damien always touched me softly and entered me gently. Damien knew if I didn't like something or if he was being too rough, he'd switch things up quickly to make sure I was always comfortable during our foreplay and lovemaking.

I loved and enjoyed everything Damien did — he was always romantic and felt so good. Mark, on the other hand, knows I hate his sexual maneuvers but does them anyway, like I love them. It strikes me that maybe I can teach him to be gentler or better than he is now. "Mark! Get off of me now." I say, pushing him off.

"What's wrong? Didn't you enjoy it?"

"Fuck no. I feel like I'm fucking a dog. Lie down and shut up," I say while getting on top of Mark.

"Who do you think you're talking to like that?" he snaps, trying to get up.

I push him back down and put my finger to his mouth, telling him, "Shh."

Surprisingly, he listens and lies back down. I grind my hips while on top of him — making sure he can feel me. He closes his eyes and moans in pleasure. I stop. "See, you don't have to fuck like a rabbit to feel something. If you want to turn me on and if you want me to stop faking with you, be a little gentle. You can't even last longer than one to two strokes, and you can't shut up when you're having sex. Do I want to hear, 'Ooh yeah, oh yeah, and you like that?' No, I don't. It gives me a headache and hurts my area." I explain to him.

He looks at me, he's mad as hell. He sits up with me still on top of him and kisses me like never before. He gets on top of me and grinds on me the way I showed him. "Like that?" he asks.

"Yes."

He smiles and kisses me again. I smile, not because I like it, but because I don't hate every second. I smile because I've got him. He's more tender and does not throw me around or hump me like a jackrabbit anymore. He strokes inside me slowly, lasting more than four strokes this time — which is the only bad part because now I have to deal with him for longer. It may not hurt as bad, but him lasting longer means I have to have sex with him longer and work overtime to hide my disgust. I hate my life right now.

It was easier to hide my disdain and revulsion when it was two strokes. Mark knows I hate him. This is just his sadistic way of holding my necklace over my head. If I'm in physical pain, I can't pretend to be with him, no matter how hard I try. I think he's fallen in love with me and has this sick obsession about me — there are too many signs. He finishes, then eyes me suspiciously. I lie on his chest. After a long silence, he finally speaks, "Why?"

"Why, what?" I say, playing dumb.

"Don't play dumb with me. Ever since we've been doing it, you've hated it every time. Now you want to tell me how to move when I do my thing. I don't get it."

"I was thinking to myself about everything. I might not like this place or you, but I'm not leaving anytime soon — I might as well make the best of it."

"Good thinking," he says and plants a kiss on my cheek. Mark finishes with me and sends me back to the basement. They chain me up to Jen, and I lie down on the hard, cold ass concrete floor. All these girls in here make it hot and stuffy. Every time I fall asleep, I have nightmares about Damien being hurt. I can't sleep peacefully without Damien. Something about him relaxes me and keeps all the bad dreams away. I miss my family — I'll never see Scotty again… although something inside me tells me he's alive.

How could he be alive when I saw him die with my own eyes? He died trying to save me, and I did nothing but run. The door opens, and I stop reflecting. They're dragging another girl down here, which is nothing new. We get new girls all the time. They chain us up down here in pairs to the wall. They chain the new girl to me — which is weird because I'm already chained to Jen. We keep quiet while the men do this. They retreat upstairs. When we're confident they're gone, Jen and I start whispering. "Jen, they chained the new girl to me."

"I know, but why? You're already chained to me."

"Exactly. I don't know; maybe they ran out of wall room." The new girl is unconscious like we all were the first time we were kidnapped and brought down.

"Nope, we have lots of room on the wall," Jen whispers back.

"I'll ask Mark next time I see him."

"I doubt he'll even give you an honest answer," says Jen skeptically.

"Yeah, you're right," I agree.

"When she wakes up, we'll ask her questions and see if we can figure anything out about her and why they chained her to us."

Jen and I stop talking. We hear the other girls whispering about the same thing we were talking about. We all talk to each other down here about everything going on, but there are things that Jen and I keep to ourselves. We don't trust all the girls down here. We believe someone is down here pretending to be a victim but is part of the trafficking ring and working along with the men.

The girl finally wakes up; her reaction is similar to mine when I first woke up here. Jen and I calm her down. We try to get to know her. She tells us her name is Theresa Pacsteli. She's from California.

She too is an American that was on a dream vacation in France —
so much for a dream vacation. She was shopping in Paris, and the
next thing she remembers was a rag being put over her nose and
mouth from behind, then a black bag thrown over her head, and
now waking up in this dark, cold basement chained to us. She has an
older sister named Tiara that she was with, but they only knocked
Theresa out and took her. Her sister was able to get away.

Chapter 39

JEN GONE

It's been a while since I've seen Mark. Jen, on the other hand, is very sick. She's vomiting like crazy; the men upstairs don't care. They give her a bucket and tell her to throw up in it. They take her, and something tells me it's not good. I speak up, "Where are you taking her?"

"None of your business!" one of them yells aggressively.

"She's sick and needs a doctor! Where are you taking her?"

"Know your place. Sit down and shut the fuck up!" one of the men yell.

Something comes over me. I don't know what it is. Still chained to Theresa and the wall, I stand up in front of him as close as the chain allows me and yell in his face, "No! I'm telling you to take her to the doctor now!" He whops me hard in the head with the back of his hand and something in it, knocking me out. Later, I wake up alone in Mark's bedroom with a throbbing headache. I hear men talking in the office part of Mark's room. A door closes, and footsteps approach the bedroom. It's Mark.

"Where's Jen?" I ask him.

"Well, hello to you too. How was your day, Mark? Well, it was quite fucked up because some dumb bitch wanted to talk out of turn," he snidely replies.

"Says the man in charge of all this, who isn't the one waking up with a headache. Would you like to know how my day was? Oh wait, I don't know since I've been knocked out for the entire day. But then again, I don't know what day it is because I've been in a fucking cage with no windows and only a tiny crack of daylight shining through. Not to mention the men I have to fuck against my will and no hope I'll ever get out of this hellhole. I've been chained to a wall and a girl that I don't know whether she's dead or alive. Shit. I can't even eat because no one gives me fucking food. I have no freedom, and everything and everyone I've ever loved has been taken away from me. It all happened in a blink of an eye without so much as a fucking warning! And — now, I have a headache from probably the back of a gun because I was worried about my best friend that I may never see again. So, sorry if I don't give a fuck about your day — Mark. No, actually, I'm not sorry, you piece of shit — you're a sorry excuse of a man. Where is Jen, and what's wrong with her?" I demand while spiraling, breathing hard, angry, and fed up.

He stares at me in response for several minutes. His arms folded with no expression — a stoic look and brash demeanor. "Hey, we feed you, and it's not even that bad. What's the difference between a girl having sex for free versus for money?"

I'm shocked by Mark's response. The sick part is that he actually believes himself. "Wow, is that what you tell yourself so you can sleep at night? You feed us when you remember to, which is not that often. The bread is old and moldy with a spit of water. The difference is a girl has sex for free with a man she cares for and loves. But in this place, girls are made to be sex slaves to men and watch others get rich off them for selling us girls to them. We girls lost our families when we were put here, but we also lost our faith here. We lose our pride, dignity, honor, respect, happiness, freedom, and most importantly, ourselves." I tell him.

He hands me a glass of water and two pills. "What's this?"

"Advil and water to help with the headache. I'm sorry you feel that way," says Mark.

"No — you're not."

"Yes, I am."

"Don't be sorry, just let us go."

"I can't."

"Then, you're not sorry. You just want me to believe you are. You enjoy this as much as I hate this, and if not more." I get up, snatch his bottle of brandy, and go to the bathroom.

"What are you doing?

"What does it look like?" I open the cabinets and find a bottle of pills. Jen is dead, and if not, on her way to being dead. I'm never going to see my family or Damien again. I'm going to die here. Why not die now by overdosing? It's better than dying a sex slave — I probably won't feel it. I remember overhearing Dad say one time that drinking on an empty stomach is dangerous. My stomach is beyond empty. I shove the pills in my mouth and wash them down with brandy. I choke at the burning sensation in the back of my throat.

Mark bangs on the door, demanding I come out. I don't answer him. I continue doing what I'm doing. He kicks open the door. I try to put another in my mouth, but he grabs it and takes it from me. I try to fight him off of me, but he's way stronger than me. He puts me on the bed, looking scared and worried; he yells, "How many did you take!"

Waiting for the side effects to kick in, "Hopefully enough to get away from you," I say and spit in his face. I lie on the bed, waiting for everything to start working. My head is pounding, and everything is getting fuzzy. I feel like I'm spinning. I'm shaking; I'm dizzy. The pills are about to put me out. I have no energy to fight it — I lie there slipping — waiting for my demise.

"You really are your mother's child," a voice says that isn't Mark's. "Dawnie, I love you; please don't leave me," Mark cries. I try to look at the other person in the room, but my eyes shut, and I drift away.

I start to dream of Damien — it's a nightmare. He's fighting, but not in a boxing match. He's fighting for a way out. He's trapped in a dark place and chained. Men are kicking and punching him and laughing. My nightmare shifts to the one I had during the Paris vacation. I'm in a dark, small place. There are three dead bodies. I take one of their guns and go upstairs. Someone's behind me — I still can't see their face or faces. Next, I'm in a kitchen, and looking through a window full of light, I hear gunfire. I run to the door, and it opens.

A bright light is shining, blinding me almost. This must be the light to heaven, but it isn't. It's the light right back to hell. I wake up in Mark's bed. I'm so mad I start screaming and destroying the room, hoping they'll get so angry and shoot me between the eyes, ending my misery once and for all.

Why didn't the drugs work? I took so many — I lost count with the brandy! I should be dead, not alive. I see Mark at his desk, looking absent-minded. He's staring at the mirror on the wall across the room. He's been crying and hasn't had any sleep. He's pale like death and has dark circles around his eyes. I take something and smash it — getting his attention. "What did you do? Why did you save me?" I shout and cry angrily.

"Hell, I thought I lost you."

"Can't lose something that was never yours."

"You passed out on the bed, and I got a doctor. He pumped your stomach and went on his way."

"You men have a doctor?" I screech — unbelievable!

"We have everything for you girls' safety," Mark replies proudly.

"How nice of you guys to act like you care a little," I say cynically.

I start making my way to the bedroom, and he grabs my wrist and pulls me onto his lap, "What the hell was that about today?"

"I don't know."

"What do you mean you don't know? I thought I was going to lose you until the doctor came and confirmed that you were going to be okay. Do you know what I've been going through these past couple of days?" he vents.

"Not as much as I've been going through as long as I've been here. I want to go home to my family. I can't take this anymore, sleeping with stranger after stranger and not being able to go outside and smell fresh air. Having to do the things I hate to stay alive, and you keep the only thing I have left that reminds me of home," I say, breaking down. I look into his eyes, as much as I hate begging, I have to today. "Please, Mark, I beg you — please. Let Jen and me go. I promise we will not tell anyone about this. Please, I beg you. I'll do anything."

He looks at me with glossy eyes, "No, I can't."

"Yes, you can. You just don't want to. You said you loved me. You won't let me go through this if you love me. You know how much it hurts me. Please, Mark, please."

"No! I can't let you go, but maybe someday you might understand my feelings towards you. You're too young to understand everything right now, Dawnie, but someday you will. I do love you. You're the only girl I've ever loved. That's why I'm doing this." His response cuts deep like a knife in my back. I fall on the floor, weeping in distress. I'm never leaving this hell hole. I'm going to be here as long as I'm alive. I'll never get to see Damien and my family again, and Scotty's dead because he was killed in front of me by Mark's guys. "Dawnie, baby, do you hear me?" he asks, holding my face in his hands.

"Don't call me that. Don't you ever call me that! My family are the only ones who call me that, and you're not one of them," I instruct him. He looks at me; he's hurt, but I don't care. I want him to hurt as much as I hurt, but no matter how much he's hurting, he'll never hurt as much as I do, not even close to as much as I hurt.

He walks to the door, "I'm sorry you feel that way. You'll be staying in here until you're better. There are no drugs for you to take, so I don't have to worry about you trying to kill yourself again."

"Where's Jennifer?" I ask quickly before he leaves.

He looks at me again and says, "Gone." Something inside me tells me he's hiding something, and she's hurt.

I run to the door and bang on it as hard as I can, yelling after him, "Where is she? What did you do to her?" He doesn't answer me. He keeps on going to wherever he's going. I'm left in this room by myself until he comes back. Questions fill my mind. Is Jen alive? What does he mean she's gone? Why is she gone? What happened to her? Did she overdose? Will I ever see her again? How can I survive without her? She's the only reason I've made it this long. What am I going to do now? Is that why that girl was chained to us? Is she going to be the next person I'm chained to? I can't believe Jen is gone.

Chapter 40

IMPOSSIBLE

It's been days since I've seen or heard anything about Jen. Mark's been keeping his windows uncovered so I can see if it's day or night — it's not much of a view, but at least it's a view. Mark forbids me from asking or talking about Jen. I refused to listen one time before and asked about her anyway. He smacked the shit out of me. Mark had never hit me until then — I felt it for days. He only used to yank me by my arm, but this time, he manhandles me and lets his men get their licks in, too. I don't know why I'm so shocked — he's the head of a human trafficking ring, so I really shouldn't be surprised — probably my naïveté.

Mark has a TV placed in the room to keep me occupied and has salads brought for me to eat; it's no longer the stale bread and dirty water they usually give me and the other girls. Mark and his men continue doping me up on heroin — it keeps me tired, often sleeping for hours. I've become very addicted to heroin; I need a hit every day. They purposely keep me drugged up so I'll stay tired and not try to kill myself — how selfish of them.

One thing's for sure, I'm still in France — at least, I think it's because the TV channels are in French. Mark sits next to me in the bedroom and watches TV with me sometimes, but that's only when he's high himself. He sleeps next to me every night. Sometimes, he's up for days at a time until he crashes hard — he sleeps for days, it seems. Heroin is taking its toll on him — he's more addicted than me. He wears long sleeves to hide his arms. The long sleeves keep him from picking at his arms — he keeps saying they're bugs in his flesh, and he needs to get them out.

Karma is catching up to him; he's slowly going crazy. He has the worst mood swings I've ever witnessed before, constantly pacing back and forth. From what Jen told me before, he's also on meth. In his own sick, twisted world, he thinks he's making love to me every time he fixes himself to get on top of me. I hate him next to me, and I hate him inside of me. I wish my vagina had teeth and could bite his dick off. Unfortunately, I have no choice but to deal with him and pretend I like it. I don't need him smacking the shit out of me again — so I live with it.

I haven't been sent to sleep with any other men since my suicide attempt. This is a good thing, but you can never tell with these people. What you may think is good is bad, and what you think is bad is good. That's the life of this dark underworld. What you think is the worst day of your life is really the best day of your life, and what you think is the best day of your life is probably your last. I live here in fear and false hope. It's a sick, demented, and evil place. I hate it here; I hate my life.

"I'm going to be away for a day or two. I have some business I must attend out of the state," Mark tells me.

"More little girls to snatch dreams away from?" I blurt out, knowing this is probably the case.

"Don't be like that, love. You have everything you need; food will be brought to you. Got to go — bye," he says, kissing me and leaving the room.

Like always, I'm by myself. I decide to watch TV. I turn the captions on to read what they're saying in English. I flick through the channels and find something that looks good on the Lifetime channel. In the movie, a girl is rummaging through a desk for something. It hits me. Mark's desk is just outside this room, and there's no one here but me. Maybe there's a cell phone in his desk, and I can call Dad!

They have me high on drugs, but I still want to escape — that's how bad it is. I'm so determined to get far and away from here — I think I'm becoming a functioning addict. I can't say the same for Tracy. She was never this motivated for anything but another needle in the arm. She was motivated by staying high and not her freedom from addiction.

Once I get out of here, Dad can put me in rehab, and I won't have to worry about being addicted to drugs anymore. They hit me earlier today, but the high has come and gone — it wears off so quickly now because my body is used to it. I've been keeping my cool, so they won't need to give me another hit. I need to stay sober-minded. For the last several days, I've been acting like I'm high and out of it so I can eavesdrop. I've got to find a way out.

The desk is locked — I'm not surprised. But Mark is less than smart. He'll have a key close by. I'm right. I find a key under the flowerpot in the room. I unlock the desk drawers and search through them, finding nothing but worthless files and a book titled *Victimology.* I open the book and read several pages.

I figure out why Mark's been acting the way he has lately by giving me things like a window view, salads, and a TV. He's trying to make me fall in love with him. It'll never happen. The book reveals how victims get attached to their capturers. It's clear Mark's sick idea is to keep me imprisoned while treating me nicely, and eventually, I'll fall in love with him. What a sicko.

I find another book. Its title is *Psychology.* Then, another book catches my eye. It's an English-to-French dictionary. Why would Mark have a French translation dictionary if born and raised in France? Isn't French his first language? It makes no sense. Maybe it's for me, but he hasn't given it yet.

Mark said he would be away for a day or two, so he'll be away for at least two days. I've caught on to how he speaks and what it means. He never gives approximates when talking to me, but I've been picking up on some of his patterns. I have exactly two days to read and memorize these two books. I start reading the books and hide them whenever one of Mark's henchmen comes in to check on me or bring a salad. I learn a lot. What interests me is that victims fall for their predators, and they stay in their captivity, ultimately believing this is the life for them. I keep reading — this is some psychological bullshit the victims fall for. I won't be Mark's victim. I won't be anyone's victim. All I have to do with Mark is make him think his little psychotic game on me is working.

I sneak the books back into the desk drawer, lock it, and put the key back under the flowerpot. When Mark returns, I'll make him think I love him. Fingers crossed, I'm hoping my plan works well and he starts taking me out — I'll escape that way. But one thing is for sure — I can't leave without Jen. She must escape with me.

I don't know how to pretend to love someone. One thing I'm not is fake. Thank God for TV — it's teaching me how. I understood some words after watching French TV, but not much. I wonder exactly when Mark is going to give me the dictionary.

Mark's back! He returns with a box in his hand. The box is nicely gift-wrapped, too. He tosses it on the bed. "Open it," he insists.

"What is it?"

"Just open it and see," he smiles. I open it. What's inside catches me off guard. Although Mark is the devil's son, he does have good taste in clothes. It's a satin white dress with a silky-like feel. It's been so long since I've received a gift or anything; it feels good.

"I love it, thank you," I say, kissing him. I give him a real kiss — one where he'll feel the difference from before. It's not the fake one I've always given him — for God knows how long. It's my real-real fake one — like I've seen the actors do on TV. I surprise him. He's pleasantly caught off guard. I giggle at his reaction and toy with him. He tells me to try it on. When I come out of the bathroom with it on, a lady with many hair tools is waiting for me.

"What's this?" I ask, confused.

"Mr. Mark wants me to tend to your hair."

"Who?" I laugh.

"Me. We're going out tonight, Dawn," Mark butts in.

"We are? To where?"

"Don't worry about it."

"I don't have shoes."

"You will after your hair is done. They're on their way over."

Getting my hair done is nice for once. She straightens it beautifully for me. Mark brings me designer black heels. I'm at a loss to understand what he's up to, but whatever it is, I'm happy. It means

I'm getting closer and closer to my exit strategy. Nonetheless, I'm also impressed with the pampering I'm receiving. I can't believe I finally get to get out of here and smell fresh air — maybe even escape. He places a blindfold over my eyes and walks me outside to the car. After a while of driving, I beg him to let me take the blindfold off. He caves in, unties it from the back, and removes it from my face. I gasp in awe. I see France, streets, cars, people, the sunset. I see everything I've been missing in life. "Thank you, Mark."

"You're welcome — where we're going, you can't scream, and you can't run. If you do, there will be nothing I can do to help you or your family," he warns firmly.

"What does my family have to do with this?"

"Everything. If you mess up, ever — someone from the family pays the price — keeps the girls in check. I'm putting my ass on the line taking you out after what you did. Don't make me regret it."

"Okay, I won't," I say, still thinking in the back of my mind a master plan.

"Good," he pulls me close to him. I'm so relieved to leave the sex slave dungeon; it takes a while for me to register that we're riding in a limo. Mirrors are all around. The seats are black leather, there's wine, snacks, and a TV. It reminds me of Brittany's limo, but Brittany's was bigger. We arrive at a huge building and go inside. It's a restaurant. I can't remember the last time I've been to a restaurant or been in the real world. This is a small taste of freedom for me — yet controlled by Mark and his sex trafficking organization. I'm convinced — maybe my complete freedom is near after all.

We sit down; I can't read anything on the menu. All my studying of Mark's dictionary suddenly becomes mentally overwhelming. I haven't entirely memorized it yet. I still have to keep learning. My French is still at the beginner level if that is correct. I have a long way to go before I can read and understand a menu in French. I must continue to act as if I know nothing when I'm around Mark, or he'll suspect something's up. Mark translates the menu for me.

Our table is lovely; we talk the entire time. I've hated Mark so much, and for so long, I've never cared enough to get to know him beyond trying to collect information from him when lying in bed —

which always led to much of nothing anyway. However, today, Mark is opening up to me. It feels nice to learn about him beyond forcing his thing on me. He's a real comedian and knows a lot of people. He's a lot smarter than I thought he was. "Mark?"

"Yeah?"

"Why?"

"Why what, Dawn?"

"Why do this job — you can be so much more?"

Stunned by my question, Mark replies, "Geez, I don't know. Probably because it's the family business, I guess. It was promised to me when I was younger."

"Promised?" I repeat, puzzled, and taking a sip of water.

"Yeah, my father and his brother started it. They passed it down to the next generation — me," he begins gulping his glass of red wine.

"Did you ever want to do anything else?"

"Yes."

"What did you want to be?"

"A special agent for the government."

"But you couldn't — because of all this?"

"Right. The only thing I ever wanted to do in life — I can't. I hate this job so much."

"So, why don't you leave?"

He chuckles sarcastically. "Sweetheart, this is not a job you can just quit. The only way out is death or to hand it down, and there's no one else to hand it to."

"I'm sorry," I tell him.

"Yeah, you see, you and I aren't so different after all," he says, finishing his wine and raising his hand for another glass. I begin to feel bad for Mark. He never wanted this life — he was forced. He doesn't want to sell girls; he has to! He's trapped in his family's business. Of all people, I know how it feels to be trapped. I'm trapped in this life, too, and so far, there's no way of getting out. I was also trapped in Earl's world until Tracy met Dad and got away — at least, we thought. We finish our food, and I have to go to the bathroom. Mark threatens me, and reminds me of every reason why I better not try to escape.

As much as I want to leave, now is not a good time to try. Mark's men clear the bathroom out to ensure no one is there when I go. I walk out of the stall to the sink and overhear two men having a conversation. The bathroom walls are very thin; I figure out what they say. One of the voices is Mark's, and the other's is a man with a very strong French accent — I'm not sure who he is — he doesn't sound like any of Mark's guys. Mark has spoken in French to everyone all evening except me but talks to this guy in English. Interesting, Mark told me no one he knows here speaks English — but this guy does. "Mark, how is everything?"

"Fine, Jeremiah, thank you," replies Mark. I remember Mark speaking to Jeremiah. He's the owner of the restaurant.

"No problem, it was my pleasure," says Jeremiah.

"I hope you're going to the ball we're having Friday. The best people in France will be there."

"I wouldn't miss it for the world. That's a fine young lady you have tonight."

"Well, you know me, I only hang with the best."

"Yes, sir, you always do. Your bill is taken care of." Jeremiah responds graciously.

"Thank you," says Mark.

"Will my order be there waiting for me?" Jeremiah asks.

"Yes, it will. Thank you again, Jeremiah. See you Friday."

"And same to you."

Mark never tells me about a ball on Friday, but then again, Mark never tells me anything. Hell — Mark's never taken me out of Satan's pit of hell until today — an odd move for him. Jeremiah has to be one of Mark's clients because he wouldn't be asking about an order if he wasn't. The only thing anyone ever orders from Mark is women. I walk out of the bathroom and to the table. Mark's mob follows me. We get back in the limo, and I'm blindfolded again. Not much later, I'm back to imprisonment. He goes to his desk. There's nothing on top of it. I follow him and sit on the desk's edge, staring off, reflecting on the events of the evening. I turn to look at him. I take off my shoes, and in my peripheral, I see Mark looking at me out the corner of his eye.

"What are you doing, Dawn?"

"Nothing, just sitting here watching you," I tell him, his face full of suspicion.

"What? I can't watch you work?" I say, knowing I don't care.

"Dawn, you never watch me work. You always stay in the bedroom watching TV."

"And you've never been this nice to me or taken me out before, but you did today."

"Oh, you want to know why I took you out today, is that it?" he inquires, smirking.

"Yes, well, it crossed my mind many times."

"Believe it or not, I listened to what you said. You were right about everything. Unfortunately, I can't help every girl here because it's too dangerous, but I can at least help you. All I care about is you, Dawn. I don't want anything to happen to you. I've said it before and I'll say it again — a hundred times if I need to; I love you, Dawn Trieger." Mark gets closer to me, pulls me in and onto his lap, and begins kissing my face all over. I watch him closely. Mark is in love with me. But the thing is, men like Mark don't fall in love, and they don't know what love is.

"Impossible, Mark," I say, hopping off his lap. I walk towards the bedroom. Something shatters from behind, scaring me like crazy. I turn around to Mark, who is charging towards me. I turn back around to run to the bathroom. Mark grabs me by the arm and yanks me in front of him. He's yelling — he's pissed. I start screaming, "Get off of me!" but he doesn't. Instead, he shakes me senselessly.

"Are you serious right now? I just poured my heart out to you, and you tell me it's impossible. How dare you!" Mark berates, shouting from the top of his lungs. I'm scared out of my mind, he's going to beat me to death.

My mouth opens, and I start spewing, "It's impossible! I'm not a person someone should love. Something always happens to me or them. I'm not meant to be loved or be in love. I swear it's not safe — you can't love me. You just can't. It's impossible!" We stand, not taking our eyes off each other. He loosens his grip on me, and we fall to the floor. What just came out of my mouth is the truth. I've always known this about myself, but never owned it. I'm not meant to be loved, and I'm not meant to be in love. It's not only me thinking Mark is incapable of love, but it's also me not being able to be loved. It's unsafe for anyone around me to love me or for me to love them, including myself.

"No, Dawn — no! This won't happen to us, I swear," Mark pleads.

"Yes, it will. It always happens. Every single person I've ever cared about is gone. I'm supposed to be alone. I'm supposed to be with no one."

"No, you're not. Nothing is going to happen, Dawn, I promise."

"You can't promise that. You have no idea what has happened in my past. It always finds me and chases me in full speed."

"Trust me, I know more than you think," Mark replies assertively.

"No, you don't, Mark. You don't know about one specific person — Earl. He'll come after you." I say, warning him. A peculiar expression surfaces Mark's face when I mention Earl's name.

"No, he won't. He won't take you away from me. Nothing can keep you away from me. I promise you that," Mark says without flinching.

"How can you be so sure?"

"I just am. You're my girl and not anyone else's," he urges while kissing me, and me kissing him back. I hate kissing him, but he took me out to dinner today. I did get a glimpse of France once more. I did get to see regular people, breathe fresh air, and learn some personal information about Mark and his family. Maybe I hate kissing him a little less for today and today only. But I'll never love Mark like I love my Damien. I mean, how could I?

For the first time in a while, I begin sitting with the thought that I'll never see Damien again. I'm never going to get out of this hell. Whether I like it or not, this is my life — I'm now Mark's. To make my life better, the only thing I can do is accept it. My hope for leaving this place is only a false hope. He said to himself at the restaurant that he would kill my family. I love my family so much that whether I see them again or not, I don't want them to die because of me. The only thing I have is myself and Mark, and he's not taking no for an answer.

I wrap my mind around the fact that Mark has changed. He gave me a beautiful dress and brand-new shoes and took me out for an exquisite dinner. Never in a million years would I have thought Mark would've done something like this for me. We kiss intently. He picks me up and carries me over to the bed. We have sex. I don't enjoy it, but I don't hate it as much. Nothing will ever be as good as Damien. I love Damien. I don't love Mark. I have no choice but to be with Mark — I'll make the best of it. My life in America is over forever. When he's done with me. Mark goes to his nightstand and pulls out a clear baggie with white powder. He makes me snort it; he snorts it too. It takes me out right away.

Chapter 41

THE BALL

Everything with Mark has been going quite well lately. A part of me is a little worried because when things are going well, it often means something is about to go wrong. He's been taking me out with him a lot. It's only out to eat, but it's better than being locked up in this place and going nowhere. He's revealed that he's taking me to the ball, and I must say, I'm excited about it. It'll be a change of scenery and a chance for me to possibly interact with other people who are free in the world.

He's arranged for the hairstylist to do my hair and buys me a lovely dress and shoes to go with it. Just like every other time, he blindfolds me when we leave and takes it off when we're close to the destination. I can tell Mark is horny because he keeps on kissing and touching me all over. Ever since the night he poured his heart out to me, he wants it more and more. I don't care for it, but if it makes him happy, I'll do it to keep things as peaceful and convenient for me as possible.

"Mark, c'mon, stop it. Not now."

"C'mon, why not?"

"We're almost there."

"No, we aren't. I told my driver to take the long way."

"You'll mess up my hair."

"I won't, I promise, c'mon," he says, undoing his pants.

One thing I know about Mark very well is that he doesn't like the word "no." The word "no," to him, doesn't exist. When you say "no" to him, he ignores it and does what he wants anyway. He gets on top of me and goes inside of me. He holds my hair and says, "I love you." He holds me tight and works his way deeper inside me and says, "Tell me you love me." As much as I don't want to, I know I have to say it. If I don't, I'll undoubtedly feel his wrath — it's never good.

I tell him what he wants to hear, "I love you." Of course, I don't mean it. I only mean it when I say it to Damien. Out of fear, I pretend to love Mark. Fear that if I don't, he'll hurt or kill me and my family. He'll even throw me back in that dark basement. At least when I tell him I love him, he believes me — keeping me and my family out of the danger zone.

He finishes and kisses me. I look in the mirror to make sure my hair is okay. He sticks to his word, not messing it up. We arrive at a huge mansion. It's beautiful. It's bigger than my house and Brittany's put together. "Wow!" My mouth hangs wide open.

"You like it?"

"Yes, it's beautiful."

"Only the best for you, love."

"Thank you."

Mark makes me snort something before we get out of the limo. It kicks me instantly, and I perk up. The limo drops us off at the front, and a man opens the door for us. We get out of the limo and head for the door. There are many people, but not too many — it's not crowded. The inside — prettier than the outside. It takes my breath away. There are many men, so many, they outnumber all the girls. I look around and notice that many men look very familiar, but I can't put it together. Most girls look tired and scared but are also jittery — they can't keep still. It's making me question what kind of ball this is.

"Hey, Mark."

"Yeah?"

"What kind of ball is this?"

"Umm, it's so everyone can get to know each other. It's how people make friends around here and stuff."

"Oh, okay, then what's wrong with the girls over there?"

"What do you mean?"

"They look jittery and sick, and I can tell they haven't slept in a while."

"Drugs, it's a big thing in France for women. It makes them look and feel younger, they say."

"Well, they lied." he chuckles to himself, and we start walking, only to be stopped by one of his friends. They're speaking in French. I have no idea what they're saying. I know a little French, but not much, especially when someone speaks it fast.

"Hey, sweetie, I'll be right back. I have to handle something real fast."

"Is everything okay?"

"Yeah, just some confusion going on." He walks away, and I turn in another direction to get something to drink. In the corner of my eye, I see someone walking towards me. It's one of the girls when I fully turn around to face her. It's Elizabeth, Uncle Brian, and Aunt Aileen's daughter! She looks so different from the drugs; I barely recognize her.

"Act like you don't know me," she whispers.

"Hey, how are you?" I say, following her instructions.

"Hey," she says in English, with a strong Irish accent. I began to notice that most women here are American and Irish.

"Yes?" I say.

"So, I see you're here with Mark."

"Yes, I am."

"Hmm, that's interesting."

"How so?" I reply while getting a drink off a server's tray walking by.

"Sweetheart, it's Mark. He doesn't even look at us girls for more than a second. What makes you so different?"

"I don't know," taking a sip of my champagne, hoping she would stop talking to me like a stranger. We casually walk away from the others to speak in private.

"Where did he take you from?" she asks; I start choking on my drink.

"Excuse me?" I say, giving her attitude, unsure how to answer her.

"Sweetheart, every girl here is getting paid for. If there's anything we all have in common, we're all price tags and property. What do you think the ball is for?" I give her a blank stare. She realizes quickly that I have no idea what the ball is for.

"You thought he was being nice to you? This is a sex ball — for high-class whores. We get showered and groomed — our price is higher. The men here are going to buy and have us. It's better than being in a dark basement — I guess." I look around; she's not lying. No wonder Mark is being so nice and dressed me up. I thought he loved me and was taking me to see his friends and family. But no — it's for his sick business so he can meet more high-class clients — the ones that'll pay way more than those that swing by the basement. I hate his nefarious ass!

While Elizabeth is still talking, I walk away quickly, not wanting to cry in front of her. I'm not trying to be rude, but she caught me off guard. I walk onto an empty balcony — no one's around — and cry. I feel so played. Why didn't I see this was a setup? Mark must've given me meth in the limo. I can't stand or sit still. I pace back and forth on the balcony, talking to myself. I'm sure I look completely insane, but I'm too out of it to care. What the hell is Elizabeth doing here? What the hell was she trying to pull off? It was really bitchy of her to do that. "Are you okay?" a voice says, interrupting my thoughts. I step back, surprised that someone is here with me.

"Sorry, I thought I was alone," I say, feeling embarrassed. I head towards the door to leave.

"No, it's okay; stay," says the familiar voice. It's Jeremiah! — The owner of the restaurant, Mark, always takes me to!

"Do you remember me?" I nod my head yes.

"Who am I?" he asks, getting too close for comfort.

"Jeremiah. You own the restaurant Mark takes me to."

"Yes, you're right. You know he promised me something-something I've been looking forward to for quite some time now. I've been very patient waiting for it... the only thing paying for his food at my restaurant."

I'm confused by what Jeremiah is saying, and I also can tell he's drunk. With the drugs in my system, I can't stand still here talking to him anymore. "Well, you must take that up with him. I don't know what he promised you," I say, walking away, but the man grabs my arm.

"He showed me you when you walked into my restaurant. He promised me you."

"No, impossible, he wouldn't."

"Oh, but he did. Why do you think you're here? — to cater to my needs, of course," answering his own question.

"No, you have me confused with someone else."

"No, not at all." Someone walks onto the balcony. It's one of Mark's guards, Alejandro.

"Excuse us, sir, I have to talk to her." Alejandro grabs my arm, pulls me into the room out of Jeremiah's eyesight, and slams me into the wall.

"What the fuck are you doing?" he demands.

"What is that guy talking about? Mark wouldn't promise me to someone else — he loves me," I explain.

"Yeah, yeah. Look, you're here for that man over there for one reason. You'll go over there and make him happy. Do what he says, or you're in big trouble."

"So, he's right? Mark promised me to him?"

"Go over there now!" Mark's henchman instructs, brandishing his gun. Tears trickle down, and my enforcer gives me a threatening look. I wipe my tears from my face and go back onto the balcony. Jeremiah is lying down on the recliner chair. While I'm walking up to him, I start taking note of what he looks like. White skin, clean cut, short haircut, brown eyes, straight white teeth, soft hands, no callouses, and wears a cross around his neck. I get on top of him. He has his way with me. During the whole ordeal, I hold back my tears. I swear I hate this shit! I hate Mark most of all. How can he say he loves me, then tell someone they can have me? Jeremiah finishes and exits the balcony, leaving me there.

After he leaves, I bawl my eyes out. How could I be so stupid and trust Mark? I sit there and think about how stupid I am. Moments later, I hear someone moaning in pleasure. It sounds like Mark. To make sure, I follow the noises. It's coming from the other side of the room. I peek inside the room. A girl is on her knees performing oral sex on a man — what do you know, it's the one and only Mark.

I swing the door wide open so he can see me. He does. "What the fuck, Mark!"

"Oh shit," he says and doesn't move. He keeps his hand on the girl's head, directing it to keep moving up and down and not to stop. "Get out!" he yells.

"With pleasure," I slam the door and storm downstairs to where everyone else is. I want to go outside, but they'll probably think I'm trying to run away if I do. I go to the bathroom instead. It's empty, and I'm glad it is. I've never experienced anything like that, not even with Scotty when we broke up. Yeah, Scotty was fucking that blonde bitch, but he ran after me when he saw me catching him in the act. The only reason he went back upstairs was out of pure jealousy. Besides, Scotty, especially not Damien, would never say they love me, then sell me to someone else. When they said it, they meant it. They're not the type to share their girl.

I miss Damien so much. I miss my family, too, but I miss Damien the most. The way he used to treat me and kiss me, even when we made love. He never hurt me. He always made me feel like I was important. I've never felt important here — only used and abused. Last week, for a moment — I think it was last week, I felt important, but that was that monster, Mark, buttering me up for today. I can't believe I'm Mark's high-class whore, and nothing more.

The door opens, and a man with a girl walks in. The man is smiling ear to ear like it's his first time having sex. The girl is faking her smile because we know we don't want to be here. The man is much older, with salt and pepper hair and tanned skin. He has to be from America because he speaks English without an accent. Disgusted, I walk out of the bathroom and am spotted by Mark. He rushes over, grabs me by the arm, and directs me to our seats. I snatch my arm out of his grip and grab a drink before I sit down.

"Enjoying yourself?" he asks.

"If you call fucking Jeremiah fun! — a warning would've been nice," I reply, a little loudly.

"I thought you'd like the surprise more," says Mark, smirking.

"Fuck you, Mark."

"I thought you already did love."

"Fuck you, Mark. You don't love me. You said all that shit to make me comfortable and less resistant." he scoffs, takes a sip of champagne, and gets up from the table.

"Follow me. I have to show you something."

Knowing this is not my choice, I follow him — dozens of eyes on us. I realize we have a mini audience. I'm so mad at Mark. He walks until he knows no one can see us, turns around, smacks me in the face, grabs my hair, and slams me into the wall. "Don't you ever speak to me like that, especially when people are around? Know your place and the reason you're here! Do you understand me?"

"Okay," I reply, staring into his soulless eyes and not giving him the pleasure of seeing me cry this time. He forces a kiss on me. I push him away. He disgusts me.

"I love you to death. I promise you that," he utters, walking away, leaving me. I fall to the floor. My tears are unstoppable. I sit here for a while, and when I look up, Elizabeth approaches me. I wipe my tears quickly, stand up, and try to fix my dress.

"There's no need to hide your tears from me," she says, hugging me.

"I can't believe I was so dumb," I say, wailing.

"Every girl here has been in your predicament once, including me. We've learned to accept it."

"Accept it? — I keep telling myself that, but I can't bring myself to do that."

"Look, we're stuck in this life; leaving here is not an option. Whether we like it or not, this life is our present and future. There's no escaping it. We can kick and scream all we want, but we're never leaving this life. Not all of us choose the life we live — it's sometimes chosen for us," she says, still holding me.

"Is that how you made it this far — thinking like this?" I sob.

"Sadly, yes. No matter how much I hate it, I had to accept it."

"And — what was that earlier — that stunt you pulled? Pretty fucking cruel of you, Elizabeth."

"I had to. I do it to every girl. It's expected of me. They would've suspected something was up if I hadn't did it to you."

"Oh, okay, you're forgiven," I say, slightly relieved by her explanation.

"Why, thank you," she says, relieved I'm no longer mad.

"How long since you've been taken?" I ask.

"I got taken right after you. The whole family was in shambles — still are — when they heard you were taken."

"What about Scotty? He got shot in the stomach, protecting me," I say, sobbing.

"He's okay. Scotty is alive and well. He was in the hospital for a while. But Uncle Steve, I mean, your dad, he's physically okay but not emotionally," she says, filling me in.

"Scotty is alive!" I screech, excited by the news.

"Yes, alive and well. However, your dad was devastated, and he's going crazy looking for you. He bought a house here in France and won't leave without you; my dad did the same thing. The whole family is here, over the pond. That's how they got me; I was snatched the day we arrived. Gus and I were out together, and they hit him on the head and took me away from him. The family was ramping up security before I was taken. You should've seen the line of security guards up for interviews. Before I was taken, everyone was about to have their private security detail here in France since you were taken from here. Uncle Steve hates himself. He blames himself for you being taken. I've never seen him so broken." she says. I can tell Elizabeth's hurt, too, but she's trying to hide it.

"Mark keeps threatening to kill our family if I don't do as I'm told," I tell her.

"Have you not been listening, girl? I told you, the family's ramped up security. You don't have to worry about them — they're safe. Just worry about yourself right now," Elizabeth insists.

"I had security when I was taken, and these people got through."

"Yeah, and they were shitty. Your dad was trying to do it alone, but the whole family is in this together now. They aren't fucking around, or at least not when I was there," my cousin explains.

I'm happy to hear my family's safe. No matter what threats that evil spawn of the devil, Mark, says to me, he won't be able to hurt them. Then it stuck in my head; Elizabeth mentioned accepting this life, "… and, if I don't accept this?" I ask her.

"C'mon, do you have to ask me that — like you don't know the answer already?" she says, giving me a look. I know she's right. I have to accept and live this life of hell. Life of lost dreams with no hope. As badly as I want to leave this life, deep down, I know I'll never get to leave.

She helps me fix my hair and wipes my face. Elizabeth hands me meth, I take a hit, and we return to the main room of the ball. I feel Mark's eyes on me walking in. I grab champagne from a server walking by to help my nerves. Elizabeth and I speak to some of the men there. I even flirt a little, making sure Mark sees. I doubt he'll care, though — he'll probably sell me to them anyway.

Elizabeth and I stay next to each other. Being close to my cousin makes me feel better, and finding out Scotty's alive and not dead uplifts my spirits. I'm so grateful my dad is alive and still loves me after everything. There's comfort in knowing he and my family are still in France looking for me. Several hours later, the ball ends, and everyone leaves. "Remember what I said, girl... accept and embrace it or die," Elizabeth whispers while hugging me goodbye.

"I'll accept; thanks for everything. I hope I'll see you again," I say, squeezing her back tightly.

"No doubt you will. This isn't the only thing they have for us," she warns with a little laugh.

I'm torn up from the ball. The champagne mixed with the meth has done a number on me. Mark has a guard escort me to the limo. He's holding me up, almost having to carry me; I can barely stand up, and I keep tripping and falling over my feet. The ride back to hell is nothing but awkward silence until Mark's ready to fuck again. I try pushing him off me, but it's no use. The drugs are wearing off; all the champagne and small bites of food I ate are the only thing inside me.

When we return to the pit of hell, we go into Mark's room, and I head for the shower. I scrub my skin nearly raw, trying my best to wash the scent of Jeremiah off me. Mark will be waiting for me when I come out of the shower. I don't want anything to do with him — not now, not ever. I put on the ugly lingerie he has out for me. When I exit the bathroom, I climb into bed. I'm tired — purely exhausted. Mark is kissing my shoulder for not even ten seconds, ready for a nightcap. I try pushing him off me with my hand. He ignores all my signs of disengagement and continues kissing me. "C'mon, Mark, I'm tired — not tonight."

"You weren't saying that to the men all over you today," he says.

"I was hiding it," I tell him, barely getting my words out.

"So, you can't hide it for me?"

"After today, not a chance in hell."

"What's your problem? You're being a complete bitch," he says, his tone increasing.

"Oh, nothing, you just love me so much you have other girls suck you off while you sell me to other men. Little did I know, my body was paying for our meals at Jeremiah's restaurant," I say.

"Oh, that girl sucking me off was nothing. She's new, and my brother was busy today and couldn't test her out, so I had to. It didn't mean anything — I only love you."

"Yeah, it didn't look like anything alright, and you never told me you had a brother."

"You never asked… and it's not important. C'mon, are you upset?" he asks.

"Mark, are you serious right now? You made me believe you cared about me, but you don't give a rat's ass what happens to me."

"That's not true, and you know it."

"Bullshit! If you love me so much, why did you promise me to Jeremiah tonight? Oh, and the way you smacked the shit out of me and spoke to me there!"

"You deserved it — you were way out of line. You need to understand that this is business. We lost a lot of money the days you were here not doing anything," he informs me.

I was in this bedroom recovering from abuse and attempted suicide, I think to myself. Like holding me here in this damn dungeon is doing me any favors anyway. "Yeah, so groom me to be your high-class whore, and everything will be okay, right?" I snap back at him.

"You're overreacting with everything," says Mark.

"Fuck you, Mark! Please leave me alone. I'm tired of being your high-class whore for tonight."

"What did I tell you about speaking to me like that, love?" he yells, wrapping his hand around my throat from behind and tightening it with no warning. I shut up, fearing he might tighten his grip more, making it impossible for me to breathe. But I had to get things off my chest.

"I don't see why you get to have sex with men, and I can't get a simple blow job from a girl. Let this be the last time we speak of this, understand me," he says in a threatening tone. I nod my head yes. He kisses me and loosens his grip. I keep my back turned to him lying down. Elevating my exhaustion, he gives me heroin, putting me into a comatose state. He hugs his arm around me like nothing happened.

Chapter 42

ALEJANDRO

I have the dream again — the one where I'm in the basement. It always ends the same way; I wake up just as someone opens the door, and a bright light beams in. The same light that jolts me from sleep at that exact moment every time. I'm not sure what bothers me more, not knowing what the dream means or that it's the only thing I keep dreaming about. I open my eyes to see red roses and a card beside me. I open the card, and it reads:

Dearest Dawnie,

I'm truly sorry about yesterday. Please understand why I have to do what I'm doing. I don't enjoy doing any of this. As I said before at dinner, I don't want this. I didn't want to give you to those men last night — I hated it, but I had no choice. My family makes me do all these things, and I don't want to do them. I know you're upset with me right now, and you have every right to be, but I also know you will forgive me and love me again soon.

Love always,
Mark.

I close the card and throw it on the other side of the bed. I close my eyes and lay my head down.

"Didn't like the card, I assume," Mark says.

"It doesn't matter what I think anymore, Mark. You made that perfectly clear."

"Not true, Dawn. What you think matters to me very much."

"I think the card is a bunch of bullshit."

"How so?" he asks, sounding pissed off.

"You don't have to do this — you just choose to," I say.

"Like you chose to be here — like you chose your life. You don't have to have sex with those men — you chose to," says Mark arrogantly.

"Bullshit, and you know it. I didn't choose this life. I tried to end my life. Maybe you forgot. It was you who decided to get a fucking doctor and save me! Well, not save me, but bring me back to this hell. But if you think I won't choose that option again — think again!"

Thinking Mark was pissed off before, I'm wrong. He's beyond pissed off now, and all I see is rage. His face is red, his eyes are full of evil, and his demeanor is sinister. He starts speed walking to the bed and smacks me full force. My face and upper body fly to the other side of the bed, landing me horizontal. While holding my face in pain and to protect it, he jerks me, forcing me on my back, now facing him. In one of his hands, he has my hands trapped in his very painfully tight grip while he squeezes my face from my chin and cheeks, forcing me to look at him with the other. "I fucking despise you so much," I scream, hatred in my voice, staring my trafficker down.

"You take those words back, Dawn! You love me, and you will always fucking love me, and only me! I remember that day you almost fucking killed yourself because it was the worst day of my life. I fucking saved your life! I'll do it a million times more if you try that shit again. You'll never be alone now, and if you somehow manage to try and do it again, I'll fucking bring you back and make sure your life is a living hell. If you think you hate your life so fucking much now... just wait and see! You ungrateful bitch! Go ahead and try that shit again — and you wait and see what happens!

Do you understand me?" he scolds.

Mark's face is so close to mine that I can feel the heat from his breath. I don't answer him. I weep in agony and lay there, pissing him off even more. He shakes me forcefully, "Do you understand me?"

"I understand. I understand that this is your sick-as-hell version of a choice. The choice to continuously be raped by random men and be tortured worse than I already am," I say, gritting.

"Exactly. You do what you do to survive, like me. You and I are no different. We're exactly alike, so we're meant for each other. I told you, this life I have, was passed down to me. I had no choice but to accept and embrace it. I can't leave it, so I might as well make the best of it — and you should too," he says, sitting down next to me at the end of the bed. Within seconds, Mark's anger begins to subside as if he didn't just beat me and threaten me with a forever life of hell.

"It's different when you're the one being sold, and the other is the sales manager conducting the transaction and watching over like a slave master," I yap in pain — rubbing my face, wondering how nasty my bruise will be.

"C'mon," Mark says, taking me out of bed.

"Where are we going?"

"Eating breakfast together," he says, leading me to the office part of his room where a table is set up for two people. "I'm showing you how much I care for you." Seconds into our meal, he gets a call, responding with nothing but a "yes" to anything the person on the other end says. "Got to go, love," Mark says to me. He leans in to kiss me, but I move my face away. He might have forgotten what happened, but I sure haven't — and won't. The pain on my face reminds me of it far too well, and the fact that it just happened less than five minutes ago. He hesitates, scoffs and hurries out the door.

I'm alone again in his office. I sit thinking about how I'll always be alone like this. Mark will come back when he's ready. I start to eat my breakfast — my appetite is shot. One of Mark's men walk in and makes me sniff something. I become tired, and it takes me out on the table. The dose was very strong.

I wake up alone and in bed. One of the guards checking in on me must've put me there. I look at the chair in the room and see a dress and shoes. It's something I don't want to see — I know what it means — another one of Mark's fuck balls. I began wondering which high-roller Mark has promised me to this time. At least the ball is better than the fucking basement he used to stuff me in. I put the dress on, and the hairstylist comes and does my hair. I tell her to surprise me because I don't care how she does it anymore. She can cut it all off or put a tree branch on it. Besides, I'm sure Mark already told her how he wants it anyway.

'Embrace this life,' what's up with everyone telling us to 'embrace this life?' Bad enough, I got to accept it, and I can barely do that. To live, I have to embrace it like I want this life. Elizabeth and Mark must be out of their minds. That's because they are. They're both on drugs, and I am, too, but I know not to embrace this life. The door opens and slams shut, and the men are laughing. I don't have to go out there to find out if it's Mark.

Mark stumbles into the room, high off of whatever he's on. His clothes are halfway off him, and he falls onto the bed. He starts taking his shirt off, and I see his arm is bleeding. I push the hairstylist away and run to the bed where he's lying. "Mark, what the hell happened to your arm? It looks like someone clawed it."

Confused by my questioning, he looks down at his arm, "Oh, there were bugs in my arm. I had to take them out before they ate me alive."

"Bugs? Like what kind of bugs? How did bugs get in your skin?"

"Oh, I don't know. I just saw them crawling in there and had to pick them out. Stop asking me all these damn questions, and get ready for the ball. I'm tired. I had a busy morning," he says.

"You're not going to the ball?" I ask, picking up on his strange behavior.

"Yeah, I'm going to meet you there."

After I'm ready, a bag is placed over my head, and I'm sent to the ball. The guard who snatched me up last time before getting myself hurt is sitting in the back with me. I can sense him there. He must be my babysitter. We sit in awkward silence, and I ask to take the stinking bag off my head. My arms become very itchy, and I'm getting chills, which is weird because it's hot outside. The guard takes the bag off my head and gives me a hit of something, but it's not enough. They usually give me more drugs than this so I can feel a buzz and be more alert for the evening. He gives me a little bit more to stop my chills and itching. "That's it?" I ask, surprised by the low dosage.

"Yup," he says, not looking at me.

"Mark and the others give me way more than that."

"Well, after you finish here, you can get more. If you want it, you've got to work for it."

"What do you mean?"

"What do you think? You know this whole play dumb thing doesn't work here in France," he says.

"I've been working my ass off here trapped in a basement and chained to a wall! I've been taken away from my family and friends. The least they can do is give me something to numb the pain a little." I say, frustrated and wanting more.

"And you also have been the biggest pain in the ass with trying to kill yourself and all."

"Sadly, it didn't work," I reply, snidely.

"Why?"

"Because you bastards called the doctor."

"That's not what I meant," he says, looking at me out of the corner of his eye and quickly ensuring I don't see him.

"Because I hate not having a say so in the men I'm forced to sleep with. I'm forced to take drugs, fuck men I don't know, and I'm locked away in hell, and barely eating is not a life I planned on living for myself."

"You'd be surprised by how many people don't choose the life they live," he says, loosening up in conversation.

"Yeah, I already learned that," I say, noticing we've arrived at the ball.

"Finally, here," the guard says.

"Yeah, what's your name so I know what to call you?"

"Alejandro," he says, opening the door for us to exit.

"Oh… it's you," I say, jogging my memory back to the balcony incident. We go inside, but Mark is still not there. I see Jeremiah staring at me, but I ignore him. I approach Elizabeth, who has two drinks in her hand and hands me one.

"They're cutting down our drug intake," I tell her angrily.

"I know. I snagged some from one of the guards when he wasn't looking. He thought I was trying to grab his cock, which I was — but with my other hand," Elizabeth tells me. We both laugh.

"Why were you doing that?" I ask.

"I needed a distraction, and that's the only thing I could think of doing at the time. Desperate time calls for desperate measures. Let's go to the bathroom before we get caught up with these men," she says, and we start cracking up.

While walking to the bathroom, Alejandro stops me and tells me Mark has someone upstairs for me. "Okay, I'll be up there in a second. I need to freshen up first," I let him know.

"I'm afraid you can't; there's a bathroom upstairs. You can use that one. Come on, let's go," he says, pulling me by the arm. I follow him; it's not like I can say no. "When you finish with this guy, you'll get more drugs," he says and waves it in front of me when we're out of sight of everyone.

"Then, we do need to hurry," I tell him, wanting another hit.

"I'm sure," he says, rolling his eyes. He takes me to a room with dim lighting. I walk further into the room and don't see anyone but sense someone's presence.

"Hello? Anyone here?" I call out, taking a few more steps in the room.

"Yes, I'm sorry. I'm just admiring your beauty. I was caught off guard when you walked in the room," says a man, walking from the dark corner of the room.

"I'm going to go to the bathroom and freshen up really quick," I say, already making my way over to the bathroom in the dark room. When I return, he goes to the bathroom, and I walk over to the bed. I'm jittery and freaking out because the drugs are wearing off sooner than expected. I take a deep breath, trying to calm myself down. I begin giving myself a pep talk, okay, Dawnie, let's keep it together. Make this shit quick, then I can get what I need — Alejandro made that clear.

I take off my dress and lie on the side of the bed facing the bathroom. Out of nervousness, I adjust my hair, praying it's not messed up. Water runs, then turns off. In a matter of seconds, he opens the door and sees me. When he walks out, he stops, and stares at me in amazement. He walks over to the bed and kisses me, pulling my hair so hard it feels like it will come out. Based on how he acted when I first walked in, I thought he was a newbie. Dang, I'm wrong. He's been doing this for a while because his shyness shifts quickly to harsh and violent. The whole thing hurts like hell; there is no pleasure in it. There are times I get numb during these sexual encounters, but this man is hurting me so badly. He's a piercing sword.

My body endures the pain while rejecting numbness. I fake a moan, but it turns into an outcry. Does he have full intentions to hurt me? Does he think my wailing is moaning? He finishes and leaves the room with me still in the bed. My high is about gone. Not only am I hurting from this horrible man, but I need drugs badly, and I need them now to numb the excruciating pain I'm in.

My body hurts so bad that when I go to stand up, I collapse on the floor, yelling out in agony. I need to get to the bathroom right now because it feels like my box was just dismembered from my body. I crawl to the bathroom, and when I pee, it burns like an inferno. I wash my hands and look in the mirror. That's when I see her. The person I'm looking at in the mirror isn't me; it's Tracy inside me. I scream and fall to the floor, sobbing in sadness. I have turned into Tracy without even knowing it. I promised myself that I'd never turn into her, taking drugs to numb the pain, having sex for money, and allowing men to take advantage of me. However, I'm not paid money for sex, but I'm paid drugs for it.

I crawl out of the bathroom and entirely collapse; the impact hurts my box even more. I cry out in pain and lie there. Alejandro hears me, and within seconds, he's next to me, picking me up from the floor.

"Are you okay?" he asks, seemingly concerned.

"Hell no! That guy is a jackrabbit from hell!" I utter, holding onto him around the neck while he carries me.

"You said, after I have sex with him, I get my drugs. Where are they?"

"I've got them right here. Let me put your dress on you first," he says. He goes to retrieve my dress on the other side of the room. I grab his hand, and he turns around and looks at me.

"No, I need it now. Can't you see I'm suffering here? Those drugs are the only thing that helps me get through the day. I can't be in this place doing these despicable things sober. I can't do it. It hurts too bad. The drugs help me sleep — they numb me — they numb the pain and help me not care so much." I beg. I begin shaking. He looks at me, and I can tell he feels terrible. From the first day I was captured, Alejandro has never displayed emotion around me or to anyone. He bends down over me, grins a little, and hands me the heroin. The high kicks in, and I start becoming relaxed, then tired. My painful body turns into heaven. I feel myself falling back, and he catches me in his arms. "Thank you," I whisper.

He forces a grin and says, "You're welcome."

I lie on the couch staring at the ceiling in a daze, with tears silently streaming down my face. I know he gave me the drugs, so I should feel relieved and happy, but I'm not. I've been so blinded by the drugs that I never saw what I was becoming, but now, I'm catching glimpses. I've turned into her is the thought that keeps replaying in my mind as I drift off to sleep. I hear a voice asking who, but I'm too high and out of it to respond. I'm clueless about what happened to me after Alejandro gave me heroin that night. All I know is that it's the following day when I wake up, or at least I think it is.

Mark has been assigning me a personal guard — Alejandro, at these high-class balls. Alejandro wasn't lying when he said he would never leave me alone again. I hadn't paid attention to Alejandro until now because I've always hated everyone and everything in this place. I'm noticing Alejandro more from the short time we've spent together. He's tall and tan, with ear-length hair and a muscular build. His serious expression always softens when he speaks to me. His hands are rough and calloused, and he's always sober and quiet. When he does speak, his accent is the thickest I've ever heard — distinct from everyone else's. Whenever I try to start a conversation, he responds with a quick, one- word answer and goes on about his business.

For the longest time here, I've been mostly by myself, and now I'm going to be with him all the time. I need to make conversation to make the daily life I live as a sex worker go by faster. Hell, if he thinks of me as a friend, maybe he'll give me a little more drugs. The cutting down on drugs they've been doing lately is killing me.

Alejandro is sitting on one of the couches reading a newspaper. I walk over to him and plop down on the couch next to him, hoping he'll engage with me, ask a question, or at least take his eyes off the paper and look toward me. He doesn't move a muscle. It's like he's a mannequin or something, and nothing can disturb him. "So…" I say, interrupting his reading.

"What is it now?" he says, annoyed by my interruption.

"What are you reading?"

"Newspaper."

"See, you've been watching me lately."

"Just doing my job."

"But why watch me all of a sudden?"

"After you argued with Mark, do you think he'll ever leave you alone again?"

"What do you do in your spare time?"

"None of your damn business."

"You don't talk much."

"Nope."

"I'm just trying to have a little dialogue with you. You barely talk, and we're around each other all the time now."

"We're around each other because it's my job to protect you. Not to be your friend," he says.

"You know, you're an asshole. I'm always by myself and don't talk to anyone but a man who claims to love me and sells me to the world. If you're protecting me, you're doing a shitty job because I'm getting hurt every day here and at that despicable ball. When they give me to those nasty ass men, I'm hurt. When I'm given drugs to forget, supposedly, but guess what? I never forget. I'm hurt. All this torment sticks to my memory worse than superglue. I've been ripped away from my family and friends. Sorry if I'm sick of being alone and having to talk to myself all the time. I need a change," I rant, rushing to the bedroom, upset.

My directness is getting out of control. I'm making bold statements and standing up for myself against evil people who can hurt or kill me. If Alejandro tells Mark what happened, I'm doomed. The door in the other room opens, my food has arrived. "Dawn!" Alejandro calls my name to tell me my food is here.

"Wait a minute, I'm coming," I reply, annoyed.

I hate eating when they say eat and do what they say or else. I was used to doing what I wanted, when I wanted and how I wanted, and eating what I wanted when I was living with Dad before I was kidnapped. But not here, not ever. The only thing they feed me is salad, even for breakfast. At least when Mark takes me out to dinner, I can get what I want, but then again, I'm paying for the food after all, or should I say working for it. I love lettuce because it's crunchy — well, I used to love it, anyway. I hate it now because I'm fed it every day.

They don't want me getting fat or anything because I'd no longer be marketable to these high rollers they auction me off to. I can't hinder Mark's business' money flow. But Mark gets to eat steak, chicken, turkey, or anything else that's fattening in front of me, but I can only watch and wish for some, and imagine eating it. Come to think of it, even at the sex balls, I nor the other girls can eat anything but salads. I reluctantly make my way over to the table and nibble on the salad. I notice there's a second plate across from me. I assume it's for Mark, but I'm wrong; it's Alejandro's.

"Don't you get tired of eating salad?" he asks me.

"Yeah, but there is nothing else to eat. Remember, you guys want to make sure I keep my figure looking nice?" I say sarcastically.

"I think your figure is fine, and I doubt you'll be losing it soon," Alejandro says.

"Why, thank you for your consideration," I say, still sarcastic.

"Here, let's switch. I need to watch my weight, and you need your strength." He takes my salad and gives me his steak, rice, and green beans. He catches me off guard. I'm speechless and can't stop staring at him. "You're welcome, by the way," he says, eating the salad.

"Thank you so much." I look at my plate and cry because I'm so happy to have anything but salad. I bite and close my eyes, taking in the taste of real home-cooked food for once. It tastes nothing like Dad's cooking but is ten times better than salad.

"Are you okay?"

"Yeah, sorry, eating anything but salad just feels so good. You have no idea how much this means to me."

"Well, I must do it more often," he says, smiling. He pauses for a second, looks at his food, then looks at me, "Who were you talking about last night?"

"What are you talking about?"

"Last night, after I gave you some drugs and put you on the couch, you said you turned into her. Who is her?" My face turns red, and becomes hot. I'm embarrassed and mad that I said it out loud and not to myself. I swallow hard and look at my plate.

"I didn't know I was talking out loud."

"It was a whisper, but loud enough to hear because I was so close to you."

"The "her" is Tracy. She's my mother but was murdered."

"I'm sorry."

"Yeah, sure you are," I say, continuing to eat my food, feeling guilty.

Chapter 43

MARRIAGE FROM HELL

Alejandro and I have been very close since he traded his steak dinner for my salad a few months ago. It could've been two months at least; who knows? Whenever Mark's around, we don't act like it. My outburst at Mark that day got him mad. My words hit him hard — like concrete because he acts completely different. When Mark leaves, Alejandro and I watch TV, eat, play around, and take naps together. I keep the TV captions on and pretend I don't understand French. I can't shake the feeling of not letting Alejandro know about me knowing a little French.

Mark is so oblivious; it's pretty funny. Alejandro is my new best friend, but Mark can never know that. I wake up, and Mark is a little too excited and cheery. Alejandro and I look at him like he's from another world because we don't know why he's so cheery. "A hairstylist is coming to do your hair today, and a tailor is coming to fit your dress," Mark tells me and dances his way out of the room.

"Okay… what's going on, Alejandro? Why is he so happy?" I whisper, baffled.

"You got me. Maybe he's getting new drugs or something," Alejandro whispers back. We both let out a little laugh under our breath. When I come out of the shower, the hairstylist is here. She straightens my hair. Suddenly, I start feeling queasy. Weird feelings begin circling in my mind about today. The tailor arrives and helps me get fitted into my white mini-dress. I'm given black shoes to wear with the dress, and we leave for our destination. "Where are we going, Alejandro? What's happening?"

"I honestly have no idea, Dawn. Mark has left me in the dark on this. He told me you didn't have any jobs today."

The bag is removed from my head when the limo pulls up to the mansion where the sex balls are thrown. Alejandro and I sit in the limo, looking out, unaware of what's happening. Mark didn't tell either of us there was a ball today, but lots of people are here, dressed in exquisite formal wear from head to toe walking in. The driver escorts us out of the limo, and we go inside. My cousin, Elizabeth, rushes over to me. "Alejandro, can I please have a word with Dawn briefly?" she asks him hurriedly.

"If you tell me what's going on here," he replies, his seriousness reappearing.

"You mean to tell me, you don't know?" says Elizabeth, perplexed by Alejandro's question.

"Know what?" I interject, wanting to know too.

"Fuck the French King! Are you both unconscious? Follow me, and I'll tell you what's going on," she says, walking over to an empty room. We follow her, and Alejandro inspects the room, ensuring no one is around.

When we're positive we're safe and alone, Elizabeth blurts, "Dawnie, this is your fucking wedding!"

"What!" Alejandro and I both shriek at the same time. I hear the shock in Alejandro's voice; it matches the same shock in mine.

"That's impossible! He didn't tell me this! He would've told me if he was getting married. Especially to Dawnie because I'm always watching her," Alejandro enrages while speaking another language and angrily parading around the room.

"I wish I wasn't lying. I found out about it this morning when I was getting ready," says Elizabeth.

"Who told you?" Alejandro demands furiously.

"Who else? Mark's cousin, Ralph," she replies.

Ralph is Elizabeth's Mark. He's the one she has to cater to, and like Mark has declared his love for me, Ralph has declared his love for Elizabeth, too, but doesn't care about her. "What am I going to do?" I panic, looking over to the balcony, believing it will give me the correct answer.

"You must walk down the aisle or die," warns Elizabeth. I look at her, and she knows what I'll say.

I start making my way to the balcony, "I'd rather die." They both pick up the pace behind me. I start running, but my heels cause me to trip and fall. Alejandro catches me before I hit the balcony floor. I struggle to break free from him. It's no use. Alejandro has me in a Kung Fu Hold. I stare over to my only way out — that I've failed.

"You can't kill yourself, Dawnie! You can't leave me here!" Elizabeth weeps, hugging me tightly.

I sob with her. I've never imagined myself marrying anyone other than Damien. I don't want to marry that monster. I hate him for everything he's put me through. He took me away from my family, sells my body for money, have men hump me like I'm nothing but a glory hole, abuses me, doesn't feed me. The list goes on. "Get out, Elizabeth, give me a moment with her — please," Alejandro interrupts.

Alejandro's eyes are affixed on me. I feel him urging to protect me — the feeling is burning the side of my skull. Elizabeth obliges him and leaves the room. I start hitting him to get off me. He holds me tighter and grabs my hands so I can stop hitting him. "Get off me! I hate you! I hate Mark… and all of you that are part of this!" I yell. He picks me up and sits us both down on a chaise chair.

"Don't you ever do that again! Do you understand me? I can't lose you, Dawnie!" he cries out, holding me by the arms and shaking me simultaneously. I sit there looking into space, hoping for someone to save me, but it's useless.

"Why do you care? You're a part of them! You're just as bad and as sick. I hate you, too! Why didn't you just let me die?" I sob.

He kneels before me and holds my face in his hands, "I'm nothing like them. I thought you, of all people, you'd see that. With everything I do for you and all we do together — I'd thought you'd see that by now. I'm here to protect you. I swear I had no idea about the wedding. Mark never told me — I would've stopped him. You should know I'll never do anything to hurt you," he says to me compellingly.

"Ha, you don't think I remember the night you slammed me into the wall and showed me your gun to force me to fuck Jeremiah!" I say, pushing his hands away as I get up to walk back into the room. He grabs my arm and yanks me towards him so I can look at him.

"If I didn't do that, they would've killed you. I didn't want you to die. Everything I've done was for you because I love you."

"Then prove it and stop this wedding from happening," I beg him.

"I can't, it's too late. There's no way I can stop it." I start crying again, and he hugs me for a bit, and we go inside. I get ready for my wedding — the one I don't want to happen. The dress is lovely. It's plain white with buttons going down the back. It looks used, though, like it came out of someone's basement or something. Tracy and Fawn would've loved it, but it's not my taste.

"Elizabeth, come here," I call her, bringing her to the balcony where we're alone.

"Yes, Dawnie?"

"I'm sorry about earlier. I wasn't thinking right. Everything that's happening is a bit too much for me, but if I'm going to have a wedding, you should be my maid of honor?"

"Dawnie, I don't think that is allowed."

"I don't care what's allowed or not. If I'm going to marry this demon against my will, I need you next to me as my maid of honor for support," I say, pleading and hugging her. She gives me a look of worry, but forces a smile.

"Okay," she agrees. We return to the room, and I tell them to give her flowers. Alejandro gives me a hit of something — so I can relax. We hear the horrible cheesy instrumental playing, "Here Comes the Bride" and start walking. Elizabeth is the only person walking with me. Not like I would've had people walking down the aisle with me, anyway — except my dad, if I were marrying Damien.

Mark is already standing up front by himself. By his facial expression, he wasn't expecting Elizabeth to be a maid of honor. The room is full of people I don't know. They all look familiar, but it's probably from the whore parties. The room is plain — no decoration, no thrill — just simple. A priest is standing in front of Mark. I reach them and face Mark. "What's this?" he says and gestures a head nod towards Elizabeth, trying not to be noticeable.

"What's all this?" I say back. I don't need to nod. He knows exactly what I'm referring to — this wedding.

"Your wedding, love." We face the priest, and it begins. The wedding flies by because I'm so high. It feels like the room is spinning. I hear awe and laughter. We walk down the aisle, and I'm placed back in the room I was in before the wedding. Mark disappears.

"Why are we in here?" I ask, dropping onto the couch.

"Waiting for everyone to move to the reception room," Alejandro informs. I go onto the balcony, and Alejandro follows me.

"Not right now. I want to be left alone," I say to him.

"Sorry, can't do that. I almost lost you last time, remember."

"But you didn't — remember." He looks at me, stands there, and says nothing.

"If you're going to stand there, at least give me something to get through the day."

"I think you've had enough for now," replies Alejandro, firming his tone.

"If I have to get through this horrible day as Mrs.…" I pause and stare off into the clouds.

"What? What is it?" he asks and looks up at the clouds in which I'm gazing.

"…I don't even know my last name. I'm married to a man whose last name is unknown to me. Talk about a marriage from hell."

Alejandro goes into his pocket and hands me whatever is there. It makes me relax. Mark comes in and whispers something to Alejandro. They give me some paper, but I'm so out of it I don't know what's happening. I'm being forced to sign something — but I don't know what I'm signing. I want to lie down — but no time for that. We walk into a room of people eating, and they begin clapping.

Mark and I have a table in the front center of the banquet room. People come up and congratulate us and mostly speak to Mark. I begin studying the room. It's all men — with hookers! Yuck. I can't believe this is my wedding day. They all look cracked out or high on something — because they are.

Mark becomes occupied with someone. I don't see Alejandro

or Elizabeth anywhere. It's the perfect time to slip away and go somewhere alone. Keeping my poise, I quietly leave the room, trying not to stumble over anything. There's a closed door. I walk towards it, slowly cracking it open and peeking inside to ensure no one's in. I need to be alone. The other room is where people are constantly walking in and out. Thankfully, this room is empty. I go inside and quietly close the door behind me. I walk out onto the balcony for fresh air.

This place is suffocating me — I feel like I'm dying. I collapse onto the balcony's floor and cry. There's nothing I can do. I'm stuck here in this sinister place and now in this ungodly marriage — I don't want to be in. I have no friends or family except Elizabeth — I barely get to see her. Yes, I'm close to Alejandro, but only because he's my guard and for no other reason. He's not my friend — at least not by choice.

Chapter 44

RECEPTION

A man puts his hands on my shoulders, scaring the hell out of me. "Holy shit!" I jump up, trying to hide the tears, and turn around in fear, only to see Alejandro. "You scared me! I thought you were someone else." I walk towards the balcony railing, pretending to look at the scenery or something. He grabs my arm, yanks me towards him, and puts his arms around my waist.

"You don't have to fear or hide your feelings from me. I thought we were past that." He catches me off guard, assuming now is the perfect time to return to our conversation earlier.

"I'm not hiding anything. I'm just getting fresh air. I wasn't going to jump, I swear."

"I didn't think you were going to jump. I saw you slip in here alone and wanted to speak to you about today."

"Yeah, I wanted to talk to you about today, too, about you saying that you love me."

"Ha, I knew you were going to bring that up," he chuckles.

"How?"

"I had a feeling you were going to say something," he says.

"No, I mean, how can you love me like this? I'm never sober and can barely remember things we speak about. I'm forced to have sex with every man in the world — I hate myself and everyone. I've never felt so low, dirty, disgusting, weak, and whorish in my life. I need drugs and alcohol to get through the day. How can you love someone like this?" I ask, distraughtly.

"Because I know this is not who you choose to be. You're forced to do this, just like I am. Don't you dare try and act like you don't remember what we've discussed? I know you choose to block it out so you won't have feelings for me like I do."

"Maybe you're right, but it doesn't change who I am now. I'm like Tracy, someone I never thought I'd ever be," I admit to him disgustingly.

"Tracy became this as a choice, not because she was forced to," Alejandro says.

"You know nothing about Tracy," I tell him.

"You'd be surprised at what I know," he replies.

"What's that supposed to mean?" I question him, wondering what the heck he's talking about.

"Nothing, I'm proving a point, that's all," he says, moving in closer to me, holding my face in his hands and kissing me gently. With everything going on, I forgot what gentleness feels like — what it's like not to be forced or abused. It wasn't a kiss like Damien's because nothing can compare to Damien — he's one of a kind. Unable to control my emotions, I kiss him back. Instantly, feelings come over me. I realize I love Alejandro, too. It's not my love for Damien but the love I'm experiencing right now with Alejandro.

"We should get back to the reception," I say, pulling away from him.

"I didn't think you'd kiss me back," he says, smiling and holding me closer.

"I didn't think any of this would happen," I say.

"Me neither, crazy how things happen," he says.

"Yes, you're right — crazy how things happen — I think we should get out of here before someone walks in. Mark might be looking for me soon," I say, beginning to feel eerie about getting caught.

"Mark isn't going to be looking for you. He's out handling business as usual." He doesn't have to tell me what kind of business Mark's doing — I already know. I've walked in on him doing his business before, and it was a hell of a surprise.

"It's our wedding day, and he still can't be faithful. That's Mark for you! Being that I'm married to him, does this mean I still have to have sex with all those random men? Please say, 'no.'" I say, wondering what kind of man would make his wife sleep around for money.

Alejandro becomes quiet. His face turns red, he turns his head, and he stops looking at me. Seeing this gives me my answer. I still have to have sex with random paying men! Even as Mark's wife? There's no benefit in being married to that sick bastard. Frustrated, I get up and push Alejandro's hands off me. "What the fuck! What was the point in him marrying me?"

"I have no idea, and I'm sorry this is happening to you," Alejandro says softly.

"Yeah, sure you are," I say, walking back into the room. "Got my bullshit reception to attend." I leave the room, spot my cousin, and make my way over to her.

"Why were you in there?" Elizabeth asks.

"Needed to get away from these people."

"I hear you on that one," she replies.

Someone catches my eye, and I stop paying attention to Elizabeth. At first, I can barely see who the girl is, but she's familiar. I walk closer to her, it's Jen! She sees me, too; I can tell by her reaction. She's with a man who is all over her; he strongly resembles Mark. "I have to go to the bathroom," I hear her telling him, detaching from his arm and walking away.

"Okay, don't take too long," he replies firmly.

Surprised to see her, I follow her to the bathroom, and Elizabeth follows me. We enter the bathroom, and thankfully, no one's there with us. Elizabeth is clueless as a fish out of water about what's going on. Jen and I look at each other and hug. "Oh my gosh, I thought they killed you!" I say, crying.

"They can't kill me anymore than they already have," she says tearfully.

"How're you, and who's that guy you're with that looks like Mark?" I ask.

"That's Mark's brother and my lover, apparently," she says, her tone apathetic and annoyed. Jen's eyes shift to Elizabeth, wondering who she is.

"Oh, Jen, this is my cousin, Elizabeth. She's also been kidnapped, and well, you know…" I say, realizing there's no need to explain further. Jen and Elizabeth greet each other.

Jen turns to me. "What the fuck, D?"

Hearing her address me as "D" reminds me of my Damien because he used to call me that. My memories of him bring a little warmth to my heart. "I had no idea I was getting married today. I found out from Elizabeth right before walking down the aisle!" I tell her.

"That's weird because Jeff and I are getting married too," says Jen.

"I don't like the feeling of this, Jen."

"Neither do I. I feel like they're planning something, but I don't know what. Listen, D, we have to get out of here. I swear I'm going crazy, and I don't know how much more I can take," she stresses.

"There's no way we can leave here. Guards are everywhere, and we don't know anything about this place. Look at all these people here. It's all of France. How do we know we can be safe anywhere here?" I stress.

"I know, but we must figure out something. We've got to use what we have now," says Jen, mentally strategizing.

"Which isn't much, Dawnie," Elizabeth intervenes. Remember what I told you? We have to accept this as our fate because there's no way out of here but death." she continues, reminding Jen and me she's here in the bathroom, too.

"I'll never accept this as my fate. And if this is my fate, I'd rather pick death without hesitation." Jen tells her with hurt and sadness in her eyes. "D, we have to leave this place. Elizabeth, if you want, you can leave this place with us too, or you can stay here in hell. The choice is yours," Jen says sternly.

"No way in hell you're doing this without me!" Elizabeth responds.

"I have to go; Jeff is waiting for me — he'll come for me for taking too long," says Jen, hugging me goodbye, then walking out. Elizabeth and I wait a few minutes after Jen leaves, then walk out. From a distance, Jeff's manhandling Jen and asking her a crap load of questions about what took her so damn long.

"There you are. I've been looking for you everywhere!" says Alejandro, grabbing my arm and taking me to the room with everyone else. "You have to sit at the bride and groom table," he says.

"Where's Mark? Doesn't he have to join me?"

"He's busy at the moment."

"Isn't he always?" I reply. Alejandro grabs a seat to the left of me. "What are you doing?"

"I'm your bodyguard. I have to be near you at all times."

I sit at the table with Alejandro and look around the room. Everyone is socializing, eating, and dancing. It's all the deplorable men laughing and having fun — the girls, not so much. The girls are high as kites. They don't even know what's going on. They're putting on facades and laughing to avoid being roughed up and lashed out by their owners. Alejandro touches my hand and circles my palm with his finger. I pull my hand away, frightened that someone would see him. "Are you trying to get us caught?" I say frantically while watching the crowd, and hoping no one sees what he just did.

"Don't worry, I'll get you out of here, I promise," he says.

"I won't leave without…"

He cuts me off, "I know you won't, and that's what makes everything so much more difficult. I'll do what I can for them as well. It'll be easier if it were only you, though," he says, staring nonchalantly at the guests but speaking to me.

"I will not leave without them," I state firmly.

The reception is finally over, and we head back to my place of captivity and go into the bedroom. Alejandro receives a phone call. He says 'yes' or 'no' to everything Mark says on the other end. I know it's Mark calling to tell him he won't be in until tomorrow — what's become his usual routine. Mark informs Alejandro what time to expect him back before they hang up.

Chapter 45

WEDDING NIGHT

I say nothing to Alejandro when he hangs up with Mark. I head straight to the bathroom to take a shower. I feel so dirty when I'm around those people. I know I didn't fuck anyone today because I just married the devil, which is just as bad. While in the shower, I hear the door open, thinking it's Mark. I freeze under the water. The hard water hits my body like it's cleaning the dirty feeling I have away. The shower curtain opens, but I don't look back. I keep staring down at the drain, watching the water go down.

I feel the person's arms caress me from behind. I know right away that it was Alejandro. I close my eyes in relief and turn around to face him. He's looking down at me. I look up at him and kiss him. He picks me up, and I straddle him. We lean against the shower wall, making out intently, his hands all over me.

He inserts himself inside me. I shouldn't be liking or enjoying this, but I can't help myself. I'm intimate with someone I desire for the first time in forever. He's not Damien, but he's as close to Damien as I can get for now. Alejandro listens to me. Our bodies stay synced the entire time, maybe because he's with me all the time that we sexually mesh. Before I know it, we're in the bedroom, and I'm holding in my moans. "What about Mark?" I whisper.

"He's out on business. He's not coming back today," he says, moving deeper inside me.

This is my wedding night, and I'm not even spending it with my husband. Although I was forced to marry Mark against my will, he's still my husband. Being with Alejandro romantically is not as good as being with Damien. Damien and I had something so real that no one can compare. I have a place for Alejandro in my heart, but it's not the special place where I keep Damien, and it will never be because Damien and I are locked in.

I fall asleep, and dream of Damien. He's no longer in a dark hole — he's in the light, and he's older, bigger, and muscular. He's fighting, but it's not boxing. He's in the street, surrounded by many men. He's beating everyone's ass. He has a knife and jabs his enemies when he has to. There's thirteen to fifteen men; he takes them all down. When he finishes, he stands there and glares in my direction. He's filled with anger, pain, sorrow, determination, and hatred. He throws a punch my way. I wake up startled, hoping Alejandro doesn't hear me.

Alejandro doesn't hear me, but he turns over, facing me. This uncomfortable feeling makes me feel that someone is watching us right now. I grab something in my hand and walk out to the living room area, fearing that Mark is there. Thankfully, he's not. I return to the bedroom and go straight to the bathroom to use it. I avoid the mirror in fear of seeing Tracy's reflection again. I get back in bed and cuddle in Alejandro's arms. He kisses me on the forehead, I go back to sleep. This time, I don't dream anything.

Chapter 46

TIL DEATH DO US PART

Mark doesn't come back, nor does he call for a few days. Hmm, he marries me and doesn't even spend time with me? After a week, Mark returns, takes a shower, eats, and sleeps. He barely speaks to me or Alejandro. He only wants me to lie in bed next to him. I lie next to Mark because I have no other choice. I've never seen Mark like this, not even when he said he had bugs crawling in his skin. He's so distant, dead-looking, depressed, and empty. Mark was always a jerk, but he was always alive, talkative, and trying to have sex with me all the time. This is not like him. He doesn't push up on me once. Instead, he lies there lifeless and fragile.

"What's going on with you, Mark?" I ask worriedly.

"Nothing, bride, why do you ask?" he replies, not looking my way.

"You don't seem or look like yourself."

"How exactly do I look?" he asks, turning around to look at me. I hesitate in fear of his reaction when I answer. He repeats himself, sitting up, not taking his eyes off me. I swallow hard, feeling the sweat build up on my forehead.

"Mark… umm… you look sick… almost like you're dying — maybe you should lay off the drugs for a bit," I say, terrified of what's going to happen or be said next. He cocks his head to the side, squints his eyes, and looks at me. He smacks me off the bed. I hit my head on the dresser.

"You, fucking bitch! How dare you tell me how I look! Have you looked in the mirror at yourself!" he says, lifting me from the floor by my hair. I scream in pain. I kick and scream for him to stop. He puts me in front of a mirror, "You look like that stupid, cunt, horrible bag of a junkie mother of yours," he says in my ear, no longer yelling, but in an evil, vindictive whisper.

"You know nothing of Tracy, you bastard."

"Oh, I know more than you think, love. How else do you think I found you?" He starts yelling at me again and pushes me forward, slamming me into the sink. My ribs hit the sink, and he walks away. I sit there holding my ribcage; I think it's broken.

"You think I want this life or marriage? You're wrong. I don't want any of this! Before you insult someone, look at your reflection before you speak, sweetheart. Might save you next time," he utters. I try crawling out of the bathroom to the bed, but he sees my hand in the doorway and kicks the door shut. I scream so loud, pulling my hand back, crying and scared for my life. This time, I think Mark is going to kill me. He's often lost his temper with me, but he usually slaps me and goes on his way. I'm in the dark about what's going on with him today. His eyes and soul are tainted with hate. Mark starts punching and kicking me on the floor. He yells at me to shut the fuck up and tells me he hates me, and yells how ungrateful I am.

I cry and scream, "I'm sorry!" but he's not hearing me.

He starts choking me and saying, "I'm going to set us both free. Til death do us part, my love." I'm convinced he's going to kill me. I try to pry his hands from my neck, but my right hand is not moving — only one hand is functional. My left hand, my less dominant hand, is useless to Mark's Jujitsu grip around my neck. I maneuver my head to see if I see Alejandro. Where the fuck is he, and why isn't he helping me? My eyes can only see so far. Alejandro is nowhere in sight.

I'm about to pass out. I see a human figure with a black tank on from the corner of my eye. He looks like Alejandro. The guy tackles Mark and pulls him off me. I gasp for air and look around the room; everything is blurry. Two men yell, thump, and fight. My whole body hurts so bad I can't move. The pain is too severe. I pass out.

I dream about Damien again. This time, he's in a dark room standing, tied up with no way to get out. Someone is next to him, and they're tied up, too, but I can't tell who it is. Damien knows the other person tied up next to him. They both try to wiggle out of whatever is binding their hands. A door opens, startling them. They look in the door's direction to see who's entering the room.

A person walks in, but their face is fuzzy and unrecognizable. They zap Damien. He screams and shakes because of the voltage going through his body. They stop and laugh and zap him again. His knees give out, and he's hanging from his arms. He lifts his head slowly and looks in my direction. He carries the same hatred, pain, determination, and sorrow. I wake up wailing in agony, my body in unbearable excruciation. I remember Mark almost just killed me. I start moving around in fear that he might be waiting for me to wake up so he can finish me off.

Unexpectedly, Alejandro is beside me, holding my face, hushing me, and telling me it'll be 'okay.' He's no longer in the tank shirt, he's now wearing the black fitted V-neck I always make him wear. I look at him and sob in pain, shock, and fear because Mark had damn near killed me — enjoying every second. "Shh, he's gone. I'm here now. He can't hurt you, and he won't hurt you again," Alejandro says, rocking and kissing me. My face is busted; it burns at the touch of his lips.

"Where were you?" I ask him, looking him in the eyes. He knows what I'm referring to.

"I left out for a moment on a business call. I heard you screaming when I got back. I immediately came in and slammed him off you."

"I thought I was going to die," I whimper.

"I know, and I'm sorry, you won't leave my sight again. The doctor is going to be here soon to check you out. He bruised your ribs badly. I think he broke them. Your neck is damn near fractured — you will have to wear a neck brace."

"What are you, some kind of doctor?" I ask.

"No, I've seen something similar to this, that's all."

There's a knock on the door, and seconds later, the doctor and Alejandro are in the room with me. When I look at the doctor, I almost stop breathing. Of all the doctors, it's Dr. Bill Stasinski, Dad's friend. By his facial expression, he's livid and bothered by my appearance. However, he acts as if he doesn't know me and as if this is the first time he's ever treated me. Alejandro steps out of the bedroom, leaving me and the doctor alone.

"Dawnie, baby, I finally found you. We've been looking everywhere for you. Don't worry, we're getting you out of here as soon as possible, and they'll all pay for doing this to you," he whispers, ensuring only I can hear him, and not Alejandro. I shed tears from the pain in my body, still feeling it as I listen to Dr. Stasinski — well, I mean Bill. I remember he went by Bill as I think about how they hadn't given up on me and how they had found me. My family has not stopped looking for me since I was kidnapped and they've now found me. Finally, a glimpse of hope — my family will save me. This is the first time I've felt this way since my captivity.

"Have you seen Elizabeth and Jen?" he asks, keeping his voice low.

"Yes," I whisper back while trying to figure out how he knows about Jen.

"Do you know where they are?"

"They're with Mark's brother, Jeff, and cousin, Ralph, but I don't know where exactly." Speaking to him is taking a tremendous toll on my body. I'm in so much pain that I force myself to talk to Bill because I know he's the key to saving me from this hellhole. He continues to examine me to avoid suspicion from Alejandro.

"We're getting you girls out of here. Don't tell anyone you know me; promise you won't trust anyone but me. If you tell anyone you know me, it'll ruin our chances of saving you."

"I promise," I say, sighing in relief that I'll soon be free from here.

"Okay, look, I'm going to finish examining you and just continue to act like you don't know me, and I have to do the same," he says.

"Okay," I reply.

Everything Alejandro assessed is wrong with me — he's right. My ribs are bruised, and one is fractured. The doctor puts a cast on my neck and one on my hand. I knew they were broken before Bill even told me. I can't move them at all. Bill is very concerned about my critical condition. His face gives it away. I don't blame him. If I were him and had seen someone in a similar state as a medical professional, I would've been very worried, too.

My right eye is in pretty bad shape. It's swollen shut, and I can't open it, but at least I can open my left eye some. My ability to slightly open my bulged left eye was the only way I could recognize Bill when he came in. My right cheekbone is broken, and my lips are puffy and busted. Bill gives Alejandro some meds and a piece of paper with instructions. "Make sure she does nothing but rest. She's been beaten badly and needs her rest to heal," Bill says and leaves the room.

"Do I look that bad?" I ask Alejandro.

"Mark did a hell of a number on you. He's been going crazy since increasing his drug usage, but this is beyond too far. I will not stand for it any longer. Dawn, my love, I promise I'll get you out of this place. You and your friends will soon be free," he says, gently kissing my forehead. He turns the TV on, and we both start watching. I try to watch TV but can't get over Bill being here. I'm so damn happy, yet reluctant to keep my excitement all inside. To mask my smidgen of happiness, I cry.

Alejandro thinks my tears are because of my ailing discomfort. I'm in severe pain, but my inner happiness that I'm about to be rescued helps me to ignore my body's agonizing state. I've never been in this predicament. I had lost all hope of ever seeing my family again, but when Bill walked in, my hope was restored. The fact that he found me means they're very close to saving me from this living nightmare. They didn't forget or give up on me. They still love me and are trying to get me, Elizabeth, and Jen out of here. But how do they know about Jen? Honestly, it doesn't even matter. I'll find out later — they need to get us out of here.

I shouldn't tell Alejandro even though he's trying to get me out of here, too. I'm unsure of my instincts, but I'll listen to them — I must listen to my intuition if I want to get out of here. I pretend to watch TV with Alejandro. I'm secretly thinking and piecing together everything concerning Bill's visit. I can't help but think about Damien and the recurring nightmares I'm having about him. Why am I having them?

Is Damien in trouble, or do I miss him so much that he's stalking my mind? I can't stop the nightmares while being held hostage in this sex prison. Who's next to him in trouble - why are they in trouble too? It's not Scotty because Damien and Scotty never hung out like that to ever be captured together. If anyone, maybe it's Snake, but it doesn't seem like it is. I've never seen so much detestation in Damien's eyes. I've never seen him like that. He's in my nightmares because he's in danger; Damien is fighting for his life.

Chapter 47

THE GET AWAY!

onths have gone by since Mark almost killed me. I've lost track of the days since Dr. Stasinski, I mean Bill, was here. The days are longer, and so are the weeks. It feels like I've been here for an eternity. Mark still comes and goes. Somewhere in between time, he apologizes to me for beating me down to the white meat. I accept his apology because I have no choice, like the wedding — I had no choice. Against my will, I was forced to walk down that damn aisle and say, "I do," while dying of rage on the inside because "I don't" — that's what I wanted to say.

My bruises are gone, and so is the swelling, but my hand and ribs are still messed up, and by messed up, I mean broken. I've been on edge waiting for Bill and Dad to come and rescue me and the girls. Every day that passes by and these prison walls are not barged or shot down drives me insane bit by bit. It's making me nervous. Has something happened to them, and that's why they aren't here yet? I'm very concerned and scared. A dress arrives, and the hairstylist comes. Ugh, without having to ask, I know what this means. Not again! I don't want to go to another whore ball. It's apparent Mark feels my time off is well overdue.

Alejandro is always anxious around me but settles down whenever Mark is around. He's tense and anxious again today, pacing around while I'm beautified for the ball. When we arrive at the ball, I see Elizabeth and Jen. I'm excited to see them — it's been a while. I shake my head from side to side in pure disgust towards the room where my dreadful wedding took place. Elizabeth and Jen notice my disdain for that room and for that day. They share my horrid sentiments.

"Oh my god, you're alive!" Elizabeth says, approaching me.

"Yeah, but barely," I say, waving my cast.

"What the fuck is that?" Jen asks.

"Mark almost killed me! My bruises and swelling have healed, but my bones haven't yet. Clearly, I've missed too much work and that's why I'm here — broken bones and all," I say, mockingly. The door opens while we're catching up, our faces turn white in fear. Whew, it's just Alejandro. He looks at us weirdly; we stare at him in fright.

"What? It's only me," he says.

"Yeah, well, we didn't know that at first," I say, tapping him with my hand.

He laughs and says, "Sorry, but I have brilliant news."

"Brilliant news — in this place?" we inquire, staring at him like he's crazy.

"Today is your freedom day — I'm busting you girls out!"

"Oh my god, you started using too," I say to him, completely disbelieving him.

"No, love, I haven't ever since Mark, you know… I'm determined to free you girls, and my mind needs to be clear. You three will sneak into the Porsche I have waiting downstairs. The license plate number is E-V-E-2000. Got it? E-V-E-2000."

"How the hell will we sneak down there without being seen? Have you forgotten about those violent guards on post?" I say, reminding him.

"My owner keeps a close eye on me, which reminds me, if I don't leave now, he's coming to look for me — he probably is already." Jen gets up and heads for the door. Alejandro puts his hand on the door, stopping her from opening it.

"You and Elizabeth are supposedly doing a threesome in a room very close to the parking lot where the car is. Dawn, no one will say anything because I'll be with you. I'll tell my cousins you two have been requested, then you can slip out the door and into the car. I'll leave it open for you. The Porsche has tinted windows. No one can see into them, only out. You'll be safe, then I'll come out and drive you three to safety. I have passports and all for you."

Jen, Elizabeth, and I look at each other in amazement at how Alejandro has organized our escape. We agree and return to the prostitution ball. No longer will I have to wait on my dad and Bill. However, something deep inside me tells me I should remain patient and not follow Alejandro's plan — and wait for my dad and Bill. I'm not sure what it is, but my gut is telling me that something is about to go wrong. I try calming myself down by inhaling and exhaling to avoid drawing attention to myself. It's probably just nerves. I don't want us to get caught. If so, no mercy will be given, and we will have hell to pay. Worse, it'll be off with Alejandro's head for devising our escape.

Since becoming best friends with Alejandro, he's around me twenty-four-seven, it seems, even at these ungodly slut balls. But today, he's barely near me — maybe because of the plan he's trying to execute on our behalf. Mark and his brother Jeff also notice Alejandro is missing. They ask me where he is and why he isn't with me on assignment. I lie and say he's not feeling well and stepped away for a moment. Jeff takes the excuse for face value and goes on about his business.

"Hey, Dawn, can I speak with you?" asks Mark — knowing it's not a question — it's always a demand. The thought of him wanting to speak to me scares me because of the last time, I almost ended up dead. Swallowing hard, I nod my head yes. I have no other choice. I look around, hoping I'll see Alejandro and he'll come too, but he's nowhere near. Where the hell is Alejandro, I think to myself. Oh god, did Mark and Jeff figure us out? Did he find out about our escape plan? Why else would he want to talk to me? If I thought I was dead before — I know I'm dead now. I start fiddling with my nails to avoid looking Mark in the face and to ignore the elephant in the room. I feel Mark's eyes piercing me. I pray that Alejandro walks in, but he doesn't.

"Dawn."

"Yes," I reply, still messing with my nails. He sits me down next to him on a love seat and holds my hands. I try to hide from Mark that he repulses me. I look away from him and over towards the window.

"Oh, so I scare you that much that you can't look at me anymore, huh?" he gripes.

"You almost killed me," I remind him, my eyes tearing up.

"I wasn't going to kill you — I didn't kill you. Look, you're alive. You're here right now... see. You just needed to be checked."

"Mark, you roughed me up badly and broke my bones. Look how long it's taking for me to heal. I still have broken bones. You didn't see the look in your eyes; your hatred towards me is unreal. You kept beating me no matter how much I pleaded with you to stop. You were out of control. If it weren't for Alejandro pulling you off me, I'd be dead right now, and we both know it."

He looks at me, caught off guard by my words. "Alejandro?"

"Yes, he pulled you off me when you were choking the fuck out of me."

"Oh, yeah, he did," he says, huffing and looking up at the ceiling, irritated — and remembering.

"Dawn, I wasn't myself, and I haven't been for a while because of the drugs I'm on — they're doing this to me," he exclaims, tears in his eyes. In my eyes, Mark is dying slowly because of the drugs and family business he never wanted. He starts crying and drops to his knees, lying his head on my lap and wrapping his arms around my waist. He looks up at me, his face discolored from his sobbing and tears running down. "I'm sorry, Dawnie. Is there any way you can forgive me?"

I return, looking back over at the window, and think about Dad and Scotty calling me 'Dawnie.' "I told you once before, and I'm telling you again, my family is the only one who calls me Dawnie." I look down at him slowly in the eyes. He's about to blow. He screams in anger, jumps up, and flips over a table.

"I've got something for you, sweetheart — I'm your family!" He sticks his left ring finger in my face and takes my left ring finger and puts it next to his. "I'm your only fucking family now, for better or worse."

"Not if I had to choose," I say back.

"But you don't get to choose. No one does. Everybody's life is chosen for them! I love you, Dawnie, and you will never get rid of me. We're bonded for life!" He gets up and holds my face in his hands, forcing a kiss, lets it go, and leaves the room. I stand there and cry. Moments later, Alejandro walks in, sees me crying, and sits next to me. He gives me a kiss and puts his arms around me.

"It's okay. I'm here, and I know you're upset, but we have to go now," he says. I nod in agreement, and he helps me up and kisses me. His kiss is solid and passionate, like it's the last time we'll kiss.

"Hell of a kiss," I say.

"For a hell of a girl," he replies, and we laugh.

We walk out of the room and see people walking into the ballroom. Mark and Jeff are also talking and walking into the ballroom, never looking our way. We walk towards the back of the place and head for the garage. No one is there — the area is empty. I'm worried that the girls didn't make it to the car. "What's wrong?" whispers Alejandro.

"It's so empty here. Why?"

"No one comes here — only the employees come here."

"What if the girls didn't make it to the car?"

"Then, we'll wait for them until they do." He opens the door, and the black Porsche is there, just like he said it would be. We get in the car. The girls are already tucked in the back seat — thank God!

"I'm so relieved you're both here. I was beginning to think you two got caught," I say, hugging them. Alejandro doesn't waste any time; he revs up the engine and puts the car into drive.

"We were thinking the same thing," they reply.

Alejandro is calm, while the girls and I are freaking out. We need to get away from here — stat! Alejandro is focused — like he's done this before. Despite our panicking, his calmness and focus are a subtle confidence that we won't get caught. We make it out of the garage on the run for our lives. We exhale in relief. "What happens if we get lost? Do you know where you're going?" I ask Alejandro, my mind racing.

He scoffs, "Don't worry, I know this country like the back of my hand." Alejandro's phone begins ringing off the hook. After several rings, he answers it. His face says it all. I don't need to see the caller ID to know it's Mark.

"Hello, Mark. Yes, your wife is with someone right now. Okay, I'll take her there in a minute. Ne tsarapay moy khlyst!" Alejandro hangs up the phone, turns to me, and holds my hand. This is the first time he's ever spoken English to Mark around me. They usually speak French around me. Then again, I'm not supposed to be next to Alejandro. I'm supposed to be getting screwed by a high-bidder right now. As quickly as Alejandro holds my hand, he lets it go. He accelerates like a madman, showing what this Porsche can do. We go faster and faster.

"Hold on!" he yells, whipping around corners and speeding down streets.

"What's going on?" I yell, holding on tightly for dear life. I put my seatbelt on in fear we're going to crash. Elizabeth and Jen put theirs on, too.

"We're being followed. They found out we left," says Alejandro, looking straight ahead. The girls and I look at each other and start panicking. I turn back around and look out the front window, my heart pounding, my breath panting — things becoming more intense.

"What's going to happen!" I shout, freaking out.

"We try and outrun them," Alejandro replies, whipping around another corner. We weave between cars and trucks, run stop signs, and almost hit people. We're still being chased — this is not ending. I'm quietly praying on the inside that we don't get caught and will get away.

We turn a corner, "Fuck! Shit! No, this can't be!" Alejandro yells, slamming on the brakes. He puts the car in reverse and slams on the brakes again. I keep my eyes closed, praying while hearing everything happen. I stop praying but don't need to open my eyes to confirm what's next. Elizabeth and Jen scream, but Alejandro is silent. Car doors slam shut from the exterior — they're coming from the trucks that were following us. I open my eyes; Alejandro is staring at me in fear.

He has an emotional outburst, "I'm so sorry, Dawnie. I love you; I swear I didn't mean to. You know I'd never hurt you." He grabs my face and kisses my lips.

I kiss him back, crying, and tell him, "I love you too."

"I swear I'll get you out. I'll find you and protect you. I love you; I promise you won't be in this for long," he cries. The door opens, and Alejandro is yanked out. They start beating him. We all start screaming, I yell for the girls to escape.

"Shut up, bitch! Get them bitches — now!" My door is nearly ripped off its hinges. Someone pulls me out — it's Mark! I scream in pain; my body can't take this. I'm still recovering from the number he did on me before.

"Why!" he screams over and over again. I say nothing, letting him yell, knowing he's going to beat the shit out of me. Alejandro yells in pain and the girls scream while the other men yank them from the car. With all his might, Mark throws me up against the car and grabs me by the back of my neck.

I scream in pain because my ribs are still messed up.

"Mark, please!" He smacks me so hard that I fall to the ground. He pulls me right back up and smacks me harder. I scream, traumatized and in pain. My ribcage is done.

"Please, what? Have mercy on you? What mercy did you have on me?" He throws me on the ground again and kicks me.

"Mark — don't hurt them! Take it out on me! It was my idea — not theirs!" shouts Alejandro.

"They made their choice when they got in the car with you. I love you, Dawnie, I do, but you make it so hard. I spill my heart out and apologize to you, but this is what you do. You betray me, and you embarrass me. What's this madness with Alejandro? Running away together?" he says, kicking me to the ground.

"Mark, please, I couldn't do it anymore! We love each other!" I beg.

"You're a stupid bitch! One day you'll learn that he loves no one — only his fucking self! I love you — not him!" Mark pulls me by my hair and throws me in the truck. A man bellows loudly in pain. It's Alejandro. Mark looks at me one last time and smacks me unconscious.

Chapter 48

WAKING UP IN A DARK PLACE!

"D, wake up," a voice says. It's Jen — shaking me awake.

"Is she dead?" Elizabeth freaks. I moan and cringe because my head and body hurt.

"I'm alive, sadly," I barely respond. I open my eyes and see nothing but darkness. My foot is heavy — I'm chained to Jen again. It must be our punishment for trying to escape, like beating and selling us wasn't enough.

"What the fuck, Dawnie!" Elizabeth shrieks.

"We're back in this bitch!" I say, agitated, sitting up. "What happened after they knocked me out?"

"Ralph, Mark, and Jeff threw us down here to rot. They don't want to see us anymore," says Elizabeth, filling me in.

"Jeff looked at me for two seconds, then turned away with the most disgusted look," Jen cries.

By the sound of her outburst, she's emotionally and physically down. The door opens, and we're blinded by the little light that seeps through. We stop talking; we hear footsteps. Something hard hits me — it's stale bread. One of Mark's goons tosses a bucket of water next to us and disappears. We don't touch our food.

"We're being sold! It doesn't matter if it's by the men upstairs or down here. The same dreadful thing that happened to the other girls is now happening to us because of our actions. The only difference is we're married and have been downgraded from upper-echelon whores," I tell them, twirling the bread around and feeling the mold on it.

"What are we going to do?" Elizabeth panics.

"Find another way out this bitch!" says Jen.

It feels like we've spent weeks down here since getting caught. There's no sense of time in this dark, cold hole. Maybe it's daytime, perhaps it's nighttime — who knows. I stop trying to figure out the time of day because it's useless. A great deal of time has passed by because my broken ribcage is healing. My physical condition is improving. Being reduced to lower-class whores that tried to escape means barely any drugs are given to the three of us. We're used to being given a hit or two every day, which helps us cope, but they hardly give us any now.

Instead, these sickos watch us suffer in pain. We beg and cry for a fix, but they do nothing. My body is still sore, but somehow, I'm gradually adjusting to the weaning off the drugs. I'm more sober than my cousin and Jen. I'm sure it's because Alejandro started to cut down my drug intake before we were caught and thrown back down here. I'm certain this a lot to do with my recent clearheadedness, I suppose. However, Jen and Elizabeth are struggling with adjusting, and I'm still kind of weak from hunger and thirst.

The door opens, and we hear footsteps coming down the stairs. The same routine is followed. A man turns on the light to purposely blind us so we can't see him. The chain on my ankle moves, and he's trying to take Jen! "No!" she screams.

With the little strength I have, I open my eyes and see a pipe on the ground in front of me. I grab it and swing at his head. He hits the floor — hard. Adrenaline kicks in, and with everything I have, I become unhinged. I hit him continuously on the head — over and over again. He's dead. I know he's dead, but my bottled-up anger unravels; I've entered a psychotic warpath of revenge.

"D, stop! He's dead!" Jen screeches, putting her hand on my shoulder. I turn around and look at her and around the room. We've been so out of it that we didn't even notice we're the only three down here.

"You killed him!" Elizabeth cries, reminding me of the man I just beat down. Blood is everywhere. His head is damn-near flattened. His brain spread across the floor. Blood is all over me. My hands, face, and clothes are drenched in the color red. The taste of blood is in my mouth. I feel a little woozy. The next thing I know, Jen and Elizabeth are shaking me awake from fainting.

"Dude, wake the fuck up! They're going to be down any second!" they panic. My mind starts working and moving. The taste of his blood has somehow heightened my awareness and my instincts surface. Elizabeth stands there, scared out of her mind. She's in shock and crying while Jen helps me search the man's lifeless body for a key. We immediately find the key.

"Find anything you can get your hands on, grab his weapon, too!" I instruct. Elizabeth stands there. "Look, if you don't fucking move now, they'll kill us. We need to leave now! Snap the fuck out of it and move or have them rape and slowly kill you!" She nods her head yes and moves. We pause. Someone's approaching the door. The doorknob turns. We switch the lights off and hide behind the steps so the person can't see us.

Fortunately, we were always chained towards the far back of the basement. The back of the basement is not visible until you come down. They won't see the body or the blood right away.

He stomps down the steps. I hit him on the back of the head, knocking him out. Jen grabs his gun from his holster, and like the other man, he suffers by the weapons I wield. I bash him into a lifeless, bloody pulp.

"So, what's the plan now?" Elizabeth blares in a panic.

"We go upstairs and pray there's a door nearby. If we have to shoot or kill, we will. Got it?" I order, looking directly at Elizabeth. She nods yes, and Jen says 'yes' right back. Jen and I are on the same page with this escape shit. We tiptoe up the step and slowly open the first door we see. We hold our breaths, terrorized by what awaits us on the other side.

There's a man sitting in a chair with his back to us. He's getting head from a girl because her knees are on the floor in front of him. We slip into the kitchen. I stop dead in my tracks when I notice a man staring at me. He's the man on watch. He fires his gun at us, and we jolt. Men yell and chase us in pursuit. Delirious by the gunfire, the man seated in the chair stops enjoying his blowjob. He shoves the girl off him and she hits the floor.

I notice a door through a hallway and signal the girls to go towards it. There's a balcony above us with men positioned at the top. Jen and I start shooting at it while Elizabeth opens the door. Men go down, but I'm unsure if we've hit them or if they're dodging bullets, or both.

We escape our imprisonment and see we're in the suburbs. We haul ass and come across a home with a black Range Rover and two sports cars parked in front of it. We race to the front door and bang on it hard. A tall, muscular, tanned man opens the door. We tackle him to get inside for safety.

"What the hell is going on?" he says, seeing us in our underwear and bras. He closes the door and locks it.

"We have to hide, please — they're going to kill us!" I say out of breath, and without thinking, he takes us to a hidden door in the closet.

"Stay here and don't speak."

There's a bang on his front door — we all jump. In fear and desperation, I look into his light blue eyes. "It's okay; I won't let them touch or find you." I nod yes and climb through the hidden door to a small room that fits the three of us perfectly. He shuts the small room door and goes to his front door. We can hear everything from the room.

"Hello," the man says while opening his front door.

"Hey, have you seen three girls running around here?" the person at his front door asks him. Oh no! It's Mark!

"Umm, no, but I'll look out for them. What are they wearing?" inquires the homeowner.

"Well, my sister and her friends took some drugs. Now they're tripping out. You know how some people get when they're on drugs." Mark lies.

"Yeah, I guess. I mean, I've tripped out on a few drugs myself in the past. Give a brief description, please."

"Well, they're in nothing but underwear and bras. The drugs gave them hot flashes, and they ran off thinking we're out to get them."

"Hmm, must've been a bad batch of drugs they had," the man replies.

"Aren't they all bad?" implies Mark, hearing the arrogance in the bastard's voice.

"Yeah, but not like that. Anyway, I'll keep an eye out and let you know if I see them."

"Merci, monsieur, and here's my card if you do."

The door closes, and someone runs upstairs. It must be the man who lives here since Mark left. The closet door opens and we know someone is about to open the door to the small place we're hiding in. We tense up in fear. What if Mark and his men have tricked us, but to our relief, it's the owner. We cry; it was a close call. He hands us clothes to put on.

"My name is Lucky. What's your name?" he asks, looking at me.

"I'm Dawn, this is Jennifer and Elizabeth, and those men are not our brothers."

"I figured they weren't. It doesn't take a brain surgeon to figure that out. It's no secret — the McCabe family are nothing but human traffickers."

"The McCabe family?" I reply, curious to whom he's speaking about.

"Mark McCabe and his family are one of the biggest in France."

"Where exactly in France are we?" I ask.

"Mennecy, France," he replies.

"Why did you lie for us, knowing how dangerous they are?" I ask, the girls standing behind me wandering the same. In my mind, only a crazy person would put their life in such danger for three strangers.

"It's obvious you girls need help from a good man like me. When you came to my front door terrified, I couldn't abandon you," he says, with glossy eyes and a red face. Not only does he speak English, but he doesn't have a French accent — he's American! I have a gut feeling there's much more to what he's saying, but I don't want to alert him to my intuition so he can turns us over to Mark.

Jen walks over to him and hugs him for a long time. He holds her embrace. Lucky's hair is black, cut into a fade on the back and sides, with a mop top that reaches down to his ears. He's clean-shaven, tattoo-free, and built like a football player. His teeth are pristine white, and he's wearing basketball shorts and a sleeveless T-shirt. He also has a pleasant scent, possibly Tom Ford cologne.

"Thank you so much," I say.

"You girls going to tell me how you escaped?" The room goes silent, all eyes are on me.

"Dawn saved us!" Elizabeth and Jen exclaim.

"Me? How did I save you? You saved yourselves. I didn't pull those triggers all on my own, and I didn't carry you out of there."

"You didn't physically, but you did mentally. If you hadn't beat the first man to death, we wouldn't have had the courage to kill the other guys and shoot our way out of there. And you gave a hell of a pep talk to Elizabeth when she was freaking the fuck out," Jen says and turns to Elizabeth. "No offense."

"No offense taken. I agree with everything you're saying," says Elizabeth.

Lucky is watching us talk; he interrupts us, "Why don't you three come downstairs and sit in my base—"

"No!" we yell at the same time — cutting him off.

Startled, he puts his hands up as if surrendering, "Hey, I'm sorry, I just don't want them coming back and seeing you girls here, then land right back where you started. The basement has no windows and is secluded. I didn't mean anything by it; I swear."

"Sorry, Lucky. We were locked in a basement for a long time and can't be in another one. Is there another room you can put us in?" I ask.

"Well, my attic is pretty secluded. Would that be okay, at least until we contact the authorities?"

"Yes, thank you so much." He walks us up to his attic; Lucky and Jenifer go downstairs to get food for us. I'm so cold from the inside out. I need a fix. I haven't had one in a while, but I'm craving one now. I doubt Lucky has heroin. They come back upstairs with sandwiches and water. He gives me a blanket, but it doesn't seem to help.

"You're experiencing withdrawals," he says.

"With what?" I question him, shivering excessively.

"Withdrawals are when addicts go a very long time without narcotics. They had you girls on drugs, and now you don't have any. It's quite normal. I'll get more blankets because the two of you will be cold like your friend over here very soon, too." He leaves the room while I sit shivering.

"What are we going to do now?" Elizabeth asks.

"Eat, warm up, and contact the authorities like Lucky said, and wait and see," I say.

"I can't wait to see Gus and our family again," she says with hope in her eyes, and Jen agreeing. "However, for some inclination, I don't want to contact the authorities. I have a terrible feeling that we aren't going to see our families anytime soon. I fear hell still awaits us. Things are not going to end yet," Elizabeth warns.

Lucky returns and hands Elizabeth and Jen blankets. "The authorities are on the way." he tells us. "Are you girls feeling a little better?"

"A lot better. We aren't in that hellhole anymore," I say.

He sits with us in the attic, and we tell him about our lives and captivity. We explain to him how we were kidnapped. Then, something occurs to me, I don't know what day it is.

"What's today?" I ask.

"November 4, 2013," says Lucky.

"What the fuck! They've taken four years of our lives away! How could they? They snatched us up, and just like that, I've missed four Christmases, four birthdays, and every holiday with my family. Four school years are down the drain — I can't ever return, now! Four years without Damien — I just can't believe it. He probably doesn't even remember me anymore," I spiral, sinking in the deep end of my tears.

Elizabeth and Jen break down in tears, too. Lucky has no idea what to do. He feels horrible for what has happened to us. It's written all over his face. The doorbell rings. It's the police! They come upstairs, and we come down from the attic. We tell them everything. They say they're going to barge that place. They take us to the station and separate us into three different rooms.

I wait in the room for what feels like an eternity. Finally, someone comes in. He's an average-height, average-built man wearing an old-fashioned hat. His fingernails are manicured, and he's dressed in a suit with scuffed dress shoes. He looks familiar, but I can't figure out where I've seen him. The man's face is full of anger and sadness. His eyes are bloodshot red. Has he been crying? Without looking at me, he throws a folder on the table. I become very uncomfortable. What the heck is going on?

"Did you check out the house?" I ask him.

"Yes, we checked it out, and there was a lot of blood everywhere and dead bodies all over the place. You, sick bitch!" he yells.

"Fuck you! I'm the one who got sold!" I shout back.

"I don't care! Do you know what you did? I'm going to make sure you burn for what you did!" he threatens.

"Burn? What are you talking about?" I shout, frightened by his words and what will happen to me. "What did I ever do? I'm the one who got sold!"

"I don't give a flying fuck what happened to you! All I know is, I have one less son and one less nephew today because of you and your whorish friends!" He throws pictures at my face, and I see dead person after dead person. They're the men Jen, Elizabeth, and I killed when we were escaping. Pictures land face-up on the table, and there are images of dead girls. What is this — we didn't shoot at any girls! I don't remember seeing any girls except the one going down on the guy in the kitchen.

He points to one of the pictures, and it's the very first guy that I killed with the pipe. It's his son! He points to another picture, and it's his nephew. He's the second guy I killed that came into the basement. For a moment, in my mind, I relive the very moment I mashed his brains into smithereens. "We didn't kill these girls. They did! They were making us have sex against our will. We had no choice but to take those men out, or they were going to kill us!"

"There's always a choice, and you've been trouble since day one, you stupid bitch. You'll see how I run this damn town and how I'll destroy you and your whorish friends. You three will go to prison for the rest of your lives and fucking rot!" he berates.

"Please, you don't understand — you would've done the same thing. We didn't do anything wrong. We want to go home and be free. We want to see our families just like you want your son and nephew," I cry.

"I don't care! All I know is that I have one less son and nephew because of you, bitches," he yells, anger evident in his voice.

"We did what we had to do to survive," I plead in defense.

"And so did they! All you had to do to survive was lie there and open your fucking legs!"

His coldhearted words make my heart stop. My tears turn into plunging waterfalls. Oh my god, he knew what they were doing to us and didn't even care. He's part of them. "If that was your son and nephew, then they deserve worse than death. The only thing I regret is that you weren't down there with them so I could've bashed your brains out, too!" I blurt remorselessly.

He leaves the room, the door slamming behind him. I scream and flip over everything in sight. I pace back and forth and bang on the door. I collapse in the corner into a fetal position, sobbing. The guards come. They take me to a filthy cell where Jen is being held. Jen sees me and runs to hug me. We bawl our eyes out, knowing nothing good is in our future — our fate is in their hands.

"Where's Elizabeth?" I ask Jen, still sobbing.

"I don't know. I'm unsure what they've done with her," Jen replies.

"They're a part of them, Jen."

"What do you mean?" she asks worriedly.

"The two guys in the basement whose brains I bashed out were the detective's son and nephew. He knows they were trafficking us and didn't give a fuck when I tried to explain. He wants us to burn and rot."

"That's because he doesn't understand what we've gone through. We have to tell him," cries Jen.

"Jen, he won't listen!"

"We have to make him listen or speak to someone who will," she says, placing her hand on my shoulder.

"Yeah, we'll see. Did you see the detective?" I ask, unconvinced any authorities will be on our side.

"Yeah, I've seen that fucker," says Jen — now mad.

"Is it me, or did he look familiar?"

"I've seen so many men over the past four years; they all look the same, other than Lucky," she says, sitting on our decomposing jail bed.

I look around, becoming aware of our surroundings. My stomach churns. The bed is black and brownish, no longer white. The frame is rusted and rotted. It's two seconds from snapping — the jail cell smells of piss and shit. Rats are running around, the toilet is inoperable, and someone left a present in it that won't flush. Jen and I should be scared, but we aren't. It's a repeat of that dark dungeon they held us captive in. We're exhausted, but we stay up waiting for Elizabeth. Where the hell is she? What did they do to her?

The weening effect of not having drugs is taking a toll on us. We shiver uncontrollably. There's no Lucky to give us blankets this time. Jen and I huddle together to stay warm. We fall asleep. I dream of the first night we arrived at the basement. The light shines on Jen and me only. We're trembling in a line waiting to be inspected. The rest of the basement is dark except for the dim light from the narrow staircase. I see someone come from the stairs, but I can't make out who it is because the light is too dim. The indistinct figure is in a trench coat. Their collar is up; a brimmed hat covers their face. I presume it's a man.

The mysterious man appears briefly, then disappears into the thick darkness. It never registered in my mind because I was scared; things were happening quickly, but the disguised man was wearing a trench coat and an old man's hat — in what I now realize was the summertime! He was trying to disguise himself. I'm able to make it all out now because everything is occurring in slow motion. I can see his face. I know who he is, it's the detective! He hates me so much!

I wake up abruptly from my deep sleep. My dream is beyond shocking. Yet worse, two giant rats are on Jen and me! We lose it. We scream and jump. The bed snaps and breaks completely. We crash hard on the floor, we're up and alert now. We're freaking out; we move and jump around like our feet are trying to dodge hot coals. Elizabeth is still missing. The guards hear us screaming and come running.

"Qu'est-ce que vous criez, bordel?," he demands loudly. (What the fuck are you screaming for?)

"Rats et lits cassés!" Jen replies. (Rats and bed broke!)

"Fermez votre gueule, ou bien," he says, and turns around. (Shut the fuck up or else!)

"Attendre... Sir notre ami est- elle revenir?" (Sir... our friend, is she coming back?)

"Vous ne demandez pas question chienne." (Bitch! You don't ask questions.) He walks away, leaving us in silence. I pull Jen to the side when I'm confident we're alone again.

"I know where he's from!"

"He? Who? Where?" she says, confused.

"The day I was taken, do you remember them snatching off my necklace when they had us lined up? They were ripping everything off me and the other girls — clothes, jewelry, everything! The basement was real dark, but there was a dim light coming from the stairs and a brighter one on all us girls. I was watching those stairs — I never took my eyes off them. I remember one of the guys coming down them. When he got down to the bottom, he stepped into the dark — like he didn't want to be seen — it was strange but I still saw his face for a split second. Jen, I know who he is! I just figured it out in my dream — everything from that day was replaying in slow motion, frame by frame. I know his face Jen, it's —"

"The detective?" Jen blurts out.

"Yes!"

"We — are so fucked!" she gasps.

I nod, regrettably, to confirm. The door opens — they ask for me. The guard takes me and walks me to a room. It's Lucky! I'm so excited to see him. I run and hug him. He hugs me back and asks how they're treating me. I inform him of the horrible conditions and tell him everything, even about the detective.

"Oh shit, Dawnie! I didn't know! I wouldn't have ever called them. I'm so sorry you girls came to me for help. I've been of no help to you. I've let you down. I'll make this right and get you girls out of here — no matter what it takes, I promise. I have some of the best lawyers here in France. They're legally required to give you a fair trial. I'll not rest until you girls are safe and free of this depravity."

Lucky's face is wet, his eyes sunken in guilt and shame. He's filled with remorse. His body language gives it away. He pleads for my forgiveness and trust. I forgive him and trust him. He's very sorry for what's happened to us. I place my hand on him to calm him down and let him know that he's forgiven. I guess Lucky isn't so lucky after all. "It's okay, you didn't know. We didn't either," I say.

"What's your family's name? I'll let them know where you are," he says.

"No! If I'm going to be locked up, or worse, killed, I don't want them seeing me like this.."

"But…," he interjects.

"But nothing! You said you want to make this up to me — this is the way. I can't have my family seeing me for the first time in four years only to have me taken away again. Do you understand?" I demand.

"Yes, I do. I'll keep my word to get you the hell out of here. I promise," says Lucky.

"Thank you."

The door opens, and the guard says, "Times up." I'm escorted back to lockup. Lucky mentioning my family, makes me think about Bill and how they found me and would rescue me.

My shackles hit the floor while walking. I reflect on how the girls and I should've been patient and waited for them. We wouldn't be in this mess had we waited. I was so eager to leave and experience the smell and taste of freedom. But look at us, our future — doomed. There's no telling what awaits us now. I haven't even told the girls about Bill, and if I do now, I'm scared they might hate me for not waiting for my family to rescue us. Instead, my eagerness to escape by Alejandro's wits has landed us here in this situation.

I wonder what happened to Alejandro. I don't think he's dead. They're probably torturing him everyday, killing him slowly, and making him an example for all in that dark world to see. I feel for him, and I hate that this is his fate.

I arrive back at the cell. Elizabeth's back, and she and Jen are waiting for me. The three of us are happy to see each other; we hug. "Why were you gone for so long?" I ask Elizabeth.

"I don't know. They left me in a small interrogation room forever. They asked me questions, yelled at me, and told me we're all guilty. They think we killed them unjustifiably. They said we're cold-blooded killers."

"Elizabeth, the two men in the basement are the detective's son and nephew. The detective is part of their organization. I remember seeing him in the basement, watching us be tormented."

"Shit, Dawnie! We're so fucking dead!" she freaks.

"Lucky is going to get his lawyer for us. He said his lawyer is the best of the best — and they can get us out. I believe Lucky. He's determined to get us out of here — he's on our side." I say, trying to instill some sense of hope.

"When did he say that?" Jen asks curiously.

"A few minutes ago — when the guard took me away, he took me to see him. I told him everything that's going on in here. Lucky's distraught."

"You think we can trust him? He was the one insisting on calling the police," Elizabeth reminds us.

"Yes," Jen says confidently, walking up. "I'm one hundred percent confident, he didn't have the slightest idea about this. He was trying to help us. Lucky might not be as lucky to us right now, but he's a guy who cares about our freedom."

"Yeah, she's right. We can trust him. He didn't know anything about our situation until we told him. I could see it in his eyes and body language. He's hurt about it all — as much as we are. He told me he's not going to rest until we're out of here, safe, and back with our families."

Chapter 49

SURPRISE, SURPRISE!

The guard comes in and asks for me again. He takes me to another interrogation room, just like the one I spoke to Lucky in, but this time, no one is waiting for me. I sit down, and to my surprise, my worst nightmare enters. It's not the detective, but it's that son of a bitch, Mark. "Hello, my lovely cunt of a wife," he says, smiling devilishly.

"Mr. McCabe, it's so nice to see you," I snarkily reply.

"Oh, so you know my last name now, huh?"

"Oh, no, you mean our last name. Did you forget I'm Mrs. McCabe now? Can't remember?"

"How could I forget, my lovely bride?" he says, with a look of demise.

"What are you doing here, Mark?"

"Well, I'm just seeing if you're okay."

"I'm in a French jail, away from my family, whom I may never see again! I left one bottomless pit only to be dragged into another. How do you think I'm doing?"

"Oh, things aren't that bad yet. They were great for you when you were in my care, but now, you have no idea how bad they're about to become for you."

"Mark, I've been kidnapped, sold, forced to take drugs, and now an addict. Beaten, cut, threatened, raped, had psychos like you fall in love with me, and forced into marriage. I was nearly killed by the hands of my husband — you! Locked away in hell, had to kill people for my safety, and almost died! I've missed four of my birthdays and so many holidays with my family, and saw my mother Tracy's brain blown out of her head. So, please enlighten me on what could be more diabolical than what I've already been through. Enlighten me, please! Now!"

"Prison de L'inconnu," he says, grinning.

"We haven't had a trial yet, idiot. There must be a trial before prison. It's the law here in France."

He laughs, "Trial? What makes you think there's going to be a trial? This isn't America, sweetheart. It's France, and it's my country. The McCabe family owns this country, especially this town. Your paperwork is all set. You and your little pawns are going to L'inconnu." He sits up in his chair and leans closer to me. "Your new home is one of the most dangerous prisons in the world. The lovely inmates there are your new family since everything I offered you was never good enough."

"Offered me? Kidnapping girls, selling them for money, killing our families, beating us to keep us in line, and heavy, rusty chains around our ankles in a dark, rat-infested basement is what you call 'good enough,' Mark?"

"You're going to wish you were with me when you get to that deadly coop." he snips.

"Anything is better than being with you. At least I'll be away from you and the drugs," I snap back.

He gets up and leaves the room. I know everything he said is true, but I couldn't let him see he was getting to me. When I know he's gone, I break down. All I want is to stop being a man's concubine and whore, be set free, see my family, and see Damien again. Instead, I get a first-class ticket to a life sentence straight to hell and no way of ever returning home.

Lucky said he would get us out, but there's not going to be a trial. His lawyer will not have an opportunity to defend us and get us out of here. I hear the guards coming. I wipe my eyes. I will not give them the satisfaction of seeing me like this. I return to the cell. The girls think I just met with Lucky again. They're thinking things are good to go with our lawyer. The cell door slams behind me.

"What did he say?" Elizabeth asks, desperately wanting to know.

"It wasn't Lucky. It was Mark!"

"Fuck the French King and his Queen!" Elizabeth gasps.

"Dude, this is France, not England," says Jen.

"I know where we are, hence, the French part. Looks like someone hasn't read the right history books lately." Elizabeth snidely remarks. "Anyway, what the hell did Mark say?" Elizabeth repeats her question.

"He said that there isn't going to be a trial, and we will be serving a life sentence in one of the most dangerous prisons in the world called Prison De L'inconnu."

"What! No trial? What do you mean? I've never heard of a prison called 'Prison of the Unknown,'" Jen says, reminding us that she understands French better than we do.

"They own this town and this country. Mark said the paperwork is finalized, and they're getting ready to transport us there now. Is that what Prison De L'inconnu means?"

"Yeah, that's what it means. What about Lucky?" Jen says, starting to worry.

"What about him? He can't do anything with the McCabe family running everything around here. By the time he finds out, we'll be inmates there already."

"This is bullshit! What have we ever done to anyone to have this kind of evil thrown our way?" Jen says, punching the wall hard — making a loud bang.

"I don't know, but God is angry with us for some unknown reason," I answer.

"You think?" Jen replies.

The withdrawals become worse. I was doing so well weaning off the drugs, but this entire ordeal has me feigning for a hit. I need to relax. I need to calm my nerves. The three of us sweat and experience body chills at the same time. My back and head are killing me. I want to die. My stomach is aching. I curl into a ball on the floor in severe pain. My body hurts so bad that I don't care about the rats, mold, or the coldness seeping through my bones from the concrete floor. I use the floor as an icepack, hoping it'll lend me some relief.

The girls are in worse shape than me. Elizabeth paces back and forth. She bends over in pain, crying. We each take turns throwing up in the broken toilet. We can't keep down the sandwiches Lucky fed us. Our digestive tracks need realigning, I'm sure. The toilet fills to the brim with our vomit. We're unable to flush it. Our jail cell is so bad that the guards are too grossed out to send for help.

Things are in motion. They instruct us to come out of our cell and escort us to a holding room. They don't usually make the inmates wash up before being transported, but we're in such bad condition they make an exception. They strip us from our clothing and snatch the necklace from my neck, the one that Damien gave me. I almost yell in protest, but I start dry heaving instead. There is nothing left in me. We can't stand up fully to wash ourselves because we're in agonizing pain. Instead, they spray us down.

The powerful water hose against my body feels like someone is stabbing my body over and over again. I know it's set to the highest setting. Every inch of water that hits my body stings. Two of the guards leave the room while one stays. The guard left behind looks sad, his face full of guilt. He wants to help us, but he knows he can't. He walks over to us and asks if we're okay. We shake our heads, no, and he apologizes for our suffering. He doesn't understand what's going on.

He's muscular with a shortcut and slightly tanned. He's paler and shorter than the others and wears eyeglasses. They look like name-brand ones. He doesn't look like he should even be a guard. I tell him to go away before he gets the same treatment. I don't want him to get hurt because he has a big heart towards us.

The other guards return and gives us clothes to put on. They drag us because we're too weak to walk. They don't send for a nurse or give us anything to coat our stomachs. Our bodies feel empty, and we're so weak. I don't know how much longer we can hold on to this almost lifeless state. They throw us in the back of a truck.

"D?"

"Yeah, Jen"

"The guard who said 'sorry' slipped me your necklace."

"Thank you, Jen. You know how important this necklace is to me," I reply, with nothing left in me. I cry from the inside. I need my necklace because it's the only thing that connects me to Damien. I thought I lost it forever. I didn't think I would ever see it again, but somehow, it always finds its way back to me. Thanks to that guard with a big heart, I have it back again.

"D?"

"Yeah, Jen."

"They're going to kill us, aren't they?"

"They will try, but—"

"I'm not dying here — and not like this!" Elizabeth buts in, surprising the hell out of me with her courage.

"Exactly. We must get better and fight. What doesn't kill us will make us stronger," I say, reaffirming my cousin's hint of grit.

"We're the strongest people in the world," Jen says.

"Girls, we must stay together and never break apart. We've been through too much to give up now. We must stay hopeful that we will get out of here and back to our families. We must remember who we are and use that as strength."

"I don't even remember who I am anymore," Elizabeth cries.

"I do. You're Elizabeth, soon to be married to Aengus, who loves you very much. I'm going to marry Damien and have a family with him. Jen, I know you must also have special people in your life. We three must always remain focused. We must keep our heads on a swivel and stay strong to get through this."

"Yes, I do," says Jen. "My family is special to me, but it's complicated. My parents aren't on the best of terms, but I miss them, especially my brother. We were always close. It's hard going through all this without him. He's always been a source of strength and encouragement to me."

"See what I'm saying? We all have something to live for. We must stick together in this fucked up prison, no matter what. We've killed before; if we have to kill again, then so be it. Do you understand me?" I say, glaring at them with confidence and authority bolting through my veins.

"Yes," they reply.

We're silent for the rest of the ride. We arrive at the prison. A guard gives us each a blanket, towel, soap, and toothbrush when we enter. Ironically, Elizabeth and Jen's cells are next to mine. As for me, I share a prison cell with a woman but I can't see her face because she's writing something on a piece of paper. "Which bunk is yours?" I ask, trying not to aggravate her.

"The top one," she replies. She continues writing, never looking at me. I put my things on the bottom bunk and sit on it silently, surprised by her English.

"You speak English?" I ask curiously.

"Yup, and so do you. What you in for?" she asks.

"My friends and I are in for murder."

"Who'd you murder? Father? Mother? Lover?" she inquires, her interest in me now peaked by my crime.

"No. Human traffickers kidnapped us and turned us into drug attics and whores. They sold us to men and locked us away in a fucking basement," I explain while becoming emotional. She stops writing and lifts her head slowly. I can now see her face. I have her full attention. She's entirely focused on me. She's beautiful and a skinny woman about ten or more years older than me, about thirty or so. Her long brown hair matches her brown eyes, and her teeth are white. Her clean appearance makes me wonder if she just arrived here, too.

"What's your name, young one?" she asks, standing up and approaching me slowly.

"Dawn Sandino. Well, McCabe now, supposedly. I was forced to marry one of the sons in the McCabe family against my will."

She stares at me and touches my face. I remain still but also scared. I have no idea what's going on. Is my prison mate going to make me her bitch in here? I don't want to be her girlfriend. I grab her hand quickly. I tighten my grip, trying to act tough, "I'm not yours to touch." I let her know. She makes this insane quick maneuver and flips me over to my stomach. With a fist full of my hair, she uses her other hand and runs it down my back and body slowly and seductively.

She breathes on my neck and whispers, "You have heart and guts doing what you just did. Don't you know that kind of shit will get you killed here, bitch? If you were anybody else right now, I'd

fuck you over and over again. You'd be my little sex slave in here."
She turns me over. I lay on my back facing her, trying to avoid eye
contact. This psycho woman has me in total fear. "I could've killed
you already and mailed your body to your family. You think you're
big shit, huh? Killing someone with a gun doesn't make you shit if
you can't fight."

"Get off of me, you bitch!" I roar, trying to sound as tough as I
can. She boffs. She's not taking me seriously — it's funny to her.

"You're lucky you're far from my type. I don't like young ones, but
I love your bravery and guts. Tell you what, I'll take you under my
wings and make you stronger. I'm going to rid you of that baby-ass
fear you have. I'll make you stronger and fearless. I'll make people
fear you." She releases my hair and sets me free. She gets off my
bed and returns to whatever she's working on.

"How can you do that? What's your reason?" I ask.

"Because you remind me of myself, and you're young. You don't
belong here like the rest of us, and you know it. You and your
friends will die without my help, and we're connected. One day,
you'll see why."

"Why 'one day?' Why not now?"

"Because you're still young, dumb, and too weak to understand."

"Try me." I retort.

"Maybe another day. Get some sleep. We have a long day
tomorrow."

It's nighttime and I'm not able to sleep for shit. I hear nothing but
rats scrambling around and inmates yelling, fucking, and banging
and clanging on their cell doors. Worse, my nightmares about Earl,
Mark, and others haunt me. My nightmares hit me like a bulldozer,
coming on at once. I've never experienced nightmares to this degree
before, not even in Mark's hell. This place must be the lowest part
of hell to make me have nightmares about Earl again. Before I know
it, the guards bang on the prison walls with their batons, waking us
up. My fellow prisoner wakes up with a smile on her face.

"Good morning. Oh god, you look like shit, sweetheart," she says
in a rough, cracked tone.

"Yeah, and why don't you? How can you sleep in a place like this?
I've had nothing but nightmares all fucking night." I reply.

She laughs, "Yeah, I used to be the same way when I first got here."

"How long have you been in?"

"Oh, baby, I don't know. After ten years, I lost count."

"Ten years! And you look like that? I thought you just got here like me."

She laughs, "No, I did not, and I'm never leaving here."

"You got life, too?" I respond curiously.

"No, not like me. You're not spending the rest of your life here. Over my dead body," she proclaims.

"Sadly, that's not up to you. Wish it was, though." I reply. She looks at me, her face and mind hard to read. She has no facial expression. She stares me straight on.

"How do you stay sane in this fucking place?" I wail.

She laughs again. "Honey, I learned to make the best out of everything. If I let everything get to me, I'd look like... hell, like you."

"I can't make the best out of mine. I'm not meant to be happy, just miserable."

"I used to think the same thing when I was your age. Shit, I even hated myself, but I learned to deal with my problems. I used to be weak and broken, but I taught myself to be strong and glued myself back together."

"You must've been through a lot."

"You have no idea what I've been through."

"Maybe you can tell me," I say, wanting to know her story.

"Maybe. Get on kitchen duty. That way, you know what's going in the food. You'll learn that kitchen duty helps you control certain things and people," she says and walks out. I follow her.

"Hello, everyone — lovely prison morning, isn't it?" she announces to the other inmates with a big smile.

Elizabeth and Jen are watching me like a hawk, wondering what the fuck is going on. I look at them and shrug my shoulders. My prison mate turns towards them, "You two must be her friends. Well, I was just telling Dawnie here that you girls are going to be on kitchen duty. Dawnie will fill you in on the details," she tells them. She prances around the hallway. Her hands are in the air, and she moves her hips from side to side.

"What the fuck is she on?" Jen asks.

"I don't know, but I need some — and as soon as possible," I say back, just as confused.

"Shit, we all do," says Jen.

"Line up!" guards yell. They pat us down and proceed to destroy everyone's cell except for my prison mate's and mine in search of something.

"What are they looking for?" I whisper, looking over to my prison mate.

She mouths back, "Weapons."

While they ransack the other inmates' cells, I see what this prison looks like. It's horrible. The railings are rusty, and everything reeks of feces. Inmates' clothes are torn and soiled, and reek of shit. The guards find something in one of the inmate's cells. They beat her and the other inmates standing around.

"Don't look any of the guards in their eyes, ever. You don't want to cause any trouble for yourself," my prison mate warns.

"Why are they beating them?" I ask.

"Because they can — they don't need a reason. They run this shit. This is just a reminder for us, so we won't forget."

They finish raiding everyone's cell. I help Elizabeth and Jen straighten their cell back up and head to kitchen duty. Somehow, we're already set up for it. It feels like we were expected here. I don't know what's worse, the kitchen or the cell blocks. Rats and roaches are everywhere, from the ceiling, floor, and sink, which is black as night. It's like this whole prison was abandoned and they just opened it back up one day and didn't care to decontaminate the place.

My job is mixing this unidentified mud in a pot and serving it. My prison mate is in charge, I assume, because she's spewing out orders. I plop some food on one of the girl's trays. She looks at the other inmate's tray in line in front of her and gives me the death stare.

"Something wrong?" I ask, wondering what the hell her problem is.

"Oui, tu lui as donné bien plus que moi," she says, spitefully. (Yeah, you gave her way more than me.)

Her teeth are rotted and nearly gone; her hair is sticking up on the top of her head, and she reeks of death. I look at Jen since she's the only one who understands French. "She's complaining that you gave the other lady more than her," Jen says.

"But I didn't. It's the same amount." I whisper back. The lady starts yelling, and Jen shakes her head in fear.

"Laissez-les tranquilles!" my prison mate shouts. (Leave them alone!)

"Davina, rester hors d'elle!" the lady screams back. (Davina, stay out of it!)

My prison mate, whose name I now know is Davina, smacks the tray out of the deranged woman's hand. She grabs her by the hair and slams her on the table, causing the hot pot of mud to spill on her. She screeches in pain. The scolding hot grime is all over her. Everyone is silent. They look scared for what will happen next. One of the guards run over, yelling, "Qu'est-ce que tout le bruit?" (What's all the noise?)

"Elle a glissé et s'est cogné la tête," Davina says. (She slipped and banged her head.)

"Oui, je la vois," the guard says and walks away. (Yes, I see.)

Everyone stays silent. They pretend everything is normal. Elizabeth, Jen, and I are the only ones in complete shock. The woman tries to get up from the floor but keeps stumbling. I start to clean up the mess, but Davina grabs my arm. "No. Serves her right! Guarantee you, she will think twice next time." I nod my head and stop cleaning. Davina approaches Jen and Elizabeth. She tells them to stop shaking in fear. They nod their heads in agreement and continue serving food.

"You, come with me," Davina instructs me. I follow her, a little scared of what will happen next.

"Why are you helping us? We don't even fucking know you, and you don't fucking know us. What do we owe you? Nothing's ever for fucking free! I'm not going to be your bitch! I'm not going down that easy. So, why?" I demand, regurgitating the thoughts in my head.

We're alone now; maybe this wasn't a good idea. I shouldn't be approaching her alone. I can't take her on by myself. She sets her pen and pad down on a table. I should start backing up. She walks towards me, but I stand my ground. I pray she doesn't whoop my ass like last night.

Davina stands directly in front of me and stares deep into my eyes. "I look at you and see a little girl who can't be no more than nineteen. Yet, you've been through more than anyone and possibly me. You were forced to grow up. You never had a childhood, and the little inclination of the one you had was quickly snatched away from you. You were taken away from people you love and love you. You're terrified, but try not to show it. Your friends look to you for direction and help. You have no idea how to help or what to do, but you try anyway. I see fear and confusion, courage, and a little girl screaming for help. I see myself in you. That's why I offer you my help and guidance. If you don't want it, that's fine. You don't have to take it. You can be controlled and abused like the others. Perhaps, raped or killed," she says, leaving me standing there alone. I never knew anyone could see all that by looking at me. I wonder what else people can see.

Breakfast ends, and we're sent back to our cages. The other inmates are very noisy. For some reason, I get a funny feeling that something terrible is about to happen. Davina must still be in the kitchen because our less-than-glorious room is empty. They don't close our cell doors, and it's loud and noisy on our wing. I lie on my bunk and glare at the one on top since it's blocking my ceiling view.

"Hey, fresh meat," a woman says, catching my attention with her horrible English.

"Hey, Davina is not here. She'll be here soon, though, if you want to come back." I tell her, expecting her to leave and come back later, but she doesn't. Instead, she walks in and sits at the desk in my room, making a small laugh. She walks over to my bunk and sits at the foot of the bed. I sit up, wondering why she's here.

"Maintenant!" she shouts. (Now!) Clueless what she's bellowing, I immediately regret that I still have not learned French. Two more women walk in. I can't lie to myself — I'm scared like crazy. I know they're going to jump or rape me, probably both. One of the girls stand at my cell door as the lookout. I stand up, fixing to open my mouth and scream, but the bitch by the bed punches me in the stomach, knocking the wind out of me.

Elizabeth and Jen hear me squeal before my mouth gets covered. They come busting in. They tackle the lookout dog. Elizabeth screams for help and kicks the other woman, who's part of the pack, down to the cement floor. The lookout gets up from the floor from Elizabeth's tackle, and Jen jumps on her back as she gains up on me. We're getting fucked up. I don't know if I prefer to have Mark or this bitch hit me. No need to think, the bitch punches me and makes my mind up for me. I prefer Mark to beat me.

She grabs my hair. I land against her chest. Her mistake and my only moment! I bite her tit as hard as I can. I feel and taste the blood that oozes out of her left boob. She howls like someone shot her in the face. Everyone in the room stops fighting and looks at us. I continue to bite down in rage and revenge. No one comes near us, not even Jen or Elizabeth.

"Stop it, you'll bite it off!" The other lady with the broken English shouts.

The bitch that has her tit still between my teeth is soaked in blood. She tries to tear me off her, but I clutch my teeth harder. The muscles between my teeth are tense, making it challenging to bite down even harder than I already am, but I push myself to do it anyway. I breathe heavily, panting in and out. In the distance, I hear footsteps running, coming near.

"Bite that shit off and teach her a lesson!" Jen shouts.

"No!" Elizabeth screams.

I do it anyway. I bite the bitch's nipple clean off. It wasn't easy at first to bite off, but all my anger and hate motivate me to finish her. If I do something this insane, I figure people won't mess with us anymore. She collapses to the floor, defeated, with blood gushing out of her. I look Jen in the eyes — we mirror each other. Her smile is filled with anger, revenge, and hate.

"Oh, mon dieu!" the guard shouts, looking at me. (Oh my God!)

"What the devil!" Davina yells, utterly stunned, entering our pen.

I spit out the woman's nipple, and it lands on her on the floor. I brace myself for the prison guards to whoop my ass. The guards come for me, Elizabeth, and Jen. They beat our asses and separate us by placing us each in tiny dark rooms alone. Once again, I'm inhaling the smell of piss and shit. The bed is soaked. I know it's some other bitch's urine. Dried-up blood is all over my face and shirt. Everything replays in my head. Everyone was shocked by my tit-biting stunt, including me. I think I've caused more problems for us. Maybe I should've waited for Davina's help.

Days pass by while being held in the prison hole. The room is so dark that my eyes flinch whenever they open the door and light beams in. I'm given food and water every day, or what they call food and water. This food is shit. It's moldy, nearly inedible. I wouldn't even feed this to a dying, starving baby. The cup my water is in is filthy and has a roach floating. I'm so thirsty and hungry; I remove the roach, drink the water, and eat the food.

The door opens, and someone comes in and sits next to me on the bed while I lie there. The door slams shut; I shriek under the tissue paper they call a bedsheet. The woman says, "Thank you." I relax, by the voice I hear, it's Davina.

I open my eyes. "Fuck, Davina! You scared the shit out of me!"

"Stop cursing so much. It makes you sound uneducated. Look who's talking about scaring people. You just sent a female off to a civilian hospital without a nipple," she chuckles villainously. "I had to disinfect the room because of all the blood," she says, bringing out a wet rag. She wipes the weeks' old of dry blood off my face. She hands me a clean shirt.

"I didn't mean to, I'm sorry. She was fucking us up, and my adrenaline kicked in. I was so scared. My friends ran in and started getting beat up. She had me by the hair, and when I looked up, her tit was in my face, so I bit it. Jen told me not to give up, but Elizabeth wanted me to stop."

"Your survival genes kicked in, and you lost it. You and Jen are very similar in ways. You must be best friends."

"No, we aren't. Well, I don't know. We were chained in a basement together, and that's how we met. We had a connection and desire to protect each other. And... Elizabeth's my cousin and was kidnapped not too long after me."

"Kidnapped and chained. Yeah, you told me that." she reminds me. "What a shame," she says.

"Yeah, four years and human trafficked!"

"Hell, I'm listening. Whew, I thought I had problems. So, who did you exactly assassinate? There is no way you're going through all this because you killed human traffickers."

"We shot our way out of there. I killed an officer's son and nephew. They were our kidnappers, though, and held us hostage for years. What's assassinate?"

"It means to murder someone of position or status. No wonder there wasn't a trial. Let me guess, they were working for them, huh?"

"Yeah, and how do you know? I never told you about us not having a trial." I say, puzzled by her having this information.

"Sweetheart, I have connections in the outside world and here. How do you think I'm here in your prison hole right now, wiping your face and giving you clean clothes? In solitary confinement, there are no visitors. Think about it. Our room was never ransacked like the other inmates, and you got on kitchen duty so quickly. Everyone wants kitchen duty. You know, access to more food. This isn't normal in this prison, Dawnie. I run this prison and always have from day one of my arrival."

"How?"

"I was tired of being dumb when I lived in the outside world. I made friends outside and with the warden and wards here. I even have a few guards in love with me. It took me some time, but I get what I want when I want now — warm showers every day, new clothes, makeup, sex, good food, not that mud stuff, and anything I demand."

"Why are you here?" I ask her, hoping she finally tells me.

"I told you; we're very similar. The same thing that brought you here is what brought me here, and I'm not talking about murder or human trafficking."

"I'm scared," I say.

"So was I. But the difference is, I was alone, and you're not. You have me and your friends."

"Davina, I can't fight, I'm dumb as fuck, and I can't speak French or understand it too well. I don't know how to make connections like you, and as far as sex is concerned, I don't want it unless it's Damien. I'm inexperienced regarding your tactics; should I continue?"

"You just bit off a woman's boob! Yes, you're young, but not like other girls. You've been through so much and experienced more than most in three lifetimes. You can't speak French well, but I'll teach you and your friends. You know how to fight; you need to remember how. I'll have the guards watch over you and protect you," says Davina.

"No!" I roar, making sure I have her attention. "I don't want protection. I want your guidance. Teach me how to fight. Teach me how to earn respect. Teach me how to speak French and other languages. Make my vocabulary bigger. Make me smarter. Teach me everything I don't know and need to know. I don't care what I have to go through. I'm up for the challenge, and I want to learn. I want to go through what you went through. Hell, let me go through worse, if I have to." I beg her.

"Are you sure?" she says.

"What happens if the guards get mad and decide not to protect me? I need to be able to defend myself. I no longer want to be weak, scared, and stupid."

"You'll always have some fear," she says.

"Not here, I won't," I say back, my confidence reemerging.

"You're not stupid, Dawnie. You lack knowledge."

"Translation for stupid," I retort.

She kisses my forehead and taps on the door so the guards can open it and let her out. "I'll check on your friends again. Last time I checked, they were okay."

"Thank you."

"No problem." The door slams shut behind her. I lie down to reflect, feeling way better than before. Davina cleaned the blood off me, gave me clean clothes to wear, and is going to help me. Thank God the girls are safe. I don't know what I'd do if something happened to them — Davina will help me through it like she has everything else, I think to myself. I start to doze off but hear people talking outside of my claustrophobic cage. My sleepiness kicks in. I ignore them, but the last thing I hear is Davina's voice telling someone, "At 4:00 p.m. tomorrow."

I have nightmares as usual. Oddly, snippets of Davina randomly appear in between them. She's younger. We're playing in someone's backyard. We're happy, but the image keeps cutting off whenever she looks up. My nightmares of Earl and Mark return. I sit up, awakened by the sound of my cell door opening. I get out of bed, and Elizabeth and Jen walk in. Maybe they're releasing us from solitary confinement. It turns out to be just a little freedom while still in the prison tank. I plop down on the bed and close my eyes. I've had no rest, tossing and turning all night because of the nightmares. Jen hands me my necklace. I put it on, and they sit on my bed with me.

"Davina seen us," Jen tells me.

"Yeah, me too," I reply, my eyes still shut.

"She's going to protect us," Elizabeth says.

"No. She's going to teach us." Jen says.

The guard comes in, "McCabe, aller à la salle de blanchisserie."

"He says, go to the laundry room," Jen translates.

"Seul vous." the guard says. (Only you.) We look at each other in confusion.

"He wants you to go alone. I don't like the sound of this at all," says Jen with angst.

"Shit. Me neither!" I reply.

"I'm not leaving you," she tells me.

"You have no choice, Jen, but you should stay here. I'll be okay, don't worry," I lie.

"Bullshit!" she argues.

Elizabeth is quiet but freaking out, given the panic written on her face. Jen and I look at each other, instantly remembering Elizabeth isn't as brave as we are. "There is nothing we can do," Elizabeth says.

"Fuck that. I'll find a way down there somehow. Try to take your time before leaving. Stall!" Jen tells me. I nod yes but do not know how I'm supposed to stall. The guard eyes me down. He wants me to move now.

"Dépêchez-vous de!" the guard yells.

"He wants you to hurry. Walk slow," Jen says.

I start walking. I look around, watching to see if someone tries to attack me. It's the longest, darkest hallway, and it's empty, but I can feel the presence of others. However, no one is in sight. "Hello?" I call out in a low voice. No one answers but my echo. I walk slowly, hoping Jen is trailing behind me. "Hello?" I repeat. Nothing again but my echoes. I make it halfway down the hallway, and a woman pops out of nowhere. She scares the shit out of me, but I don't jump, I hold my stance for a second. I back up and bump into two female inmates standing behind me. I'm about to get another ass beating. "Shit!"

I try to scream and run but one of them covers my mouth and holds my arms back, leaving the front of my body exposed. The other red-headed inmate closes in on me. My instincts kick in. I raise my leg and kick her in the face. She hits the floor hard. I spit on her. The other girl with a scar on her cheek runs up and punches me in the face, wanting my face to match hers. The one holding me throws me to the floor. I'm losing, but still manage to get some punches in. I hear Jen yelling. She sprints down the long hallway and joins the fight. In seconds, Jen is right next to me on the floor. A door opens and see Elizabeth running down the hall with a guard in tow and yelling something. With all her might, Carrot Top head punches my lights out before they reach us.

Chapter 50

INFIRMARY

I try to wake up but can't open my eyes or speak. I go crazy and start thinking the worst. Someone gently touches my arm. Instantly, I know it's Davina. I calm down, still feeling somewhat tense. I'm worried about Jen and Elizabeth. "Shh, Jen is okay — just got knocked out. Your eyes are swollen shut, and your jaw is wired closed because it's broken. If you talk, it's going to hurt. It'll also be too hard to understand you. I'd stay quiet if I were you for the first week or so. Elizabeth is in the other room, asleep. There's a guard on duty watching her," she informs me.

I relax a little more, but not entirely because I'm still in pain. "You fought back," Davina says proudly. I nod my head, agreeing. How did Davina know I fought back? Too bad I can't ask her because I can't move my mouth. It literally won't move. I try to open it but shut it just as quickly. She wasn't lying; it hurts like hell.

"You said you wanted to learn how to fight — what better way to learn than to get thrown in one. You girls surprised the hell out of me, I swear. Dawnie, you didn't punk down, and Jen came blazing in to help you. Elizabeth went to get help. Keep your friends close, especially Jen, because she's a true friend. Jen will be in the trenches with you, and Elizabeth is the girl who bails you out. You'll never be alone as long as you have Jen. She's your ride or die," she says, touching my arm again.

Davina's words keep repeating, but I don't know why. I fall asleep and dream of Davina. She's younger. She's with Uncle David and Grandpa Sal and who must be Alex because there are two Davids, Andrea and Fawn.

It's a family barbecue, and I'm much younger. I play with Alex, then swim over to Davina. We play in the pool together. She has a vibrant and unforgettable necklace with an intriguing and captivating Phoenix as its charm. "Aunt Vina," I say as she picks me up in the pool.

We're all playing, but I'm mainly attached to Davina. Everyone is happy. It's a true family. Andrea is also present but keeps leaving the family gathering and returning. Everyone else stays. We're now eating and laughing at the table. Alex is wedged between me and Fawn while we eat. Davina is on my other side, and we're all smiles.

"Dawnie… Dawnie… Dawnie…," Davina repeats. The sound of her voice wakes me up. I try and open my eyes, but they're too swollen. "Raise your hand if you're awake." I do what she says, cringing in pain. "The doctor is here to check on you." The doctor conducts his checkup and leaves the room. Davina presses my broken ribs. I scream in pain. "Silence. You must learn how to endure pain. If something hurts, you can't let anyone know. Show no weakness. Pain is only weakness that leaves the body," she says, adding more pressure.

I'm about to pass back out from the pain but hear Jen screaming next to me — she's in pain, too. I fall back asleep. Are these real memories I'm having, or am I imagining things? These dreams feel so real, and my memories are so strong. Maybe they're memories. Perhaps these are actual events I'm remembering. I wake up briefly, my eyes still closed. I'm so tired I pass back out. My dream repeats. We're in Grandpa Sal's backyard. Uncle David and Alex are play-fighting. Grandpa Sal watches with Fawn on his Lap. I'm with Davina, and she's teaching me how to fight. I throw a punch and miss. She punches me hard in the face, causing me to fall.

I sit up, holding my cheek, crying. I don't think anyone sees me, not even Grandpa Sal. They all continue with what they're doing. Davina bends down to me and whispers, "Shh, it's okay. You must learn how to defend yourself. You'll need to know how to do more than anyone else someday. I know it hurts, but you must learn how to endure pain. Become one with pain, and it won't hurt so bad." I nod my head, letting her know that I understand, and stand up to play fight with her some more. I notice her necklace again dangling in front of me. I go to touch it, but she grabs my hand.

"Trust me, Dawnie, you don't want this necklace."

"But it's so pretty, Aunt Vina."

"Baby, you don't know what I've done to earn this. Hopefully, you won't have to know what it is to be a Phoenix. This is something you earn and the book that's written about us." I wake up again. This time, I open my eyes a little to peek. The doctor is flashing a light in my eyes, I turn away in pain.

"She's healing faster than anyone I've ever seen before," says the doctor.

"Yeah, it runs in the family blood," Davina says, confirming that everything I dreamed was real things that happened. She's my aunt. For once, I'm happy. But what happened? Why haven't I remembered Grandpa Sal, Uncle David, Davina, Andrea, and Alex? Why didn't they remember me? Why did Alex leave? What did Davina do? Why is my aunt in jail? Days later, I become well enough to open my eyes fully and speak. I'm not sure how long I've been here, but my entire body still hurts. I decide not to complain in fear of Davina touching my bruises and making them worse. She's sitting in a chair next to me, reading a book. I can't see the title.

"How long was I out for?" I ask, my voice slightly cracked.

"Long enough, Dawnie," she replies, never looking away from her book.

"Elizabeth and Jen?"

"Fine. They're both sleeping in the other room. They have guards." There's a long silence that feels like an eternity. "You talk in your sleep," Davina mentions.

"Sorry, I wasn't aware of that," I reply, feeling the soreness in my jaw.

"Well, you need to be. Don't want you giving out vital information because you can't keep quiet during shut-eye."

"You're right, Auntie Vina," I say, looking at her. She smiles.

"Knew it was only a moment before you started remembering, especially after hearing you sleep-talking."

"So, when were you going to tell me?" I ask her.

"I wasn't. You were going to find out, which you did."

"So, what happened? Why, when I met Grandpa Sal, Uncle David, and Andrea for what I thought was the first time, they acted as if they didn't remember me?"

"Because Grandpa Sal and your Uncle David don't remember you."

"Why don't they?" I ask curiously.

"Why didn't you?" she questions me back.

"I… don't know." I utter, slowly realizing her point. "What happened to us? Why don't I remember anything before the age of nine? Your necklace? The book?"

She laughs and looks up, "This is something only you can answer. The book is somewhere no one knows," says Aunt Davina, giving off mystic vibes.

"You don't know why? What is the book about?" I ask, eagerly wanting an explanation.

"I didn't say that; the book is about you, Dawnie."

"You're not going to tell me what happened? What do you mean it's about me?"

"You're a smart girl, sweetheart. You've always been more determined, anxious, and curious. You were far too knowledgeable for your age and still are — full of questions without answers. Sadly, whoever knew or knows this about you is to blame for your downfall. The book is about your life. It was written before your conception."

"So, it's my fault they forgot? How is a book written about me?"

"No, it's not your fault at all. I've said too much already. I can't say anymore."

"Why can't I find out now?" I persist, still desiring answers.

"You already know the answer. It hasn't come to you because you're not ready for the information."

"How do you know what I'm ready for?" I shoot back.

"Because if you were ready for it, then you wouldn't be asking me to be—"

"Because… I'd already have the answer if I were ready for it?" I say, finishing her sentence.

She smiles, "Exactly. You learn quickly; you always did."

"What did you go through when you got here?" I ask.

"Hell — and more," Aunt Davina replies.

"Are you taking it easy on me?" I ask.

"Yes."

"Why?"

"Because you've already been through a lot. I don't want to put you through more than you can handle."

"I can handle a lot; you'd be surprised," I say, confidently, pushing through my aches and pain.

"We can handle more than a lot," Jen says from the other side of the curtain. Davina slides the curtain open, and Jen and I look at each other.

"You're awake!" I say.

"Yeah, and so are you." She turns to me, "If you have to go through something, I am too. You said that we were in this together when we were being transferred here. That meant something to me and still does, or I wouldn't be here. I can't speak for Elizabeth, but I doubt she'll be for it."

"I don't think she will either. She insists on the easy way out," I say, agreeing with her, looking over to my aunt.

"Yes, she's vulnerable, and when someone is vulnerable, they become a liability," Davina adds.

"We can't just abandon her," I speak up.

"You aren't abandoning her. I'll take care of her, and so will the guards. She'd rather be watched over than taught how to defend herself," says Davina.

"We have to inform her we're leaving," I mention.

Davina turns away and walks towards the window. "You girls must understand what you're asking me to do. When I came here, I was beaten and tortured every day. I've been through things that I still have nightmares about. This haunts me, and I toil with them every night and day."

"But it transformed you. You became strong and not weak. You taught yourself to fight and to endure pain. You fear no one, but everyone fears you," I say, reminding her of her words.

"You girls won't be here anymore. You'll be in a camp that will try to break you down and end you. The conditions are far worse there than here. The basement you were in is like heaven compared to this place. They'll try and break and destroy you like—"

"Like they tried to do to you?" I respond, cutting her off. "I know they tried to destroy you, but they didn't. What they did was resurrect you. You were like us, weak, afraid, and naïve. That camp killed the old Davina, then a stronger and wiser Davina was born. I don't see you as broken or destroyed. I think of you as a Phoenix because you were killed and renewed by your pain. You're stronger, wiser, and fear nothing."

"I'm tired of being scared and helpless," Jen butts in.

"We're trying to say that we want to be a Phoenix. We don't want to be sad, always scared, crying all the time, weak, and helpless. We want to be like you!" I look my aunt in the eyes; she's trying to hold back the tears. She nods her head up and down.

"You remember the necklace?"

I give her a nod. "Hopefully, I'll know what it feels like to be a Phoenix and earn that necklace and learn about the book and about us. But if it kills the weakness inside of me and makes me stronger, I'll kill to be a Phoenix and earn the necklace."

She looks at me and Jen. "Then it's done. I'll arrange for both of you to go to the camp. I'll bring Elizabeth in so you two can say your goodbyes. I'll tell you this — don't let anything or anyone separate you from each other, or you won't make it out alive," she advises sternly.

"What do you mean?" I ask, feeling nervous.

"I mean what I said. You won't make it if you don't stick together like you do now. Be partners, unify, and become one, as you have already started to do, but be very careful not to let anyone know how close you are, or they will try to destroy you. Put on a front, don't let others take over your friendship," she instructs. We agree to her terms.

Before Davina walks out to get Elizabeth, I stop her. They've been calling me "McCabe," and it's driving me insane to be called by his name. "Aunt Vina, the McCabe name is driving me crazy. How do I stop it? How do I divorce that bastard? I'm connected to him here because I have his name, which makes me sick."

She looks down towards the floor and rubs her forehead, "About that, I looked into your marriage with Mark. I didn't think the marriage was legal since you were underage, but somehow, you're legally married to him, and that's your name."

"What the fuck! How? No! How is this possible? How can they do that? I was hoping the marriage wasn't legal. I never signed anything. I'm not a McCabe. I'm a Sandino!"

"Sweetie, I have no idea. Someone signed your name for you, but the records are sealed. Unfortunately, your marriage to Mark is legal."

"I don't know how, but the McCabe family has moved up from the bottom of the barrel. That family has much power."

"What do you mean?"

"Well, they used to be the cleaners and picker-uppers. You call them if you need a body or situation to disappear. The Sandino family used to be on top, but I don't know when that changed. Looks like the next generation of the McCabe family decided bottom of the barrel, no more. They started making things happen. They've become so powerful, it's nearly impossible to put them back in their place."

I rub my head in disbelief at what I'm hearing but quickly stop because my head is aching. "Wait, a minute. Are you talking about mobsters and gangsters? My family isn't part of the mob or in a gang — they're businessmen. My dad barely curses, not an evil bone in his body. He's not into selling people, that's for sure."

"Sweetheart, not all mobsters sell people. Just those sick bastards do."

"Okay, this argument is for another day. Let's get back to the divorce and changing my last name."

"I know you hate it, but I think it's best to keep it. You never know when it may come in handy. He's only trying to get under your skin. Show him that he can't. Not to mention, he'll lose his shit when he finds out that you disappeared from this place without his knowledge. Remember, you have the upper hand right now because you're in control."

"I hate him so much and everything that has to do with him," I gripe.

"I know, but if you file for divorce now, it'll delay your training and bring you unwanted attention. Keep the name for now. You're a clever girl. You'll figure out how to use it against him eventually." she says.

Jen clears her throat, "Umm, about that last name thing, Dawnie. Jeff made me do the same thing, too, but it was done secretly — only Mark was there."

"But why? Shit, I'll still testify against him in court!" I say.

"You won't be able to." Davina chimes in. Jen and I are dumbfounded. We look to Davina for an explanation. "Our world has different laws," Davina says.

"Our world?" we repeat.

"It's a long story, but in short, we have different laws and judges in our underworld. We're in a prison that you have never seen or heard of. You can't google this place if you tried," says Davina.

"What the heck is going on, Aunt Vina? What exactly is the Sandino family into?"

"Sweetie, something that our ancestors got us into that we haven't been able to get out of for centuries."

"I want to know more about this," I say.

"You'll learn more at the camp like I did. Every family involved has their own book and story."

"So, not only is there a book about me, but a book about all these dark family secrets?"

She nods her head, "Yup, pretty much." Jen and I look at each other in disbelief. There's not much we can say or do until we discover more. Aunt Vina turns and leaves the room to get Elizabeth. It's time to tell my cousin that we're leaving and that she's staying here.

"Jen, you don't have to come," I tell her, trying to give her a way out.

"Yes, I do! We're connected somehow, D. I'm going with you! We've been connected since being chained to each other in the basement. I know it's not all for nothing. We can sense when each other is in trouble or pain. It's like, we're destined to be sisters or something. We're in this together and will always be. You're not getting away from me ever. Only death can separate us, and that's a promise. We must find out about the books and different laws that control us. We're going to figure it all out, D!"

"Figure it all out? Fuck that! I'm going to burn that shit down to the ground! It's ruined our lives, and now, we will ruin it!" I declare with every bit of strength left in me.

"Yeah, if we can. D, you must promise me we'll be in this together," says Jen.

I smile, "Till death do us part."

Chapter 51

BREAKING THE NEWS TO ELIZABETH

"We're leaving this place," I say to Elizabeth.

She begins smiling, clearly misunderstanding me.

"What! When?" she says with disbelief in her voice.

"No, Elizabeth. You're misunderstanding us. Dawnie and I are leaving. We're going to a dangerous camp for training. We — won't — be — here — anymore," Jens says slowly while clapping her hands on every syllable for Elizabeth to comprehend.

"Wait! What? You can't leave me here alone! What about me? We're supposed to be in this together, remember?" Elizabeth cries, pacing back and forth; tears spew from her saddened eyes.

"You'll be fine. Davina and her guards will take care of you here. As for us, we're going to a place where we'll be tortured and treated far worse than the basement or this prison. This is somewhere you don't want to go. You wouldn't survive, but Jen and I must go."

"You don't have to go! Stay here with me and follow Davina. She can teach us everything we need to know and save us," begs Elizabeth.

"I don't want to be saved! We want to learn. We won't ever learn here. This training camp is going to push our limits. Our lives will be tested like never before. Elizabeth, you're not built for this. This will be lower than the pits of hell we've already been through," I try explaining but soon interrupted.

"To what?" she demands. "Haven't we been through enough already to last us a thousand lifetimes and then some?" she cries.

"No, not like this. We're so damn tired of being scared, weak, and helpless!" Jen chimes in.

"What about me? You're abandoning me here?" Elizabeth continues to cry.

"We aren't abandoning you. We'll be back, I promise," we say reassuringly.

"I don't want to be separated from you two because you're all I got," whines Elizabeth, feeling defeated.

"You can't go with us! You're fragile, Elizabeth. We need you to stay here. You can't take any more of what you've already been through." I cut in, not allowing her to finish her thoughts. We sit silently on the edge of her bed for a few minutes.

"This is goodbye, I guess, huh?" Elizabeth sobs. The three of us have a moment and weep, realizing that our little sisterhood trifecta is splitting up after four years of being in captivity together.

"No. It's not goodbye; it's we'll see you before long. We have to go away. We must do this, but we'll be back," I keep reminding her.

"Think of it as we're going away to boarding school or something," says Jen, placing her hand on Elizabeth's back to comfort her. The three of us share a group hug. We embrace each other tightly, scared of what's to come.

Jen and I contemplate our fate. Whatever awaits us, we know, is nothing good.

Chapter 52

THE ROAD TO HELL

Davina prepares everything for Jen and my departure in just three weeks. Our trio spends as much time together as we can. Jen and I do our best to console Elizabeth before we leave. We're not sure when we'll ever see each other again. Davina tells us we can't take anything with us. Her instructions don't matter because we have nothing to take.

Jen keeps doing this breathing exercise. She practices holding her breath for as long as she can. She says she might need it one day. Her goal is to reach five minutes. Her best time right now is a little over four minutes. I try to practice holding my breath, but I'm not nearly as good as her. My best time is barely three minutes, generously speaking.

"I hate that you had to come here, but I'm so happy I got to see you again before I die. Remember everything I told you, and you'll persevere. Don't either of you worry about Elizabeth? She's in good hands," Aunt Vina reassures, hugging and kissing us both on the cheek.

Elizabeth is standing by herself. As expected, she's taking it hard — twin rivers are streaming down her cheeks. The three of us cry. "Hey, wipe those tears off your face. We're only going to school to better ourselves, remember?" I say, trying to cheer her up. She wipes her eyes and hugs us.

"Don't go. Please stay here with me. How am I going to survive without you two?"

"You will survive, and you'll be okay. You have Davina watching over you. She's the best of the best," Jen says.

"But—" Elizabeth interjects.

"No. You must be strong. We have no choice but to do this. It's for our good," says Jen, becoming assertive.

The three of us hug one last time. We release our embrace, and the guards chain Jen first, then me. They put us in the prison van and secure us. We're ready for transport. They close the doors. It's pitch-black inside. We can't see anything. Jen and I are hauled off to the militia camp — it's just us. Our prison shackles rattle as the paddy wagon begins to move.

"D," Jen calls my name in a low voice.

"Yes."

"I'm scared about this camp."

"Yeah, me too, but we have to do this. We're predestined and will come out better in the end."

"You're right. This is the only way for us to resurrect like the Phoenix and become one like your Aunt Davina." Jen replies, regaining her confidence by my words.

I conjure up a chuckle, "Yeah, a Phoenix."

"To becoming a Phoenix," she says.

"To becoming a Phoenix," I repeat.

The prison van pulls over abruptly. The back doors swing open, a dusk of light beams in, and our eyes try to adjust. Two men with cloths in their hands enter the back of the van. I shift my body the best way I can to resist whatever they're trying to do to me. It's useless — they have me, but I try to make it hard for them. Jen sits there calmly and looks at them. She knows she's next. They put the cloth over her nose. Jen takes it. However, I don't make it easy for them. I maneuver left and right — Aunt Vina never warned us about chloroform.

One man unlocks my shackles from the paddy wagon floor. Next, he pulls my chain and slams me to the van's floor. He shoves the cloth over my mouth and nose. Jen is leaning on the other man. He's doing the same to her. I glance her in the eyes. I can tell she's doing her breath-holding exercise. I wish I had taken those breathing exercises a little more seriously.

This is why she didn't run. It's a tactic! She sits there calmly and doesn't run out of air. Unfortunately for me, I inhale some of the chloroform being shoved in my face. It's only a matter of time before this stuff takes me out. Jen's eyes droop. Maybe her breathing technique didn't work. She looks unconscious. I don't get tired. I'm still alert. How can this be? Maybe I should pretend I'm unconscious. The two men exit the back of the van and close the doors, leaving us alone. I open my eyes. It's back to being dark. Jen gasps for air. She quickly covers her mouth to keep things down.

"Damn, you're good," I whisper.

"Yeah, but you're way better. I didn't know you were holding your breath," Jen whispers back.

"Umm, that's the thing, I wasn't holding my breath. I held it momentarily but can't hold my breath for a long time like you."

"How did you know it would work?" she whispers again.

"I didn't. I told myself not to inhale because I knew it would put us out. I chanced it!"

"You know, the crazy thing is, before Jeff and his men took me, I overheard them saying to one of their trainees that chloroform would put a girl out in just a few minutes. Anyway, how the heck are you immune to chloroform?" she questions, her voice more elevated this time.

"I have no idea! Maybe they didn't use enough or grabbed the wrong rag or something."

"Maybe," Jen replies with speculation. I'm not so convinced, either.

We're terrified out of our minds, but we're here now. It's happening. No turning back. We've been through so much, the worst life has had to offer. Dad, Scotty, Alejandro, and Davina couldn't protect us. We landed here, not knowing how to defend ourselves but to lean on each other. If this brutal and merciless induction can dismantle the terrified and pathetic little girls we are and resurrect us into indestructible immortals, then so be it.

A Phoenix we'll become, a Phoenix we'll forever be. We'll never be broken. We'll never be destroyed. We'll be transformed into better. We'll never be knocked down. We rise.

About the Author

Amanda Mercedes Sotomayor, originally from Egg Harbor, New Jersey, and now a proud Virginian, brings a vibrant, bold voice to the world of storytelling. Her love for the beach and tropical escapes reflects the dynamic energy she channels into her writing. With a seasoned career in IT, Amanda uniquely fuses innovation with narrative, crafting suspenseful, twist-filled tales that keep readers breathless. Her debut, The Phoenix Awakening, is the first installment in an intense odyssey thriller series that promises a journey of psychological depth and exhilarating suspense. Amanda writes with a passion for pushing boundaries, leaving readers immersed in works where courage and resilience are extracted for every challenge. Her philosophy — "what won't kill you will make you stronger" echoes through her work, creating a reading experience that's not just thrilling but also deeply meaningful. Amanda Mercedes Sotomayor's books are not just reads; they're emotionally charged rides that captivate from the first page to the last. Once you start, you won't be able to put her stories down.